He had to find the man with the snake tattoo.
The man who killed his wife.

"This is my fault. It's entirely my fault. I created Mithras Court."

Love is not enough to keep Lewis Wentworth from the horrors of Mithras Court, the place where the dead walk and the living hide, the place where God has fled and mankind waits for an unquiet grave. He is drawn into the Court by his vengeance, his need to destroy the man with the snake tattoo.

"Let me provide you with another clue. Missing artifacts from an archaeological dig in Rome, 1857."

Other people are drawn into the Court at the same time, and they have the same question: why are we here? But the answers are unpleasant, if they can be found at all, and one man must bear the guilt for creating the Court that traps them now, while another finds to his horror that the crime he was the victim of is the reason he has come here.

"You must choose, love. You have always known what to do. Do not falter now."

None who experience the Court at its finest—or its worst; they are the same—will forget it. They will bear the memories for as long as they live. They will carry scars, visible and not, and they will suffer their losses with the pain that they cannot use to save themselves.

But that time is short. And it is growing shorter.

"[*Surviving Frank* is] a fun tale, well worth a few hours of your time . . . his next book should be worth a look."

- Tom Easton, *Analog Science Fiction & Fact*

HEAVEN'S BONES
Samantha Henderson

MITHRAS COURT
David A. Page

DAVID A. PAGE

Mithras Court

Wizards
OF THE COAST
®

MITHRAS COURT

©2008 Wizards of the Coast, Inc.

Cover art by Android Jones

First Printing: November 2008
9 8 7 6 5 4 3 2 1

ISBN: 978-0-7869-5068-3
620-23939740-001-EN

U.S., CANADA,   EUROPEAN HEADQUARTERS
ASIA, PACIFIC, & LATIN AMERICA   Hasbro UK Ltd
Wizards of the Coast, Inc.   Caswell Way
P.O. Box 707   Newport, Gwent NP9 0YH
Renton, WA 98057-0707   GREAT BRITAIN
+1-800-324-6496   Save this address for your records.

Visit our web site at www.wizards

Dedication

I would like to dedicate this book to my beautifully talented wife, Jen, whose boundless creativity, humor, and love have been an endless well of inspiration.

Acknowledgements

I would like to take a moment to thank some of the people who have helped me survive this whirlwind, hardcore novel-writing extravaganza. First, I'd like to thank my parents, Dan and Marilyn, my Grandmother Monks, my sister Jeannie and my brother Fil for their continued support. I'd like to thank my step-daughter Alia for listening to me talk about this book over and over again without going crazy. Special thanks to my twin girls, Violet and Aria for their excellent advice spoken in the babble of toddlers. I don't know what they were saying, but it sure sounded important. Thanks to John DeTurk and Chris Muffoletto, two members of my three-person writing group, for excellent writing feedback. I'd like to thank Jaime M for her thoughts on my original synopsis and for being a great cheerleader for me. Thanks to Brent for cracking me up with repeated "Victorian speak" and to Cara for early advice on the Victorian era.

I'd like to thank my editor, Cortney Marabetta for not only being a great editor, but for her witty banter that made this an even greater experience than I thought it could be. And finally, I'd like to thank my wife, Jen, for turning her excellent "reader's eye" in my direction and for backing me up with lots of kid duty. This has been a crazy year as I wrote a novel whilst simultaneously working fulltime and juggling twins and I could not have made it through without all the people mentioned above and the friendship of many others who I have not named. If I missed anyone, my apologies; after this year, I'm lucky I can remember my own name.

DECEMBER, 1892
LONDON

Chapter ONE

An ominous shadow fell across Lewis Wentworth's path as he strode across the worn cobblestones of the plaza. He pulled his black overcoat tight against the chill of the dark London night and paused to take a closer look. The dim shape of the Monument's massive fluted column loomed over him, its giant outline barely visible in the night's gritty coal fog. For most passersby, it was a somber tribute to the destruction of London during the Great Fire of 1666. For Lewis, it had a different meaning. Climbing its worn stone steps had been one of the last things he and Elise had done together.

It had been a perfect spring afternoon surprisingly devoid of the fog that so often blanketed the city. They had stood above the city for what seemed like hours, staring out at the view, sneaking looks at one another. Despite the scenery, all he could remember were the gentle black curls cascading over her shoulders, framing her delicate features and accentuating her dark eyes as she looked lovingly at him. He had looked back with fondness.

She had been so young, so beautiful, and above all, so full of life. To her, their future was filled with boundless possibilities. Such optimism had never come easily for Lewis, even before his leg injury had brought his military career to an abrupt halt, but she had turned that around, the effervescence of her boundless spirit making him whole again—almost.

He sighed. Such things would never again be possible. He pressed a hand to his chest, feeling her wedding ring on the chain around his neck beneath his shirt.

The clatter of hooves drew him back to the stark reality of the winter night. A horse-drawn carriage sped past, a black silhouette against the soft glow of the gas lamps on the far side of the square. The sounds of laughter and conversation drifted toward him out of the fog. A well-dressed gentleman in a stylish gray overcoat, with an attractive raven-haired woman on one arm, materialized out of the murk, strolling leisurely in Lewis's direction. The man pointed at the Monument and leaned in toward her, murmuring into her ear.

Lewis glanced back and exhaled. The flames that had consumed Charles II's London could not match his need to find and kill the man responsible for Elise's death. The tender love she had poured into him had curdled within, becoming bitter hatred until he could not be certain which held more importance: the joy he had shared with her or the hate that had consumed him since her death. And her death had been his fault. He had not been there to defend her, had not chosen to travel with her that night, had not felt it important.

The guilt dragged on him, making him feel heavy, dead inside. He closed his eyes for an instant, focusing his attention. Finding her killer was the only thing that mattered now, the only thing that could grant him some measure of peace. He should have been there for her, but he hadn't. The only cure for his guilt was to exact vengeance. With new resolve, he limped quickly across the street toward a row of soot-stained four-story homes, using his cane to relieve the pain of his old wound.

A four-wheeler drew to a stop near the walk.

"That'll be one and six, guv," the driver informed his passengers, an older gentleman in a dark suit and top hat, and a younger man similarly attired. The older man paid their fare and he and his companion disembarked.

Lewis pressed on, toward the opposite side of the square. The tall stone buildings along Monument Street slowly came into view as the dark shroud hanging over the plaza thinned. Dozens of gray shapes coalesced into men and women, moving about their evening business. He scrutinized each man carefully, never bothering to glance at their irrelevant faces, focusing only on their left wrists. The boy who had survived the Underground Massacre had reported seeing a snake tattoo coiling up the arm of Elise's murderer. Armed with only that fragment of information, Lewis had spent the better part of two years scouring the city, from his home in Coniston Court to Whitehall, to the docks and beyond, ending each night with a ride on the very train on which she had died.

It was little enough he could do, but she deserved no less.

Bright gas lamps atop fluted iron poles illuminated King William Street Station, its narrow front curving sharply away down side streets. The soot-smeared sign over the three arched entrances read City and South London Railway. Smartly-attired gentlemen in long tailcoats and ladies in silk gowns that showed beneath their coats mingled with less well-to-do men in sack suits and women in simple dresses and wool shawls; the railway did not recognize wealth or class. They pressed against one another as they came and went from the station. Lewis walked through the arch and down the granite stairs into the depths; his gaze darted from one wrist to the next.

Despite the absence of the thick smoke found in London's other underground rail stations, the air grew heavy and oppressive as he descended. Once, this place had been a technological marvel to be experienced with Elise, the same as the bicycle—or playing lawn tennis, or so many other novelties they had shared. The advent of the electric underground had revolutionized transportation, but now—and forever—the conveyance only reminded him of his wife's slashed and bloody body.

Lewis closed his eyes and stopped for a moment as the vivid image of her, lifeless on the cold morgue table, jolted his mind. He saw her there every time he closed his eyes and every night in his dreams, and each time, his heart shattered all over again at the loss of her bright light. He had always felt comforted by her presence, always happier as a result of her attention. And yet, that wonderful affection had not been enough to convince him to join her that night. In his mind, she would return home, as safe as always. He had always known that one of them would die before the other, but that thought had been wrapped in the comforting knowledge that they had time, that death would separate them when they'd reached old age after a lifetime together, not when Elise had barely reached thirty. He grew dizzy and had to lean against the white-tiled wall.

"I say—you don't look entirely well."

Lewis blinked and saw a white-haired man in a well-kept, if dated, gray coat and dented top hat. The man stroked his pale beard as he looked at Lewis; something about the stranger made Lewis's eyebrows rise with alarm. There was something familiar about the man's eyes, but Lewis could not place him. He glanced at the older man's wrist, but saw only unmarked skin. And this time, for the first time since he had started this quest, Lewis wasn't sure whether he was relieved or frustrated by the lack of a tattoo. Frustration, certainly—not finding Elise's killer simply prolonged his quest. But relief came to the fore as well. He had often pondered the consequences of his quest for vengeance. Would the police capture him? Would they understand why he had done what he would?

They were fleeting thoughts. The truth was that he lived for vengeance.

"It's nothing." Lewis nodded curtly and rejoined the throng moving downward. Consequences be damned.

With the gas lights pushing away the shadows on the broad stairs, this was the most effective location to search for his quarry. And yet, all the illumination in the world could not peel back the sleeves of the hundreds of people who rode this train each day. Finding the man and seeing his tattoo would take a lifetime of luck, but Lewis could not care. There was nothing else for him to do. He would never stop, would find the man if it took him the remainder of his life.

At the bottom of the staircase, a wide lobby funneled passengers into a large chamber. A low, arched brick ceiling above the platform stretched along the electrified tracks. The iron train waited there, the arched tops of its cars mirroring the ceiling of the tunnel. Made up of three linked carriages with narrow slits for windows, it stretched down the platform. Standing at the doorway to each car, a porter in a blue uniform and round cap stood ready to assist as passengers disembarked.

Several anxious travelers shouldered past Lewis as they queued up to board. The cacophony of myriad conversations, noisy children, and shouting porters echoed through the underground, but Lewis was focused on his task. He gripped the knob at the top of his walking cane tightly and glanced at wrist after wrist. But for every one he saw, four others were concealed by long sleeves or gloves. And yet, he had no other option than to keep searching. Elise deserved no less—and far more than this ritual.

As the last of the passengers disembarked from the carriages, the waiting crowd surged forward. Lewis pushed toward the closest car, one of the first to board. He reached for one of the brass bars running along the curved wooden ceiling, leaving the seats for the ladies, and watched his fellow passengers as they entered. The white-haired man who had spoken to him on the stairs stood at the opposite end of the train, his rumpled hat in one hand. Lewis dismissed him and observed the rest of the small carriage.

Two long benches ran down each side of the car, their cushions providing comfort for the women and the occasional gentleman, though most of the men remained standing. With its lacquered wood and polished brass, the interior of the carriage offered a luxury to which some of its passengers were not accustomed, judging by the way several of them surreptitiously ran their hands along the furnishings. One man in particular, with the rough hands of a laborer and a suit that labeled him a factory man, or perhaps a blacksmith, gazed around the interior with quiet awe. Next to him, a woman in a simple gray skirt and delicate white blouse and wool cape held his left hand tightly. Seeing no tattoo on the man's wrist, Lewis looked away.

"All aboard!" the porters bellowed abruptly. A moment later, they closed the doors from the outside as a low hum sent dull vibrations through the car. With the crackle of electric sparks, the car eased forward, gathering speed quickly.

A lanky, dark-haired man near the center of the car grabbed hold of the brass bar to brace himself against the motion. The sleeve of his modest gray sack coat slipped, catching Lewis's eye. He sucked in a breath when he saw the tattoo of a coiled serpent on the man's left arm.

The lights dimmed as the carriage entered the tunnel; Lewis stood frozen in the darkness.

It was a strange feeling, as if the train car were growing longer somehow, and he had the impression that he was falling backward. He bit back a scream, enraged that the man stood by so casually, free of regret, without a care in the world—but he had taken Lewis's love, his dreams, his future when he took Elise. Lewis suddenly shook as cold rage chilled him. Honor demanded that this man die; Lewis's hate wanted him to die in pain.

He took a lunging step toward the lanky man, but hesitated as doubts assailed him. What if the child witness had been wrong? What if this man had not murdered Elise? What if this man did not exist? All of it could be a figment of Lewis's desperate mind, the tattoo a trick of the light, all a complex illusion to answer the obsession that enslaved him.

Faced with the culmination of his hopes and efforts for the last two years, Lewis paused. It could not, some part of him said, be that easy. He had thought so long about this quest, thought so little of what would happen on the other side, and here he was, faced with that choice.

He blinked hard, his gaze riveted on a single point on the back of the tattooed man's head. Cautiously, his hand slid into his coat pocket and closed around the comforting grip of his Webley revolver. He contemplated whether to kill the man slowly or swiftly. A swift death was far too kind for such as this, he felt. Yet in a public place, Lewis had little choice but to act quickly, lest the other passengers stop him.

Steeling himself, he stalked down the aisle, drawing the gun, oblivious to the motion of the car. Passengers cried out in alarm as they saw the weapon, but he ignored them. Everything but the tattooed man faded into nonexistence. Only his prey mattered.

He raised the revolver, allowing it to lead the way. It clicked almost imperceptibly as he pulled back the hammer and a cartridge slid into place. A loud rushing rang in his ears. The tattooed man turned, his dark eyes widening as he came face to face with the gun's muzzle.

"You!" Lewis said. "Son of a whore!" But something in the man's level gaze made him pause.

"Aye, my mother was a whore." The man's gravelly voice was steady. His oddly dark eyes twinkled and the corners of his lips twitched as if he found Lewis's statement comical.

"Who are you?" Lewis held the gun closer to the man, his mind screaming at him to pull the trigger and be done with it, but something in the man's comment, his utter calmness in the face of the gun, jarred Lewis, derailed him from what he knew must be done. His muscles froze as doubts crept into his thoughts, daring him to question the man further.

"Take care, both of you! There are ladies present. Such language and violence are reprehensible!"

Lewis recognized the voice—the white-haired man who had spoken to him on the stairs of the train station. As his rational mind reasserted itself, Lewis realized that he needed more than just the man's death. He needed to assuage his doubts and know why the stranger had done it, why he had taken Elise. Lewis's grip on the Webley relaxed ever so slightly.

"If this man truly is guilty of some crime, then this should be handled by the Yard. This type of rash behavior can only lead to your own undoing." The white-haired man had moved up beside him, speaking quietly.

"This is a matter of justice." Lewis hesitated despite himself, impressed by the old man's honest bravery. "Righteousness will be served. My wife's memory will be honored." As he struggled with his words, desperate to find the perfect phrase that would draw the truth out of the tattooed man, his eyes lit on white fog, curling along the floor. He dismissed it. The fog—or was it smoke?—was not something to fear, merely something that conveyed greater urgency to the task at hand, to finish and be away from the car.

"Justice? There ain't no such thing." The tattooed man did smile now, revealing straight teeth that were too perfect. "Not for me, not for you . . . not for her. You kill me and you'll never know why."

"You bastard!" The smoke, the man so insistent on the Yard's involvement, all of it melted away in a hot, corrosive rage. The arrogance of the man infuriated him, the way he spoke so casually of Elise enraged him, but the thought of someone else pulling this man's strings halted him again. His finger eased up on the trigger. "Tell me, you miserable cur! Why did you kill her?"

"Fire!" a woman cried as the smoke thickened abruptly, curling along the floor and swiftly rising to knee level, giving no sign of stopping.

Some remote portion of Lewis's mind noted that it wasn't smoke. The vapor was cold and damp. It sent shivers up his spine, but he could not spare it more than a thought. He stood eye to eye with the tattooed man, and if he was honest, Lewis did not mind dying if it meant that the tattooed man was brought to justice. He had no desire to flee the fog as he glared into the man's eyes, trying to force him to speak.

But others were screaming, not realizing that the vapor wasn't smoke. The carriage filled with sounds of coughing as panic seized the passengers.

Lewis had known war, the terror of battle, how it could affect people. This was no different. The chaos that was beginning to erupt would take his moment from him; he had to shoot, even though he had no answers. The man had admitted to slaying Elise, and that cold fact surely trumped any explanation he might give. To delay, even in the hope of learning who might have pulled the man's strings, would be to lose his opportunity forever.

The tattooed man's smile broadened as he looked fearlessly down the barrel of the gun. The mist had filled the car to Lewis's shoulders by now.

The lights flickered twice and went out.

In the darkness, Lewis squeezed the trigger, cursing himself for his moment of doubt. The muzzle flash revealed that the tattooed man had disappeared amid the panic and the smoke. The lights flickered again, coming back on as the car slowed, and a metallic screech drowned out the passengers' screams. Lewis stared in disbelief at the empty space before him, and at the bullet hole that marred the car's wall.

Rough hands closed around Lewis's wrist as the laborer took hold of him. Two other men in fine-tailored coats grabbed his left arm, knocking his cane out of his grasp. It hit the floor with a staccato rap and rolled against a bench where two women wearing elaborate evening dresses pressed back into their seats, as if they could sink through the wall and escape the commotion.

"Let me go!" Lewis struggled against his assailants, determined to maintain his grip on the pistol no matter the cost. The tattooed man had obviously somehow hidden among the passengers, but he could not have run far in the crowded car. If he acted quickly, Lewis could catch him.

The car's brakes squealed again as the train jarred to a sudden stop. Using the momentum, Lewis freed himself of the three men and swung his revolver toward them, stepping backward until his coat brushed against the front wall of the car. They would not take him again.

"Enough of this!" The white-haired man stepped in front of him, his dented hat still clutched in one hand. "Lower your weapon before someone is injured. If that man has truly committed a crime, then it is a matter for the police, not you. Duels are illegal!"

"The man must die!" Lewis held the Webley steady as he shouted into the car, "Show yourself!" He risked a glance past his assailants and saw the frightened faces of the other passengers, but even in the light his quarry was nowhere to be seen. The man had vanished.

Lewis staggered and his breath caught in his chest. Impossibly, the man had escaped, and now *Lewis* was the one cornered, as though he were the madman. His shoulders slumped; he fought to keep his feet as his strength fled with his botched opportunity.

He had been so close. Every day since Elise had been taken from him, Lewis had envisioned discovering the man. He imagined him pleading for his life, the way Elise had probably done. Surely her death by stabbing had been filled with pain. The thought of her dying, scared and alone, burned through him. That torment could only be driven away by the tattooed man suffering, and ultimately dying at Lewis's hands.

And yet, with the man in his sights, he had not been able to take his revenge. He swallowed the bitter hatred, clenched his teeth, and pushed his spinning thoughts aside. He needed to escape, to find the man again. And this time, he would not hesitate. Elise deserved no less than his full dedication.

"Steady now." One of the gentlemen who had held him was speaking calmly. He was a tall, broad-shouldered man with a thick walrus moustache. "We do not wish to frighten the ladies any more than they already are."

"We can't let you . . ." The white-haired man quickly glanced around the car. "I don't understand . . . where has the smoke gone?"

"That was no smoke," the taller man said confidently. "It was cold—it must have been mist."

"I've never heard of such a mist in any rail tunnel." The man's demeanor was authoritative, and Lewis hoped that the oddness of the moment might distract the passengers from taking further action against him.

A loud click interrupted their debate as the bolt on the outside of the car slid back. The door opened with a pop to reveal a dimly-lit platform beyond. The cloying smell of damp earth assailed Lewis's nose, inexplicably filling him with dread. As he considered, he realized why—the smell did not belong there. The other passengers either did not notice, or did not care, as they bolted. Some left behind their bags, others abandoned articles of clothing, hats, even a coat, in their haste to get away from Lewis, the imagined fire, or both.

"Come on, Reggie!" the woman in the plain dress said as she tugged at the sleeve of the laborer who had tried for Lewis's gun. She risked a fearful glance at Lewis, her lips pursed as if about to berate him, but thought better of it.

Reggie glanced at Lewis, then his wife. He sighed and allowed her to lead him away.

Shame at the fear he had caused and a dull confusion weighed on Lewis. As the passengers fled, he saw no sign of the tattooed man—as if he had disappeared with the mist.

"Where are we, Gregory?" the gentleman with the walrus moustache asked of a clean-shaven man next to him, all the while keeping a wary eye on Lewis. He shifted his position to see Lewis, his friend, and the open doorway all at once.

"I'm not certain, sir." Gregory risked a quick look through the door at the platform beyond. "But something is not right. The London rails are something of a hobby of mine, and I have ridden this electric train dozens of times. I can say with complete assuredness that there should not be a station here."

Lewis's sense of danger, honed in battle, led him to agree that something was very wrong. It wasn't merely the smell, either, though that was a portion of it. He met the gaze of the white-haired man and saw something he had not noticed in their initial meeting and subsequent confrontation. Behind his outward kindness lay a haunted but grim look of determination that Lewis had only seen in men who had known the horrors of war. The man nodded, as if understanding passed between them. Lewis decided that he could trust this man.

The old man pivoted and looked at the tall gentleman, his eyes widening in recognition as he recognized him for the first time.

"You are Lord Geoffrey Crandall." He stared at him with wide-eyed awe and, oddly, a slightly curled lip that barely concealed his contempt.

"Indeed, I am. And who, pray tell, are you?"

"Sir Robert Drake, Professor of Antiquities at Cambridge."

"Is that meant to impress me, Professor?" Lord Crandall arched one eyebrow. Lewis had the distinct impression that he had deliberately used the man's professional title rather than the salutation afforded a knight.

"My position stands on its own merit—not on the opinions of others," Drake responded. He paused, then added, a bit more stiffly, "Given the present situation, I suggest we put any differences aside until we can ascertain what has happened here." He glanced at Lewis. "Provided, sir, that you will agree not to point that pistol at any of us."

"Of course," Lewis nodded. He had not survived the horrors of war without knowing when to back down.

"Very well." Lord Crandall reached up to stroke his moustache, glancing sidelong at his friend. Gregory, undoubtedly Crandall's employee, merely nodded.

Lewis lowered his revolver but did not return it to his coat pocket. He was determined to be ready—for the tattooed man or any other danger. He carefully crouched down, and without taking his eyes from the men, felt around with his free hand until his fingers closed on the lacquered wood of his cane. He straightened, and moved with the others to peer through the open door of the train car. Only the four of them remained inside now. The sputtering gas lamps cast a feeble light, creating long shadows across the platform and making it difficult to see the ceiling and walls of the station.

A group of perhaps nine men and women from their car milled at the center of the station. Beneath a wrought-iron gas chandelier, all of them held their hands over their noses and mouths, clearly warding off an unpleasant stench. Several of them pointed toward the car and spoke; at that distance, their words were unintelligible.

Lewis watched as two women and a gentleman in a gray top hat approached the ticket counter, a small wooden booth in the far corner of the station at the very edge of the light. A shadowy figure wearing a railway hat sat motionless behind the metal bars of the small window.

Lewis glanced to the other side of the platform and noted a broad stairway that ran along the right-hand wall, leading into a tunnel about ten feet above the station floor—that would be the exit, he thought. The dim outlines of other people hung back in the deeper shadows, their movements strangely erratic. They shifted back and forth in place, evidently awaiting something.

A porter stood to the right of the open car door, mere feet from Lewis, his back to the train car.

Lord Crandall and his man stepped out and nearly gagged.

"Dear God, what is that foul odor?" Lord Crandall asked, a monogrammed handkerchief appearing in his hand. He covered his mouth.

"It smells like a charnel house," Gregory gasped. He grabbed his own cloth and brought it to his face.

Lewis thought it odd that he could not smell something so potent from within the coach—he smelled something unpleasant, yes, but it was not as strong as the other men were suggesting. It was, he thought, as if the open doorway shielded them from the stench to which the others reacted.

"There's a man with a gun on board!" shouted the gentleman leading the charge to the ticket counter, but his voice was barely audible to Lewis, as the place devoured the very sound. "Call the constables immediately!"

Lewis was not sure why the man and his female companions had not alerted the porter who had released them from their car. But given the haughty tone in the man's voice, it was entirely possible that he did not wish to bother with an underling. Or with too many underlings, at any rate.

Lewis gripped his revolver tightly, and with Professor Drake at his side stepped onto the soot-stained platform. As he crossed the threshold, his body tingled and the hairs on his arms stood up. It felt as if lightning had struck nearby. Barely had that thought registered when the stench of death assailed him, nearly knocking him back into the train car. He looked down as he covered his face, trying desperately to push away the images of bloody carnage that the scent evoked in his mind. Something terrible had happened there, he was certain of it, but it boggled the mind to imagine what it could have been.

Drake gasped and dropped his top hat as he doubled over and nearly retched. Lewis heard the sounds clearly. The train car had not only protected them from most of the smell, but had also dampened the sounds coming from the bizarre station.

"Are you all right, Professor?" The question was the one he would have asked of the men serving under him in his cavalry unit; it was not motivated by concern for the man's life, but by the unknown that awaited them in the station—and by Lewis' need to understand it before he risked the danger.

"Yes, yes." Drake waved him away. He straightened, but pointed to the floor suddenly.

Lewis's eyes went to the pavement below their feet, where tiled letters spelled out strange words. "Mithras Station," he read aloud.

"I've never heard of this place," Drake said. "Gregory was correct about that."

"Nor have I, and I've ridden this train every night for two years." Alarm scattered his thoughts at the realization that he might have missed something as big as a train station in his nightly journey. If he could miss that, then his senses were suspect, but it was equally not possible that an entire train station had just *appeared*. "Something's very wrong."

He turned to glance at the train and took a step backward in shock. Only the engine and the single car remained on the tracks. The lead car and the end car had vanished completely.

Drake followed Lewis's gaze and stared in disbelief.

The black metal door to the engine compartment opened and a short, stocky man in the uniform of the rail service stepped out. He was younger than Lewis expected, although his red hair and freckled face might have given the impression of youth. The engineer looked at the orphaned car and blinked in confusion.

"What's happened?" he demanded of no one in particular. "There were three separate cars! My boss will have me head!"

"I say, man, are you deaf?" The gentleman at the ticket window across the station was yelling at the clerk again. He removed his hat and tossed it down on the counter as if throwing a gauntlet in front of the man. "How can you—"

The woman next to him shrieked as dark, vaguely-human forms suddenly left the shadows. Even from where Lewis stood, frozen in shock, he could see clothing hanging in tatters from sickly-thin bodies as they shambled forward, their motions jerky and palsied.

The trio at the ticket booth was struck dumb, and the creatures were upon them before anyone could react. Swiping at the women with long talons, their clawed hands sliced through clothing and flesh, drawing blood as the women wailed, fear turned to shock and pain.

"For the love of God!" the man bellowed, lunging forward to help the ladies. "Somebody call the police!"

"Bloody hell." Lewis's oath was quiet. Two years of focusing only on himself and his vengeance fell away in the face of true terror. His honor, tarnished but not lost, demanded that he aid those hapless people. He moved toward them but stopped as dozens of newcomers staggered forward out of the darkness, coalescing out of the shadows. They surged toward the cluster of passengers at the center of the platform.

Even in the low light of the guttering lamps, their distorted and decaying faces were visible. They had been living beings once, but death had overcome them. Lewis had seen enough corpses to know that some of them, with most of their flesh intact, were only recently deceased. Others that were almost skeletons had been dead for years, even decades.

Bile rose in his throat. He bent, but managed to keep his eyes on the mob even as he fought the urge to vomit. As the passengers screamed in sheer terror, Lewis forced himself to stand straight. He blinked and saw that the people near the ticket counter had vanished—probably pulled into the shadows. Only a crumpled shawl and a bent top hat lay where they had stood. Lewis fought back his panic. If the survivors did not react quickly and smartly, death would have them all.

He leaped into action, ignoring his aching leg, and quickly crossed to where the porter stood next to the train. He grabbed the man's shoulder. "You must summon the police at once!"

But the porter only hissed as he slowly turned, revealing another of the walking dead. The fetid stink of the monster's breath from its decaying lungs washed over Lewis. The porter glared at him with burning hatred in its empty eye sockets. Its pale skin did not appear decayed, but its eyes had been plucked from its head.

Lewis recoiled, trying desperately to move away, but the creature seized him by the throat with supernaturally strong hands, colder than ice. Terror grabbed at him, and his pulse hammered against the thing's dead fingers as he fought against its grip.

"Shoot it!" Drake yelled.

The fiery resolve that had forced him to drag himself off a distant battlefield during the Zulu War burned through his consciousness, and his training took over. He swung his pistol up, aimed at the monster's head, and fired at point-blank range. A tongue of flame erupted from the pistol's muzzle as the bullet hit the abomination, blowing the side of its face off. The dead man's grip on Lewis's throat loosened. The porter's body slumped against the train and Lewis wriggled out of the deadly embrace. He pushed the creature away and wished he could purge the memory of its touch from his mind.

"Protect the women!" Lord Crandall ran forward, the tails of his coat flying behind him like a cape in the wind. Gregory followed on his heels.

The shrill screams of the terrified and the dying echoed around the station, bouncing off tile and stone. The din sounded as if hundreds of people were embroiled in the scuffle, rather than the dozen who had disembarked from the train. As loud as it was, however, it was not enough to drown out the dull, scraping footsteps of the shambling corpses as they moved across the platform.

Lewis limped swiftly forward, using his cane, and saw several passengers on the ground. A half-dozen walking dead leaned over them, blood pooling around their feet as they clawed and bit at their victims. Several women shrieked in terror from the cluster of survivors, drawing Lewis's attention. The men had formed a ring around three women and were trying to fend off the devils with their bare fists. One woman crossed herself and clasped her hands together as she prayed, loudly and clearly enough that Lewis could hear her over the sound of the assault. Another woman stood, hands raised, ready to swat at anything that came near and a third woman kicked at the monsters as they pushed against the men. Lord Crandall and Gregory plowed into two of the assailants, knocking the creatures to the ground, but others took their places.

Focused as he was on reaching the surviving passengers, Lewis failed to notice the slick dark fluid pooling in front of him. He slipped on the brick platform and would have gone down if not for the quick action of Professor Drake. The old man appeared on his right, caught his arm, and steadied him. Lewis thanked him with a look. Together, they ran forward.

"Lewis . . ." A soft voice whispered his name. He halted a few yards away from the closest monster, blinking in disbelief.

"Elise?" Her wedding ring, hanging from a gold chain around his neck, grew warm against his chest. "Elise?" Astonishment crashed against him and he dared not speak her name again, fearful that he had imagined her voice. Had madness gripped him? He held his breath and hoped for her to say something else. He cursed the loud beat of his heart, too loud for him to hear another soft whisper from her.

"I beg your pardon?" Drake paused with him.

"Run, Lewis! Run to the surface!" Her voice cut through him like a blaring war trumpet. It echoed against the inside of his head and he bolted with the automatic response of a soldier. He abandoned the mystery of her voice and her presence; it would matter little if his life ended there at the hands of those clawing horrors. More of the living dead were coming out of the shadows. It would be only minutes before the survivors were overrun.

"Elise." He breathed her name again as the heat from her ring faded. Her voice was a gift he would tuck away. He would explore the idea of her return with the greatest of care, a delicate jewel he had happened upon. If the living dead were real, it lent credence to the possibility that he had really heard her voice. Lewis snapped himself back to the moment, glanced about for Professor Drake, and darted ahead.

Whether he had gone mad or not, however, this was the time for swift action.

Years earlier, after the Zulu war, after his injury and convalescence, Lewis had been a civilian instructor at the Royal Military College at Sandhurst, where he had instructed men on how to become soldiers. He had seen some rough recruits in his time, but he had repeatedly proven that he could make any man battle-ready. As he neared the last cluster of survivors, Lewis raised his Webley and fired two shots into one of the creatures that was half-skeleton as it flanked Lord Crandall. The corpse, draped in rags that had once been a stylish frock coat, jerked backward as the bullet bit into its shoulder. It fell over, leaving a gap in the direction of the stairs.

"My thanks!" Lord Crandall shouted as he and Gregory regained their balance. They launched themselves at the skeletal corpse of a woman in a dirt-smeared wedding dress.

"Listen to me, all of you! We must reach the surface! Everyone make for the stairs . . . *now!*" Lewis had to shout to be heard over the din of the station. He squeezed the trigger again; the muzzle flashed and another corpse went down in a heap, its brittle bones cracking with staccato pops. Lewis hobbled swiftly, using the pain in his leg to help him focus, and he quickly reached the bottom of the stairs.

"Do as he says!" Drake shouted, falling in step just behind Lewis.

"Someone call the police!" a woman yelled.

"The police can't help us. If you wish to live, climb the stairs!" Lord Crandall ordered. He grabbed her by the arm and pulled her toward the staircase. "Go, now! Hurry!"

"Stay together and go quickly!" Gregory pushed another woman after the others.

"Come on, Mary!" On the opposite side of the crowd, Reggie, a pocketknife in his hand, slashed at a tall corpse in filthy overalls and a leather vest. As the dead man gave ground, Reggie grabbed his wife's hand and pulled her toward freedom.

The train engineer dodged several creatures and sprinted the remaining distance to Lewis. Lewis had seen men lose their wits in battle too often, and knew that the engineer was on the verge of total panic.

"What are we going to do? We'll never make it out alive!" He babbled wildly as he reached Lewis, panting in fear more than exertion.

Lewis slapped him across the face.

"Get hold of yourself, man." He turned away and thrust his cane at Drake. "Take this and lead them up the stairs. I'll hold the rear." He risked a quick look up and saw dim light filtering from an archway where the stair curved upward and opened into a low tunnel. The archway remained free of the dead, walking or otherwise.

Drake accepted the cane. "Very well. You men, assist the ladies! We are leaving!" He glanced at the engineer as he climbed the first steps. The stocky man hurried after him.

"Pull the cane's knob!" Lewis called to the departing professor.

The old man did as he was instructed, pulling free a slender rapier. He nodded grimly, and with the empty cane in one hand, the blade in the other, led the engineer up and out of sight. Several passengers hurried past Lewis, racing up the steps and away from the insanity of the station. Reggie and Mary ran arm in arm and were several yards away when three of the dead caught them with their clawing hands.

"Reggie!" Mary's shriek was a clarion cry as the undead tore at her dress. She kicked and pushed at the creatures to no avail and screamed her husband's name again. Her cries for help reverberated through the station. The sound changed with each echo until Lewis thought he heard Elise's voice instead of Mary's, pleading for his help from the past—help that had never come.

"Get away from her!" Reggie shouldered into the creatures, knocking two of them back, but the third, wearing the shredded remains of a monk's robe, slashed him across the face, spinning him around and forcing him to one knee. Mary grabbed her husband's shoulder but her grip failed and she stumbled away from him.

"Use your pistol!" Mary ran to Lewis's side and seized his sleeve. "Help him!"

"Follow the others up the stairs!" Lewis stepped toward Reggie and fired. His bullet caught the dead monk in the back of the head, dropping him instantly.

"Come on!" Lewis grabbed Reggie's arm and yanked him to his feet.

Jarring pain seared his right shoulder as another of the walking corpses speared him with its long fingernails. Lewis whipped the Webley around, pressed it against the skull of the skeletal thing, and squeezed the trigger.

It clicked but did not fire. The creature reached for him, and though it moved slowly he almost did not dodge in time. The sound of its claws ripping the air in front of his face was a sound that would stay with him for a very long time.

He pulled the trigger again and again, to no avail, the hammer striking empty chambers. For a moment, Lewis was dumbfounded. The realization that he was out of bullets hit him as a physical blow, and he felt his energy drain away. A second corpse caught him by the shoulders from behind. It pulled at him with inhuman strength, dragging him backward, away from the stairs and toward the shadows where its brethren lurked. Lewis's right shoulder burned where the first creature had gouged him, and his leg wound blazed so intensely he wondered if he had taken another spear in his thigh, but this was not the Zulu War.

It was far worse than any war could ever be.

And yet, he fought with every bit of strength he could muster. The man with the snake tattoo was still alive, he felt that in his soul, and until he found him again and delivered justice for Elise, he could not, *would* not, yield. He gritted his teeth, roaring a battle cry as he heaved against the corpses, and for an instant he surged forward, but his leg gave out. As he fell to his knees, he wrestled against the dead flesh and skeletal limbs—and the hopelessness of it all. He *had* to survive.

More fiends lurched toward him, tearing at his clothes.

"In the name of God, unhand him, fiends!" Lord Crandall appeared behind Lewis and his attackers. The gentleman wrapped his arms around one of the creatures and yanked it off its feet, heaving it away as Gregory struck another in the head with his fist. The weight lifted from Lewis as they fell away.

"Come on, man! We have but a moment!" Lord Crandall kicked at one of the creatures on the ground, sending its head skittering across the floor, its body jerking with the blow.

Lewis pushed off the ground. He half ran and half limped to the stairs, reaching them just as Reggie disappeared into the tunnel. He followed, climbing the steep steps with all the speed he could muster. He did not risk a look back.

MITHRAS COURT

CHAPTER *TWO*

Dim gas lamps illuminated the arched brick stairwell every few yards, casting flickering shadows against the soot-stained walls. The dank air sent chills along Lewis's bare hands and face, amplifying his discomfort and sense of panic. The undead were not pursuing. He took a moment to steady his breathing and collect his thoughts. What on earth had they just witnessed?

He wanted to rationalize away the horrors he had seen. The decayed flesh of the dead could have been a trick of the light, brought on by the disorienting panic of the crowd. The attackers could have been human—savage vagrants that preyed on unsuspecting travelers.

But an internal voice, one that hid in the deepest shadows of his mind, whispered the truth. Though it was the logic of a nightmare—those creatures were real. The terror of it was unbearable, he thought; and the terror was not yet reconciled, exactly as Elise's death was not. He had spent months trying to escape the pain and the knowledge of her murder. The attacks in the train station were still raw. If he was to live through this, he would need to act, not reason away the dreadful truth. He could come to grips with these events later.

He silenced the nagging voice that pointed out he had not come to grips with Elise's death even now.

". . . pray for us sinners, now and at the hour of our death . . ." The praying woman's frantic voice echoed down the tunnel, followed by snatches of muffled conversation. There were no screams, at least for the moment. Lewis took heart from the familiarity of the words.

"I suggest you reload that revolver." Gregory took Lewis by the arm and helped him to climb faster. Normally, Lewis would have shrugged off such assistance. Under the circumstances, however, he welcomed the help. Gregory and Lord Crandall had saved his life, and he would not dishonor them or himself by appearing ungrateful.

"Gregory's right—and be quick about it, man." Lord Crandall fell into step on Lewis's right. "Those things are still following us."

"Of course," Lewis said, suddenly out of breath from the swiftness of their pace. "Thank you . . . for saving my life." He paused and added, "Please know that I meant no one else harm." His sense of honor craved their understanding that he had not sought wanton violence. His conscience called only for the death of the tattooed man.

It flustered him to realize that the more he tried to convince them of his intentions, the more he might seem like a raving lunatic with a gun. He clenched his jaw and willed himself to keep quiet. Calmly and slowly, he opened his Webley, dumped the spent cartridges and reached into his pocket for more. He had only twelve rounds, a fact that he cursed himself for in hindsight. His plan had been simple: put a bullet into the skull of Elise's murderer. Never in his wildest imagination had it occurred to him that he might need ammunition to fight a legion of undead. But then, another voice pointed out, there was no reason it should have.

With the bullets loaded, he spun the cylinder and pocketed the revolver.

"What you intend will have to wait. For the moment, we have more pressing matters," Lord Crandall countered. "But I will have your name, sir."

"I am Captain Lewis Wentworth, retired, formerly of the 17th Lancers and more recently instructor at the Royal Military College at Sandhurst."

"Indeed?" Gregory asked. "That would explain your aim."

"Aye," Lord Crandall agreed, huffing from the exertion of their climb. "The Lancers are notoriously good shots."

"Only when my gun is loaded." Lewis's attempt at wry humor surprised even himself. He closed the revolver, spun the cylinder, and risked a glance over his shoulder.

They had travelled at least a hundred feet, perhaps more, and he could no longer see the entrance to the station below. The stairs descended into a darkness that the feeble gas lamps could not vanquish. A good dozen yards away, though, several shifting gray forms clumsily clawed their way upward, their broken bodies contorting as they climbed on all fours; Lewis was reminded of rabid animals. He patted the revolver in his pocket and rubbed at his aching thigh. It was hardly a comforting thought.

"They'll never catch us before we're out." Gregory wiped sweat from his brow.

"I hope there are none ahead of us," Lewis said.

His companions did not respond, but judging by Gregory's clenched jaw and Lord Crandall's narrowed eyes, they shared his concern. They climbed in silence, Lewis holding his gun at the ready, watching for any hint of a side passage or any indication of danger. The climb was swift and rigorous, but Lewis kept pace with the others.

His thoughts turned to Elise. In his panic, he had forgotten about her voice in the heat of battle, but as he climbed towards whatever fate awaited them, he took time to ponder it. He considered two explanations. Either he had lost his wits, or she had crossed the void and spoken to him.

He had never questioned his sanity before, and did not plan to start. The events in Mithras Station had occurred, had been real—people had died, and they had not been killed by shadows or illusions. If the dead had truly risen from the grave, it followed that Elise and her love for him could bridge the afterlife as well.

That opened endless possibilities, some good and others bad. But it meant that his search for Elise's killer had ended not only in discovering the man, but perhaps also in finding her again. If he truly could speak to her, then he could beg her forgiveness. She had died because of his desire to remain at home rather than travel with her that night.

Lewis had no way of knowing whether anyone else had heard her voice. He put aside the idea of speaking to her aloud. He did not want his fellow survivors to think him insane for hearing voices that remained hidden to them. His survival required his credibility as a military man, which would allow him to lead the others into doing as he commanded. In his mind, he implored her to talk to him again, however.

Light shone ahead of them, distracting him from his musings. It bathed the blackened walls in its warm glow. Lord Crandall and Gregory still flanked him, and the corpses hadn't gained on them. Given the swift nature with which both men had responded to the crisis, Lewis suspected that both had served in Her Majesty's Armed Forces in their younger days. He would ask that question when their crisis had resolved.

Until then, he would assume they were brothers in arms.

Two shadowy figures stood framed in the light, watching and waiting. Lewis raised his pistol, but relaxed when he saw that one of the silhouettes carried his cane sword.

"I say, down there!" The strain in Drake's voice was unmistakable. "Are you all right?"

"Yes!" Lewis said, before Lord Crandall or Gregory could answer. "And you?" He quickened his pace at the realization that they might actually survive the night. Whatever had happened down there, surely they could find their way back to a station they knew.

Lord Crandall glanced sidelong at Lewis, apparently annoyed that he had spoken first, but called out to Drake. "Are any of those fiends up there?"

"Not yet. I suggest we regroup and contact the authorities post haste." Drake shifted uncomfortably, as if his fear prevented him from standing still.

"A good plan." Lord Crandall nodded in satisfaction.

They had drawn close enough that Drake's weathered features were visible. Next to him stood the red-haired engineer, his eyes darting back and forth nervously. Both had bloodstains on their jackets, their hands, and their faces, leaving Lewis to wonder if any of the survivors had died on their flight to the surface. He had not noted any corpses.

"We appear to be safe for the moment." The old man drew back so Lewis and his companions could get a clear view of what lay beyond.

The tunnel opened into a broad cobblestone court, similar to the one Lewis had passed through to enter the underground earlier that evening. Unlike that one, however, this formed a perfect square with one street leaving in each direction. Ringed by brightly glowing gas lamps on ordinary metal lampposts, it was brighter than the station, but a dark haze of smoky fog hung in the air, making the terrace houses and other buildings at the edges of the square difficult to see. Lewis could make out pinpoints of light coming from many of the houses.

The statue of a military man in the uniform of a modern British soldier, complete with tall hat and bandoliers, stood in the center of the square, though its face appeared to have been sheared off; whether on purpose or due to time and the elements was impossible to tell. An arched sign above the statue spelled out *Mithras Court*. The survivors huddled near it. Lewis unbuttoned his overcoat, surprised that the evening was much less chilly than he recalled. In fact, it was a good deal warmer. The others had removed their coats in recognition of this.

An aging, gray-haired woman wearing a long-sleeved maroon dress leaned against the base of the statue, whispering fervently in prayer. Next to her, a young lady of no more than eighteen years wearing an elegant blue dress and a smart velvet coat sat on the flagstones and sobbed. A young man stood between them, holding the young lady's hand. He held a wool overcoat over one arm and appeared barely old enough to shave. A portly man leaned against the statue near the gray-haired woman, his breathing heavy. His right arm hung in a makeshift sling and he gritted his teeth as if in pain, but remained silent. Not far from them, evidently divided by class, Reggie sat on the ground next to his wife, who dabbed at the blood oozing from the gash in his cheek with the sleeve of her dress.

"Hold still, Reggie," Mary said.

"It stings." Reggie winced as she tended his wound.

Lewis turned to the gentleman and the professor. "I've never heard of Mithras Court."

"Nor have I." Lord Crandall kept pace with him. "Which begs the question—where the devil are we?"

"None of us has heard of such a place existing in London."
Professor Drake paused as if he might say more, but kept silent
in the end.

"There he is! He's brought this menace upon us!" The gray-haired
woman glared at Lewis.

"Please, Josephine," the portly man said gently. "No man can
conjure the dead."

"How do we know it's not his fault that we are here to begin with?"
The young man's accent identified him as American. "Everything
happened after he drew his revolver."

"You're right! He's a sinner and God has judged him and brought
this disaster upon us." Josephine narrowed her eyes at Lewis. "To
trust him is to destroy us all!"

"Be silent, Josephine!" the heavy man said. "Do you really think
God would send legions of the dead after innocent people just to
get the one who sinned?"

"It's a ridiculous notion." Lord Crandall waved at them in irritation. "As is the supposition that this man could have brought us to
this Mithras Court, or raised the dead."

"God works in mysterious ways, Edgar." Josephine glared at the
fat man, but her voice softened, the wind taken from her sails.

"I don't care whose fault it is, we need to get away from here."
Panic flushed the engineer's freckled face.

"Everyone, please calm yourselves." Lord Crandall raised his
hands, quelling the bickering with the gesture, and a glance at the
recalcitrant Josephine. "We are safe for the moment and our next
actions must be chosen carefully, lest we place ourselves in greater
danger." He pointed at the engineer. "You, rail man. Are Gregory and
the professor correct? Is Mithras Court an unknown station?"

"There isn't any such station on this route or any other." The
engineer doffed his black conductor's cap and wiped his sweaty
forehead with a meaty hand, but Lord Crandall's question had
apparently calmed him. "And even if there were, no one could make
the other train cars vanish or rearrange themselves. Something's
happened here—something evil." He shuddered as he settled an
accusing gaze on Lewis.

"I am not responsible for any of this!" Lewis's cheeks flushed with anger. He met the engineer's glare with confidence, then turned to face Josephine's anger head on. "I *am not* an agent of the Devil." Such hysterical musings would not help them find a way out of their predicament. As Lewis had seen in the past, such accusations had all the markings of the battlefield ramblings that always followed a defeat.

"Then perhaps you are the Devil himself!" Josephine shouted back.

"That is superstitious nonsense." Professor Drake folded his arms across his chest. "Let us not return to the dark ages because we have witnessed a horror. There must be a logical explanation for these events."

"What other power could cause the dead to rise? It's Armageddon! We must cast this man out or be taken with him!" Josephine was rapidly approaching hysteria.

"Enough!" Lord Crandall turned to her. His lip curled in obvious distaste. "We must determine our next course of action immediately. We haven't *time* for your nonsense."

Lewis turned away from them, his guilt overwhelming his anger. He could hardly blame them for turning their terror in his direction. It was true that he had been intent on killing a man in cold blood, and murder was contrary to the laws of God, whether in war or as an act of vengeance.

And yet, God, if he existed at all, had allowed such atrocities as Lewis had witnessed during the Zulu war. In light of those horrors, he could not see God lifting a finger to help them now. Lewis's experiences had led him to believe that God's plans included atrocities.

He peered into the gritty fog, pushing their accusations and his doubts from his mind. At the edges of the light, shadow-draped alleys between several clusters of buildings yawned forbiddingly. He squinted, trying to discern anything that might lurk there. Several shadowy figures jerked forward a step, as if sensing his gaze.

"Son of a whore . . ." He raised his weapon.

"I beg your pardon, Captain Wentworth?" Lord Crandall glanced at him.

"He's a captain?" The American frowned. "On whose side?"

"More of those things are out there, in the gloom." Lewis pointed to the alley where the creatures watched them.

"What? Where?" Edgar straightened, his gaze flicking over the alleys. "What if they come for us? We must find shelter now! We can't rely on this man and his pistol to protect us if there are more than one or two of those things!"

"Get hold of yourself, man!" Lord Crandall peered into the murk. "They appear to be afraid of the lamps."

"We must not panic!" Drake said. "What we must do is leave this square straightaway and locate a safe place to hide until morning. Perhaps some of the local residents will assist. There are lights coming from many of these buildings. There could be survivors taking shelter from this plague of the dead."

"And what if there aren't any survivors?" Edgar puffed out his rotund chest, and for a moment, Lewis thought he might actually beat it like an ape. "What if everyone has drowned in this evil?"

"The entire world cannot have perished during our short train ride." Lord Crandall frowned. "Drake is right. We must question the locals, or at least gain their assistance."

"But these locals, this place . . ." the engineer said. "This district has to be in London . . . we've not come so far that we could have left the city. The tracks don't go that far. Where in God's name are we, and what kind of people will we find here?"

" 'Tis a big city," Reggie said, his tone gentle. "I've heard stories of entire neighborhoods getting lost and forgotten, except by those who live in them."

Gregory rubbed his jaw thoughtfully. "That is preposterous."

"Perhaps not." Drake turned in a full circle, studying the buildings. "How many of you know the exact location of Petticoat Lane? After it was renamed and cleaned up, it became lost to most. And it was hardly the only one."

"I see your point." Gregory nodded.

"Gentlemen," Lewis said finally, in the commanding voice he used to motivate his troops and recruits in the direst situations. "And ladies. We need to leave . . . now."

"Where do we go?" the American asked.

"We go in the opposite direction from wherever this *captain* wishes us to go," Josephine said haughtily.

"Enough, Josephine," Edgar said, but his shoulders slumped in defeat. "We need to find shelter for the night. As much as I hate to admit it, we should stay together. There is strength in numbers, I think."

The pious woman crossed her arms over her chest and glared angrily at him, but remained silent. Lewis ignored their byplay and studied the nearest buildings. He saw a sign hanging over the arched doorway of a three-story terrace. He could not make out the words on it, but could clearly see the image of a mug of ale painted on it. It seemed a logical choice.

"There!" He pointed to it. "If there are survivors, they'd naturally seek a public place with food and drink. I suggest we head there at once."

"You might not be an agent of the Devil, as some have suggested," Lord Crandall said, in a quiet voice intended for privacy. "But how do we know you aren't a villain nonetheless?"

"I'm a decorated veteran of the Zulu War, where I served the Queen well!" The pride of his past overcame his guilt-ridden quest for vengeance. "I nearly lost my leg to a Zulu spear, and I was discharged with full honors. I did not apply for my position at the Royal Academy; rather, my superiors submitted my name, and the Academy came to *me.* If you like, you may consult my colleagues for a reference. Or, you may join in Josephine's hysteria. I'm sure within the hour she'll be accusing me of being Jack the Ripper!"

Gregory studied Lewis in silence for several moments. "Let us, for the moment, accept your statements. Why would you seek vengeance upon that man?"

"The man with the snake tattoo," Lewis's eyes burned with anger, "killed my wife, and for that he will die. But I swear to you, I know nothing of what has happened to us, or of the creatures that attacked us. I am no agent of evil!" The memory of Elise's face, her perfect skin and penetrating blue eyes, flitted through his mind, and he thought again of hearing her voice in the station. For a heartbeat, he wondered if their survival mattered, if this place offered the chance to be with her, talk to her, see her.

He shoved the thought away as Drake spoke.

"If that is true, then I am sorry," Drake said. "This conversation will be academic, however, if we do not make haste."

"I will give you a full accounting of my behavior when we're safe. And should you require it, I swear to you I'll turn myself in to the police." Lewis met their skeptical glares straight on. He had changed over the past two years, but he was still a man of honor and principle. That honor demanded that he remain with the others rather than set off on his own. As the only man with a weapon, it fell upon him to protect this group. He had not been present to save Elise, and he would never make such a miscalculation again, whatever his personal thoughts about his companions.

"I accept your explanation and your word for the time being." Lord Crandall motioned toward the pub, satisfied by Lewis's promise. "Lead on." He turned to the others. "I suggest you follow."

Lewis raised his gun and limped across the plaza.

CHAPTER *THREE*

Heels tapped on the cobblestones and mumbling voices echoed behind Lewis as he led the survivors across the courtyard. Strangely, a calm feeling settled over him, the way it had when his mounted brigade had ridden alongside him during the war. As they crossed the square, he heard Drake introducing himself to the others, as if not knowing everyone's name was too much for an English gentleman to bear. Lewis almost laughed at the irony of good manners in the face of the walking dead. But by listening in, he learned about his companions. There was the American, Thomas Bainbridge, and his wife, Anne—school teachers on their honeymoon. Ben was the train's engineer. Edgar was a banker, and Josephine was his wife of twenty-six years. And there were the others whose names he had already learned during their brief acquaintance.

An uneasy tension flowed between them all, palpable and unnerving. They spoke to each other in tones that betrayed their nervousness and reminded Lewis inexorably of soldiers arriving on the front line for the first time. The wide-eyed stares as they glanced around, the fast speech, and the sweat he saw beaded on many a brow all spoke of their fear of what might come next that night.

Lewis made a note to watch them, especially the ones who had no training in war. Without question, someone would lose his or her nerve, just as the occasional infantryman did in the field. It was inevitable. This group had just witnessed the most horrifying event of their lives. He considered himself fortunate to have known the heat of battle, and as terrible as the attack in the station had been, even with the dead walking among the living, nothing would ever be as horrifying as learning of Elise's death.

The memory of the constables standing outside his door, with that look on their faces as they told him the news, came unbidden to his mind. He pushed the memory away, consciously focusing on survival.

The creatures still watched from the shadows, the hatred burning behind their decaying eyes, as if they remembered life and hated those who still had it. Yet they made no attempt to approach. Lewis swiftly climbed the worn stone steps of the pub, but paused halfway up to look at the sign hanging over the entrance. The words The Laughing Gargoyle were painted in blue letters above the mug of ale. A stout gray creature with a hideous face squatted in front of the mug itself. Had Lewis seen the grotesque visage from the other side of the courtyard, he might have changed direction; something about the eyes of the thing made it look alive. Below the sign, a stone archway jutted forward, creating an alcove before a thick oak door. A small, barred peep-door was closed against the foggy night.

"I don't like the looks of that," Josephine said from a few steps back. Lewis wondered if she liked the looks of anything. She struck him as a woman whose sole purpose in life was to complain at every turn.

"The purpose of gargoyles is to ward off evil spirits," Drake said from the step behind Lewis.

"It doesn't appear to have worked." Lord Crandall pointed to the door. Looking closer, Lewis spied claw marks gouged in the surface. He tightened his grip on his weapon and stepped closer. He had not yet put the revolver away, and after what he had seen tonight, he was not sure if he ever would again.

"The question is, did the door hold them back?" Gregory stepped up next to him and looked up at the stone ceiling of the alcove, clearly expecting someone to pour boiling oil on them through invisible murder holes.

"It must have prevented these walking dead from gaining entry." Lord Crandall balled his fists, prepared for a fight. "However, I suggest we make ourselves ready."

"I agree." Lewis did not find that very comforting. "If these dead have gotten inside, they would not have shut the door behind them. They don't seem to have that kind of intelligence."

"Are you an expert on the dead now?" Edgar frowned. "You have no idea what drives these devils, or what they are capable of."

"I'm an expert on sizing up an enemy." Lewis stepped up to the door and knocked three times. "They didn't make it into this establishment."

The soft scrape of metal against metal sounded as Drake slid the blade from the cane. The others held their collective breath as heavy footsteps echoed on the other side of the entrance, and a soft click broke the silence as the peep-door opened. A round, unshaven face appeared in the small opening. The man narrowed his eyes.

"What do you want?" The voice was heavy and gruff.

"We've been assaulted by . . . creatures in the underground rail station. We need shelter and medical attention," Lewis said.

The man grunted and closed the door before Lewis could say anything else.

"In the name of God, help us!" Josephine said from the rear of the group.

A heavy bolt slid back and the door opened to reveal a burly man, taller than Lord Crandall and wider than Edgar. He wore a long white apron over a tan shirt. His sleeves were rolled up and he held a flintlock pistol in one hand.

"Get inside, quickly!" He stepped aside so they could enter.

If the courtyard was the picture of danger and desertion, then the pub was its exact opposite. A high, beamed ceiling gave the place a spacious appearance, though so many tables, chairs, and patrons filled the room that it felt cramped. A roaring fire blazed in a hearth along the right wall, and heavy smoke hung over the room, a pall fed by the fire, pipe tobacco, and cigars; the coal fog contributed as well.

Coats of arms, swords, and a few muskets adorned the walls, and a massive tapestry hung in the rear. A narrow wooden stair at the back led to the second floor, where, no doubt, rooms could be rented. A long polished bar, complete with brass fittings and swiveling stools, occupied the left wall. Mirrored shelves behind it bore dozens of bottles. Several kegs of beer stood visible on the floor below them.

Three serving girls in plain gray dresses meandered about, catering to the many patrons. Dressed in styles of clothing that crossed the class divide, from regal gowns and stylish frocks to simple homemade clothing like the kind worn by Reggie and his wife, the customers hunched over their tables, their low voices a dull murmur that reminded Lewis of the sound of a small brook. It ceased as they entered the room, and all eyes turned toward them.

Lewis ignored the challenging stares and led the others inside. No matter how hostile the crowd might seem, it was preferable to what lay outside. If the claw marks on the door were any indication, then surely these patrons could understand their plight.

The instant Edgar had crossed the threshold, their burly bene-factor slammed the door hard. He turned a massive key near the handle and slid a thick metal bolt into place.

"The name's Frederick." He turned to them with surprising speed and grace for one so large. "I'm the proprietor of this establish-ment." He glanced at Lewis's gun and looked at his own weapon as if suddenly remembering that he still held it. He shoved it into his belt and murmured, "Sorry about that. You can't be too careful." He extended his hand toward Lewis.

Lewis slipped his own revolver into his coat pocket and shook the man's hand. Lord Crandall frowned at this and took a step toward them.

"What the hell are they doing outside during first night?" a man said from somewhere in the crowd.

"And without a lantern?" a woman said. "Are they daft?"

"Are they trying to get themselves killed?" another man said from near the fireplace. "Or endanger the lot of us?" Angry glares punc-tuated the questions and a tense silence fell. Lewis did not flinch as they watched, though their stares were as palpable as those of the corpses. To show any sign of weakness could endanger them all.

"That's enough! These good folks are clearly new to Mithras Court," the big man said in a booming voice. "And they're my guests."

This seemed to placate the crowd. They returned to their con-versations and Frederick motioned with one massive arm to an unadorned door at the side of the bar.

"You look like you could use some privacy." He grabbed a bar-maid's sleeve in a gentle grip. "Chloe, take drinks and some food to the parlor."

"Of course." The blonde woman looked at them, her blue eyes displaying both concern and mild interest, but she headed through another door behind the bar without saying more.

As the door opened, a blast of delicious aromas, including stewed meat and potatoes and boiled cabbage, assailed Lewis's nostrils. He caught a glimpse of a small kitchen where several older women stirred a massive iron pot and prepared other foods. His stomach churned and his mouth watered as he suddenly realized that he had not eaten anything in at least half a day.

Frederick led them through the common room, charting a zigzag course between the crowded tables. Judging by the snatches of con-versation Lewis overheard, everyone in the place was talking about them; some wondered where they had come from, while others were afraid that the newcomers would draw attention to them. All of them seemed to think that their arrival was significant. None exchanged more than a passing glance with Lewis. It made Lewis think they were hiding something.

As they neared the rear of the pub, Lewis studied the tapestry. It depicted an idyllic forest scene with birds flitting about in the foreground and flowers in bloom. Tall oak trees stretched skyward in the background. He paused as he realized that several peasants lay prone in front of a hovel of stone and wood on the edge of the forest. Red-eyed wolves, with drool-covered fangs bared, stalked toward them. As he looked closer, he realized that the heads of the peasants lay tilted at odd angles and their eyes stared blankly into the sky. He shivered and looked away from the disturbing piece of art.

An odd-looking raven-haired man of middle years wearing the gold-buttoned coat and loose trousers of the gypsy folk sat directly below the hideous scene, grinning at Lewis and displaying white teeth. He waved, revealing a missing pinky finger on his right hand.

"What a disgusting tapestry," Lord Crandall said; he'd paused beside Lewis to study it.

Frederick raised his eyebrows ever so slightly. "Tonight it is." The big man walked past the bar, opened the door, and disappeared from sight.

"What the devil does he mean by that?" Drake glanced from the open doorway back to Lewis and Lord Crandall.

"I have no idea," Lord Crandall said. "Something is very wrong here, more than we thought." A frown slipped from beneath his moustache. "We should watch ourselves."

"Always." Lewis said.

The gypsy nodded, continuing to smile at him.

"Are we going to follow the innkeeper or not?" Edgar pushed past them impatiently.

Lewis turned away from the gypsy and walked to the door. He paused just inside as an odd tingling sensation itched his back directly between his shoulder blades. The gypsy's penetrating gaze was focused on that exact spot, Lewis knew instinctively. He shivered involuntarily, not entirely sure why, and followed the others inside.

════MC════

The sitting room was simple but comfortable. A blue divan, tan sofa, and comfortable cushioned chairs were spaced around an odd-looking rug made of a thick grayish fur that covered the hardwood floor almost entirely. Two gas lamps hung on the wall to either side of the door, their soft glow providing sufficient light and even a little warmth against the evening chill. Thick burgundy drapes had been drawn across two tall windows, preventing them from seeing outside, or anyone else from seeing in. Knowing what lurked in the darkness of the alley upon which the windows opened, Lewis was glad for the drapes. Elevated from the level of the street as they were, and with the bright glow of the gas lamps, he felt certain that the walking dead could not gain entry. Knowing that the patrons in the other room felt safe enough to sit down for meals and flagons of ale, Lewis decided that they were as safe as they could be.

"Chloe will bring your food shortly. I'll have one of the other girls fetch some fresh bandages." Frederick turned to leave.

"Just a moment, my good man." Lord Crandall caught him by the arm. "Why don't you tell us what the devil is going on here?"

"What do you mean?" Frederick narrowed his eyes and looked down a good three inches at the other man.

"Don't you wish to know who or what attacked us?" Crandall asked.

"Not especially." The big man shrugged. "People get attacked all the time in the Court. It doesn't make much difference to me."

"We weren't attacked by thugs in the street," Lord Crandall said, in the impatient tones of one who expects to be obeyed without question. "We were attacked by the dead risen from their graves. You must summon the police at once."

"Yes! And call for a priest!" Josephine pointed at Lewis from where she sat on the sofa. "Evil is among us!"

Frederick laughed.

"Have we—have I said something humorous?" Lord Crandall's face flushed. "Do you doubt my word?"

Lewis groaned. It was never a good idea to impugn the word of a gentleman. Surely an innkeeper would know that.

"The police can't do anything about the dead." Frederick shook his head at Josephine. "And a priest can do even less."

"Then you know what we're talking about," Lewis said. "You've seen them?"

"Aye. Every first and second night they rise from their graves, or wherever it is they rest during the daylight hours." Frederick glanced at the window. "Everyone knows to bring their own lantern or a torch if they have to go into the Court at night. At the very least, you must stay close to the street lamps and avoid the dark places."

"Surely Scotland Yard can do something about these fiends!" Professor Drake said.

A puzzled look crossed Frederick's face, then vanished quickly. "No one can do anything about it." His eyes narrowed. "Least of all you. It's better to stay out of their way."

"None of this makes any sense." Thomas Bainbridge stood up from where he had been sitting with his wife on the divan. "Are you telling us that in this neighborhood, the dead walking amongst the living is commonplace?"

"Aye, that's the truth." Frederick turned to leave. "You're in Mithras Court. The police can't help you." He moved toward the door.

"That's insane!" Bainbridge took a step toward the innkeeper.

Indeed it was, Lewis thought. The Metropolitan Police Service had a presence in all areas of London and the surrounding villages. Wherever they were, they were not out of reach of the Met. To claim the police could do nothing made no sense.

"But where is Mithras Court?" Drake asked from an armchair between the windows. "In what part of London does it hide? How far away from the Monument have we come, and how long has this terrible trauma been going on here?"

Frederick paused before he laughed aloud. After a moment, he sobered. "You're new, but you'll learn. In the meantime, you can stay here as long as you like, as long as you can pay."

"Money is not an object." Lord Crandall puffed himself up. "Nor is it the issue here. We——"

"Good. I have patrons to see to." Without another word, Frederick left, closing the door firmly behind him.

"Impudent wretch."

"What an infuriating man," Josephine said. "I fail to understand why he refused to send for the police."

"And I don't understand what could possibly be humorous about this situation." Edgar took a seat next to her and wrapped an arm around her shoulders. She slid closer to him.

"Edgar's right," Bainbridge said. "The man made no sense. None of this makes any sense."

"It's like I said." Reggie spoke from the corner where he stood behind his seated wife. "This place got lost and London forgot about it. All we need to do is figure out what districts are around us and we'll know where we are."

"What we need to do is survive until morning and locate the local constabulary," Lord Crandall said.

"We seem safe enough for the moment." Lewis paced across the rug. He slipped his hand into his pocket and touched the comforting steel of his revolver as a clergyman would reach for his cross to find solace. "The people here do not appear afraid. In fact, the only thing that seemed to scare them was the thought that we might have brought some of those creatures in with us. Which suggests that we're safe in this pub."

"Yet even that did not truly frighten them." Professor Drake struck a match and lit a pipe that he had produced from an inner coat pocket.

"I'd be willing to bet they'd act differently if the gas stopped flowing to the lamps." Gregory looked at the frosted glass chimney of the nearest light.

"An excellent point," Lord Crandall agreed. "But the question is, how long has this been happening, and as Edgar queried, what are those things out there?"

Lewis blinked at the man's restatement of the questions they had all been asking since their arrival. Surely they had discussed this enough. But he said nothing as he paused in the center of the room, realizing that Lord Crandall watched him with raised eyebrows. The man expected an answer. Lewis dredged his memory for anything that might serve as an explanation. His thoughts touched on the tales his soldiers had told as they camped on the grassy African plains.

"During the Zulu War," he said finally, "there were stories of dead soldiers rising from the battlefield to stalk the living, but I always dismissed them as sheer fantasy." Such tales had usually been shared after too much drink had flowed. Lewis had never given them credence—until he arrived in Mithras Court and the tales came true. He and his companions had witnessed things that no person was meant to see. Images of the passengers who had been torn apart on the platform flooded his mind. Such horrors would surely haunt them all to the end of their days.

"I heard similar stories as a boy when visiting our summer estate in Yorkshire," Lord Crandall said. "The servants used to talk of drowning victims who would rise out of the muck at the bottom of the Thyne and walk among the living in search of revenge." He fixed Lewis with an intense gaze.

"I assure you, I am quite alive," Lewis said, drawing a few muted chuckles from the group, despite their circumstances.

"Yes, of course." Lord Crandall did not look as though the matter was quite settled.

The door opened, interrupting any further conversation, and Chloe entered, balancing a tray of food on her shoulder. Two young men carrying a table followed on her heels. They set it in the center of the room and the girl lowered her tray onto it. It contained more than enough food for all of them, including a slab of braised boar surrounded by vegetables and roasted potatoes. Another platter bore sliced cheeses, fruit, and small loaves of bread. The aromas took hold of Lewis's nose and tantalized his taste buds. His stomach grumbled and his mouth watered; he found himself across the room without realizing he had moved. One of the serving boys returned with a stack of plates.

"Jenna will be along in a tick with them bandages," Chloe said, and disappeared with her helpers.

Lewis and his fellow survivors descended upon the tray like savages, tearing into the food as if they hadn't eaten in days. It was odd, really; this incredible hunger they all shared felt slightly out of place somehow. In war, some men worked up ferocious appetites, but just as often, Lewis had seen men refuse to eat for days at a time. Given the horrors they had just witnessed, he would not have expected them to feel like eating. But he could not deny the raging hunger they all felt.

Lewis picked up an apple and felt himself edged away by Edgar. He maneuvered toward the potatoes, mindful of not bumping the ladies, but barely controlled himself from shoving them aside. He sensed the others desperately clinging to gentility and manners even as they surrounded the food like a pack of wild animals.

CHAPTER FOUR

"Well, that was rather embarrassing." Professor Drake sat back in the arm chair near the windows and motioned with his pipe to the bits of food scattered over the table. Chloe moved around it, picking up debris and wiping the rug with a wet towel. She glanced at him, her eyes narrowed. After a moment, she returned to her work.

"Appalling, I would say." Josephine brushed breadcrumbs from her skirt. "It must be this terrible place."

"Mithras Court has affected us all," Anne agreed from the divan. "More than I thought, if I might eat like that." She wore a small smile, an attempt at humor. Lewis returned it, but the expression did not feel right in this place.

"Indeed, I haven't been that famished since serving in the Transvaal," Lord Crandall said thoughtfully. "In fact, I am not certain I have ever been that hungry."

Lewis perked up at that. His suspicions had been correct. Crandall had indeed served in Her Majesty's Army in the conflict that immediately followed the Zulu War. He studied the man again. Crandall carried himself with an air of authority that might have meshed nicely with Lewis's ability to lead, were it not for his arrogant, off-putting demeanor. Still, as far as the nobility was concerned, Crandall was tolerable.

A grunt from Edgar drew his attention and he focused on the portly man. He was eyeing the leftover morsels greedily as Chloe cleaned up.

"Does anyone else need bandaging?" Jenna asked. The barmaid had arrived with clean water and bandages as promised, and had helped to dress their wounds, including Lewis's shoulder. Jenna had the same round face as Chloe, marking her as a sister or perhaps a cousin, but her darker hair and brown eyes set her apart. Lewis saw a surprising kindness in her eyes that seemed absent from Chloe and the other people they had seen so far. He rubbed his shoulder. It was sore, but it felt better than it had since the dead man's long nails had pierced it.

"I believe you have helped everyone in need of aid," Professor Drake said. "Thank you, my dear."

She curtseyed and gathered up the remaining bandages and bowl of water from the table. "You'll be lettin' me know if you need anything else, then." She smiled and exited.

"I fail to see the point of this meaningless conversation," Josephine said. "Our situation has not changed because we've eaten."

"Indeed it has not," the professor said. "However, there appears to be little we can do tonight, unless you'd care to return to the courtyard outside?" He arched an eyebrow in emphasis.

"We can't just sit here!"

"What would you have us do?" Lord Crandall looked at her. "Light a signal fire on the roof?"

Gregory and a few of the others snickered.

"Listen to me, all of you," Lewis said. He moved to the center of the room, drawing everyone's attention. "This is not the first time I have had to fortify a position against a superior force. Believe me when I tell you we must remain here. We have ample supplies, this structure is sound, and there are enough of us to hold out against a small army if you count the other patrons. I recommend the men stand guard outside this door in a rotating duty shift two at a time, while the others get what sleep they can. At first light, we can figure out a way to contact the police."

"I agree with the Captain's assessment of the situation." Crandall nodded in satisfaction. "It seems prudent for Captain Wentworth to take the first watch, perhaps with Professor Drake?"

Drake nodded his approval. But Lewis watched Crandall in silence, wondering why he had suddenly yielded authority to him. Lord Crandall did not strike him as a man who wasted words or actions. He surely had a reason for everything he did. This turn of events did not comfort Lewis.

"I volunteer Gregory and myself to take the second shift."

"Just a minute." Thomas straightened, jarring his wife, who leaned against him, her eyes shut, though Lewis did not think she slept. She startled at the abrupt movement, her eyes fluttering open. "I'm sorry, my love. Go back to sleep." He turned to the others. "I believe the Captain owes us a full accounting."

Lewis frowned, but as all eyes turned toward him, he shrugged. If he could convince them that he was innocent of any crime and that they could trust him fully, it would make their next hours more smooth. He felt strongly that command should rest in one man's hands. That would make them all safer, himself included.

"Very well. I'll be brief." He pulled up a small side chair and took a seat, gathering his thoughts and steeling his resolve. This task would not be pleasant. "As you probably know, shortly after the City & South London Railway opened in December of 1890, twelve people were slain after their train departed from the King William Street Station."

"I do recall the incident." Lord Crandall tweaked his moustache thoughtfully.

"As do I, but what does that have to do with anything?" Josephine glared at him.

"My wife was one of those killed." Tears brimmed at her memory and with his wish to see her again, and he made no effort to keep them back.

"Oh, my." Mary gasped and Reggie leaned forward to embrace her reassuringly.

"And that man you tried to dispatch on the train . . .." Gregory said thoughtfully. "He must have been involved."

"The only survivor of the massacre was a ten-year-old boy who reported seeing a man with a snake tattoo on his forearm. The man I tried to kill—on the same train where my wife was killed—has that tattoo." Lewis bowed his head, unwillingly imagining, as he had for two years, Elise struggling against the man as he stabbed her again and again. He took a deep breath and straightened himself. The tattooed man deserved no quarter, and Lewis would give him none.

And yet, he had paused rather than shooting him outright. His lip curled into a sneer of disdain for his weakness. To have come so far, cornered his quarry, and then to have allowed a moral conundrum to divert him from his course, smacked of an incompetence he had not thought he possessed. In war, such second guessing would have gotten him killed, he knew, but this was not war. War was an affair of honor.

This was revenge.

"Captain?" Drake coaxed him. "Are you all right?"

"That man must die," Lewis said coldly. "And I *will* pull the trigger."

"And what of your word to turn yourself in to the police?" Josephine said, studying him through narrowed eyes, clearly waiting for him to break his promise.

"I gave you my word. Unless you change your minds, I'll turn myself in once we're safely away from this place and these walking monsters." Josephine might doubt him, but he knew that honor demanded that he guide these civilians to the local constabulary and to safety.

"Just like that?" Josephine asked.

"I, for one, believe him," Lord Crandall said finally. "And I am an excellent judge of character." He met Josephine's stare and did not flinch even as the tension grew.

Lewis resisted the urge to laugh. The gentleman's contradictory statements and constantly changing attitude toward events made his judgments suspect. Combined with his general feelings regarding the gentry, Lewis did not trust the man. He would not have trusted him in any situation, but it was made that much easier since Crandall's actions did not inspire trust.

"If we're all in agreement, then." Drake's statement broke the deadlock. "I suggest we ask our host for some bedding and call it a night."

As if he had been listening the entire time, the door opened and Frederick strolled inside holding a washbasin. Several white towels hung over his arm. He set the bowl on the table.

"As promised," he said gruffly, turning to leave.

"I say, Frederick." Crandall stepped between him and the door.

"We'll need some bedding. There is hardly enough room on these couches for all of us, and I do not relish the thought of sleeping on the floor without bedding."

So much for the tough war veteran, Lewis thought. Crandall might have seen combat, but even in war, he had certainly slept in luxury. Lords might play at war, but most could never truly understand what a typical soldier experienced. Lewis had led men in the field, in the thick of combat that sometimes was the result of poor planning on the part of lords and generals. He had seen firsthand what real fighting did to men, and how they could be spurred to greatness or misled to ruin.

"The boys are fetching some." Passing Crandall, Frederick seized the doorknob.

"Where do your other patrons sleep?" Drake asked suddenly.

Frederick paused at the question—suspiciously, Lewis thought. The answer couldn't be that hard.

"They double or triple up on rooms upstairs, and some sleep in the common room."

"How long has this been going on?" Lewis could not imagine that the situation had been so bad for very long. No one could withstand such tension. "Surely the police or the army is trying to rid you of this scourge of the dead."

"The police are working on that." Frederick squinted at him for an instant. Seeming satisfied, he stepped through the door into the quiet tavern beyond.

"That man is hiding something," Edgar said.

"Yes," Lewis said matter-of-factly. He resisted the temptation to compliment the portly fool on his keen intellect. It would be obvious to a first year cadet that Frederick could not be trusted. He slipped his hand into his pocket, closing it around the handle of his revolver. A new gesture, yet one the last few hours had made comforting. "Perhaps we should move a piece of furniture in front of the door while we sleep and keep watch from the inside."

"Do you not trust him?" Ben asked. "He seems an honest fellow."

"No." Lewis frowned, wondering why the engineer would be

taken in, but he seemed merely naïve rather than stupid. Although Lewis did not feel threatened by their host—not the way they were threatened by the dead—the secrets the man clearly harbored could prove dangerous. Lewis had learned to take nothing for granted, to trust no one lest they be a betrayer.

"Nor do I," Lord Crandall said.

"Yes, but does that opinion have anything to do with us, or the creatures that attacked us?" Drake said.

"It doesn't matter." Lewis drew his revolver. "We can use this to keep him honest if he proves he is not to be trusted. We need only survive until morning, and we will be done with this whole affair." Unless the dead had spread everywhere in London. If they had overrun an entire neighborhood, there was little reason to expect that they had not moved into other parts of London. He shivered at the thought and resolved himself to put his vengeance on hold should that prove to be true. If the dead had invaded the entire city, it was his duty to stand with his queen, regardless of his personal feelings or his quest.

The door opened again and the two lads brought blankets, pillows, and a few bedrolls. When they had gone, Lewis directed his companions to move the sofa against the door. This done, his fellows settled in for the night with he and the professor taking the first watch.

"Tell me something," Professor Drake said. He spoke in a hushed tone so as not to wake the others. He and Lewis sat on the sofa in front of the door.

"Yes?" Lewis leaned closer. "What is it?"

"You said you were in the Zulu War, correct?"

"I did." His voice was cautious; the man was friendlier than the others, but at night in this place, it was easy to think of treachery.

"How many men did you kill?"

Lewis thought back to the dusty countryside surrounding Ulundi. The battle still raged in his mind as if it were yesterday—the clash of the infantry, the distant nighttime Zulu war drums that so unnerved some of the soldiers, and the final charge that crushed the might of the Zulu army. More than that, he recalled the dead and dying soldiers around him as his horse thundered past. So many Zulus had died in what amounted to a slaughter—whatever the British, who suffered barely a hundred casualties, called it. There was honor in war, but none in such a slaughter. He still felt the shame he had first experienced upon seeing the dead Zulus next to the river and scattered across the plains.

Lewis knew exactly how many corpses could be attributed to him. He had slain fifteen men—fifteen warriors—who had faced a far more advanced enemy with only their spears, their shields, a few scavenged muskets and rifles, and their bravery. Those primitives knew more of courage than the British lords—more than the leaders who had brought them into so many conflicts around the globe ever would.

"Perhaps a dozen . . . perhaps a few more." Shame burned his cheeks both for the lie and for the truth. The fifteen men he had killed had been the tiniest fraction of the thousands of massacred Zulus, but they forever tied him to the dishonorable event.

"And how did that feel?" Drake stared intently at him, as if he could read Lewis's soul through his words.

"Killing doesn't ever feel good," Lewis said. But something in him argued that point. It would feel good when the tattooed man fell to a bullet from his Webley. He shoved the thought down; it was no proper thought for an honorable man. "But we were there at the behest of Queen and Country, and we did our duty." That last part was utter nonsense and Lewis knew it. What the war had accomplished for British colonization in Southern Africa was partially undone by the disastrous Boer War two years later, when the Dutch colonists retook much of the Zulu lands Lewis had fought to conquer. In the end, those he had killed and the men he had lost had truly been thrown away for nothing. Yet he could not bring himself to say such a thing for fear of betraying the memories of those who had died on both sides.

"And what of this tattooed man? You won't be killing him for the service. Are you really prepared to strike a man down in cold blood?" Drake's brow furrowed. "For revenge?"

"Is there any better reason? In war, I killed proud warriors defending their homeland. There was no justice in the deed. But this . . ." He clenched his teeth as the familiar anger seethed inside him, ever hotter. "This man killed my wife. He will die for it." It was said flatly, no threat but a promise.

"Did it not occur to you that some things are better left in the hands of the police?" Drake was clearly looking for a specific answer, but Lewis sneered at the thought. There was no justice for him, no more than there had been for the Zulu.

"I pursued that course, but the police were useless." Lewis picked up his revolver; he had discarded his overcoat shortly after reaching their refuge. He leaned toward Drake and conveyed his deadly earnestness with a look. He would do what the officers of the law would not do—he would search for Elise's killer to the end. "It rests solely with me to avenge her, and I will *not* fail. I *will* watch the tattooed man perish."

"There is no swaying you from this course, then." Drake sighed, a cloud coming over his expression. "But I admit that I understand. I, too, have lost someone dear to me. My brother died as part of the Charge of the Light Brigade in the Crimean War."

"A tragic event." Lewis could sympathize with the man's loss. But deep down, he could not equate the loss of a brother to the death of a spouse, and surely the man could see that. Still, Lewis was interested to learn that Drake's brother had been part of a cavalry division, as Lewis had been. It gave him a sudden small connection to the man. "Was he a member of the 17th Lancers?"

"He was actually part of the 13th Light Dragoons. Now they're the 13th Hussars, I believe." Drake paused and offered him a grim smile. "Forgive me; it's easier to focus on minor details. Regardless of what they called themselves, the event was just as disastrous. Poor military planning, arrogance and blatant stupidity lead to the deaths of far too many men. Malcolm was wounded in the action and died shortly thereafter." The old man's fists balled; pain flashed across his face.

"I'm sorry." Lewis meant it. The Charge of the Light Brigade was the stuff of legend for the average Briton, due in large part to Lord Tennyson's poem—but even more so for the dragoons.

"Yes, well." Drake paused and composed himself. "It was a long time ago, and my own brand of vengeance was served." He looked down for a moment, and when he looked up, the set of his jaw and the hardness in his eyes betrayed the same grim determination that Lewis saw in the mirror each morning. "So you can believe me when I tell you that the act of avenging a loved one serves only to separate you from their memory. Vengeance takes a toll on one's soul. I have seen it. I have lived it."

"Indeed? Have you killed for it?" The hardness in the professor's eyes could not match the hardness of Lewis's own gaze as he watched the man, trying to determine how serious the professor felt himself to be.

"Killed? I am not sure," the professor said. "Destroyed, certainly, and I can tell you that such an act rips a piece of your heart from your chest. I have never been the same." But he did not look ashamed, and Lewis approved of that—he would not be ashamed to destroy the tattooed man.

"Even so, I'd wager it a price worth paying. I will keep my own counsel on that matter." Lewis was not certain what brand of vengeance Drake was guilty of or how it had affected him; he only knew that he would never forget Elise and how much she had meant to him. For her memory, he could never turn away from his duty.

Drake grabbed Lewis's wrist and forced him to meet the professor's gaze. "Honor your wife's memory in some other way, Wentworth. Nothing good can come from vengeance. I know."

"This is none of your affair," Lewis snapped, drawing his arm back, unwilling to face the professor's hard stare. He stood and walked to the other side of the room, carefully avoiding the sleeping forms on the floor. Pulling the curtain back, he peered out the window into the darkness below.

Drake knew nothing of Lewis's life, of what he should or shouldn't be doing. The man's suggestion that he renounce his goal was enough to stir the ever-present rage; this wasn't a quest to honor his wife's memory, it was a quest to honor her death. And it was not merely a task he had taken upon himself to pass the time. It was his life now. There was nothing else. *He* was nothing else. He would kill the tattooed man. Nothing could hinder him from that objective. He had carelessly lost his opportunity, but he would not make that mistake twice.

He considered what he would be willing to do to have his revenge. Would he die for it? Certainly. Would he go so far as to kill a gentleman such as Drake or Lord Crandall if necessary? Perhaps.

He realized he was nodding grimly to his own reflection in the dark glass of the window. He noted the truth hardly troubled him. In fact, it was a comfort.

The window looked out onto a dark, narrow alley between one row of houses and the next. Most likely a home for dust bins, it offered a shortcut to the next street. Diffuse light shone through the heavy mist from the home across the alley, emanating from every window, no doubt to keep the denizens of the night away. In the dim illumination, dark shapes shuffled through the mist, appearing and disappearing as the light waned or the mist thickened. He could not clearly see any of them, and doubted they could see him, but he could feel their hungry gazes fix on him. He drew the curtain closed and stepped back, wondering how long the citizens of Mithras Court had dealt with this scourge.

"I take it they are still there?" Lord Crandall rose to his feet. He had wakened quietly, and Lewis had not realized it.

"Yes," Lewis nodded. "But they aren't moving any closer. As long as the lights burn, we appear to be safe."

"Very good. I believe it's time for Gregory and myself to relieve you." The gentleman held out his hand, palm up.

Lewis glanced down for a moment, knowing what he wanted but unwilling to provide it. If he gave up his weapon, he would have no defense from his fellow survivors. Or the walking dead.

"Come, Captain." Gregory stood up nearby. "If we can't trust one another, what chance have we got of getting away from these beastly things"—he gestured out the window—"alive?"

"Very well." Lewis handed the revolver to Crandall, though his fingers lingered on it a moment. He did not particularly like or trust the man, but Lord Crandall was certainly intelligent enough to understand that leaving before dawn would be suicide. Additionally, he had to know that remaining with Lewis and the group would be the safest option until they could reach a police station. And their combined skills were better than one alone.

"A fine piece." Lord Crandall ran his fingers along the barrel lovingly. He cracked it open, folding the muzzle downward, and counted the cartridges. Satisfied, he closed it and spun the cylinder. "Now, what if I require more ammunition?"

"There." Lewis motioned to his coat, where it lay over the arm of the chair nearest the door. "There are additional rounds." If only he had brought an entire box of bullets, but he had been pursuing only one man, not a horde of walking dead.

Crandall nodded, and he and Gregory seated themselves on the sofa by the door. Lord Crandall looked at Drake with one arched eyebrow.

"Professor?" Something in Crandall's tone indicated to Lewis that he did not fully accept Drake's title—as if he questioned the title as much as the man. Lewis made a mental note to investigate that situation at a more appropriate time, assuming that they lived through this ordeal, and that they did not have him arrested.

"Of course." Professor Drake blinked in confusion at the man. After a moment, he shrugged. "Good night." He negotiated the crowded floor and settled down on the bedroll Gregory had vacated, even though Crandall's was closer. Whether this was more of their argument or merely the professor's honor, Lewis could not tell.

"You should get some rest, Captain," Lord Crandall said to him. "You've been in the field—you certainly know that you should take what you can get when you can get it. We have no idea what tomorrow will bring."

The comment grated on Lewis, but the man was correct. It was vital that he use this opportunity to sleep. He paused to glance from Lord Crandall to the professor. He did not know why the gentleman disliked the scholar, but the enmity was obvious. Dissension could place them all in jeopardy, but for the moment, the conflict appeared controlled. He made a mental note to learn more as the opportunity presented itself, and made his way to the other bedroll. He lay down on his back and drifted immediately to sleep.

Chapter FIVE

"Lewis . . ." Elise spoke, her voice a mere whisper in his ear. "Wake up, love."

Lewis stood in the fog of a dank London day, only the cobblestones beneath his feet visible. A faint light diffused through the vapors around him, providing a dull glow. The troubling scrape of bone on wood echoed in the mists as dark silhouettes circled, vague and indistinct, but drawing ever closer.

"Lewis . . ." Elise's voice trailed off again.

A dozen figures suddenly coalesced out of the mist, forming a barrier on all sides. Black curls quivered around their identical faces as they turned their heads to look at him. They wore a variety of dresses from Elise's wardrobe—the dress Elise had worn in Hyde Park, her favorite sapphire blue silk, the black gown in which she had been buried. Each of them bore an identical resemblance to his lost love, though their expressions ranged from a happy, smiling Elise to a sad, pouting Elise who stared at him with accusing eyes. Lewis's breath caught in his throat.

"Lewis," they said in unison, a bizarre chorus of identical voices. They stepped closer and he saw Elise's beautifully smooth skin, her bright blue eyes, and her perfect teeth on all of them. The difference in their expressions confused and agitated Lewis and his heart beat swiftly, pounding against his ribcage in an attempt to escape. His soul prickled as something scratched at it from inside.

"Elise?" The fog swallowed his voice, making it sound small.

"We need you, Lewis." They took another step forward. "Help us!"

But an icy wind stirred the mist around him, obscuring them for an instant. When the women emerged again, their dresses were covered with dirt; their hair was tangled and in disarray and the flesh had fallen away from their faces, patchily revealing gleaming skulls.

"Elise!" Lewis's eyes opened wide and fear seared his skin, as hot and harsh as if he stood at a glassblower's furnace. He screamed helplessly.

He was surrounded by nightmares.

Upon hearing the news of her death, and ultimately seeing Elise's still form that night in the city's mortuary, he had felt himself falling helplessly into an endless pit. It was as if that feeling, that fear, the very embodiment of her death, had multiplied and returned to stalk him. As they watched him with empty sockets, their very existence a mockery of his love, that feeling crept up from deep within him, causing his heart to beat in an odd rhythm against his chest. The fear tearing his insides froze in silent dismay as he realized that his wives moved to the same beat, their feet falling as his heart pounded.

The demons that resembled his wife tilted back their bony heads and shrieked.

Lewis staggered backward, flinching at the last instant as he remembered that there were more of them, more of *her* behind him. He cried out and whirled around, desperate to find a way out. He had to escape their wrath, the punishment that they clearly intended to levy.

But there was no way out, and as the Elises closed in, he could not escape . . .

"Captain?"

A familiar voice pierced the gloom abruptly.

"Captain, wake up!"

The fog retreated and drew his dead wives with it.

CHAPTER SIX

Lewis's eyes snapped open and he jolted upright with a start to find himself sitting on the parlor floor. Lord Crandall knelt before him, one hand on his shoulder. The other survivors stirred around them; some were just waking up, while others were already on their feet.

"Is it morning already?" Lewis wiped the sweat from his brow.

"It appears so; the sky is lightening. However, according to the clock, it is barely three in the morning." Crandall stood up and motioned to the drapes.

The curtains had been pulled back and Professor Drake and Gregory stood at the windows looking out into the morning fog. Although thick, the vapor could not completely obliterate the sun. The world outside had brightened enough that the other buildings and the alley were visible.

"I don't understand." Drake shook his head. "It is December. It should not be light for another five hours or so."

Lewis stood up, but looked at Lord Crandall rather than out the window. This time, he was the one who extended his hand expectantly. The big man straightened, his hands going to the lapels of his coat, but he said nothing.

"I'll take the gun, if you don't mind." Sarcasm overlay his voice as he took a step closer. He would not give up his weapon again, not until he knew they had safely escaped this place.

"Don't give him that pistol!" Edgar suddenly stood between them. "I still don't believe we can fully trust the man."

"It's his gun," Reggie said, next to Lewis. "And from what I've seen, he knows how to use it better than any of us. Personally, the wife and I feel safer if he has it. And besides, if he'd wanted to kill us, he could have done it last night."

"I agree," Professor Drake said calmly. "If there are more of those creatures between here and the station house, then I would like us to be able to defend ourselves to the best of our abilities. Wentworth is the best shot of all of us."

"Well, I don't see how——" Josephine said.

"I am a man of my word." The sentence dismissed everyone and brooked no argument. Lord Crandall never broke eye contact with Lewis as he handed the weapon to him.

Lewis could tell that Crandall was good to his word as well, at least in some matters, but would oppose him if he deemed it in his best interest. And sometimes his best interest was not the group's, Lewis suspected. This was a man he could understand, he thought, as he took the revolver.

The gun felt comfortable in his hand; it was with reluctance that he donned his coat, picked up his cane, and slipped the Webley into his pocket.

"How can it be daylight?" Edgar, his voice chastened, carried his injured arm gingerly as if it hurt again. He glanced at a gold pocket watch.

"Maybe the clock is wrong?" It was only the second time Lewis had heard Anne Bainbridge's voice, but he noted the melodic quality of it with appreciation, especially in contrast to Josephine's peevish tones.

"Is Edgar's watch wrong as well?" Josephine glared at her as if the suggestion that Edgar could be wrong was ludicrous. No, Lewis decided, it was more annoyance that anyone other than herself could contradict her husband.

"Maybe," Anne said, meeting her stare levelly. It sounded like the voice of a person trying to convince herself of something that could not be true.

"Let's ask our host." Lewis crossed to the door, hopeful that his actions would stop another fruitless conversation. The last thing they needed was a committee guessing at decisions. The heavy door swung open easily on well-oiled hinges to reveal the dimly-lit room beyond. As he crossed the threshold, Lewis realized that not only was the room utterly silent, the lights were turned low. The large common room was empty, the fire burned down to glowing embers and the stools had been placed upside-down on top of the bar.

"Where the devil is everyone?" Lord Crandall stopped to take in the sight.

"I don't understand." Gregory said. "We were up against this door the entire time and didn't hear any commotion, certainly not the kind of disturbance that a mass exodus would have made."

The others fanned out as Lewis stared, dumbfounded, around the place. His eyes fell upon the grim tapestry under which the gypsy had been sitting the previous night. Something was different about it, and he moved to examine it. Lewis realized that the wolves, as well as the villagers that had been lying on the ground, had vanished, as completely as if someone had pulled out the stitching that made them.

A chill bit into his flesh as if a breeze had crashed over him as he realized that pairs of red points peered out from the embroidered forest. Lewis blinked at it in shock and turned away, repulsed. Something was nauseatingly wrong with that tapestry, the inn, and all of Mithras Court. He would be glad to be gone from it.

"Where has Frederick gotten to?" Edgar asked. "I'd like to hear an explanation for all this from him."

"Never mind him," Professor Drake said. "I'd like to know how an entire tavern full of people can empty out without our noticing. Where have the lot of them gone?"

"Frederick made it clear that although it's dangerous to move about at night, there is safety during the day. More than likely, the patrons have simply gone about their daily business. Or perhaps they're still asleep upstairs," Thomas said.

Lewis ignored them as he stepped back to the tapestry, peering into the forest at the red pinpricks. As his eyes focused, interpreting light and shadow, the dim outlines of the wolf pack became visible. He jerked back suddenly, the tapestry seeming even more wrong.

Evil, his mind insisted.

"Are you all right, sir?" Reggie appeared at his side.

"Do you see them?" Lewis pointed at the forest on the tapestry.

"All I see are trees." Reggie drew closer to it, examining the scene intently.

Lewis pointed at the exact spot in the forest, but when Reggie didn't say anything, he looked again. The wolves had vanished.

"I don't understand. There were wolves and villagers——" But he stopped himself. His eyesight was as good as ever, and he could see clearly that the wolves were gone. Nothing in Lewis's experience could explain how such a thing had occurred. He immediately ruled out hallucinations. He had visited an opium den in India as a young soldier and knew how those vapors could skew reality. Given everything else he had seen in Mithras Court, he was inclined to trust his senses. If ever there was a place where the truth did not make sense, this was that place.

"If you two are finished looking at that pedestrian wall hanging," Edgar said, "could we get on with finding Frederick?"

"Are you speaking to me?" Lewis pried himself away from the strange tapestry and turned around to see the heavy man glaring at him from the center of the room, where he stood with the majority of their small group. "A detailed study of our surroundings can only lead to a stronger position. Do you wish us to be vulnerable?"

"Of course I'm speaking to you, Captain!" Edgar visibly puffed himself up; Lewis thought he looked like a peacock. "I don't see how critiquing the wall art can help us with anything."

"Of course you do not; you have no experience in studying a situation with an eye toward learning the best methods for defending oneself. Your refusal to look at what you call a pedestrian wall hanging means you've missed a key detail that the tapestry has provided. Furthermore, *any* detail can be important in gauging a potential ally or enemy."

"And which is Frederick?" Edgar's question surprised Lewis, despite the lashing he had just given him.

"I am not certain yet," Lewis frowned.

"Then I suggest we find out," Edgar said, his arrogant tone replaced by a more determined voice.

Lewis could find nothing more of interest in the tapestry. He turned to the others.

"Very well. We shall conduct a room-by-room search. Reggie, please remain here with the ladies. Lord Crandall, will you please take Gregory and search the rooms on the left side of the hallway upstairs? Ben and Thomas, I'd like you to check the kitchen and any other rooms on this level. Professor Drake, will you accompany me upstairs to check the right side of the hallway?"

The men nodded in agreement, although Lord Crandall could not keep from scowling. They went their separate ways and returned in less than a quarter hour.

"The kitchen and store rooms are deserted," Thomas reported.

"As are the bedrooms upstairs," Lord Crandall added.

"And we found not a soul," Drake said.

Lewis stood silently, studying the group and contemplating their next move.

"We've wasted enough time," Lord Crandall complained. "We should be making our way to the police station."

"And how are we supposed to do that?" Josephine stepped into the conversation. For once, she sounded curious rather than angry or querulous. "We don't know where the local police are, do we?"

"We can ask directions from someone on the street." Ben rubbed his hands together nervously but looked resolute.

"What other choices do we have? There does not appear to be anyone here, other than us," Professor Drake said.

"Well." Lewis drew his weapon. "In that event, there is no reason to delay. You may all stay and argue if you wish. I will go to the police station at once." He moved to the door, curious to see who would join him, and hoping that some would stay behind.

Lewis guessed correctly that Lord Crandall would be the first to volunteer. The man spoke up immediately. "Gregory and I will join you."

Lewis looked at him. The man's grim demeanor revealed that he meant to accompany him regardless of Lewis'ss opinion about the matter. It surprised him that he felt glad of the company. He did not relish the thought of venturing into Mithras Court on his own, despite holding the best weapon in their group.

"Very well, Lord Crandall," he said, deliberately doing his best to sound as if he were granting permission. "I welcome your company."

Drake cleared his throat. "I'm coming with you as well."

"And I." Edgar negotiated the crooked path between the tables to stand with them, a pugnacious look on his face.

"We've no intention of letting any of you out of our sight," Josephine said, joining Edgar, a distrustful look on her face.

As the others chimed in, Lewis realized that all of them would be going to the police station. It frustrated him, but he could not forbid them to leave the pub. And it made sense for them to remain together, despite his desire to be alone. Lewis had become so accustomed to being alone that even in the face of danger, he wished for solitude. It was foolish, he knew. There was, more often than not, strength in numbers—but that implied a certain amount of trust. He knew he could count on himself, but none of the others—with the exceptions of Drake and Reggie—had proven themselves useful or trustworthy. Lewis could see the value in having the rest of them where he could keep an eye on them, rather than out of sight and potentially working at cross purposes.

He cleared his throat. "If all of us are intent on going, I suggest we depart immediately, without wasting any more time." He limped toward the door without awaiting a response. Lord Crandall and Gregory fell into step after him; the professor and the others straggled behind.

A heavy wooden bar had been lifted from its brackets and laid against the wall next to the door. A quick look through the open peephole revealed that no one was near the entrance outside, so Lewis took the handle. The latch clicked and the door opened inward, revealing the dank, fog-enshrouded courtyard beyond. Even in daylight, the gritty vapor was so thick as to make the line of sight only slightly farther than the previous evening. As Lewis breathed in, coal smoke stung his throat and scratched at his lungs.

He wondered how people could live in such pollution. He had

lived almost exclusively in the London filth for the better part of a decade, and since his return from the war, the city felt dirtier and fouler. He and Elise had been considering moving to her family's country estate, but her murder had made that choice irrelevant; he would not leave her killer in London.

He closed his eyes tightly for a moment, remembering her running over the grassy hills of the estate, her hat in her hand. She had spun around in circles and smiled up at the blue sky overhead . . . He gritted his teeth and pushed the memories away, returning to the matter at hand.

The gas lamps remained lit, glowing beacons even in daylight. They helped him discern the outlines of the buildings around the square. He shivered as his eyes fell upon the station's gaping entrance and the stairs descending into blackness at the center of the plaza. From his vantage point, the words Mithras Station were clear. He doubted if even in daylight there could be any safety so deep under the ground, where the dead walked amongst the living. The light could not possibly reach far enough.

The others around him wore expressions of fear and revulsion as they, too, spied the entrance. He knew without doubt that some of them would not survive another such encounter, even if they were physically unharmed. It surprised him that none of them had gone mad considering what they had seen. Civilians were not trained for such things, and the army labored very hard to train its soldiers to expect the horrors of war.

Lewis saw no indication of the creatures that had attacked them, or those who had lurked in the alley outside their window, or of any living people. An eerie calm had settled over the place, as if the entire neighborhood had been abandoned in the night.

"It's very quiet," Mary said from the back of the group, hugging her arms to her chest. She shivered in the chill of the fog.

"It's just the mist, love," Reggie said gently to her. "Sound is funny when it's this thick."

Lewis was not so sure. It had the feel of the uncomfortable silence on the plains near Ulundi just before the attack.

"There—that street appears wider than the others. I suggest

we begin there." Lord Crandall pointed to the left. His coat sleeve slid back as he did so, revealing a diamond cufflink on the white shirt beneath. It gleamed even in the diffuse light.

Lewis frowned. He thought it foolish to wear such items, especially when riding the train at night as they had been. But then, the gentry could be naïvely fearless. As if that thought had set the nobleman to action, Lord Crandall went down the street with Gregory in tow. Lewis sighed at the man's headstrong action, but followed nonetheless. Sometimes being a leader meant making quick decisions, even if they later turned out to be the wrong decisions . . . clearly, Lord Crandall had learned that lesson. Sometimes survival meant not being the first one to face the unknown. If Lord Crandall wanted to wear the bull's-eye . . . so be it.

Their booted feet echoed against the flagstones, a dull rapping that accompanied the higher-pitched heels of the women. Lewis caught up with Crandall and Gregory as they stopped on the corner in front of a rounded three-story brownstone. Constructed of large sandstone bricks, the fog and the London rains had left the building pitted and scarred. Despite that, lights shone through its age-warped glass. The structure marked the start of another city block that stretched away into the murk across the street. A brightly-lit butcher's shop on the ground floor beckoned with an open door; it was out of place amid the desolation. Human figures could be seen inside, moving about in front of a counter. Snatches of conversation drifted from the open door.

"God be praised!" Josephine said, sounding genuinely grateful. "We aren't alone."

"Of course we're not alone," Edgar said. "This is the most populous city in the world! I don't believe it's possible to be alone in London."

Relief that other people were going about their business flowed through Lewis, but a street sign drew his attention. "Cannon Street," he read aloud. "I've heard of it."

"It's in Whitechapel." Professor Drake rubbed his white beard. "But I've never heard of it connecting to a place called Mithras Court."

"Nor I." Lord Crandall took a step to cross the road, but stopped as horse hooves suddenly echoed loudly around them. An instant later a hansom cab emerged from the mist, moving toward them at a brisk trot. Lord Crandall raised his hand and whistled. The driver drew rein and brought the cab to a stop. The horse kicked its front legs, apparently annoyed at the sudden halt, but settled down as the driver muttered to it.

"Day, guv," the weasel-faced driver said, doffing his cap and slouching a bow from atop his seat. "Where would you be goin' this fine day?"

"We require directions, my good man," Professor Drake said abruptly, drawing a scowl from Lord Crandall as the professor took charge. He reached up as if to remove his own hat, a surprising gesture given that this man was only a cab driver. But his hat had been lost in the previous evening's encounter. He lowered his arm and clasped his hands behind his back as if that had been his intention.

Lewis smiled. The gentry could be so amusing even in the worst of times. Even after what they had witnessed, the gentleman's manners remained intact; appearances still mattered. Surely the dead would not care.

"Those'll cost you, too." The man rubbed his hands together and smiled, revealing several good teeth.

"Here." Lewis drew a shilling from his pocket and pushed up next to Lord Crandall to hand the coin to the driver. "We're trying to find the local police station."

"Why do you want to go there?" The man took the money as a timid expression crossed his weathered face.

"That's none of your concern," Edgar said, as rudely as ever.

"Forgive my companion." Lewis stepped to the left, blocking the portly man from the driver's immediate view. "We were attacked last night in the train station. We must alert the police."

"Oh!" The driver's eyes widened in surprise, and he could not stop a furtive glance to either side—Lewis had the strong sense he was seeking an escape route, or witnesses. He tensed, wondering if he might have to defend himself against some unknown danger, but the driver eventually returned his attention to him. "You're new! Why didn't you say so!" He pointed down the street. "Follow Cannon Street two blocks until you come to Caesar's Way. It's on the corner on this side of the street. You can't miss it. A big ugly building . . . looks like a church . . . almost."

"Thank you." Lewis offered the man a nod, relieved that no new troubles had found them.

The driver frowned as he cracked his whip against the rump of his horse. It leaped forward, pulling the carriage away from them. They vanished into the fog a moment later, and all sounds of their passage died abruptly. Lewis stared after the cab, straining to hear the horse or any other signs of life, but the street was eerily silent.

After several breaths, a noise reached Lewis's ears—it was the muffled sound of the butcher shop. He found it oddly comforting to hear ordinary people moving about their ordinary routines. Perhaps the horrors of the past day had unnerved him. Clearly, the disappearance of the cab had been a trick of the fog.

"What are we waiting for?" Edgar tugged on the lapels of his stylish but blood-stained vest. His fingers jerked away when he remembered the condition of his clothing.

Lewis shook himself. He glanced at the fat man and strode swiftly down the brick sidewalk in the direction the cab driver had indicated. As much as he had come to dislike the banker, Edgar was correct. They were wise to make haste.

"Wait for us!" Josephine hurried after them.

The sounds of other horses, of people talking, and the general din of the city reached them suddenly as they walked. The sounds were sometimes loud, sometimes soft, as if the fog controlled the volume by whim. They encountered people on the sidewalks now: a young couple with baskets of fruit and vegetables, an older gentleman walking his dog, others; neither Lewis nor his companions spoke to them. In his mind, there was nothing to say to anyone other than the police.

On both sides of the street, visible at the edges of the fog, four-story terraced houses, their bricks well worn, gave way to older Italianate dwellings mixed in among a few Elizabethan buildings.

The majority appeared to be homes, but every now and again a tradesman's shop nestled in between them.

In the course of their swift walk, Lewis led the survivors past an apothecary, a clothier, and a small bookshop, among others. Some were open and some even had customers, but Lewis stayed on course, noting them and just as quickly dismissing them.

Moments later, a large building rose above the others around it. Made from blocks of quarried granite, blackened from years of coal soot and decorated with ornate gargoyles and other statuary on every corner of every floor, the structure looked like a cross between a castle and a cathedral. A broad stone stairway topped by an arched entryway led to four ironbound doors. Letters on the curved arch read Metropolitan Police.

Lewis stopped in front of the station and stared, his mouth agape. Something about the building felt oppressive, as if the structure were leaning out over him, threatening to topple and crush him. It did not look like any police station he had ever seen before. However, given the threat in Mithras Court, perhaps it made a certain kind of sense.

"Well, it certainly looks official." Edgar brushed past Lewis, climbing the steps two at a time. Josephine picked up her skirts and followed on his heels.

"Wait!" Lewis said. "We should stay together!" But it did no good. A moment later, the five that Lewis thought of as the weakest in the group were running after Edgar. Professor Drake, Lord Crandall, Gregory, and Reggie and Mary remained behind, all looking as uneasy as Lewis felt.

"This is a rather large building for a Whitechapel police station," Professor Drake said, warily alert for trouble.

Lord Crandall took a hesitant step. "Something is odd about this place, and it's not just the size and audacity of the building . . . you would think that for a station this large, officers would be moving about outside."

Lewis did not answer, but the man's statement rang true. The station appeared even more odd than the rest of Mithras Court, and that did not bode well. He wondered whether the dead could have attacked this place, removing the guards from their posts in front, but why would there not be officers moving around now that the attack was clearly over? If all of the police were dead, they were in a far worse situation than he had suspected.

"The police are no friends of laborers," Reggie said. "They never have been and they never will be."

"What do you mean?" Gregory looked down a step at the shorter man.

"The police protect gentlemen such as yourselves—merchants, soldiers, gentry . . . but not common folk like us. There's only so much they will do to help the likes of us." Reggie glanced around at the others gratefully. "Me and the missus are happy to be in your company and not rushing up the stairs with them."

"I'll see to it that neither you nor your wife are forgotten," Lord Crandall said. Lewis couldn't help but hear the patronizing tone. "It's my solemn duty as a lord."

"A bit archaic, perhaps, but an agreeable sentiment," Professor Drake said, never taking his eyes away from the place. "Now, I think we'd best hurry before our friend Edgar causes some mischief."

"There's nothing archaic about a man's honor." Lord Crandall scowled. "You're correct, however, in your assertion. We should not allow Edgar to talk to the police without us." He turned to go, but paused to look up the stairs.

Edgar and the others had reached the doors. The fat man grabbed a large ring and pulled hard. Lewis could practically see the sweat on the man's brow as he hauled the door open. An instant later, the banker led the others inside and disappeared from sight.

"I think perhaps it's too late for that." Lewis sighed and took the first step, hoping that the fool banker would not do anything that might cause them harm.

"Beware . . ." Elise's voice echoed across the lane.

"Elise?" Lewis spun around, desperate to catch a glimpse of her. "Where are you? Talk to me, please!" His own doubts about her voice would be resolved if the others could hear her. He had not realized until that moment how much he needed to know that her voice was real. If she was not really speaking to him, then the entire encounter in Mithras Court might be suspect. And if she was really there, truly reaching out to him, then he might talk to her, tell her he was sorry and promise vengeance.

"Who is Elise?" Gregory looked at him, surprise in his eyes.

"Did you not hear a woman's voice?" But even before he asked, Lewis knew it was a pointless question. He could tell by the man's confused expression that he had not.

"I'm afraid not."

"Nor did I." Lord Crandall frowned at him.

As they started up the steps, the others murmured their agreement, and Lewis's elation deflated. The sound of her voice, such a welcome occurrence in his dreams for so long, added to his fear that perhaps he suffered from a brain fever of some kind. That was a comforting thought, for it might also mean that he had imagined the walking dead. As he considered that, Elise's ring again grew warm against his chest; it gave him a brief moment of peace and his doubts fell away as his certainty of her presence grew in strength.

"Captain?"

"I'm sorry?" Lewis realized he had stopped halfway up the stairs. The others looked back from a few steps ahead of him.

"I said, we should remain together," Lord Crandall stated with an indignant huff.

"You're right, of course." Lewis hurried after them. The warmth faded as his attention focused again on the police.

"Are you all right?" Concern warmed Professor Drake's tired eyes.

"Yes, quite," Lewis said, eyeing the building with trepidation.

"I suggest we make haste." Lord Crandall turned toward the looming doors. "Before Edgar visits more bad luck upon us."

Lewis followed them up the stairs, keeping to the rear. A faint odor of burning wood mixed with the coal fog, and the smell of cooking meats and vegetables drifted unexpectedly out of the mist. It lent an air of normalcy to the place. And yet, it remained sinister somehow.

He sighed. He knew they had not understood something crucial. It was not just the size or construction of the police station, not just

Elise's warning—but some gut sense set him on edge. At the top of the stairs, the massive doors suddenly opened partway, and two officers in long blue tunics and spike-topped helmets exited. Each carried a wooden truncheon. They paused at the top as the doors closed behind them. What daylight reached them reflected off the badges on their helmets.

"Are you Captain Lewis Wentworth?" The shorter of the two, a middle-aged man with a large moustache not unlike Lord Crandall's, patted his left hand with his truncheon to make it clear he meant business.

"I am." Lewis tensed at the tone and gesture as much as the words.

"We'd like you to come with us. We've some questions to put to you." The officer added, "And we'll take your pistol, if you don't mind." He held out his hand toward Lewis; he would have the weapon whether Lewis minded or not.

"We've come here to report an assault that resulted in the deaths of a number of our fellow train passengers." Lord Crandall gained the top of the stairs and stared at the man, putting the full weight of his class into his words.

"And who might you be, sir?" the shorter man said. His taller, younger companion, a strapping lad with bushy red hair sticking out from beneath his helmet, watched carefully, clearly prepared if anyone offered resistance.

Surely, Lewis thought, Edgar had not been able to tell them enough that these men would be on edge already. He wondered if perhaps the man with the snake tattoo had arrived here. If that were the case . . . he tightened his grip on his weapon.

"I am Lord Geoffrey Crandall, and I tell you that Captain Wentworth has done nothing wrong. His bravery and valor saved lives during the assault in the train station."

Lord Crandall's willingness to defend him surprised Lewis. It had been a long while since anyone had granted him the benefit of the doubt. Judging by the expressions of the officers, however, it had not helped. Lewis wondered why Lord Crandall had suddenly allied himself with him. He did not believe the man did anything without good reason, and it made him anxious that Crandall saw advantage in being on his side.

"I'm sorry, sir." The shorter man did not lower his truncheon. "I'm sure what you say is true, but we've got orders to disarm you and bring you inside."

"Maybe we should do as they say," Professor Drake said. "We do need their help."

"Very well," Lord Crandall decided, looking at Lewis with an unfathomable expression. "I agree with the professor."

Lewis thought about running, but to what end? The professor was correct that they needed police assistance in order to safely navigate out of Mithras Court. At that thought, he remembered that he did not wish to leave the district, not yet, not until he found the tattooed man. The thing he needed most to fulfill both of his missions was information. They had precious little, and he hoped that the police might be able to tell them more about this plague of the undead and anything that might allow him to discover the whereabouts of the tattooed man. Surely the police would know of such a knave in their district. Slowly, he pulled the revolver from his pocket.

The men tensed, truncheons rising a bit higher.

"Of course." Lewis turned the weapon around and handed it to the older man, butt first. He motioned toward the door. "Lead on."

Chapter SEVEN

Lewis looked up in awe at the impressive foyer that was like no other he'd seen. Huge marble columns rose perhaps thirty feet to meet a massive vaulted ceiling. On its surface was a faded painting of a toga-clad young man wrestling a bull. A dog, a raven, a giant scorpion, and a snake stood near the man's legs, supporting his efforts—somehow.

The artwork reminded Lewis of the frescos in Elise's family's country estate. He smiled at the memory. Elise had never liked the Romanesque style her father seemed intent on filling their homes with. No doubt she would have found this building distasteful, although the ornate woodwork surrounding the painting would have been to her liking. It extended to the walls in all directions and continued all the way to the floor on one side, next to a broad white marble stair that led to the upper levels. It wasn't merely the foyer; the whole building was unlike any police station Lewis had ever been in.

In his amazement, he had failed to notice a small wooden stall against the far wall between two massive metal doors. A heavyset older man with a well-kept white beard sat at a small desk inside it. He watched the group curiously, but said nothing to disturb the silence of the place. Lewis strained to hear any sounds other than the breathing and movement of his companions, but he heard no audible noises whatsoever. The atmosphere was more suited to a cathedral than a place devoted to catching criminals.

A chill breeze wafted past, making him shiver. He frowned. Not only did the building look different than any police station he had ever seen, the air felt strangely charged and the silence was deafening—a noteworthy contrast to his expectations of the place.

Professor Drake stopped in the center of the atrium as the painting caught his attention. He stared up at the ceiling with avid curiosity.

"Is something wrong?" The shorter officer paused to look back, but did not sound sympathetic.

"I was admiring the painting." Drake stroked his close-cropped white beard. "If I am not mistaken, it is a depiction of the god Mithras wrestling the primeval bull, is it not? As the mythology goes, he dragged the creature back to his cave, where he killed it and released its life force for the benefit of humanity."

"I fail to see the relevance of a stale and forgotten god to our predicament," Lord Crandall said. "Obviously, this district was named for an ancient pagan religion, but what does that mean to us? We are modern Britons, not Romans."

"Actually," Lewis said, "I believe the god was originally Persian." He had heard soldiers talk about it during in his early military days in India.

"I see you know your mythology." Drake nodded, evidently impressed. "However, the cult of Mithras actually traces its origins back to 1400 BC India. Of course, I wouldn't expect just anyone to know that." He looked pointedly at Lord Crandall.

Crandall glowered at the professor. Before Lewis could ask a question, the police interrupted.

"Gentlemen." The shorter officer cleared his throat. "This history lesson is interesting, but we have duties to perform." He pointed his truncheon at Lewis. "You, follow me. The rest of you will go with Officer Macleod."

The younger man stepped forward, motioning for the others to follow with a wave of his arm.

"I insist that you allow us to remain together." Lord Crandall raised his chin in defiance.

"The inspector would like to ask Captain Wentworth some questions. In private." The man patted his open palm with his weapon. "You will do as you are instructed."

"He can ask us together." Lord Crandall set his feet a shoulder's width apart, bracing himself. He reminded Lewis of a stubborn child.

"It's all right. I'll go with him. I did, after all, give the others my word."

Crandall's show of solidarity surprised Lewis again. Finding such a stalwart companion in war or in peace was rare, especially considering the circumstances in which they had been introduced on the train. But he could, he reflected, count on Crandall to take the opposite side of whomever spoke. Had he found a true stalwart, or merely an obstinate gentleman? With luck, they would escape Mithras Court before Lewis learned that answer. Then he could continue his search for the tattooed man without any further distractions.

"Very well." Crandall glared at the officers. "But I warn you, if he is mistreated, I shall hear of it. And so shall your superiors."

"No one will be mistreated by anyone here." The right side of the officer's mouth lifted into an odd smile and he motioned toward the stairs with his baton. "Now, if you don't mind."

"Of course." Lewis walked slowly across the foyer.

The officer walked behind him as if he expected Lewis to flee. Lewis had no intention of doing any such thing. He did not believe that he would see his home again without their help, let alone be free to find the tattooed man. And he had given his word to go to the police, he reminded himself. It was imperative that they enlist the aid of these constables—he suspected that they knew something of what had happened to this Mithras Court and its bizarre inhabitants. They might be helpful in many ways.

He slowly climbed the marble stairs, his eyes searching for anything out of the ordinary, though that was no easy task in this building. Catching sight of the ceiling painting again, he wished he were back at Elise's family estate before that fateful night. The stairs in that home would have taken him to their second floor bedroom, where she would be waiting . . .

"Keep moving, Captain." The man jabbed at him with his truncheon in emphasis.

Lewis sighed and climbed the stairs wearily, his left thigh throbbing slightly.

=====MC=====

"According to your fellow passengers, you tried to shoot a man on the underground train." Inspector Andrew Newton leaned forward across the table. As with the three other constables Lewis had seen during his brief walk through the mostly empty halls of the station, Newton was older. His gray hair and lined face marked him as a man of at least sixty. Unlike the officers who had brought them inside, this man wore a shorter, snug blue police coat, the two insignia pins on his shoulder tab denoting his rank as inspector.

Despite his apparent age, the barrel-chested man looked formidable and Lewis had to admit to a little fear. It was not the man's size that he found unnerving, but his cold gray eyes. They were not haunted by past experiences the way Professor Drake's seemed to be. Rather, this man had clearly seen darkness in the world and instead of making him timid or afraid, it had made him stronger and colder. He doubted the man would think twice about killing him or anyone else, were it in his interest. Whether it was in the line of duty might also be negotiable.

Lewis leaned back in his chair behind the large oak table and turned his attention from the man to the room itself. Ornate gas lamps provided light, and intricate wooden molding ran along the ceilings, indicating that this room had once served some other, more grandiose purpose. Yet only the table and two chairs occupied the space.

"I asked you a question, Captain Wentworth." Newton straightened. "Did you attempt to murder a man on the train?"

"Don't you think the dead men and women who attacked us in the train station are a more pressing matter?" Lewis asked. It was an attempt to divert attention from himself, but it hadn't worked before and he doubted it would work now. The inspector was curiously uninterested in the dead. "You seem to have a problem with them all over Mithras Court."

"I'd hardly consider the departed to be a major problem here. They're scavengers." The inspector pushed his chair back and rose to pace across the room. "Think of them as trash collectors, sweeping the refuse from the streets."

"They killed at least half a dozen of my companions!" Lewis sprang to his feet, heat rising in his face as anger burst through his carefully-maintained calm. "And clearly, they've been menacing this district for weeks!"

"Regrettable, but purely accidental. Had we known you were arriving, or had you brought lanterns with you, the incident might have been avoided." Newton went back to the table. "Sometimes these things just happen."

"Are you daft, man?" Lewis leaned across the table, pressing his palms to its surface and placing his face mere inches from the inspector's, trying to use his physical presence to force the man to see reason. "People died down there, and you're telling me that this scourge of the dead is something we should simply accept? Have you not thought to contact your superiors for assistance? Surely Scotland Yard is not content to let something like this continue!"

"Let me explain something to you." The inspector straightened, his face cold. "We're not *in* England anymore. We're in Mithras Court, and that means that things are different. The law is different. Life is different and there is precious little we can do about any of it. We can, however, do something about the attempted murder of one of our new citizens."

Lewis jerked back, dropping into his seat as if struck. "What do you mean we aren't in England? What in the name of hell are you on about?" Surely, he thought desperately, the man had lost his mind. Their train could not have left the city limits during such a short journey. Ben had said so, and Lewis had known it himself. It was a preposterous thought.

"Take care, Captain Wentworth!" Newton opened and closed his fists, a clear threat.

"Be careful, love . . ." Elise's ring warmed against his skin even as her voice whispered in his ears.

Lewis had to force himself not to call out to her, to beg her to speak again. The purity of her lovely voice contrasted sharply with the dark emptiness that had consumed his every waking moment since her death, but he did not wish to alert the inspector to her presence. Nor did he wish to prove or disprove her existence, he had to admit. It seemed increasingly likely that her voice was not a figment of his own imagination. In that case, he truly did retain full command of his faculties.

"Did you hear . . ." The inspector paused and looked around, clearly startled. "I thought I heard . . ."

Lewis's eyes widened with surprise. If the inspector had heard Elise, then perhaps madness did not yet stalk him. He blinked away his surprise and leaned back in his seat, pondering his answer to the inspector's question, unsure what he should reveal.

"Say nothing of me," Elise said, her voice soft and seeming far away this time. "They cannot know."

"Did I hear what?" Lewis arched one eyebrow as he looked at the man. Clearly, she had not meant to be heard, or had not realized that anyone could hear her other than Lewis. He wondered why his fellow passengers had not heard her. Perhaps he was different somehow, but whether from living in the Court or something else, he could not begin to guess.

"I could swear I just heard a woman's voice." Newton narrowed his eyes as he studied Lewis.

"I didn't hear anything." Lewis leaned forward, trying to distract the inspector from the question of Elise. "Now . . . what in God's name do you mean we aren't in England?"

The inspector scrutinized him. "It's as I said. This entire district has been cut off from the rest of London for quite some time." The gravity of his statement was emphasized as the lights dimmed slightly.

"Cut off how?" Lewis breathed slowly, trying to remain calm. How could an entire district become lost to the rest of the city? It would take an army to cordon off an entire district, and he had seen no indication of such a force. Or at least, he amended silently, not an army of the living.

"We don't know." Newton turned away for a moment. When he looked back, his jaw was set in grim determination. "The mist that rings the Court prevents us from leaving. Occasionally, it brings it new people to us, as you were brought here."

"Are you saying the fog is so thick as to prevent you or anyone else from finding a way out? Why not just form a human chain and walk though it in a single file?" Neither coal smoke nor water mist could prevent such an organized band from discovering a path to safety even if the attempt cost a few lives.

"Don't you think we've tried?" Newton laughed at that. "The fog is easy enough to get through, but then you hit the mists. Stepping into that soup results in one of two things . . ." His jaw tensed. "Either you end up back where you started in the Court or . . . you die."

"That is ludicrous." Lewis had heard men spout ridiculous stories, especially when drunk or under the influence of opium, but the inspector did not show signs of either. On the contrary, the man appeared lucid, leaving Lewis to conclude that he was playing games with him for some nefarious purpose. Perhaps it was to disorient him, to force him to confess to something. And yet, he did not appear overly concerned with the law. Edgar and the others had told of the episode with his revolver on the passenger train, and of any slander they could imagine, but here he sat, having a conversation with the inspector. And not the conversation he'd expected.

"You've seen the dead walk among the living?" The inspector's tone was casual, as if he were asking which church Lewis attended.

"Yes. I told you I had."

"Then why would you not believe that this is possible?" the inspector asked. "Why can forces capable of such a feat not hold us here against our will?" The man searched Lewis's eyes as if looking for something. It took him a moment to realize that the inspector sought acceptance of the things he believed true.

It was a good argument. Lewis did not know why the ramifications of the dead walking the streets had not truly struck him until Newton pointed it out. Any force capable of such a feat *could* cordon off an entire district. It could probably do many other things as well—like make him think he was hearing Elise when he wasn't. The gates holding back his fears burst; his heart raced as sweat broke out on his forehead and his body twitched. He felt like an animal trapped in a very large cage, the way the Zulu prisoners must have felt during the war. But in that case, dozens of them had been crammed into small wooden boxes. Lewis stood alone, but no less trapped.

"How long has it been this way?" He tried, but failed to keep his voice from shaking. If the police had accepted defeat, then what hope did they have of leaving this place? They were all trapped, if the police and the common people had not been able to find a way out. Lewis's thoughts raced, his mind refusing to accept such a monstrous fate.

His panic drained away when he realized one key fact.

If no one could leave, then the tattooed man would be trapped in the district as well. Lewis's hunger for vengeance came sharply to the fore, and he had to resist the urge to smile grimly. Instead, he breathed slowly and nodded to the man, trying to appear calm.

"You're finally believing me, I see." Newton misread his grim determination for an expression of acquiescence. He sat down and thought for a moment. "Twenty years—maybe more. It's hard to say."

"Twenty years!" Lewis had thought perhaps several days, perhaps a week. He jumped up in surprise—surely no one could live like this for that long! "Twenty years?"

"Aye." Newton's voice was low and deadly serious.

"You've had no contact with the outside world that entire time?" A chill rolled up Lewis's spine. To think that these citizens had been cut off from Mother England for such a long time and that no one had come looking for them was terrifying—it bespoke an isolation that Lewis did not like, even if it gave him the chance to kill the tattooed man. His plans did not include being trapped somewhere forever, and it sounded as though that was what Mithras Court offered. The inspector had to be lying—didn't he? "None whatsoever?"

"That is correct." Newton's cheek twitched slightly. The topic was evidently wearing on him, for he suddenly looked haggard. "This does not, however, mean that we are without law, and I return to my original question. Did you attempt to murder one of your fellow passengers?"

"Be careful, Lewis," Elise's voice was even softer this time, barely audible. "Tell him the truth, but do not trust him."

"I am not certain I wish to answer that question, Inspector." Lewis crossed his arms.

"I beg your pardon!" Newton's eyes widened in surprise. Lewis noted that the inspector did not seem accustomed to being contradicted. Nor did he seem to want to become accustomed to it.

"If this district is truly removed from London, where, then, do you claim your authority? Who is truly in charge? Is there a mayor? Because if you do not answer to a civilian government, then your legitimacy is in question and I am under no obligation to answer any of your queries." Lewis narrowed his eyes and scrutinized the man. Would he take the bait in his statement?

"Impudent wretch!" Newton stood up, his hand resting on the butt of his pistol. "I am chief constable and as far as you are concerned, I am the law, the judge, and the jury. And if need be," he smiled dangerously, "your executioner."

But Lewis looked into Newton's angry eyes and saw something behind that dangerous ire . . . fear. For a man such as the inspector—who had surely killed men on a whim—to have fear, even in the back of his mind, meant there was more that he was not saying. Lewis did not think so highly of himself as to assume that the inspector was afraid of *him*.

"You're serious." Lewis swallowed. He had to tread carefully. But he needed to learn more.

"Yes, Captain. Extremely serious." Newton's hand closed on his weapon. "I suggest you answer me . . . now."

"Very well." Lewis tensed. "I did shoot at a man last night." Elise had given him good guidance in life; he would trust her in death. His instincts, as well, told him that to lie now would be both foolish and dangerous.

"Go on."

"The man admitted to slaying my wife. The others heard his confession. Some of them will vouch for me." Lewis watched the inspector.

Newton studied him for a moment, his hand opening and closing on the pistol handle. Finally, he nodded. "I believe you."

"Do you?" Lewis had thought the others would betray him. It

surprised him to learn otherwise, and he wondered who among them had had the strength to tell the truth. Surely not Edgar.

"I always know when a man is lying to me. You, sir, are honest." Newton's hand fell away from his weapon. He drew out a small notebook and began scrawling something in pencil. Lewis breathed a silent sigh of relief. Elise's advice had been sound.

"Might I ask you a question, Inspector?"

Newton inclined his head and continued to write. It did not seem a guarantee of answers, but he could ask his questions.

"If you have been trapped all this time, how do you get food and water? Where do you get the raw materials used in the making of the things in your shops?" Lewis had seen evidence of manufacturing in several of the shops they had passed on their way to the station, to say nothing of the shops that sold finished goods.

"The Vistani bring in all that we require." Newton continued to write, not even looking up. He spoke in a matter-of-fact tone, answering questions he'd no doubt answered many times before.

"The who?"

"Gypsies. Or not exactly, though they are close enough that you'll never see the difference." The words carried a sneer. "They're called Vistani here." Newton lowered the pencil and placed it on the table with the notebook. "They can come and go through the mist as they please."

"They can return to London?" So there might be a way out of Mithras Court after all.

"They can leave, but I don't think they go to London." The inspector watched him, making Lewis feel that he was on the witness stand.

"What do you mean?" Lewis frowned. "Where do they go?" But it did not materially change the hope that suddenly flowered in him that they could buy, or beg, or somehow leave the Court. Certainly, anywhere other than Mithras Court would be desirable if they truly had been trapped for so long. He wondered why the denizens of the Court remained there.

"It doesn't matter. I know what you are thinking, and the answer is, the Vistani will not help us. Those who have tried to coerce them end up dead." Newton answered his unasked question, but that would not stop Lewis from trying further.

"Surely there must be some way to gain their assistance." He recalled the dark-haired gypsy in the Laughing Gargoyle. That would be the place to start after their exit from the police station. Perhaps he could find a way to motivate the man.

"Impossible." Newton's tone took on a decidedly frustrated tinge. "I don't know who they owe allegiance to, but it's not to us any more than it is Lucius Knight."

"Lord Knight." Frederick had mentioned the Lord of Mithras Court as well, but had given scant details on the man. At the very least, if Lewis could get more information about the mysterious ruler of the district, then his trip to the station would not be a waste.

"Lord Knight is . . ." Newton glanced at the wall nervously. "He is the law and the leader of the small government of Mithras Court. He rules from an old manor house in the center of the district, and we obey his commands."

"And has he not attempted to organize you into a force that might compel these Vistani to aid you in fleeing this place?"

"Lord Knight can't leave. He's . . ." Lewis could see fear rising to the surface. "There is nothing else I can tell you." His tone made it clear he would not speak further on the subject. "Now, Captain." Newton arched one eyebrow. "Tell me how you knew this tattooed man was your wife's murderer before he confessed. Were you a witness?"

"There was a boy . . . he witnessed it." Lewis gritted his teeth against the memories of Elise's lifeless corpse. "He saw a tattoo on the man's left forearm . . . in the form of a snake. When I saw him on the train—"

Inspector Newton's head jerked back and the color drained from his face. "I've heard enough. You're free to go." He got up to leave.

"What?" Lewis did not understand the man's sudden change; there had been no provocation, and the man sounded afraid, not merely dismissive of someone taking up his time. "I haven't even explained—"

"You weren't trying to kill anyone, were you? You just wanted to bring a murderer to justice. Since there is no body, there is no victim. No one can tell me what happened to this mysterious tat-tooed man, so there is no crime. You're free to go." He moved to the door so quickly he was nearly running.

"Wait—Inspector!" Lewis got to his feet.

"I told you, you are free to go!" The inspector did not even turn back before he opened the door and leaned out. "Officer Macleod, see this man and his friends outside at once. There is nothing we can do to help them."

The man straightened to attention as he nodded.

"You can't just throw us onto the street! You're supposed to pro-tect the citizens in your jurisdiction!" Lewis moved swiftly around the table. "We need your help!"

The inspector glanced back, eyes darting to and fro nervously. "Good day to you, sir." He whirled about and disappeared around the corner.

"Come with me, sir," Officer Macleod said. He had a Scottish accent, Lewis noted, and wondered if he'd lived in London or come to the Court some other way. He stepped in front of Lewis, barring the way the inspector had gone. "I'll show you out." A wave of his arm made the direction even clearer.

"Are you a butler, or an officer of the law?" Lewis asked the young man, as nastily as he felt. "Is it not your duty to help citi-zens in need?"

"I hear that things used to be that way 'round here, but this is Mith-ras Court now." Macleod took him by the arm and guided him from the room into the long, dimly lit hallway beyond. "I'm sorry."

"What is that supposed to mean?" Lewis did not appreciate being handled, but acquiescence was easier, and he allowed the man to guide him down the dark-paneled passage. He saw multiple stout oak doors on either side, extending down the entire hallway. Light spilled into the hall from beneath several of them, but most appeared dark. Portraits of white-haired men in police uniforms hung every so often between them. The eyes in the weathered faces seemed to follow them as they passed.

"I can't tell you anything else. I'm sorry." Macleod paused to stare at him, and Lewis saw guilt, along with the same fear he had witnessed in Newton's haunted eyes. "Take this. You might need it."

Lewis pried his attention from the austere faces in the paintings and looked down. Macleod held his revolver. The officer raised it higher, holding the butt toward Lewis.

"Thank you." Lewis took the weapon. He caught the haunted look in Macleod's eyes and sudden chills of dread settled into his bones. He and his companions might be trapped, but he prayed they would never give up the way these officers had. Had been forced to, a voice in his mind clarified.

"Come on, now." Macleod broke eye contact and walked ahead.

Chapter EIGHT

"You can't do this to us!" Lewis yelled, as the officer and the younger Macleod pushed him outside onto the landing in front of the massive building, where Lord Crandall, Gregory, and the rest of his companions stood in a group.

"You'll hear from my solicitor!" Lord Crandall said from the top stair. The small crowd shouted angry agreements with raised fists.

"Good day, gentlemen. Ladies." The officers slammed the doors shut and the group heard the heavy bar slide into place behind it. Having seen the doors, Lewis knew it would take an army to regain entry into the station. Even if he had such a force, it would be pointless. They could expect no help from those cowards.

"How can they do this to us, Edgar?" Josephine sounded as though she had been crying, but there was only a trace of it left in her voice. She sounded more resolute than Lewis had ever heard her.

"I don't know." He wrapped his arms around her and held her close, a surprisingly gentle gesture.

"How can they do this to *me?*" Lord Crandall demanded. "My family is well known in London and in the circles of the law. Such an act is tantamount to political suicide!"

"It would seem that in the eyes of the police of Mithras Court, you are as ordinary and desperate as the rest of us," Professor Drake commented, a sardonic smile playing about his lips. "How does that feel?"

"I don't think I like your tone, *Professor.*" Crandall took a step forward, his face reddening as they leaped to their burgeoning quarrel.

"And I don't believe I like your arrogance, sir." Drake glowered at him. "Your reputation precedes you, Lord Crandall. I know all about your machinations. You move through the houses of power, brokering backroom deals with members of Parliament—deals that will only benefit you and your family. Until now, I doubt very much you've ever felt such indignity as the average Briton feels on a daily basis."

"Oh, very good, Professor." Lord Crandall clapped his hands slowly, emphasizing his sarcastic tone. "So you *do* know who I am. Well, I know of you as well. Professor Robert Drake, convicted looter of Roman antiquities."

"Those charges are preposterous!" Drake raised his arm as if he might swing at the larger man, but stopped himself. "I've never removed a single artifact without the permission of the local governments who hold jurisdiction over my digs."

"Oh, for the love of God." Edgar shook his head in disgust. "We don't have time for this! We must find a way out of this place!"

"Enough!" Lewis stepped between them. "I don't care what feuds you have with one another. These officers have chosen to turn their backs on us. We therefore must remain together as we seek help from another quarter. Or you may perish alone, but you will not take up our time on this matter. Save your quarrels for another day."

For an instant longer, the two men glared at one another. A cold wind stirred the fog around them, making the professor cough and breaking their gaze. He pulled a handkerchief from the pocket of his coat and dabbed at his face. Lord Crandall watched him for another moment, then took a small step back.

"You're right, Captain." Crandall breathed out slowly. "My apologies."

"I agree with Edgar." The voice came as a surprise to Lewis. Thomas Bainbridge stood with his wife a few steps below. His face was pale, but they both looked determined. "If there is a way out."

"The other constables must have related a similar tale to you." Lewis saw the despair in their eyes as plain as day.

"That we're trapped in Mithras Court and separated from the rest of London?" Thomas asked.

"Yes, exactly. And that only these gypsies—what they call Vistani—are granted access through the mists around us," Lewis added. "Furthermore, Lord Knight, the leader of this district, does not appear to care."

"Do you really believe we're trapped in this neighborhood?" Josephine clung to Edgar's hand as if he were the only thing keeping her afloat. "It's utter foolishness." She did not sound certain of her words.

"Given what we've seen since we got here, I'm willing to believe anything," Gregory said. He had been standing apart from the others, glancing up at the front of the building. "Those men were afraid—of us *and* of something else. Whether it is true or not, I think they honestly believe what they told us . . . that they've been trapped here for over twenty years."

"This is his fault." Josephine pointed at Lewis. "You brought us here and it is because of you that even the police have abandoned us! You are the devil!"

"Cease your superstitious drivel!" Lord Crandall never spared a glance for her, instead gazing at Lewis. He arched an eyebrow. "She does have a point, however. The officers treated us with some amount of dignity until the inspector returned from having spoken to you. Do you have an explanation for our expulsion?"

"Perhaps," Lewis said thoughtfully. "When I mentioned the tattooed man, Inspector Newton grew agitated and practically ran from the interrogation room. As he fled, he ordered Officer Macleod to escort me from the building." Lewis looked at his revolver. "The young constable seemed to feel some sympathy for our situation, I will say. He returned my Webley before he ushered me out the door where I found you waiting." Lewis paused to crack open his gun and count the bullets. Satisfied, he snapped it shut and dropped it into his pocket.

"Just like that?" Lord Crandall narrowed his eyes. "Without any explanation?"

"He told me that there was no body and therefore no crime. He had no reason to keep me." Lewis raised his chin defiantly at the man. He was growing tired of Crandall's constant mistrust.

"That does not make any sense," Edgar said.

"No." Lewis turned to glare at him. "It does not. However, I give you my word as a soldier and a gentleman, that it is the truth."

Both Lord Crandall and Edgar scrutinized him for a moment.

"The constables did tell us something similar," Thomas Bainbridge said.

· "Did they?" Lord Crandall swiveled toward the American.

"Yes, sir. Before you and the others entered the station."

"Interesting." Lord Crandall glanced at Edgar.

"It doesn't matter. The man is still not to be trusted!" Edgar waved a hand toward Lewis. "Whether the police in this God-forsaken place care or not, we all saw him try to kill that man."

"And we've witnessed him acting with honor and bravery in an effort to save all of us," Professor Drake said. "I suggest we trust the captain, at least for now."

The professor's vote of confidence helped Lewis to focus. Indeed, none of the others said anything in response, as if each weighed the statement and could find no fault with it. Even Lord Crandall simply nodded. Lewis had retained control over the group, at least for the moment.

"Shouldn't we be leaving then, before the police change their minds?" Reggie stood on the lower steps with Mary. They looked at the others with the same fear in their eyes, but also a determination that made Lewis smile. Reggie was a man who would not give up and would never fail to protect the woman he loved, nor would she refuse to defend him. He was honest and straightforward, and after the debates of the past night, Lewis found that refreshing.

Lewis spoke finally, when no one else seemed about to. "Whatever has happened to these people does not concern us. If these officers do not have the courage or the honor to assist us, then we'll simply follow Cannon Street out of Mithras Court and locate the constabulary in the next district."

"What about this Lord Knight, who wields the power in Mithras Court?" Edgar said. "The officers seemed to fear him, but surely the leader of this place is capable of aiding us?"

"If we are to believe what Inspector Newton said, Knight is trapped here as well." Lewis shook his head. "In fact, the inspector was afraid of the man, and that trepidation is not to be taken lightly.

Whatever these constables have been reduced to, anyone who rises to the title of Inspector does not frighten easily, especially in a place like this. We would do well to avoid this Lord Knight, I think."

"Perhaps that fear keeps these poor souls in Mithras Court?" Professor Drake said.

"The only way we'll know that for certain is to look at this mist ourselves and attempt to leave the district," Lewis said. "And I suggest we do that immediately."

"It's odd, this lord ruling over a district in the city," Drake rubbed his beard thoughtfully. "I mean, let us say for the moment that these people are truly cut off from the rest of London. One would think that a civic leader or representative of the people would be elected, possibly even a ruling council, not some feudal arrangement."

"That is a naïve statement. You strip away our civilization, remove us from the modern world, and any of us can become savages." Lord Crandall shook his head. "I have seen it in other parts of the world. Feudalism makes sense."

"I would hardly say that civilization has fled from this district, regardless of what has happened to it," Lewis said, his impatience at their inaction growing.

Lord Crandall frowned. He turned to the others. "Let us assume this Lord Knight is not to be trusted and seek our own manner of egress from this place. I find the assumption that there is no way out of this district to be ludicrous."

"Agreed." Lewis nodded.

"What if they're telling the truth?" Ben's freckled face was flushed with anxiety. "What if we're all trapped here?"

"Bah. Crandall is right," Edgar said. "It's rubbish."

"That's *Lord* Crandall." Lord Crandall glared at him. "And if we're all in agreement," he pointed down the street in the opposite direction from which they had come, "Captain, would you do the honors?"

The Webley gripped tightly in his right hand and the cane in his left, Lewis led them forward.

=====MC=====

The fog wrapped icy hands around them, draping them in a veil that limited sight. Disorienting sounds echoed through the street: women calling to one another, babies crying, men singing, horses clip-clopping past, all just out of sight, but all still the sounds of day, however hard it was to see. As they pressed on, dozens of people appeared, moving in and out of the vapor. They paid Lewis and his group little heed, despite Lewis's revolver. In fact, many passersby, both men and women, carried flintlock pistols or antiquated black powder revolvers. One gentleman carried a breech loader across his arm. Josephine noted haughtily that the clothing styles varied greatly, and were far more outdated than those seen on even the shabbiest streets in London. Lewis wondered if that lent credence to Inspector Newton's claims. Apparently, the Vistani had not seen fit to update the Court's fashions.

As they crossed Jupiter Street, a thoroughfare that none of them had heard of, the terrace houses and the other buildings grew decrepit. Papers and refuse blew past in the breeze, and many of the streetlights were dark. Shops appeared to either side: a blacksmith, a brewery, a cobbler, a tailor, and many others, though none were as appealing as the ones they'd passed earlier. As Inspector Newton had said, they had no shortage of raw materials. Each business had lights on and customers purchasing their wares.

As the group passed the third block from the station, the fog grew thicker, reducing visibility to mere feet in front of them. A sign at the crossroads read Bacchus Way. From the left came raucous laughter—boisterous men belting out drinking songs accompanied by an odd assortment of instrumentation. Lewis noted that Reggie, Edgar, and Thomas had linked arms with their wives.

Ahead of them, some of the structures appeared partially burned and completely abandoned. A few paupers clad in dirty rags scurried back and forth at the edges of the light cast by the two working gas lamps there. Lewis paused momentarily to watch them. As they drew nearer to their destination, he wished that Elise would visit him again. Surely they remained in danger, and that danger had caused her to speak to him since their arrival in Mithras Court. The next time she spoke, he would insist that she talk with him rather than offering fleeting warnings. He needed to speak to her—needed to tell her how sorry he was for not accompanying her that night . . . for not protecting her . . . for allowing her murderer to escape from his clutches mere hours earlier.

"I don't like the look of this." He pointed his Webley forward.

"As long as we remain together, we'll be safe from the pick-pockets and cutthroats." Lord Crandall crossed his arms over his chest.

"Are you so sure?" Professor Drake eyed the downtrodden denizens of the new street and frowned. "Perhaps we should try another direction."

"Perhaps . . ." That suggestion did not feel correct to Lewis, though, any more than going forward did. He took a few steps into the street, straining to see more of what lay ahead.

"We can't go there," Josephine said. "Who knows what rogues lurk in the fog?"

"It's not the criminals that scare me. It's those walking dead." The engineer's face was so pale that his freckles stood out like stains as he peered into the gloom.

Lewis walked unerringly toward the edge of the district, pausing when he reached the far side of the road. His new vantage point revealed more buildings in even worse condition than the last. No people—living or dead—could be seen. The buildings were scorched and crumbling in places, as if artillery fire had bombarded them. None of the street lamps were lit. The empty windows and doors of the devastated homes gaped—black maws leading into blasted ruins. They had presumably once housed the living, and now, possibly, housed the dead.

"There is danger afoot." Elise's voice tickled Lewis's ear. He straightened as his wife's wedding ring grew warm. Although he would not use any passage out of Mithras Court until he killed the tattooed man, he wondered if exiting the district would affect his ability to hear her. He wondered if slaying her killer would set her free, and she would vanish once again.

On the other hand, perhaps something about Mithras Court bridged the gap between worlds, and if he continued to hear her . . .

he doubted he could bring himself to leave. Being ahead of the others, he found his opportunity to finally question her.

"Is it really you?" He spoke in a voice barely above a whisper.

"Yes." Her voice had an odd, trailing quality. It was not so much that she trailed off at the end of her sentences—Elise had always been definite—as that something affected her speech, making it seem distant.

"How can this be?" His heart pounded in his chest as her voice conjured up memories. The first time he had heard her voice, he had been lying in a hospital bed, his leg wrapped in bandages. He had not cared to look as yet another nurse entered to tend to him. Upon hearing her speak, however, the concern and warmth in her musical voice touched his soul. As an involuntary motion, he had rolled onto his back to see what beauty could possibly match her song. He took her in as he would a work of art. Beyond her physical attractiveness, however, her blue eyes had pierced him to his core. He had been smitten immediately.

And all these years later, after so much had been won and lost, all he could think of was to question the moment. His face flushed. He should tell her that he loved her, he missed her, he was sorry.

"I don't know, my love." Her voice was softer this time, as if she were moving further away. Tell her, you fool, he chastised himself.

"If we leave this place, will I still be able to hear you?" He gritted his teeth in anticipation of her answer and peered into the gloom ahead, wondering if indeed there could be a way out on the other side and if he could take it, could walk away. Even as he thought this, he knew he would not until she had moved on . . . whatever that meant.

"You must leave. It's not safe here . . . for any of you." Her voice was so soft that he blinked as he wondered if he had even heard her. Her answer caught his breath in his throat. He had searched for her killer and had not only found him, but had found her again. The thought of losing her brought back all the pain of the past years. It crashed over him like a tidal wave, tearing at the frayed strings of the fabric of his love for her.

A hand gripped his shoulder, turning him. He braced for an attack, trying to raise his pistol at the same time.

"What the devil are you doing, man?" Lord Crandall peered past him into the murky depths beyond. "I see. That does not look inviting."

"No." Lewis breathed out slowly and lowered his weapon as he silently cursed the man for interrupting his conversation with Elise.

"Indeed, it does not." Professor Drake appeared on Lewis's left.

Lord Crandall narrowed his eyes as he looked at the older man, but—for once, Lewis thought—he said nothing.

"We'll reach the boundary of this neighborhood at the end of the next block if the constables told us the truth," Gregory added, joining them. "I don't see anyone up ahead, and given that those creatures do not appear to move about in daylight, I think it's worth the risk."

Lewis could only stare at them.

"Captain?" Professor Drake waved a hand in front of him. "Are you all right?"

Lewis wanted to tell them to go on without him, that he had decided to stay with Elise . . . if he could. But they, more than likely, would need his gun and his expertise if they were to reach another district. Two vows competed within him—his promise to slay Elise's killer, and his responsibility as an honorable soldier to escort his fellow passengers to safety. If he left now, he might not find a way back. The desire to leave this place, leave Elise again, felt remote. Going home suddenly felt like the difficult action, not returning. No, he could guide them out of the district, transfer leadership to Lord Crandall, and then return immediately. He did not trust Crandall entirely; however, the gentleman would surely relish command and the attention he would get for it upon guiding them the remainder of the way home. Yes, that was the choice—the only choice for him.

"I'm sorry. I was lost in thought." He nodded grudgingly. "I agree with you both. I believe we're in danger as long as we remain here. We must forge ahead."

"We must find a church!" Josephine lifted her skirts as she hurried along with the others. They slowed their pace as they reached Lewis and his companions.

"Why in God's name would we do such a thing?" Lord Crandall frowned at her.

"If those monsters exist, then so too must God's power. We will be safe with the local vicar until help can arrive."

"Rubbish. If the constables spoke the truth, then these people have been trapped here for years," Gregory said. "There is no evidence of God aiding these people any more than we can expect help to come."

"We must help ourselves or remain ensnared by this place," Lewis added, motioning toward the gloom with his revolver. "The way ahead is the only path for us."

"And what if we can't leave?" Edgar stepped ahead of his wife.

"Then we return to the pub and reorganize," Lord Crandall said.

Lewis resisted the urge to disagree with the gentleman, not wishing him to feel empowered. He knew from experience that if he allowed a man such as Crandall to think he was in charge, he would never be able to corral him into doing as he wished in a crisis. He decided it did not matter. In moments, with luck, he would be rid of the lot of them.

"We must seek the Lord's guidance!" Josephine's eyes blazed with more emotion than she'd shown all day.

"My wife has never accused me of an abundance of religion." Edgar stepped next to him. "But if we can't find our way out of this place, then I want your word that you'll guide us to the nearest church, as Josephine has asked."

"You're not in any position to make demands." Lord Crandall pulled at the lapels of his coat and raised his chin indignantly.

"The idea has merit." Professor Drake glanced sidelong at the gentleman. "Surely if the dead can rise from their graves, then that is proof that greater forces are at work in the world. I think that if there is such a force for evil, then there must also be one of good. Where else but a church would such a thing be found?"

"You have my word that I will take you to the nearest church if this fails," Lewis said, surprising himself as he cut off further debate. He had not been friends with God in a very long time. Any God who could allow such slaughter as on a battlefield, such pain and suffering, was not a deity that Lewis could accept. The professor was correct—greater forces were at work than he had ever believed possible. Elise was proof, and although he did not feel that a church housed such a force, it was a good place to start.

He turned around and crossed to the other side of the street.

Lewis, Gregory, and Drake, only a step behind, hurried after him. The others followed at a slower pace.

Chapter NINE

"Wait." Lewis held up his hand, bringing the group to a stop next to the shattered remains of an overturned carriage. Wrapped in the dense fog, thicker than any they had seen so far, it was the only thing they could see other than a smashed lamp atop its bent post and the pockmarked paving stones of the street's surface. Silence reigned, and as they neared this point, even the distant sounds coming from the other streets faded away. As the group halted, only their breathing broke the quiet.

"What is it, Captain?" Professor Drake licked his lips nervously as he eyed the broken cab.

"I don't know." Danger was near, he was sure of it.

"Look." Lord Crandall pointed to the front of the broken vehicle.

Lewis's eyes opened wide as he realized that the front section of the hansom had not broken off, as he had first thought. Rather, it was lost in a solid wall of grayish mist that seemed far denser than even the fog through which they had walked.

"It's that mist the constables spoke of." Gregory rubbed his jaw. "They said it forms an impenetrable wall." He stepped closer and reached out a hand to touch it.

"Wait!" Lewis grabbed his arm. "I'm not sure that's wise."

"Just because it's thicker doesn't mean it's dangerous," Lord Crandall said.

"The inspector told me that this mist can kill," Lewis said.

"Surely you don't believe that?" Edgar said from behind. "Even at sea, a fog cannot kill."

"Unseen gases kill miners all too often," Professor Drake said.

"God shall protect us," Josephine said softly. "If it is His will."

"Perhaps." Lord Crandall scrutinized the mist.

"I may have a solution," Lewis said. He raised his cane, drew the blade from it, and stepped up to the mist. He plunged the wooden casing into it until his hand was mere inches from the fog. He could feel the unnatural chill coming off the barrier. He felt as if he had walked up to an open grave and touched Death. He shivered, drawing the scabbard back swiftly. Upon examination, it appeared undamaged. An inanimate object might have fared well in that vapor, but his instincts told a different tale about the living. Now that he had seen the mist and felt its effects, he no longer doubted Inspector Newton's tale.

"It is untarnished." Professor Drake looked at the cane.

Lewis shrugged and slid the sword back into its casing.

"Perhaps it's only dangerous to the living," the professor said. "There are such things in mythology."

"Perhaps—or perhaps one of us must enter it to be certain," Lewis said. He stood tall and pushed his shoulders back to ready himself for the task. "I'll go myself. If it is safe, I'll return for you." He narrowed his eyes and steeled himself for whatever lay ahead. Facing the Zulu warriors of Africa was surely easier.

"Just a moment, Captain. If anything happens to you, we lose our only weapon," Bainbridge said.

"And I don't trust you to come back." Edgar positioned himself next to the school teacher.

"Very well." Lewis grudgingly handed his pistol to Lord Crandall. "If you would take this, sir." It pained him to trust the man, but the gentleman had steadier hands and more experience with firearms than Professor Drake, whom he preferred to trust.

The taller man accepted the weapon with a curt nod.

"Will that be acceptable?" Lewis glanced from Bainbridge to Edgar.

Both men nodded.

"If I do not return swiftly, consider this barrier deadly." Lewis turned to face the mist.

"A brave thing, this." Professor Drake clapped a hand on his shoulder. "Godspeed."

"Thank you." Lewis glanced into the old man's eyes and was surprised to see genuine concern. This man, whom he had met only the day before, truly cared what happened to him. Beyond that concern, however, was something else . . . not the fear that had lurked behind Inspector Newton's hard exterior, but something different. As he noticed it, the Professor looked away, swiveling to observe the mist. Lewis did not question Drake's emotion, though he marked it and remembered it. The other man had shown him great kindness and sympathy, and he felt a sudden bond to the scholar.

"We'll see you in a few moments," Lord Crandall said confidently.

"Of course." Lewis wished he believed that, but in light of all that he had seen in the past two days, especially the past minutes, he was not sure what was about to happen. He peered fruitlessly into the depths of that impenetrable barrier of gray, trying to discern anything. Seeing nothing, he steeled himself and stepped inside.

One pace ahead and all sound vanished as if a thick blanket had been drawn about Lewis's head. Not even his boots made sounds as they hit the flagstones. He peered around, turning from side to side, but saw only the thick gray mist in every direction. Turning back, he realized that nothing was there, not even the outlines of his companions or the missing portion of the hansom. It was as if he had been dropped into the middle of a fog bank on a tiny island at sea. That would have been preferable, for at least he would hear the surf pounding against the shore.

"Hello?" His voice sounded muffled and distant, even to him.

No response.

"Professor Drake? Lord Crandall?"

Again nothing.

"Elise?"

Not even she answered, and her ring remained cold against him.

On their trips to her family's estate, Elise had often awoken early to run through the morning fogs that clung to the moors. On such mornings, she thought the world was a wondrous and magical place. She would laugh as she joked about finding fairies or leprechauns. Lewis had chased her through that mist, laughing with her even as he searched for her. He had never felt threatened, never felt the icy grip of death that now clung to him, teasing his exposed flesh. He shivered and realized that he could not remain long without succumbing to the chill of the elements. He took a breath, turned a precise one hundred and eighty degrees, and walked away from his companions.

The paving stones vanished, replaced by what felt like a thick carpet of moss, but nothing became visible. He could barely see his own legs, and his feet had vanished altogether. If not for the fact that he could feel them and could still walk, he might have assumed they had been amputated.

A gut-churning panic seized him as he took another few steps forward. The air grew even heavier around him, pressing down the way the oppressive humidity and tension had in the moments before Ulundi . . .

A swish of movement behind him broke the deafening quiet. He whirled around, his hand going to a gun that wasn't there. He cursed himself for allowing Crandall to retain the pistol and instead drew his sword. But despite his panic, he found only the Mist looming over him, around him, and even beneath him.

The high-pitched scrape of metal against metal shrieked to his right, something else gargled and rasped to his left. His heart pounded in his chest as he felt unseen terrors closing in around him. He backed away, turned, and limped as swiftly as he could, trying desperately to put some distance between himself and the horrors that stalked him.

Glowing red coals pierced the impenetrable vapor above and ahead as if a giant creature loomed over him. Lewis halted, crying out in a show of cowardice and surprise he deemed pathetic, and nearly fell over backward. He threw his arms up to block what would certainly be a killing blow from some massive beast, but as he blinked, the eyes disappeared. Lewis found no relief, however—the grinding metal drew closer, mere paces away, a cacophony of loud, unyielding, and unharmonious sounds.

"Who's there?" Lewis's voice shook, but he gripped his sword and stood his ground as he realized that he could not outrun whatever charged toward him. He did not need a pistol to defend himself, he said in the privacy of his own head, trying to steel himself against the unknown. He had seen hand-to-hand combat, had fought men with his fists after being dislodged from his horse by Zulu spears.

"Who's there?" It was a deeper parody of his own voice that answered.

A cold dread crashed over Lewis as a tide of fear threatened to swallow him. His senses screamed at him to flee and he knew enough to listen. He angled away from where he had seen the glowing eyes and ran, uncaring that he could not see where he was going. The soft mossy ground changed, replaced, he guessed and hoped in one, by smooth stone. His feet slipped on the moisture clinging to the sheer surfaces, and he nearly fell, but somehow managed to retain his footing.

Small, sharp thorns poked at his right side, piercing his clothing and flesh. He cried out, but did not falter as they ripped free. The sound of metal blades grew louder, as if a dozen men slashed their swords together in pursuit of him. The sound nearly reached him, despite his best efforts to outrun them. Bright eyes, this time of green flame, flared ahead of him, fanned by some inhuman force. He hurled himself to the side, slipped, and fell hard onto the stones. Pain lanced through his shoulder where the walking monster had pierced him during the escape from the station, keeping him down. The blades surged toward him, so loud that he might have been lying next to a blacksmith working a blade against his grinding wheel.

The enormous green eyes ripped away the Mist above him. More thorns pierced him on his arms, legs, and face, dragging jagged gashes over his flesh and sending searing pain through his body. He felt as if he were on fire, and the unwelcome thought occurred: perhaps he was. He rolled, kicked out with his feet, and flailed his arms, desperate to keep his attackers away. Whatever these things were, they would not take him without a fight.

The glowing eyes descended toward him, their heat scorching his face. He closed his eyes against them and bellowed a battle cry at the top of his lungs. Then, with all his strength, he rolled away and pushed himself onto his feet as fast as he could. He hurled himself into the mist, in the opposite direction of those terrible eyes, knowing full well that he could never outrun whatever hunted him. He would die having failed in his quest for vengeance. He cursed himself again for not being good enough or fast enough to slay Elise's killer, and for allowing her to go to her death in the first place. Surely he would face judgment and punishment in the next life for it. Perhaps that was as it should be. He deserved no quarter, no mercy. He gritted his teeth, resigned to his fate as the murky death shroud dropped down on him.

CHAPTER TEN

He was still screaming when, a moment later, he crashed into someone's legs.

"By God, Captain, are you all right?" Lord Crandall said.

Lewis blinked and saw the man looking down at him. Gregory and Professor Drake stepped into view next to him, concern on their faces. Lewis patted his face, hands, and legs, frantically searching for the terrible injuries caused by the creature he had faced.

But his clothing was untouched, and the only wounds he bore were from the encounter in the station.

"What the devil are you doing, man?" Crandall tweaked his moustache, looking perplexed.

"Are you hurt?" Gregory's eyes were wide with surprise and fear.

"What happened?" The professor held out a hand. "Did you find the way out?"

"I . . . I'm all right." Lewis raised his arms, allowing the men to haul him to his feet. He glanced back at the impenetrable fog and shivered. "How long was I in there?"

"You were gone but a moment." Professor Drake released him and brushed off his coat.

"That's impossible." Lewis grabbed hold of the overturned hansom to steady himself as the shock of battle nearly overcame him. "I . . . I walked for at least ten minutes before . . ." He trailed off and shivered as the memories swept over him.

"Out with it, man!" Edgar stepped up to their group. "Before what?"

"The constables are right . . . evil things are lurking in there." Lewis forced himself to stop shaking and straightened up, controlling the tremors in his voice and body. "We cannot escape that way." They could never again attempt such a thing.

"Do you mean more of the dead?"

"I'm not certain. There were terrible sounds . . . I was attacked by . . . something." He shook his head. "There is no way out—I'm certain of that." In life, he knew, some things were so horrible that he could not describe them accurately. He hoped the group would accept his word; if they decided to ignore his warnings, there was little he could say. No words could do justice to what had happened to him in the Mist.

"You sound as if you're hallucinating." Professor Drake leaned forward to study his eyes. "I don't smell opium, but perhaps this mist has a similar effect."

"That might explain why he thought he was injured, but was not." Lord Crandall nodded and stared challengingly at Lewis. "If true, then perhaps we can hold our breaths and simply run through without suffering the same ill effects."

"Don't be a fool, Crandall—it is not merely gas! If it were, the citizens of this place would have figured that out long ago!" Lewis glared at him. "You cannot go in there! It is grave danger to anyone who tries it!"

"That's *Lord* Crandall to you, Captain. But I suppose your bad manners can be pardoned, since you are clearly not in your right mind. I would not expect an officer of the Queen to be such a coward." Lord Crandall patted him on the shoulder, but his arrogance spoiled the comforting effect he'd no doubt intended. "I'm afraid we'll have to see for ourselves."

"You can't go in there. It's not safe!" Lewis grabbed the sleeve of the man's coat, the allegation of cowardice irrelevant. "You must believe me! I was lucky to escape with my life!"

"Then perhaps I should take this with me." Lord Crandall raised the revolver. "Don't you agree?"

Lewis did not wish to lose the gun, but after his experience in the Mist, he thought the weapon might prove valuable; he did not wish any more deaths to occur. Too many had died that he could have saved. "If you must—but take care. You will become disoriented in there. Do not lose your bearings and shoot one of our companions." He backed up a pace. "Or me."

"I'll bear that in mind." Lord Crandall nodded curtly. He turned to face the Mist, but other voices chimed in before he could enter.

"We're coming with you." Bainbridge stood arm-in-arm with Anne; both looked hopeful.

"And Edgar and myself as well." Josephine pointed at Lewis. "Without the Captain, perhaps we have a chance."

Lewis did not reply. If she thought his absence would make the experience more successful, she was gravely mistaken. He sighed. Some things had to be learned through experience. He hoped that they would survive. Each of them stepped forward to gather near Lord Crandall. Professor Drake held back. Lewis glanced at him, arching one eyebrow in surprise.

"Someone should remain here with you. This neighborhood is clearly not safe."

"Thank you." Lewis nodded and drew the sword from his cane. After what he had witnessed, the sword was better than nothing.

"I see each of you has made up your mind," Lord Crandall observed. "So be it. Remain together." He nodded to Lewis and the professor, then stepped into the mist.

"What did you really see in there?" The professor looked sidelong at Lewis, concern making him appear older and more tired.

"Flaming eyes in the Mist and . . . that's all." He could not describe it, but Lewis knew he had seen death in that cloud.

"Where in the name of God are we, and what is this mist?" Drake rubbed his beard. "How can any of this be possible?"

"I wish I knew."

At that moment, further conversation was interrupted by a woman's shrill scream. Anne burst from the wall of Mist as if it had spat her out. She careened forward, colliding heavily with Lewis. He steadied her.

"It's all right! You're safe now."

"It was terrible! O Lord, protect us!" She sobbed against his chest as he held her. "The endless beating of the drums . . . the burn of the ice."

A gunshot echoed from within the murk, followed by distant shouts and screams, then another shot.

"Take that, you devils!" Lord Crandall dove through the barrier. He crashed to the ground, then twisted as he hit the paving stones so he could fire again.

"Wait!" Lewis barked. "You're out of the Mist!"

Lord Crandall's eyes darted left and right, but slowly stilled. He breathed heavily as if he had been running for miles, and his face was slick with sweat. Slowly, he nodded and lowered the pistol. As if that had summoned the others, the rest of the group emerged all at once from different points along the wall, some shouting, some screaming, and others sobbing as they pleaded for assistance. Anne released her grip on Lewis and ran to her husband, who appeared shaken. None appeared to have sustained any injuries.

"God has abandoned us!" Josephine wailed. "We are damned!"

No one else said anything. The husbands and wives held each other close. Ben mumbled to himself and Lord Crandall and Gregory stared at the Mist as though they feared something else might emerge. The wall of Mist swirled faster, seeming conscious of their scrutiny, but all else was still and quiet.

"What did you see?" Professor Drake stepped closer to Lord Crandall.

"I don't know." The tall man frowned, a haunted look coming over him. "What I do know is that Captain Wentworth is correct. We cannot escape through those Mists."

Others murmured their agreement, and even Edgar did not argue the point. Lewis took the opportunity to reassert his leadership over the group.

He reached over and took the pistol from Lord Crandall's still-shaking hand. The man allowed him to take the weapon without argument. Lewis cracked it open and discovered that three of the six rounds had been fired—yet he had heard only two shots. The Mist clearly defied logic, he thought as he turned to face the group.

"I suggest we break into four groups and ascertain whether these Mists truly encircle all of Mithras Court." Lewis did not like the idea of splitting up even as he said it, but they had little choice. The longer they remained in Mithras Court, the longer they remained in danger.

"An excellent suggestion. Although given what the constables told us, I doubt we shall have much luck." Lord Crandall motioned to Lewis's gun. "Our limited weaponry also concerns me."

"I don't see that we have any other choice," Lewis countered. "Speed is of the essence."

"Perhaps we can purchase additional firearms?" Gregory hugged his arms to his chest as if trying to fight off a chill. "I would feel considerably safer if we can defend ourselves effectively."

"Aren't you all forgetting something?" Josephine's voice resonated loudly.

"Indeed?" Lord Crandall queried with an arched eyebrow and a tweak of his moustache.

"You gave your word that if this attempt to escape from this place failed, you would escort us to the nearest church." She glared at Lewis with the look an angry mother might give her children as she scolded them.

"Don't you think that what we've seen just now alters the situation?" Lewis said. "Given what we've seen of Mithras Court, I believe it is not a stretch to say we are in constant danger. We must move swiftly if we are to stay ahead of those threats."

"I don't see that at all," Edgar said. "We're in no immediate danger as long as it is daylight. We've tried it your way, and it is time to try ours. I expect you both, as the men of honor you claim to be, to keep your word and guide us to the nearest church." He sneered. "Personally, I trust neither of you, but you have the weapons and the skill to use them." He made the last part sound more curse than talent.

Lord Crandall glanced at Lewis, his eyes questioning. Lewis realized that the man wanted his counsel. They had indeed made a promise, one that they would have to honor lest they risk a mutiny in their ranks. Although such a rebellion might remove several annoyances from Lewis's life, he felt that there was strength in numbers. Furthermore, although he did not trust all of them, his fellow passengers could certainly be trusted more than the denizens of Mithras Court. He would be wise to maintain good relations with them.

As for their desire to find a church, Lewis conceded that they might possibly be correct, and that a church could offer protection, though he doubted that very much. Any belief in God that had remained after the war had been lost when Elise was killed. He looked at Crandall and nodded once, slowly.

"Very well," Lord Crandall said finally. "We shall remain together and deliver any who wish it to the safety of the local parish."

"Follow me, then." Lewis glanced one final time at the swirling Mist and turned away. He moved swiftly toward the lighted street-lamps at the nearest intersection. As he strode toward the comforting glow, he noted that the weak light had dimmed slightly. He blinked, all his attention focusing on his surroundings, looking up into the fog-enshrouded sky—but he dismissed the thought. Their clocks had said the day started at three o'clock in the morning, but that had been only a few hours earlier. Night could not yet be falling. More than likely, a cloud had obscured the hidden sun. The others did not even notice, or no one said anything, and Lewis put the thought firmly out of mind.

The dim outlines of the decrepit and burned-out buildings became visible again as the fog thinned slightly and they reached the intersection, where they were greeted by the songs and shouting of the adjacent neighborhood. The echo of hooves grew louder, and as Lewis stepped into the road, the shadowy form of a hansom emerged from the fog, its driver cracking his whip. Lewis was reminded of the dappled stallion he had ridden during the war. He'd been a good horse, and although Lewis had never discovered his fate, he hoped the beast had survived after Lewis had been dislodged from the saddle. He wished he were mounted just then. He missed the safety and speed of sitting atop a horse. Even if the dead returned, he would certainly be able to outdistance their threat.

Lord Crandall whistled and waved at the cab driver, drawing Lewis from his thoughts.

The driver clearly intended to ignore them, but at the last instant he drew reins and pulled the cab to a halt. Lewis recognized the rat-faced man who had given them directions to the police station earlier. The man glanced at them, eyes narrowed.

"What can I do for you this time?" He grinned, and the expression crinkled his face with lines beyond his years.

"We're looking for the nearest church." Lord Crandall handed the man several coins without being asked.

"Why do you want to go *there?*" The man reached up to scratch his head. His fingers poked out the ends of his frayed gloves. "God doesn't visit Mithras Court."

"Surely that's not true," Josephine said with an edge of challenge. "God is everywhere."

"I only says it like I sees it." The man shifted nervously, his eyes glancing anywhere but directly at them. Lewis did not like the looks of him. Was he afraid because he feared God, or because of the force that had placed him in Mithras Court?

"You've been paid, man," Professor Drake interrupted. "Simply tell us what we wish to know and be on your way."

"All right, guv. This is Bacchus Way." He pointed in the opposite direction from the boisterous noise down the road. "Follow this street and turn right on Venus Road. You can't miss it."

"Thank you." Lord Crandall waved him off.

"Good day to you. Again." The man cracked the whip, spurring his horse forward. It leaped ahead, the cab bumping along behind it. An instant later, it vanished into the fog. This time, Lewis wasn't surprised when the horse's hooves and the carriage's wheels went silent.

Chapter ELEVEN

This end of Bacchus Way was quiet and tidy. Modest four-story dwellings lined each side and street lamps glowed warmly. Working class people strode past, some carrying groceries or other goods, while some were simply out for a stroll. The men wore the clothes of laborers, the women the austere faces of those who have known hardship.

Seeing such people living in homes that surely had once been quite nice surprised Lewis, though he had seen older neighborhoods in London in which the homes of the gentry had been handed down to the lower classes as populations changed and new groups moved into districts. He thought it odd that the people did not appear unhappy, but none of them smiled, either. They moved about their daily tasks, even those taking a walk, as if it were something they had to do, not something they *wanted* to do. He had witnessed similar expressions on battle-weary soldiers. After a while, they became numb to the horrors of war and simply went through the motions of life.

"These people—they are beaten." He paused in front of a tenement constructed of worn brick and old stones. The building might have been nice at one time, but dirt smeared its leaded glass windows and the walls bore the blackened grit of years of coal soot. An old man and woman sat upon a sturdy bench at the top of the steps, next to an open front door. They stared blankly ahead as if they had nothing to say—and had not for years. Lewis had seen couples who had been married for many years end up like that, and had once wondered if he and Elise would become so distant—or if it was simply familiarity that went beyond words. Lewis would never know. His future had been taken from him by the tattooed man.

"They seem to have lost their will to survive." Lord Crandall came to a stop near Lewis. He scrutinized the couple the way visitors might stare at a painting in a museum, unsure whether they liked or hated it.

"What are they looking at?" Professor Drake drew up as well. He glanced from the couple to the terrace houses across the street, but found no ready explanation.

"I don't believe they're looking at anything," Gregory said. "But they are *seeing* something."

"What do you mean?" Lewis tilted his head toward the man.

"They're seeing memories—terrible memories, I would wager." Gregory pulled his coat closer about him. It seemed a nervous gesture rather than a practical one. "Will we end up like that, I wonder?"

The old man looked down at them suddenly and Lewis nearly jumped. "Everyone ends up like this in Mithras Court." His voice was thick and low.

Lewis frowned, but before he could utter a response, distant bells echoed from several streets over, breaking the quiet of the street. Others joined in until a jarring cacophony of ringing rent the night. This was no ordinary bell-ringing.

"What in the name of hell!" Lewis put his hands over his ears as the noise intensified.

Without a word, the elderly couple stood up and disappeared inside, closing the door behind them and bolting it shut. A breeze blew in, swirling the fog. It thickened until they could barely see across the street. Two men in suspenders and cotton shirts accompanying a young woman in a simple work dress moved into view. They hurried toward Lewis and his group but ignored them. They walked with their heads down, clearly intent on running past without saying a word. Lord Crandall stepped in front of them.

"I say, where are you headed?"

The taller man, a lean fellow with long gray sideburns, blinked as if waking from a dream. "What?" he said, genuinely confused. "What did you say?"

"I asked you where you are going." Lord Crandall's expression soured.

"Can't you hear the bells? We're going home." He moved to pass by, but Crandall stepped in front of him again.

"But what do the bells mean?"

"Are you daft, man?" The tall man closed his hands into fists. "Let us pass!"

"Father, they're new." The woman stepped forward, her brow furrowed in concern. "Otherwise they wouldn't be standing here asking such a question. They don't know."

The man squinted at Lord Crandall, then looked at the others.

"Aye." He nodded thoughtfully. "It's second night. The bells mean second night is coming. You should be hurrying to your homes or wherever you're staying. Before they come out." He took his daughter's hand, turning his attention back to her. "Come on, lass. Let's get you out of the fog." He pulled her past, the other man following swiftly after them. None looked back.

"Frederick mentioned second night," Professor Drake said. "But from what he said, I'd no idea what it was. Perhaps we should heed their warning and return to the Laughing Gargoyle."

"Ridiculous," Lord Crandall said. "There can't be two nights."

"And the dead cannot rise from their graves, either." Lewis raised his pistol. "I suggest we follow the professor's advice. We can find the church tomorrow, in the daylight."

"The church is closer!" Edgar argued, sounding as though he'd been cheated.

"Yes, the church. We must reach the church." Josephine said. "The Lord will help us!"

"I am sick to death of your rantings about the church." Lord Crandall turned to Lewis. "Captain, let us drop these folks off at the minster and be done with it." He waved vaguely, indicating Josephine and anyone on her side—certainly Edgar and Ben, and perhaps Anne and Thomas.

Lewis did not like the gentleman's demeaning tone, nor did he relish the idea of accepting a suggestion from the man. He had seen too many of the gentry make foolish and seemingly arbitrary decisions, in times of war and peace alike, to allow Lewis to let him assume the mantle of command. For once, however, he agreed with him. Furthermore, he had given his word that he would deliver them to the house of God. He shrugged, resolved to give Lord Crandall a rare victory.

"Very well. Follow me." He took the lead; as the one with the revolver, it was the only position that made sense.

The clanging of the bells echoed loudly around them, faster, and with a power that caused the ground to shake. Lewis glanced up and saw that the sky had grown unquestionably darker. Ruefully, he admitted to himself that darkness had probably been falling since he had first noticed it.

"They were right," Gregory said as Lewis noted the sky. "Night is coming again."

"How can that be true?" Professor Drake said. It wasn't really a question.

Lewis handed his cane to the professor, who nodded grimly. "Keep moving!" Lewis said to the others in his most commanding voice. The last thing he needed was for the group to lose focus when danger was so close.

Several more men and women hurried past in a panic, disappearing quickly into the fog behind them. The wind whipped up, swirling the vapor, and as the light faded, it was nearly impossible to see anything more than a few feet away on any side. As Lewis's fear of the unseen dead surged to the front of his mind, the familiar heat of Elise's ring warmed his chest.

"Hurry, Lewis, they are rising!" she said, this time loudly enough that Lewis thought the others might have heard, were it not for the clanging bells. "They hunger for the living!"

Despite the pain in his thigh, he leaped into the street and veered to the right as they reached the crossroads of Venus Road. The signpost stood out starkly, its white letters glowing in the light of a nearby street lamp. Lewis slowed, allowing the others to catch up. When they matched his pace, he pushed onward.

Lewis was relieved to see that the new street was nicer than the last. The brick buildings were well kept, and trees lined the sidewalks ahead of them. The trees in their fall colors rose eerily out of the dim light and thick fog. As Lewis hurried past the first street lamp, he realized that the neighborhood was completely deserted.

Edgar slowed abruptly, looking around the deserted streets, despite Josephine pulling on his arm.

"Hurry!" Elise said.

"I am moving as swiftly as I am able!" Professor Drake's voice sounded strained.

Lewis's eyes widened. Drake had heard Elise! He glanced back and saw the old man at the center of the group, his expression one of steely determination that told Lewis Drake had mistaken Elise for one of the other women. He had feared that only the locals of Mithras Court could hear her, and he would never convince his companions of her existence. His command of the group would be lost as they would surely consider him insane. Relief flooded him as he realized that her voice could help him save them all.

"The lights!" Gregory's shout drew Lewis's attention to the path ahead. "They're out!"

A section of the street was completely dark, its street lamps either extinguished or missing altogether—it was too dark to be certain. Faint illumination from the lamps on adjoining streets allowed them to see the outline of a church looming to their right, a forbidding shape in the fog. Lewis slowed as he looked up. The shadows stretched outwards from the massive structure; it seemed that they were reaching for the survivors. The bells ceased abruptly, plunging them into an empty silence that was more disquieting than the noise had been.

"Keep going!" Josephine ran past. "We're almost there!"

"Wait!" Lewis tried to catch her, but she moved too swiftly. "Something isn't right! There is no light whatsoever coming from the church!" He dashed after her. Edgar and the others joined in the chase.

But Josephine ran swiftly up the broad stairs at the front of the structure, her skirts held high. She stopped halfway, as if the pure darkness into which she had run finally became apparent to her. A frown creased her features as she looked up. Lewis reached her a moment later, his eyes drawn to the church—a massive affair that was out of place in the neighborhood. Not a hint of light spilled from the structure. As the last bells of distant neighborhoods faded to echoes, a frightening silence descended on them. Even the footsteps of their companions, as they hurried after them, seemed muffled. Even in the middle of the night, the other areas of Mithras Court had showed visible signs of life. They saw here no sign of any living man, woman, or child.

Lewis squinted at the minster. Clearly, it had once been a cathedral, deepening the mystery surrounding Mithras Court. Surely someone among them would have heard of such a district within greater London had it contained a cathedral.

"This place should not be dark." Lewis took hold of Josephine's arm as gently as he could. "There is no safety here. There is no priestly, nor even godly, presence. We should leave at once and return to the pub."

As the others caught up, all could see that night had truly fallen. The shuffling of dozens of feet scraping against the flagstones echoed around them in the fog. Lewis raised his revolver and swept over their surroundings, cursing the lack of light and the ubiquitous fog as it thwarted his attempts to glean anything new.

"We need to leave *now*," he insisted, pulling Josephine back from the minster. "All of you, we must retreat to the pub at once!" The sense of impending doom was palpable, as it had been at Ulundi— this time, it was not Zulu warriors hidden in the tall grasses who would assault them, it was walking dead lurking in the darkness and the fog on all sides. He could feel them watching . . . waiting. Time was running out.

"Unhand her!" Edgar pushed him back, his face flushed with anger and exertion. "How dare you!"

"Damn it man, there is danger here!" Lewis said, keeping his grip on Josephine's arm.

"Let her go!" Edgar threw his weight at Lewis, dropping his good elbow into Lewis's bicep and causing him to release the woman.

The instant she was free, Josephine charged up the stairs again, even swifter than before.

"What the devil are you doing?" Lewis pushed the fat man away and put his Webley up to his head. "I'm trying to protect you and your foolish wife!"

"We don't need your help now that we're here!" Edgar looked toward Josephine as she neared the top of the stairs. "You've delivered us as promised, Captain. You can leave now." Edgar did not wait for an answer. He turned and followed Josephine as quickly as his portly form would allow.

Edgar had called his bluff. Lewis had never intended to waste a bullet on him, not when there was an infestation of the dead in Mithras Court. He watched the man and considered making his escape.

"Fools!" Lord Crandall said, scorn in his voice. "There is no aid to be found here! This church is dead!"

Lewis agreed with the gentleman's assessment. It was not only dead—most certainly, Edgar and his naïve wife were walking into incredible danger. Lewis was tempted to leave them, but he had sworn to protect them and deliver them to safety. This church could hardly be considered safe. He cursed under his breath at their stupidity and his damned honor. But too many had died since their arrival in Mithras Station, and he could not allow them to come to harm. He hurried after them, taking the stairs two at a time, ignoring the pain in his leg.

As he drew closer, details emerged from the dark fog and the sense of wrongness was confirmed. The building was charred and burned, its stained glass shattered, its doors scorched and hanging ajar. Collapsed beams, slick with moss from the exposure to the fog, lay scattered inside. Shuffling sounds emanated from the interior. As he listened, he heard a chorus of rasping moans floating on the air.

"Surely these dead cannot have desecrated a house of God!" Anne said, somewhere behind Lewis.

Josephine paused near the door and suddenly smiled. Lewis stopped a few feet from her, frowning at her sudden joy. Before he could say anything, she turned to Edgar.

"Isn't it beautiful?" She beamed at Edgar as he drew close. He stopped behind her, eyeing the door with trepidation.

"Josephine, the church is dark," Edgar said, trying to wave her back down the steps. "Get away from the door, woman."

Lewis realized how close to the open doorway she stood. She looked poised to run inside.

"Don't be silly! It's beautiful and bright." Josephine took another step into the archway.

"What the devil are you talking about, woman?" Lord Crandall stopped next to Lewis and shifted nervously. "The minster has been destroyed."

"I can hear the choir." She stepped into the doorway before any of them could pull her back. Josephine put a hand to her ear as if trying to draw in the sounds. "The tenors are especially wonderful tonight."

"Josephine—listen to us!" Edgar stepped toward her, reaching out to take her by the arm. "This church is in ruins. No one is inside."

"Don't be silly. I can see the beautiful lights, the stained glass. I can see the priest and his choir beckoning to me. Come inside, Edgar. The Lord shall protect all his children." She pointed to Lewis dismissively and added, "Even him."

Lewis gasped, a chill washing over him. Nothing awaited them within that burned and gutted hulk—save death. He edged toward her, fearing that a sudden movement might cause her to run inside and out of reach, and take Edgar with her. Clearly, Josephine was not in her right mind. With proper care, she might come to her senses, but for the moment, she was lost. Lewis had to act swiftly if he was to avert disaster.

"My dear, there's nothing for any of us here." Professor Drake motioned toward the street. "We should leave this place at once."

"I'll do no such thing!" Josephine took a step away from them. "I must listen to this truly gorgeous music. It will keep the dead away."

"She's gone mental," Ben said from several steps below. He sounded awed.

Movement from within the doorway caught Lewis's eye. He lunged for Josephine, but was too late; several shadowy figures rose up around her. She had drifted further into the arch. They reached for her with clawed hands as they hissed. Lewis raised his pistol and fired as they neared. The first shot struck one of the monsters in the chest, knocking it back. The others were not deterred.

"Take her hand!" Lord Crandall darted toward her. Edgar grabbed her left arm and pulled, but the dead within were too close. Claws and teeth sank into Josephine in half a dozen places, tearing through her maroon dress, slashing her skirts and raking gashes in her flesh as they drew her inexorably toward them. She did not notice the pain, even as one of the dead stabbed her in the chest with a sharp claw. Lewis could only stare in horror.

"The parishioners have accepted me into their embrace!" she cried in a tone of glorious relief, even as blood trickled from her mouth.

"Let her go!" Lewis recovered his senses and fired again into the cluster of corpses, knocking one of the dark figures back. It fell out of sight, only to be replaced by another hideous shape, and another.

"Edgar, join us!" The woman's ecstatic joy echoed through the court as the creatures rent her flesh in sprays of blood.

Anne shrieked and Ben wailed like a child at the sight of her arm tearing away. Blood soaked her dress and poured down on the stones she stood upon.

"Snap out of it, woman!" Lord Crandall grabbed at Josephine, but a creature stepped in front of him, the dim light revealing a half-decayed face and the tattered remains of a frock coat over its shoulders. It reached skeletal arms toward him, teeth bared in a deliberate smile. Gregory shouldered Crandall out of the monster's way.

"Please, somebody help her!" Edgar's grip on her arm loosened; her white glove slid down her blood-soaked arm.

"Forget about her!" Ben said. "Save yourselves! Run for the light!"

"Wait!" Reggie shouted. "We must stay together!"

Lewis did not spare an instant to look behind, and didn't care if the lot of them ran. He fired again, and again, but there were too many creatures. Each time one of them dropped out of sight, two more human husks rose from the shadows to take its place.

"They're behind us, Captain!" Thomas's voice rang out, jerking Lewis's attention away from the cathedral.

"Edgar!" Josephine's glove slid off, falling limply in Edgar's grip. With it went their only hope of saving her. She fell backward into the throng of undead, disappearing between the scattered timbers and hunched forms. The last thing Lewis saw of her was her bright, joyous smile. He could not accept the incongruity of the moment. She had gone willingly into her death. Would Mithras Court drive them all mad? Or, like the other citizens of the court, would they simply accept their fates like mindless cattle? Both possibilities sickened him.

Edgar lunged after his wife. Despite knowing what his fate would be, he seemed determined to join her. Lord Crandall interceded, catching him in a bear hug and hauling him back.

"She's gone!" he said. "You'll do nothing but sacrifice yourself, and I won't stand for that, man!"

"We must go now." Gregory stepped up to assist, grabbing the man's arm and tugging him away. The task was made easier when a gut-wrenching wail split the night, marking Josephine's death.

"Captain!" Thomas' voice shook. "We are not alone!"

Lewis fought against the frustration of his inability to save the woman. But his instincts did not let him grieve or feel guilt for more than a few seconds. He backed away from the door, which for the moment remained empty as the creatures focused on their first victim of the night. He risked a glance at Bainbridge and saw other shadowy figures appearing at the edges of his vision. Shrouded in the tattered remains of their clothing, they moved through the thick haze.

Bainbridge stood with his wife, his arm tightly around her. Anne's face was pale, but she retained her senses and her composure. Perhaps the terror of life in Mithras Court had strengthened her, but perhaps she had that innate strength in her previous life. Reggie and Mary stood their ground, though fright was evident on their faces. Ben had disappeared, though Lewis did not think him dead—his thought was confirmed when he saw a familiar figure up the road. The coward had fled toward the nearest light without waiting.

"Let me go to my Josephine!" Edgar said, still fighting to join her in death. The buttons on his vest popped. In the emotion of the moment, he either believed that she still lived, or he did not care that trying to reach her would mean his own death.

Lewis turned around and saw tears streaming down the man's face as he struggled in vain against Lord Crandall and Gregory. The men pulled him away from the church and hauled him toward the stairs. Lewis frowned at the delay.

"Leave her be! There is no saving her!" Lord Crandall dragged the man, finally reaching the top of the stairs. Edgar ceased struggling and fell into step with him. "Had she been in her right mind, she would have told you to run!"

"We need to leave—now!" Professor Drake hurried over to Lewis, sword in hand. "The devils are trying to flank us!" The undead on the street slowly climbed the stairs toward them on both sides, though a path down the middle remained open.

"Stay close to me!" Lewis took a few steps toward the street, allowing the Webley to lead the way.

The murky fog swirled around them, thinning for an instant here and there to reveal dozens of shambling dead in every direction. Lewis paused, searching for a way through, but saw none. Fear churned in his stomach and a remote part of his mind noted that he had not eaten in a long time; surely he would have lost his supper at the carnage he had just witnessed. The mob of walking corpses alone was enough for that, after all.

"We're surrounded," Lord Crandall said grimly.

"They won't take me without a fight." Reggie brandished his knife in one hand and pulled Mary closer to him with the other. She looked less frightened and more determined than she had since the station.

"I'll try to clear a path for us with my pistol." Lewis searched for a weak spot in the enemy ranks, but found none. Decaying corpse upon decaying corpse shuffled toward them from every direction. Even if his fellows all carried pistols, he doubted they would be able to escape their predicament.

"Help me!" Ben's scream drifted through the fog. Lewis redoubled his search, looking for a way to reach the engineer, but found none.

An instant later, Ben's scream ended abruptly in a gurgling wail and silence took hold once again. Lewis clenched his teeth, knowing with certainty that the coward had perished. In war, he would have had little sympathy for such a deserter, but no one deserved the kind of death the man had surely just experienced.

Suddenly, Elise's ring warmed again as the wind whipped up. It was not the chill breeze they had experienced earlier—this wind pushed away the vapor, forming a clear corridor between them and the nearest lamp post. A glowing blue figure stood in the center of the path. Behind her, the street lamp shone brightly down the corridor. The walking dead moved out of the path as if in pain, disappearing into the fog.

"This way—hurry!" the figure in the channel called.

Even from his distance, Lewis knew Elise stood before him. His heart skipped a beat, then another, then it hammered inside his chest. For an instant, he forgot about the others, the dangers on all sides, and bolted down the steps, reaching out to her. He had to touch her again, had to embrace her.

"Who is that?" Lewis heard Professor Drake inquire.

"Wait for us, Captain!" Lord Crandall called, following swiftly behind.

Lewis slowed, allowing the men to drag Edgar along with them. When they caught up, he looked to Elise, still a dozen feet away, and back to them.

"That, gentlemen, is Elise . . . my wife."

CHAPTER TWELVE

Lewis was unable to look away from Elise. There was no question it was her—her black curls, her penetrating blue eyes, and the smooth skin of her beautiful face shone even in the dim light. It was as if she had climbed out of her dark mausoleum and found him. The black dress she had been buried in clung to her as it blew about her in the wind. She beckoned to Lewis with her finger. Lewis stared at her, unable to concentrate on anything else.

She was truly there. He had not gone mad. A whole new future opened up before him and he wondered how Mithras Court played into it. Had this odd place brought her to him? Or had she come in response to his danger?

"But she's dead." The note of fear in the professor's words jarred Lewis.

"She doesn't appear to be like these other corpses," Bainbridge said quietly. He sounded, in fact, analytical. "She's translucent . . . as if . . . my God, she's a ghost!" His brow furrowed in confusion. "But will she . . . will she harm us?"

Lewis smiled, though he thought Bainbridge to be a fool. This was Elise, his lost love. She could never harm anyone, let alone Lewis or anyone under his protection.

"It doesn't matter. She's helping us!" Lewis ran down the narrow corridor of light toward her. He had to reach her before she vanished, had to talk to her, touch her! As he drew closer, he understood Bainbridge's concern. For an instant, he allowed himself to consider that she might somehow be alive. But she was outlined by that strange blue nimbus, and she visibly wavered between solidity and transparency. He slowed as he neared her, unsure how to react, afraid his hand would simply pass through her.

"Hello, love." She smiled at him, her lips unusually red against her features. She reached a hand out as if to stroke his face. "You look so very tired."

"Elise . . . how can you be here?" Tired did not begin to describe the fatigue he felt, but at the sight of her, he felt an infusion of vitality.

"I don't know." Her smile faded, her face abruptly pinched with exertion. "I can't . . . you must hurry." She pointed to the lamp. "There is safety in the light!"

"Incredible." The professor paused next to Lewis and stared at her. "You have somehow reached out to us from the other side, from the very jaws of death."

"Elise, I'm sorry." Lewis ignored the scholar and tried to touch her arm, but his hand passed through her as if she were made of mist.

"For what?" Her eyes spoke of undying love, and he felt that she needed no apology, but he could not withhold it from her. Warmth spread from her wedding ring against Lewis's chest—her reply that his love was ever enough to satisfy her.

He had allowed her to travel alone, he had abandoned her and she had died. He would not accept forgiveness for her death.

"For allowing you to be murdered."

"It wasn't your fault, love." Exertion showed on her brow. "But you must hurry. I can't hold back the dead much . . . longer." Her image flickered, losing strength, and her words came harder, straining. "Someone else is coming."

"What do you mean?"

"I can't . . ." She gritted her ghostly teeth and shook her head, clearly frustrated. "Go! He must not see me!"

"Who?" Lewis looked around, but no one came near. Even the dead were falling back.

"Move to the damned light!" Lord Crandall shouted. Edgar ran alongside him, but his face was ashen and his eyes blank. Gregory followed, moving in step with Thomas and Anne. Reggie and Mary brought up the rear.

The hissing of the dead increased as Elise's strength faltered again, and they pressed closer to the survivors as the corridor she had made narrowed.

"Lewis, please . . ." Elise glared at him, her strain as palpable as her love. "Go!"

"Come on, Captain!" Drake grabbed him by the arm.

Lewis allowed himself to be pulled away, but his heart wasn't in the struggle any longer. He smiled wanly at Elise, before he finally turned and ran toward the light.

"What just happened? Who was that woman?" Anne's face was pale as they all took shelter under the lamp post.

"My wife. She cleared a path for us and saved our lives," Lewis said curtly.

"Apparently, she has manifested as a ghost," the professor said.

"But you told us your wife died two years ago." Anne shivered visibly, staring at Lewis as if seeking reassurance. But Lewis had none to give.

"She did." Lewis did not bother to explain, could not explain; he did not understand it himself.

"How . . ."

"How is anything possible in Mithras Court?" Lewis said, before she could finish. "Somehow, she crossed the barrier between this life and the next and opened that gap in the fog that allowed us to escape. No explanation will ever make sense—we know only what *is*." He glanced around and quickly took stock of his companions. Thankfully, those who had reached the lamp post remained together and whole. He bowed his head for a moment. When he looked up, Elise's shimmering form winked out and the corridor of light vanished.

Sudden sorrow pierced his heart. Seeing her for only a few moments was almost worse than never seeing her at all. Her appearance revived the grief he had thought raw already, reminding him of all he had lost. Whatever he'd thought, he hadn't really understood grief until that moment. His resolve to escape his entrapment and destroy the tattooed man—shooting was too easy, the man must suffer!—grew as he thought of Elise, resting uneasily in her grave.

"What do we do now?" Reggie's words drew Lewis back to the matter at hand.

Lewis glanced at the fog around them and listened to the moaning of the dead that were closing in. Elise had saved them. He had to honor her efforts by surviving. His eyes narrowed and met Reggie's frightened stare. As if his attention bolstered the man, the laborer straightened and nodded. In that moment, Lewis realized that he truly had taken the task of saving them upon himself. Having seen his love and renewed his vow to avenge her death had not released him from his promise to keep these men and women safe.

"We'll form up as a unit of the Queen's army would, staying together and moving as one, and we will make our way back to the pub. You will remain silent the entire way, with absolutely no argument, or the next time someone does something foolish, I'll not lift a finger to help, nor will I let anyone else. Am I clear?"

Most of them nodded, and even Edgar straightened up at Lewis's firm words.

"If we are prepared, then lead on!" Lord Crandall said wholeheartedly. "I, of course, reserve the right to interject on our course as needed."

"Of course." Lewis bit off an angry retort. Crandall's arrogance grated on his nerves, but in the interest of making haste, he let the comment drop.

"What about your wife's warning that someone else was coming?" Professor Drake's statement drew another glare from Lord Crandall, but it focused Lewis even more intently on the task at hand.

"All we can do is move as swiftly as possible." Lewis wanted to see Elise again, to talk to her, to ask questions, but he would first need to survive. He gripped his revolver tightly and glanced at the next lamp, twenty feet away. The shining light spread into the fog, pushing back the darkness and joining with the illumination of the other lamps down the road until they disappeared in the fog. Shadowy forms hovered at the edges of the light, but did not approach. Lewis judged that the group could reach the pub if they were cautious.

He narrowed his eyes and strode purposefully toward the next street lamp.

══════MC══════

As Lewis led the group back along the course they had followed earlier that day, their path beneath the lamps remained free of the denizens of Mithras Court, both the living and the dead. Despite the threatening gloom, Lewis remained confident that as long as the gas flowed they would return safely to the Laughing Gargoyle. He forced himself not to consider the chance that the gas might be somehow cut off.

His companions stayed silent, communicating only with nervous glances or hand gestures as they eyed the darkness with trepidation. It was a welcome change from the chatter that had followed Lewis since the group left the train station. Josephine's and Ben's deaths, combined with their very-apparent inability to leave Mithras Court, weighed heavily upon all of them.

Lewis was bolstered by his visit from Elise. He had searched for her killer for so long, never imagining that the trail would lead him back to her. He was more determined than ever to find her killer. Surely the fact that the tattooed man had not been punished for his crimes was keeping her from ascending to the afterlife.

It was ironic. He had rejected the thought of an afterlife when he turned away from God, but surely, if a ghost could exist, then there must be such a place. He pushed away the thought. He was not ready to confront God. He worried that Elise could not move on to whatever existed beyond the veil. It was his solemn duty to help her as she had been helping him.

The dead kept their distance at the edge of the light, appearing as dim shapes, their inhuman hissing mixing with the footfalls of Lewis and his companions. As Lewis neared the square adjoining the train station, something changed in the cadence of their rasping. Their hisses became rhythmic, unified—words that were just beyond hearing. Lewis paused on the corner, chills running the length of him as the sudden realization that they *were* speaking dawned. Primeval fear gnawed at his insides. He raised his hand, doing his best to keep it from shaking as he signaled the others to stop at the junction of Cannon Street and the square.

"What the devil is that?" Lord Crandall's voice sounded small as he and the others halted abruptly. The color had drained from his face.

"This is something new." Professor Drake raised the sword. "And I don't believe I like it. We should hurry."

"No, wait." Lewis raised his arm to block the others from getting past him. He peered into the murk ahead. Elise had warned of something else coming, something she feared, even as a ghost, something that should not see her. He did not take that lightly.

He could not see much of the square, and the row of buildings that stretched to his right vanished a mere dozen yards away in the thick fog. The vaguest shapes marked the walking dead, but they appeared rooted in place, their restless shifting stilled. Their rhythmic hissing continued unabated, even as something new and sinister joined their cries.

A new sound slowly crept into the hideous chorus. The scrape of scales slithering along the cobblestones echoed from every direction, as if many large snakes slipped along the ground beneath the fog.

"What is that?" Anne asked, her eyes wide. "Are those . . . snakes?"

"Yes." Lewis flashed on a memory from Ulundi. He could see the rolling hills, the tall reedy brown grass swaying gently in the breeze, feel the burning heat of the day. Serpents slipped along the ground, moving deftly across the savannah, the scaled bodies making a sound he had found strange and frightening at the time. It matched the noise echoing through their fog-enshrouded prison. On those distant plains, the reptiles had maneuvered always to avoid humans, horses, other beasts. They posed no danger to an alert man. Here, the snakes were moving toward them, drawing closer with each second.

"I don't see them," Reggie said quietly. The strain of tension filled his voice.

Lewis saw him squinting into the fog and gripping his knife tightly. Lewis doubted the value of the small blade, but he admired the man's bravery. The slithering grew louder until it overshadowed the rhythmic rasping of the dead. The fog thickened, swirling before them and pulling the darkness with it as a person might pull a blanket over their head.

•

"Back up against the lamp post, now!" The role of commander came as easily as breathing to Lewis. "And for God's sake, stay together!"

The group hurried to obey, ringing the lamp post and preparing to defend themselves. Professor Drake held his sword drawn. Lord Crandall and Gregory raised their fists, ready to fight with their bare hands if necessary. Lewis pointed his Webley toward the ground. He could never kill dozens of snakes with his pistol, but if he was to die, he would die fighting.

The vaporous fog halted mere feet from them. The hissing and slithering shifted and Lewis thought he could see hints of long, shadowy reptilian shapes moving along the ground just at the edges of the murk. The dead crowded forward, keeping to the edge of the feeble illumination. Their half-decayed bodies twitched as they stood, mouths agape. In no instance did any of the creatures violate the sphere of the light.

"They've halted their advance!" Lord Crandall said over the cacophony.

"Something else is moving out there." Professor Drake peered into the dark, his eyes following something. Lewis saw movement at the periphery, but could not fully examine it lest he let his guard down.

"The snake comes." Elise's voice was just loud enough for all of them to hear. They looked around in confusion. "Prepare yourselves!" Lewis realized that she did not fear being heard so much as being seen.

"Help us!" Anne cried suddenly. "Push back the darkness again!"

Elise did not answer; her ring had grown cold.

"She's gone." Even as Lewis prepared to face whatever Mithras Court had sent at them, he could not get her image from his head.

"Why did she say 'the snake' instead of 'snakes'?" Professor Drake's voice was curious, almost detached.

"Who the devil cares?" Lord Crandall said sharply. "Only a scholar would notice the distinction in the face of impending doom."

"The professor is right." Lewis frowned as the slithering intensified again and he caught glimpses of indistinct shapes disappearing into the fog there. Elise had always spoken with great precision. Her choice of words meant something—but what was it? The motion ceased around them abruptly, jarring him from his thoughts. The rasping of the dead grew louder until they were doing more than just chanting in unison. They were speaking.

"Lucius."

"Lucius . . ." Professor Drake repeated the word.

"Lucius."

"My God!" Lord Crandall raised his hands, palms outward, as if ready to push the things away with his bare hands.

"Lucius."

"God has nothing to do with it," Lewis said, gripping his pistol tightly.

"Inspector Newton said nothing about Lucius Knight being the man who controls the walking dead," Drake said. "That explains why the police are so afraid! Their liege lord has inflicted this upon them!"

"He isn't just *a* leader." This was a new voice, but one that Lewis recognized—the tattooed man. His statement echoed around the square, and the condescension was clear. "He isn't just *your* leader. He's your lord and master. And he bids you welcome."

"Why did you do it? Why did you kill Elise?" Lewis demanded. "Did Knight order it of you?" Lewis burned to know—vengeance would not be sated until he knew why she had died.

Laughter was his answer.

"Speak, coward!" Lewis's blood churned through his veins at the man's arrogance. "Why did you do it?"

"Why not?" The man's tone did not match his carefree words, as if he truly knew the reason and did not wish Lewis to discover it. As the fog swirled around them and the dead chanted, Lewis realized that the reasons did not matter if trying to discover them caused him to lose another opportunity to slay this man. He had wielded the knife that had killed Elise . . . and that should be enough for Lewis.

The cold-hearted cur would not escape him a second time. He raised his gun and narrowed his eyes, searching for the faintest hint of the man in the fog. One shot was all it would take to set Elise's spirit free!

"Not yet, Lewis Wentworth . . ." He laughed from the fog. "But soon . . ."

"I'll have your name, you murderous bastard!" Lewis strained to hear any sound. The man would reveal himself to Lewis in the murk.

"I am Richard Bailey, servant of Lord Lucius Knight . . . killer of men . . . and women." His laughter suddenly escalated to a mad cackle; it came from the murk directly in front of him.

"Steady now, Captain." Lord Crandall put a restraining hand on his arm. "He's deliberately trying to unnerve you, perhaps entice you to waste your ammunition before you have a target."

"Yes." Lewis had realized that, but was nonetheless certain that Bailey stood wreathed in the fog directly between him and the Laughing Gargoyle, an easy shot. He clenched his jaw, pushing back the years of rage and frustration, and squeezed the trigger. The muzzle flash was blinding in the dark fog, the sound piercing and painful. The bullet tore a hole in the mist, but nothing cried out in pain.

Laughter echoed around them.

Lewis fired again and again until his cartridges were spent. Heedless, he squeezed the trigger, dry-firing the weapon over and over.

"Easy, Captain!" Lord Crandall reached out to grip his arm. "You're empty!"

"Good-bye, Lewis Wentworth!" The fog rolled back and the laughter receded. A moment later, the lamps flared to full intensity, pushing back the darkness and the dead with it.

Lewis allowed Lord Crandall to force his arm down until the pistol was aimed at the ground. Twice he had encountered Elise's killer, and twice he had failed to end his quest. He was a pathetic, incompetent fool! How could he fail to engage the enemy twice in as many days? In the field, men died for such failures.

"What in the name of God just happened?" Edgar pushed his way to the front.

"That was the murderous knave who stabbed my wife to death," Lewis said. "He stabbed her a dozen times, tearing into her with his blade, killing her with each stroke over and over again. And I, presented with the chance, with a weapon in my hands . . . failed to kill him. Again." He stared into the fog, numbness spreading through him.

"Twelve other people lost their lives that night too," Gregory said. "Your wife was not alone."

"Yes, one of them was my very own servant." Lewis heard his voice as if someone else had spoken, so distant had he become in that moment. Still, Gregory's statement rang in Lewis' ears as the truth of what he had said penetrated. Had he become so obsessed with vengeance that he had forgotten that their lives had mattered too? He pushed the thoughts away. It was not his job to care about everyone, nor was it his job to avenge their deaths. It was for him to answer Elise's murder only. Something had happened this night—greater forces had been at work for him to miss his target. His wits about him once again, he cracked open his revolver, dumped the spent cartridges onto the street, and reached into his pocket for his last six. He would not give up—would never give up.

"It would appear that this Bailey is an agent of Lucius Knight." Lord Crandall stared into the fog. "And I think it's fair to say that Knight is *not* our friend."

"I find myself in agreement with you. Not only is he not an ally, but he appears to be our number one enemy. Pursuing him would be foolish in the extreme." Lewis glanced ahead and realized that with the restoration of the gaslight, the way to the inn had opened again. He turned to the others, ignoring the still-chanting dead things that remained fixated upon them.

"Let us get to safety and recover ourselves as we had planned." He motioned toward the Laughing Gargoyle. "Then we will devise a strategy to combat this foe."

"I quite agree." Lord Crandall nodded grimly.

Lewis double-checked his weapon, held it at the ready, and strode cautiously down the sidewalk. He forced out all thoughts of vengeance, instead focusing watchful eyes on the dead at the edge of the light as he led his group up the stairs of the inn. He glanced up at the structure and wondered if it was the only safe haven they might ever know again.

CHAPTER *THIRTEEN*

"I tried to warn you." Frederick, still clad in his stained shirt, stood in the parlor of the Laughing Gargoyle. He frowned, remorse in his blue eyes—but also something else. Perhaps, Lewis thought, fear.

When Lewis had knocked on the door to the Laughing Gargoyle, their host had opened it as swiftly as if he'd been waiting for them. As he had the prior evening, he held a flintlock pistol as he ushered them swiftly inside. He locked the door behind them and led them through the common room without comment; no one paid them any mind. Barely a third of the patrons of the previous night were back, and most were asleep in their chairs, heads down on their tables, or lying on the floor on makeshift bedding. Frederick guided them around the sleeping forms and led them into the parlor, where they found that the bedrolls and pillows from the prior evening had been folded and neatly stacked in a corner.

Lewis tightened his grip on the gun as anger burned through him in a sudden rush. This innkeeper had failed to warn them about what they might encounter in Mithras Court, failed to tell them of the dangers they would face. He had offered no warnings of any sort. Whatever his reasons, his inaction had resulted in Josephine's and Ben's deaths. In Lewis's mind, the man was as guilty as if he'd pushed them into the undead himself. It was all he could do not to point his revolver at the man.

"I don't recall you doing any such thing," Lord Crandall said. The gentleman leaned casually against the back of an arm chair but his eyes were intense, focused on their host. "In point of fact, you abandoned us completely this morning. You failed to direct us to the local constabulary, to do any of the things manifestly in your power to protect us, or to warn us adequately about this second night."

"Indeed." Professor Drake stopped pacing in the center of the room and glared at their host. "Your statement lacks truth. Had we been warned, we might have saved two lives."

"I think you'd better explain yourself, innkeeper." Thomas spoke from the divan, where he cradled Anne's head in his lap, his hand resting on her shoulder.

"I agree with the professor." Lord Crandall crossed his arms. "Why didn't you tell us about this second night? Or about this barrier known as the Mists, or any of the other dangers of this place? Your comments were too vague to be useful, and now two of our number are dead."

Frederick licked his lips and glanced from Crandall to Lewis, as if Lewis might offer assistance. Lewis was not about to defend the man. He lifted the gun a bit higher, his look conveying that he was prepared to use it if he did not like what Frederick had to say for himself.

"I'm sorry. I really am." Frederick looked around the room at them and sighed. "I wanted to help you, but we have strict rules here." He pulled the door shut, giving them more privacy. Or, Lewis thought, protecting himself. "Lord Knight doesn't let us do more than offer lodging when new people arrive in the Court. If I had told you anything else, he'd have killed one of my daughters. Now that you've survived . . ." He spread his hands helplessly. "I can tell you more."

"What the devil are you saying?" Lord Crandall straightened, horror on his face. "This man *wanted* to endanger us?"

"That is exactly what I'm saying." The emotion drained from Frederick's face and he looked defeated. "The lord of Mithras Court enjoys watching newcomers die—even more so in a good struggle. Most newcomers to the Court are dead within days of their arrival. Only the rare individuals survive long enough to mix into the general population." Frederick ran a hand through his greasy hair. "There's nothing any of us can do about it."

"What kind of man would allow this? If your lord is so unjust, then why not fight him as Cromwell fought back against the aristocracy?" Professor Drake said.

"Some of us tried once . . . a long time ago." Frederick's cheeks reddened; Lewis took it to be shame. "Those of us who survived still bear the scars. So you see, no matter what I wanted to tell you last night, I couldn't. Mithras Court does not offer much of a life, but it is still a life. Better than those undead."

"Then what, my good man, are you permitted to tell us now?" A dangerous glint appeared in Lord Crandall's eyes, the sarcasm in his voice complementing it.

"Yes, out with it, man!" Gregory stood up from the sofa where he had been sitting with Reggie and Mary. He had removed his coat, and with his sleeves rolled up, he looked as if he might take a fighting stance.

"I can't tell you much more than you likely already know." Frederick suddenly looked tired, the lines on his face longer and deeper. "We have been trapped in this place since June of 1857—"

"Dear Lord!" Professor Drake's eyes widened and he recoiled. "Thirty-five years!"

"The constables said it was twenty," Reggie said, rubbing his red-rimmed eyes.

"As if that makes it any better." Edgar finally looked up.

"Most folks living here have lost track of the days. I've managed to keep it in my head." Frederick tapped his skull with one finger.

"You've been here for thirty-five years with no contact with the outside world? You expect us to believe that?" Thomas's voice was incredulous.

"Aye." Frederick bowed his head. "None of us knows why, but the Mists ring Mithras Court, preventing any of us from escaping. Only the Vistani can leave, and where they go, nobody knows."

Lord Crandall stood, paced across the room, and turned when he reached the windows. "Surely the Vistani simply pass through the Mists into London proper?"

"Have you ever seen a caravan of gypsies in the city?" Frederick asked.

"Never," Professor Drake admitted.

"We aren't part of London. We aren't even near it," Frederick said. "I don't know where the Vistani go, but it is not to London—that much I know for certain."

"Inspector Newton said as much." Lewis lowered his Webley, relaxing his arm. "About the Vistani, I mean. But if what you say is true, then how did Richard Bailey escape? And why would Lucius Knight wish Elise dead?" Lewis believed that Elise's murder had been under orders, and Bailey had claimed Knight as his master. Which meant Knight was also to blame.

"Who?" Frederick's brow furrowed.

"The man with the snake tattoo killed my wife. He must have found his way out of here. Perhaps with the aid of Lucius Knight. All that matters is that he did it, and he will pay." Lewis spoke through clenched teeth. He wondered if Elise was watching them at that moment. Without a doubt, she stood by him—invisible, watching, waiting.

"The Snake killed your wife?" Frederick looked at the window nervously as if something might leap through at any moment. He gripped his vest with both hands and tugged at it as if he wanted to pull it around himself for protection. "That is grave news indeed."

"You didn't answer my question—how did Bailey escape here to murder Elise and the others on the train?" Lewis reminded him.

"There is no way out of Mithras Court," Frederick repeated. "This Bailey—whether he's the Snake or not—is as new here as you. Lucius Knight could not have helped him escape. We learned very quickly after becoming ensnared in Mithras Court that our lord and master is trapped here along with the rest of us."

"And yet you clearly recognize the description of a man with a snake tattoo," Professor Drake said.

"Yes."

"I say, man, would you stop being cryptic?" Lord Crandall frowned. "How can you recognize this snake-tattooed man and yet not know his name?"

"Many have worn the mantle of the Snake." The color drained from Frederick's face, and his eyes widened as he stared at the window. "I'm sorry. There is nothing else I can say."

"More of your rules?" Lewis scowled at the man, sickened by his cowardice. "Do you never break them?" If Frederick knew of the Snake, he might be able to lead them to the murderer, and damn Knight's rules.

"Not . . . anymore. Not since Lord Knight's punishment."

"If I might take this questioning down a different path." Professor Drake took a step closer.

"I'm listening." The innkeeper's brow relaxed and some of the color returned to his cheeks at Drake's gentle tone.

Lewis opened his mouth to interrupt, intent on demanding answers, but thought better of it. He did not wish to push Frederick so far that he stopped talking altogether. He relaxed again, easing his grip on the revolver as he glanced at the professor.

"How many people live here in Mithras Court?" the professor asked. "And how large is this district?"

"It's about four square city blocks, give or take a few score feet." Frederick's shoulders eased as he relaxed—apparently, this was in the category of questions he could answer. "I'm not sure how many of us there are exactly—it depends on how many newcomers and how many deaths—but I'd guess around three or four hundred. Not counting the Vistani or the walking dead."

"I can certainly see why you would not include the dead, but why exclude these gypsies?" Professor Drake's eyes appeared more haunted than normal—more than they should, Lewis observed. He studied the scholar intently, but said nothing.

"They never stay here after dark." Frederick's voice grew quiet. "Except for Dragos. He's always here, night or day."

"Who?" Gregory said.

"The gypsy you saw during first night." Frederick's eyes were downcast. He looked embarrassed, Lewis thought. "The other Vistani banished him for helping us during our rebellion. We never had a chance."

"Perhaps we should speak with this gypsy," Lord Crandall said.

"You're welcome to try." Frederick shrugged. "He's daft. Hasn't said anything to anyone since he was banished. All he does is sit there and smile. We try to keep him comfortable, but that's as much as we can do."

"None of this makes any sense, and I think I see why." Edgar suddenly stood up, reached into his pocket, and pulled out a handful of coins. "Tell us how to leave this place and this is all yours. I can offer you much more when we get back to London. You would be a rich man!"

Lewis blinked in surprise at the man's sudden shift from depression to action, and the incongruity of the move. Money would have little meaning to the trapped citizens of Mithras Court—could he not see that? Was it trauma brought about by Josephine's death? His loss appeared to hit him in waves from moment to moment, a fact that Lewis found disconcerting. It bore close attention. Elise would have told him to show the man compassion and understanding, to create a common bond between them, but Lewis had no intention of forging a friendship with the despicable man.

Frederick stared at the money for a moment as if he could not understand what it was, but comprehension dawned and he laughed. "Now that's funny!" He laughed until he shook so hard with mirth he had to put a hand on his gut to keep himself together. Tears streamed down his face and he gasped for air, finally saying, "Nobody's tried to bribe me in a good long time. I wish it was that simple." He sobered. "But you, like the rest of us, are trapped here."

"If Mithras Court isn't in London, then where is it?" Anne sat up, still clinging to Thomas's hand. "Where are we?"

"Damned if I know." Frederick shrugged.

"Rubbish. I don't know what's going on here, but if this innkeeper can't help us, then perhaps we should talk to this Lord Knight." Edgar ignored Frederick's angry glare. "A good leader learns wisdom over time—maybe he has discovered a few things about this place. We must make him understand that we don't belong here! Convince him to allow us to leave!" His voice shook.

"Have you heard a word that has been said here? Dealing with Lucius Knight is out of the question!" Lewis crossed his arms and stared at the man. He would not let the fool get himself or anyone else killed by such a rash act.

"The Captain is right." Frederick frowned. "Don't go looking for Lord Knight. You will only speed up your own deaths. Unless, of course, you are that ready to join your wife."

"That's enough!" Lewis interjected, before Edgar could speak. "Have some respect for the dead."

"I have endless respect for the departed, for they are all around us." Frederick shook his head. "You must not approach Lord Knight."

"I do not need you to leap to my defense, Captain," Edgar fixed Lewis with an angry glance, then sighed. "You were right when you told me Josephine would not wish me to die." He turned to Frederick. "You, innkeeper, are a simpleton. I am a business man. I know how to deal with men of power and wealth, and if we can't appeal to his reason, then we can appeal to his vices. Every man has a price. Lord Knight must have one as well."

"You're the real fool here," Frederick said, shaking his head. "It's true that Lord Knight rules this place, but he's not the one who brought us here. And he doesn't control the Mists. Even if he did, he is no one to go looking for. Most everyone in Mithras Court stays out of his way. The ones who don't aren't seen again."

"What kind of a man can fill others with such dread?" Lewis asked, before Edgar could respond. The portly man sputtered as his retort was interrupted. Lewis could not tolerate Edgar's unwillingness to believe what Frederick was saying.

"Few of us have seen Lord Knight, but most believe that he is not human—"

He was interrupted by a loud rapping on the window that jolted them all. Lewis whirled around, pistol ready, while the others stared nervously. The banging continued, loud and insistent. It sounded like a bird that sought entry by hitting the glass with its beak over and over again.

"Is it those hideous snakes?" Anne shook and Thomas slipped his arm around her. "Could they be beating against the windows?"

"Nonsense—it's a swallow or other bird." Lord Crandall looked at her, a little more gently, Lewis thought, than he would have looked at any of the men. "Your fatigue and our experiences in this terrible place have gotten the better of you."

The noise grew louder—if Crandall's hypothesis was correct,

then at least a dozen birds now beat against the glass. It rattled in its frame with every impact.

"There must be more than one." Lewis looked at the window, shifting his weight as his body tensed. He was ready to spring into action if needed, but the draperies made it impossible to see anything.

"Why would birds be flying about in the dark?" Reggie said.

"More likely, they are bats." Professor Drake paused, his brow furrowing. "However, bats generally avoid light. These creatures seem drawn to it."

"I doubt that enough light is escaping through those drapes to justify that assumption," Lewis said, staring at the window.

"It's the Raven." Frederick stared at the window, eyes wide, face white. Lewis realized their host had been silent for a time—his mouth hung agape in shock and fear. "He must have heard us!" Frederick turned and nearly tore the doorknob off trying to open the door. "Good night!"

"Halt!" Lord Crandall roared, running toward the door. Before he could reach it, the big man had slammed it shut.

"It's stopped!" Gregory pointed toward the window. The silence drew everyone's attention.

Lewis turned to the window and listened. His ears detected only silence; the banging had ceased. He strode purposefully across the room and pulled the drapes back.

The alley below remained empty, save for several corpses standing at the edge of the light, looking up at them.

"Nothing but the dead," he said finally.

"You say that so casually." Professor Drake stepped up to the window and glanced out. "Have we adjusted to this situation so readily?"

"We've accepted this state of affairs as the truth, at least." Lewis turned to the others. "We need more information if we are going to devise a way out of this situation, and we haven't got the time to deny or dwell on the existence of these creatures."

"He's gone." Lord Crandall stood in the open doorway.

In the main room, the rest of the patrons had retired to rooms or settled down on the floor. Two barmaids moved about, wiping down tables. They appeared so tired as to be haggard, their hair hanging limply about their shoulders. Their faces were flushed and dark circles rimmed their eyes.

Lewis wondered suddenly if he and his companions looked as spent. Far more had happened in the past twelve hours than at any point in his life. Fatigue pulled at him, making his limbs and eyelids heavy. He would have to sleep soon if he were to keep his wits about him.

"Never mind him," Edgar said. "What about those damned birds—or bats—or whatever they were?"

"And the snakes in the street!" Thomas added. "Are we the targets of a variety of animals in addition to these walking dead?"

"And what about your wife?" Anne looked at him with a mixture of awe and fear. "We all saw her shimmering there . . . a spirit in the fog. How can it be possible? Is it divine providence, or the work of the devil?"

"She saved our lives." Lewis forced himself to breathe out slowly. The suggestion that Elise could be an agent of evil was ludicrous and insulting. "And there never was a woman of more purity and goodness. If she has been sent to us, then it is by God and none other. I'll not have you sully her memory by suggesting otherwise." Lewis said it with such vehemence that he shook. As he tried to calm himself, he pondered a thought: the God he had abandoned so long ago could have had a hand in sending her to him. He did not wish to consider that possibility, yet there it was. Her very existence as a spirit could be proof of an afterlife, and that in turn could be proof of the existence of God.

"If what Frederick has told us is true, and we are no longer in . . . London . . . or England, or perhaps on the very Earth itself . . ." Professor Drake pulled the drapes closed and turned to face them. "Then different natural laws might apply here. Our God might have nothing at all to do with this."

"That is quite a leap in logic," Thomas said, doubtfully.

"Is it really? We find ourselves in a place where the dead can rise from the grave, ghosts can talk to the living, and the cursed Mists can prevent us from leaving." The color drained from his face. "We could be on another plane of existence altogether . . . we could be in purgatory . . . in any case, I find it unlikely that God has a hand in our predicament."

Lewis spoke up. "My friends, we are in a strange and difficult situation, but I do not intend to simply give up. Nor do I intend to place my fate in the hands of superstition."

"Nor do I, Captain." Professor Drake moved next to him. "I have a suggestion, however. Would it not be wise to attempt to enlist the aid of Elise?"

Lewis shook his head. "I've tried with my thoughts and whispers to get a response, but I have not been able to contact her. If she is here, and I believe she is, then she is either afraid to show herself or is too exhausted to speak. She has done quite a lot." The concern in the professor's eyes surprised Lewis again. He wondered if the man could truly feel friendship toward him. Recently, he had desired camaraderie in his life—and perhaps even from this man, yet something about him, perhaps his clash with Lord Crandall, caused Lewis to withhold his trust, despite the man's evident good intentions.

"A pity," Lord Crandall said, genuine remorse in his voice. Apparently, he was smart enough to take any help he could in this situation, even from a ghost.

"I will attempt to contact her again. However, we cannot count on her to save us. We must take it upon ourselves to learn all there is to know about this place. We know much, but we do not yet see the way out. We must devise a strategy geared to thwart this Lucius Knight, and with luck, guarantee our rapid departure." He crossed to the door. "I intend to talk to the other patrons at first light. In the meantime, I suggest we all avail ourselves of what time we have to sleep and recuperate from the night's ordeals. I'll volunteer for the first watch."

"Bugger that, Captain." Reggie stood up. "You've had less sleep than the rest of us. Let me and the wife take the first watch." He glanced at Lord Crandall. "You need sleep too, sir."

"I hardly think you're in a position to dictate—" Lord Crandall started, but stopped short as if suddenly realizing the absurdity of talking down to the man, especially in light of Reggie's offer. "Forgive me. It's a generous offer. I would welcome the rest."

Lewis glanced at Lord Crandall, trying not to show his surprise at the man's sudden change of heart. Perhaps their situation had finally forced the gentleman to act like a soldier, not a spoiled lord. Lewis paused and returned his attention to Reggie, acknowledging the man's suggestion with a nod.

"Very well." Lewis handed him the revolver. "You'd better take this."

Reggie took the gun, holding it with reverence before him. His gray eyes met Lewis's blue and a look of understanding passed between them. Lewis had saved this man's life, and Reggie was ready to give his in return. Battlefield honor was not something to be undervalued or rejected. Lewis offered him a brief smile.

"What about Frederick?" Edgar stepped toward the door.

"The man fears for his life," Thomas said. "Whatever this Raven is, it scared him half to death. I'm certain that the other residents of this place will be equally as frightened. We might have to find clever ways to draw the information out of them."

"Thomas is correct," Lewis agreed. "For the moment we are safe, and I do not think it wise to risk alienating the only man who has provided us with shelter, regardless of what he has or hasn't done."

"But he's responsible for Josephine's death!" Edgar closed his hand into a fist.

Lewis tensed, ready to fight the man if needed. He would not allow anyone else's vengeance to interfere with his own, or with his vow to protect his companions.

"She climbed the stairs to that church of her own volition. She need not have died, but we cannot blame Frederick for that." Lewis took a deep breath, preparing to reveal a truth he was certain Edgar wouldn't wish to hear. "Mithras Court drove her mad!"

Edgar stared at him, his jowls shaking, his face red, but he said nothing. His shoulders slumped in defeat and he just stared.

"I'm sorry for your loss, Edgar. I really am," Lewis said, bracing for an attack, but none came.

Edgar shuffled over to one of the bedrolls, looking even older. He lay down quietly, turning his back to the room. Lewis wished he could help the man, but there was little he could do. He had done his best to save Josephine, but whether her mind had snapped or Mithras Court had done something to her, nothing could have stopped her. And yet, the guilt weighed heavily upon Lewis.

"I suggest we rest while we can." Lord Crandall nodded toward the bedrolls. "Let us seal this room up and find Frederick in the morning, when there are fewer threats to consider. We're all exhausted. If an attack came now, we would be useless."

"Agreed." Lewis nodded. "I've seen what happens to soldiers when they continue without rest." He pulled the door shut and bolted it. "I suggest we move the sofa in front of the door.

"We aren't soldiers," Thomas said fearfully, as if that idea scared him as much as being trapped in Mithras Court.

"You're wrong," Lewis looked at him. "We have seen battle and death, and have survived both. Whatever we were in our past lives, whatever vocations wait for us back home, we must act as soldiers here and now in order to survive." They had seen the horrors of war—and far more—and survived. The fact that only Josephine had been driven to madness was an impressive fact that was not lost on Lewis. They had complained far more than a soldier would or should, but they had remained together and determined.

"I supposed you're right." Thomas sighed, his expression that of grim acceptance.

"Indeed." Lord Crandall moved to the end of the sofa. "Gregory, if you would."

Gregory jumped to the task. They moved the sofa against the door and took seats on the comfortable cushions. Seeing that they had things in hand, Lewis sought his bedroll. He chose a spot near the divan where he could keep clear of the window. He was certain the dead would leave them alone, but he was unsure about the strange animals.

As he closed his eyes, even as the dark chasm of sleep pulled at his consciousness, he wondered how Bailey could have become a servant of Lucius Knight without ever having been to Mithras Court. Or if that were true.

More than that, he wondered how Elise could be there, and he wished desperately to see her once more.

Chapter FOURTEEN

Lewis stood in the dank fog, alone and weaponless. The coal scratched at his skin, making his hands and face itch and his throat feel as if he'd been drinking kerosene. A single lamp shone nearby, bathing him in the weak light that diffused through the mist.

No monsters were in sight, but Lewis could hear their distinctive shamble in the murk. They were closer than they'd been since the station. The light was too dim to keep them away and Lewis flinched at every step, expecting to feel their claws each time they moved. The sickening pop of their decaying muscle and sinew and the squish of their half-rotted feet on the pavement made Lewis's stomach churn. He backed up against the lamp post, praying to a god he didn't believe in that the light would remain on. He saw no way out.

"Lucius."

A slippery writhing suddenly resounded through the darkness as dozens of snakes added their odd slither to the symphony of the damned. Their lithe forms appeared at the edge of the light, so many of them moving in unison that they appeared as waves on the sea.

"Lucius."

But the beating of wings overhead drew his attention from the snakes. Looking up, he saw black ravens swooping out of the fog just above him; he recoiled in shock and nearly stepped on a snake with his boot. Before it could attack, he pulled away, sickened by how close he'd come to disaster.

"Lucius."

Before he could regain his senses, a clattering sound, like hundreds of tiny porcelain feet, echoed through the night. He could only think that it sounded like crabs walking along the rocks on the ocean shore.

"*Lucius.*"

His eyes darted to the ground to catch the sight. Somewhere close, a hound bayed.

"*Lucius.*"

"Leave me alone!" Lewis pressed against the lamp post so hard that the fluted metal dug painfully into his back. A small voice in his head whispered that dreams shouldn't feel this real. He wished desperately for his Webley, or his old carbine rifle, though he could never carry enough ammunition to shoot all of those creatures. Still, if worst came to it, he would have at least had the option of shooting himself.

"*Lucius.*"

Red eyes opened in the fog. It was comforting to note, with some detached part of his mind, that these were merely human-sized. A wind whipped up sharply, blowing thicker fog with it. The light Lewis huddled in shrank and the red eyes vanished, reappearing as if the mist itself had blinked.

"*Lucius.*"

The voice was soft and sonorous. "Welcome, Lewis Wentworth. Enjoy what freedom you have left, for soon, you shall serve *me*." Certain that the red-eyed creature meant him only harm, Lewis was nonetheless drawn to the sound as if it held his soul captive and his free will had been taken from him.

"*Lucius.*"

"Who . . . who are you?" he stammered, forcing himself to remain in control, failing.

"*Lucius.*"

"I am the life's blood of Mithras Court . . . I am Lucius Knight!"

Chapter FIFTEEN

"He's coming!" Lewis bolted upright, and was startled to find himself sitting on his bedroll on the floor near the divan, just as he was supposed to be. The dream had been so very real.

Unlike the prior evening, the parlor was empty and the door to the common room was open. He could see Thomas and Anne seated at a table in the pub. Chloe delivered plates of steaming eggs and biscuits to their table. Lewis's mouth watered at the sight. He observed several other tables of patrons sitting around them, but he saw no other members of his own group. The eggs drew his attention again. Elise had cooked him breakfast each morning, and nothing could compare to her fried potatoes and eggs. In the years since her death, he had tried and failed to recreate it.

"What did you dream?" Professor Drake's voice sounded tired and worried.

Lewis startled again, whirling around to see the old man sitting in the corner of the room, in one of the dark blue armchairs next to the window, the Webley in his lap and a smoldering pipe in one hand. The man's white eyebrows were raised in question. Next to him, the drapes had been pulled back to reveal diffuse daylight illuminating the fog outside.

"How long did I sleep?" Lewis gripped the edge of the divan and pulled himself to his feet. He eyed the pistol warily.

"Over six hours. It's beginning to get light, but I thought I should not wake you." He took a puff of his pipe as he lifted the revolver. He pointed it at Lewis.

Lewis tensed, ready to dodge to the side. He had no idea why the professor would wish him dead. But as with Josephine, Mithras

Court could drive a person mad. Lewis opened and closed his palms, ready to spring into action.

"Oh dear, I didn't mean to frighten you. I'm not very good with firearms." He turned the grip toward Lewis and held it out. "I much prefer you have this."

Lewis breathed out audibly, glad that he had not so misread the man. "I'm surprised Lord Crandall would let you keep it." He took the gun quickly and slipped it into his belt, relieved to have it. The desperation in his dream had stayed with him.

"I insisted with the same vehemence I argued for your need to sleep. As a military man, Captain, you are the best chance we have for survival, whatever anyone thinks." He stood up. "I felt it vital to allow you to sleep, and thought it equally important that you not be deprived of your weapon."

"Thank you, Professor." He could not argue with the man's logic or deny his own need for rest. He felt more in control, more focused and awake, than he had since before boarding the train.

"You're welcome. But you haven't answered my question."

Lewis had hoped the man had forgotten, but as the professor stared at him, he knew he could not avoid the query. "I dreamed of Lucius Knight." Lewis shivered as a sudden realization slammed into him with the force of a punch. "He told me to enjoy my freedom, for soon I would serve him."

"Fascinating." Drake frowned. "The others had similar dreams about the creatures, but none of them dreamed of the master of this place. Perhaps this man, or whatever he might be, can touch the world of dreams. Most distressing."

"Which part?" Lewis retrieved his coat from the divan and slipped it on as if it could somehow protect him from harm.

Drake looked reluctant to speak, but Lewis gazed at him until the scholar sighed. "I believe I dreamed of this man in the days before I boarded the train that brought us here. I remember glowing red eyes, urging me to go to the King William Street Station, over and over again. Finally, I had to satisfy my curiosity and I went. And thus I ended up here with you."

"Then perhaps you were meant to be here. Perhaps Lord Knight does have the ability to influence who enters this domain, despite what Frederick told us." Lewis considered that. It would make sense of many things.

"What are you saying? That somehow he has control over me?" Drake's white eyebrows rose in shock.

"No, of course not. But it could mean that some of us were influenced by him in some way." Lewis did not know why Lord Knight would want the professor there—or any of them—but if he was indeed the man who had caused Elise's murder, then he could have any sort of twisted reason.

"An excellent point." Drake relaxed. "And if you follow that logic, then this Bailey fellow might have been contacted by Lord Knight as well." He paused and looked out the window. His voice was a murmur against the glass when he added, "Interesting, that thought."

"What do you mean?"

"The snakes, the raven, the dog . . . and those skittering creatures were scorpions, I'd wager." His hands trembled slightly. "This means more than you realize."

"Why would you think that?" He moved the pistol to his coat pocket without taking his eyes from the professor. "What can it mean?"

"I do not know that any of us are safe. We are in Mithras Court." The professor's voice became more formal, as if he were teaching a student. "I do find our shared dreams of interest, though that perplexes me at the moment. You see, the ancient god Mithras is often depicted slaying a bull, with a serpent, a raven, a scorpion, and a dog in the scene, in what is called the tauroctony. It is the scene we saw painted on the ceiling of the police station."

"I'm not familiar with that word." Lewis had no reason to doubt the scholar's interpretation of the creatures in his dream; the only one he didn't know for certain was the scorpion. "Why did you not mention this before?"

"I did not think it important. Since the neighborhood is known as Mithras Court, it made sense to me that they would have such art. Given all that has happened to us, I see now that this is somehow related." Drake stroked his beard thoughtfully.

"So this tauroctony . . . what is it?" And why does it matter? Lewis wondered.

"The tauroctony is the Mithraic bull-slaying scene. Mithras is depicted slaying a massive bull while the other creatures, perhaps his minions—certainly his allies—aid him in the fight. It is a brutal and barbaric scene."

"You sound like a textbook," Lewis said.

"My apologies." Drake gave him a smile, and if it was not as full-spirited as it might have been in other circumstances, it none-theless broke some of the tension. "Historical and mythological subjects tend to bring out the scholar in me." He frowned. "It means that the Mithraic mythology is intertwined with the very fabric of this place."

"Are you suggesting that Knight is Mithras?" Lewis's eyes wid-ened. That thought was ludicrous. Despite Lewis's recent revelations about the potential existence of God, he was not ready to accept that there could be other gods as well. "Even after the horrors we've witnessed, I find that hard to believe."

"I'm not sure what I'm suggesting at this juncture. However, would you really not take our disastrous encounters here in Mithras Court as proof of some form of divine or supernatural influence in the world?" Drake scratched his beard.

"Do you mean demonic?" Lewis said.

"I mean that if the dead can rise from the grave, if ghosts exist, and if all the bizarre events we've witnessed can be true, then does that not also necessitate the existence of a divine power for good diametrically opposed to the horrors we've seen?"

"My wife is no horror." Lewis's face reddened as he raised his voice in protest. "And the occurrence of supernatural events hardly means that a god is involved, or even exists." Although he had won-dered about this as well.

"I meant no disrespect." Drake narrowed his eyes thoughtfully. "In fact, the existence of your wife as a spirit tends to prove my point, that God could be real. Surely if spirits exist, then so, too, must an afterlife . . . and if that is true, there must be a power over that realm . . . that is, *God*."

"Perhaps." Lewis was not convinced. Spirits and gods were two separate things. Just because he too had considered this did not mean he was ready to accept it.

The smells of sizzling bacon and frying eggs wafted past, tickling his nose and making his stomach grumble. He was beyond hungry—he was famished, and as he thought about it, he realized that he had not eaten in more than a day.

"We should continue searching for a way out of this place before we lose any more time." And locate Richard Bailey, he added to himself. The man with the snake tattoo would die before he left this place. And when that knave uttered a death scream at Lewis's hands, he would savor the moment, draw it out until the man felt what Elise had felt. Perhaps Lewis would merely wound the man at first to prolong the agony, and truly quench the vengeance within him. Yes . . . a slow, painful death.

As he crossed into the common room, he realized that Thomas and Anne had gone. He reached for his weapon, reflexively thinking that something had happened to them.

"It's all right." Drake put a restraining hand on his forearm. "The others have gone off to perform their tasks."

"Tasks?" Lewis turned warily toward the man.

"While you were sleeping, Lord Crandall gathered us together, organized us into four groups, and assigned each the task of testing this barrier of mist in different areas of Mithras Court. The goal is to determine if it truly encompasses us on all sides. Our first encounter with this mist is being regarded as the north, although without the sun as reference, it's difficult to get a sense of direction." The professor patted Lewis's arm and Lewis put the gun away. "You and I are to explore the "northwest" section at the end of Bacchus Way. After you try to contact your wife again, that is."

"I believe Elise is here, and has been the entire time we've been in Mithras Court." Lewis could almost smell her lilac perfume in the air. "I believe that she is with us even now, and fully cognizant of our conversation. If she could help us in any way, I believe she would. Perhaps spirits require rest. In any event, we must carry on with our plans rather than waiting for her to come to us."

A pulse of heat suffused her wedding ring against his chest.

"Yes . . ." Her voice was barely a whisper.

"Egads!" the professor said.

"Elise!" Lewis startled despite himself. "I love you."

"Love you . . ." Her voice trailed away and was no more.

"You were correct, then," the professor said. "She really is here."

"So it would seem." Elise had found a way to reach him. Their love still bound them together. Lewis smiled, unable to contain his sudden joy. If Elise could hear him now, then perhaps she had heard him for the past two years as he talked to the empty space she should have occupied beside him. "She is with us . . . with me." He bowed his head, suddenly overwhelmed.

"Are you all right, Captain?" Drake lay his hand on Lewis's shoulder.

"Why not?" Lewis brushed him off, standing straighter. "I've heard and seen my dead love. How many men can say that?" That fact should have dulled the pain of his loss more than it did. His guilt and his vengeance would not allow anything more than a fleeting moment of peace. His failures had prevented him from finishing off the Snake.

"I told you I lost a brother over thirty years ago." Professor Drake's brow furrowed. "Even after all this time, I think of him often. When I consider how it might make me feel to see his spirit here and now, I believe I would feel great joy but greater sadness that I would have to relive the loss of him. I just want you to know . . . I understand."

"That is very . . ." A new truth came to him suddenly, and Lewis gasped. "That is very insightful. Thank you." Whether he set her free by slaying the Snake, or found his way out of Mithras Court, he would lose Elise again. The very thought sent a wave of pain through him. How could he walk away—how could he leave her behind? Surviving that loss once had nearly destroyed him. He did not know if he could do it again. And yet, if Elise was to find peace in death, then he had to help her, had to do anything he could. He would endure a thousand deaths for her.

"You're welcome."

"Now, my friend, you will be happy to know that I am altering Lord Crandall's plan." He paused. "And while I am on that subject . . . may I ask about the nature of your feud?"

"The truth be told—I am not sure." Drake's shoulders slumped. "The man has been at me since the moment he realized who I was. I cannot fathom why." He paused. "Now, what was it you were saying about our plans?"

Lewis studied him for a moment, looking into his eyes for any sign of deceit, but saw none. If he wished to learn the truth of it, he would have to interrogate Lord Crandall, something that was perhaps overdue. He nodded.

"Very well. We *will* test the barrier mist, but first, I think a hearty meal and an equally hearty interrogation of our timid innkeeper are in order." He clasped the man's forearm. "Don't you agree?"

"Indeed I do."

═══MC═══

The main room had emptied out completely during their conversation. Only Chloe and Jenna moved about, clearing dishes and washing tables. Lewis and Drake saw no sign of Frederick behind the bar or anywhere else.

The tapestry fluttered gently in the cool breeze that blew through the inn's open front door. Lewis paused to glance at the ornate fabric and had to blink to be sure he was seeing it correctly. The tapestry had changed—or had been replaced. The eyes in the forest had vanished. He saw a woman, her long gray hair in disarray, her bloody body lying on its side before the hut. Her knees were tucked against her chest and her hands stretched out in front of her, locked together in prayer. The remains of a maroon dress clung to her broken form. Next to her, a short, red-haired man lay on the ground, as if he were a sheet of paper that someone had crumpled into a ball and then discarded.

"Josephine . . . and Ben . . ." Lewis said. He blinked, dread coalescing in his stomach. If someone had changed the tapestry to taunt them, then it meant that others at the inn were aware of their recent tragedies.

"An uncanny resemblance." Professor Drake paused beside him to examine the elaborate stitching. "As I recall, it showed wolves the first time we saw this."

"Yes—but there is no sign of them now. Nor of the eyes that I saw the second time I looked at it. It's altered, somehow." He peered into the woods beyond the tiny hut, but the eyes had definitely vanished. "Perhaps they have several similar tapestries?"

"Including one featuring a woman and man that bear a shocking resemblance to our dead companions?" Professor Drake arched one eyebrow. "That seems unlikely."

"It's the same wall hanging," a woman said from behind. "It changes all the time. It's unpleasant, but harmless."

Jenna appeared next to them, a tray in one hand. She looked at Lewis, her brown eyes searching his as if looking for something. A smile crossed her lips and she made him feel calm and at ease somehow. He offered her a smile in return; he had not smiled in so long that it felt foreign to him.

"But how is that possible?" Lewis looked at the tapestry, and the stitched corpses sent a chill down his spine.

"No one knows. It's like the thing is making fun of us," she said. "I've never liked it."

"Maybe it is," Lewis said. "Why doesn't your father take it down?"

"He says he can't." Her brow furrowed as if the question were somehow complicated. "He won't say why."

"Where did it come from?" Professor Drake stared at it.

"Dragos gave it to my father, back before . . ." She looked down.

"Before?" Lewis arched an eyebrow in question.

"Before they tried to fight Lord Knight." Her eyes filled with tears.

"I'm sorry." Lewis reached out and rubbed her arm reassuringly. The subject of the tapestry obviously caused her pain. For some reason, Lewis felt suddenly protective of her.

"Oh, it's all right. I was just a little girl . . . too young to remember it." She brightened and turned away from the tapestry. "Can I get you some breakfast?"

"That sounds lovely." Lewis grinned, and the brief feeling of calm settled even deeper into him. It evaporated swiftly, though, as he remembered his duty. "I'll need to speak with your father," he added in a more serious tone.

"I'm sorry—he's gone to the market." She turned away before he could protest and hurried toward the kitchen behind the bar. "I'll bring you some eggs!" She disappeared through the batwing doors.

"If I were a suspicious man, I'd say Frederick is avoiding us." Professor Drake took a chair at the nearest table and sat down. "And his daughter is aware of that fact." His pipe puffed as he watched Lewis.

"He can't ignore us forever." Lewis seated himself across from the professor.

No sooner had he planted himself in the chair than Jenna returned from the kitchen with two plates of steaming eggs and two mugs of an exotically spiced tea. She hurried away, then returned with a basket of bread and a crock of butter.

"That was fast," Lewis remarked. He wondered if the cook was supernatural, and the thought gave him a moment of amusement. He kept it to himself, despite a smile that threatened.

"Thank you." Jenna curtseyed formally, the grin on her face keeping it friendly and not stuffy. She hurried toward the fireplace to wipe tables.

The delicious aromas drew Lewis in. He picked up his fork and set about devouring his breakfast.

Chapter SIXTEEN

"This air is worse than London." Professor Drake put a handkerchief to his mouth. "As if all the coal that burns here remains trapped along with us."

"Perhaps it does." Lewis took an experimental breath. He nodded as the gritty air scoured his lungs.

They paused at the junction of Cannon Street and Bacchus Way to observe their surroundings. In the daylight, the sooty fog glowed around them, highlighting the buildings on each corner. Ahead, Lewis could see the shabby section through which they had traveled the prior evening. He shivered involuntarily as he stared briefly into the murk, remembering what horrors lay beyond. He pulled himself away and pivoted to the left, where the sounds of myriad people talking, horses moving, and peddlers hawking their wares could be heard in the distance.

"You've been very quiet since breakfast." Drake's brow furrowed as he looked at Lewis. "Are you well?"

"I've had little to say, I suppose." Lewis had said virtually nothing since they had eaten. Thoughts of Elise, of vengeance against Bailey, and of their predicament in Mithras Court plagued him, swirling through his mind over and over, taunting him. He brought his military training to bear, focusing diligently on each conundrum, searching for a solution that included killing the snake-tattooed man, finding a way out of that terrible place, and somehow helping Elise, if in fact she needed his help.

No solutions presented themselves. Until they had more information, he could not reason or plan his way out of his predicament. No answers could be gleaned from the meager facts the group had collected.

"We must be on guard. Jenna said this market is pure chaos." Professor Drake gestured with the cane in the direction of the racket. "From the sound of it, she was correct." He pulled his coat more tightly about himself with one hand.

"Agreed." Lewis reached into the pocket of his coat, his hand closing on the butt of the Webley in case Mithras Court presented additional surprises. He strode into the fog toward the market, eyes searching for Frederick.

The fog thinned as they drew closer. Dozens of people appeared just ahead of them, crowding around tables, booths, and brightly-colored tents set up in the middle of the street. Banners hung from the buildings to either side, adding to the vibrancy of the market. For a moment, Lewis and Professor Drake might have stepped back into London.

On closer examination, they saw the differences more than the similarities, for the citizens of Mithras Court pressing past each other represented all social classes. The well-dressed gentry paraded like peacocks, the men in their coats and hats, the women in their layered dresses with their perfectly coiffed hair and jeweled rings on their fingers. The modestly dressed servants swarmed around them like small dogs yapping at their masters' feet. The laborers in their wool, and bureaucrats in their austere suits milled about, mingling with the lower classes—men and women clad in dirt-smeared, sometimes tattered clothing. All meshed together, it was a strange pattern that disappeared into the gritty fog. Elise would have loved such an eclectic and vibrant market; it would have scandalized her parents. Lewis smiled at that.

"We should move as swiftly as possible." The professor pulled out a silver pocket watch. "It's already nine o'clock and Lord Crandall requested we meet at the inn by eleven."

"I have a better idea." Lewis stepped forward without elaborating.

"Captain?" The professor hurried after him. "Much as we might dislike Lord Crandall, I thought we had agreed to follow his plan?"

"There's more to be learned about Lucius Knight, the Snake, and these other minions before we accede to Lord Crandall's request. I intend to start finding some of the answers we so desperately need."

"I say." Drake grabbed his arm and pulled him up short. "I think you're allowing your feelings about Bailey to cloud your judgment. Our only duty is to find a way out of this place and alert the authorities. These people need help. We can't simply—"

"My duty," Lewis shook off the man's hand, "is to my dead wife first, and until this Bailey fellow has been held to account, I have no intention of leaving, even if we find a way out. We might be able to glean additional information in that area as well by listening to the denizens of Mithras Court. Now, follow me. Or not, as you choose, Professor." He strode into the crowd, narrowly avoiding a collision with a dirt-smeared youth. The boy dodged to the side and darted away.

Lewis reached down swiftly, touching his purse for reassurance. Pickpockets often frequented such places. But his money remained safely against his side. Given the nature of the prison in which the dwellers of Mithras Court had been trapped for so long, he wondered if money had any meaning. There might be little value in being a cutpurse there.

That did not mean that other vices weren't practiced.

"Hello, love, give us a kiss?" A tawdry woman with wildly unkempt brown hair leaned forward in her low-cut blouse, her skirts pulled up to reveal one leg.

Lewis scowled at her and brushed past. Although many soldiers availed themselves of the services of such women, he had never been interested.

"Captain, wait!" Professor Drake pushed through the mob to catch up.

Lewis glanced over his shoulder without stopping, not wanting to remain near the woman.

"How about you, grandfather?" the woman asked the professor. Her smile revealed numerous blackened teeth.

"I'm afraid not, my dear." Drake bowed politely and continued on.

Lewis stopped in front of a tanner's shop and allowed Professor Drake to catch up. Various hides, some from cows, others not so identifiable, hung from a wooden rack in front of the place, reminding him of his father's shop in Warrington. The pungent odor of skins in the early stages of tanning wafted out of the shop on the breeze, and for an instant, Lewis thought he could close his eyes and hear his father's voice. He sighed. Those days were long past and his father had been dead for nearly ten years; it had been much longer than that since he had spoken to Lewis. Lewis regretted it, but there was nothing he could do. His choice to join Her Majesty's armed services had never been in question, nor had he ever felt guilt about it. He had done what he felt he had to do for Queen and country. That his father had disowned him for it still hurt nonetheless.

A thin reed of a man in a greasy apron stepped out of the open door and stopped next to them, jarring Lewis from his thoughts. The man motioned toward the darkest of the tanned skins.

"Good day to you, sirs. Step up and look at the finest leathers in the Court. You'll find that these offer excellent protection against the walking dead." The man looked at Lewis, his eyes hopeful.

"Indeed?" Lewis stepped closer to examine the hides. He remembered enough about the family trade to know that this man's work was mediocre at best. No doubt his father would have scoffed at the man. In any event, Lewis doubted the claim that they were protection against the dead creatures. Yet Lewis knew that if he had any hope of getting the man to talk to him, he had to appear friendly.

"Fine work, my friend." He nodded admiringly. "But I'm afraid my purse is nearly empty."

"A shame." He looked Lewis up and down. "For a gentleman like you, I'd be happy to hold an item until you come into more coin." The man scratched his nose. "If you're serious."

"That would be acceptable, but I'm new to the Court and do not yet have a job. Perhaps you know of someone who might be looking for a skilled laborer?"

"New, you say?" The man took a step back, his lip twitching. What it meant, Lewis could not tell. The man could not have been completely surprised that Lewis and the professor were new to

Mithras Court. "Well, you might see Jonas, the blacksmith, about a job. He's always on the lookout for dependable help."

"Thank you. I'll do that." Lewis turned to go, but paused as if struck by a thought. "Can you offer any advice regarding the dangers we might face in Mithras Court, other than the walking dead?"

"I'm not sure what you mean, sir." The man's smile faded and he licked his lips nervously. "If not for the walking dead, Mithras Court would be a paradise. There is nothing else to fear." His tone changed ever so slightly, and Lewis knew he was lying.

"I've heard that Lucius Knight bears ill will toward recent arrivals." Lewis kept his voice low, and spoke through a smile so as not to arouse the suspicions of any passersby. If fear motivated the tanner to lie to him, then he had to tread carefully lest he push the man further into a corner and gain nothing from him.

"Lucius Knight seeks only to maintain a balance here in the Court." The man glanced around at the steady throng of people on the sidewalk and street. "His efforts to weed out those who shouldn't be here keep the rest of us from running out of the necessities of life. The Vistani can only bring in so much, after all."

"What do you mean 'those who should not be here'?" Professor Drake spoke up, as quietly as Lewis. "Who is he to decide such things?"

"He is our lord and master . . . *your* lord and master. Don't you recall your history? The lord holds your lives in his hand. You'd be wise to remember that." The tanner's gaze darted to and fro, as if he were looking for a way to escape.

"We're just two new arrivals looking to survive." Lewis thought a calmer and more rational approach might help to shake the man out of his rhetoric. "You can speak freely." He eyed the crowd and noted that none of them seemed interested in their conversation, and returned his attention to the tanner.

"I'm sorry, sir. I can't help you. Now, if you please . . . you're frightening away my customers."

"You didn't feel this way when you thought we were just average Mithras Court dwellers looking for some goods," Professor Drake said. "And the only one who seems scared is you."

"Perhaps we had better continue on." Lewis put a hand on the professor's shoulder.

The tanner turned on his heel and darted into his shop, slamming the door hard.

"Coward." Lewis resisted the urge to spit at the spot where the man had been standing. "This entire place seems to be populated by fools. No one should tolerate such subjugation or live in such fear." The pathetic nature of the citizens was beginning to irritate him. He had thought they required assistance, that all of them needed rescuing . . . but now he questioned that assumption. Perhaps they had become so acclimated to their situation that they found comfort in it.

"If this Lord Knight is as powerful as Frederick and the others seem to think, then perhaps they are justified in their cowardice." Professor Drake had a thoughtful look on his face.

"There is no excuse for such behavior. Even in the face of overwhelming odds, it is better to fight than to submit to one's enemy." Lewis would never accept a life such as the one the citizens of Mithras Court tolerated. "Even if it means one's death."

"Perhaps they have families to consider?" The professor's eyes grew distant. "Threats against one's relations can make a man do many things he never thought himself capable of. Frederick has indicated that Knight does not scruple in that area."

"Do you speak of your brother? Or have you lost others as well?" Lewis had not given any thought to whether the professor had a wife or family in London, left behind after he had been trapped in Mithras Court. He hoped suddenly that he had not poured salt in the man's wounds. Drake's calm assurance and intelligent discourse made him more than a comrade; such was not to be thrown away lightly with an insult.

"Only my brother." Creases appeared at the sides of his eyes as he squinted against the pain of his loss. He suddenly looked older.

"Forgive me for prying into your affairs," Lewis said kindly.

The professor nodded and opened his mouth to speak, but a small group of shoppers jostled him as the crowd surged by.

"We should keep moving." Even at the edge of the crowd on the busy street, Lewis suddenly felt exposed. A population of sheep was not the best place to hide; the wolves tended to stand out, and for the moment, they were the wolves. He led the professor into the throng, pressing through the gawkers, the shoppers, and everyone else as he moved along the sidewalk.

Their encounter with the tanner weighed on him. Not only had they learned that they could expect little help from the constabulary, they had discovered the same fear among the common people. If a tradesman, someone who used conversation to make sales, could not speak to them, Lewis had little hope of finding anyone else who might. Should he continue to ask questions, he might get someone into trouble, either with the citizens of Mithras Court or its lord.

As they walked, Lewis scanned the faces for Frederick and Bailey. Neither revealed themselves. Terrace houses rose up on either side. They were in good repair; their bricks were polished and their windows had been washed. Their fresh décor contrasted sharply with the other streets of Mithras Court.

The pungent odors of exotic perfumes mixed with the mouth-watering aromas of sizzling meat, tempting Lewis's nose and his palate. Seaton Market back home had never offered such a broad variety of goods, although when he had last gone there, Elise had been with him. She had a fondness for the sausages sold by shabbily-clothed vendors on every corner.

Pushing her from his mind, he strode deeper into the throng, hoping to escape the memory. He could not, for everywhere he looked, he found himself searching for her dark curls. She did not reveal herself. Perhaps there was too much commotion.

The constant noise of the myriad voices was punctuated by the sporadic shouts and cries of the shopkeepers and seemed wildly loud, but as Lewis neared the center of the market, the volume increased. People pressed forward, hurrying toward some spectacle that enticed them all. Oddly, the ever-present fog had dissipated, allowing Lewis to clearly see where everyone was going.

A group of twelve brightly-colored wagons had drawn up to form a circle in the center of the street. Swarthy men dressed in embroidered shirts and close-fitting pants, along with women clad in brightly-colored blouses and long skirts, stood among the wagons selling a variety of items: food, fabric, spices, grains, live chickens, pots and pans, jewelry, and more. The merchants seemed cold and withdrawn as though they did not care to be interacting with the citizens of the Court. The patrons, on the other hand, were orderly and respectful during their transactions with the gypsies. It was a strange reversal from the attitudes Lewis had witnessed in the interactions between the gypsies of Europe and the general citizenry.

Two tall, broad-shouldered men stood at the center of the throng, their stillness revealing their roles as watchers and guards. They reminded Lewis of the sentries posted in British army encampments during times of war, though these men carried only knives in their belts. They watched the crowd, their dark eyes steady, and any who saw them immediately drew up short, slowing to a careful walk. If the people of Mithras Court showed deference to the other Vistani, they showed downright fear of these two men. Lewis wondered at the tanned skin of the gypsies, for he had not yet seen sunlight since he had arrived.

"I believe we've found the Vistani," Lewis said to Drake. "They appear to have everything these people could possibly need for survival, which lends credence to Inspector Newton's tale." Lewis strode forward slowly, cautiously. He pointed out a few of the carts. "Wheat, fish, ore of some kind, coal, timber . . . none of which could be found in Mithras Court. All of which is essential."

"Then they must truly be able to pass through the Mists." The professor's voice lifted slightly, touched by sudden hope. "If we could convince them to aid us . . ."

"I agree. If they can move through that barrier, and yet Lucius Knight cannot, then it stands to reason they are opposing forces," Lewis said. Had they been allies, the Vistani would have granted Knight the means to escape. "Perhaps it is possible for us to reach some kind of an accord with them."

"The enemy of my enemy is my friend," Professor Drake quoted. Some of the years slipped away from his features as his eyes brightened for a moment.

"Let us see if we can find their leader and learn the truth of it." Lewis moved toward the space between two of the wagons that provided a passage into the inner circle. As he entered, he saw that within the ring of wagons, dozens of people crowded around the outlanders in their bright clothes. The wonder and excitement they provided was clearly worth as much as the goods they brought.

Lewis searched the crowd and the gypsies, and turned his attention to the wagons, but saw no obvious leader. Elise's ring grew warm against his chest.

"Take care with these Vistani," she said softly. "They are different, somehow."

"What do you mean?" Professor Drake asked in a hushed tone, before Lewis could speak. "Can you tell us?"

"They are not your friends, nor are they your enemies. They serve a higher purpose in this place and cannot ally themselves with any faction. More than that, I do not know." Her voice grew softer again.

"Elise, don't go, please," Lewis said under his breath. "Tell me how you can be here and how I can hear and see you."

"It is difficult . . . I have been with you always."

"Did God send you to help us?" Professor Drake said. "Surely if you are here, and have saved us, some form of divine aid must be at work."

"Professor, please!" Lewis glared at him.

"I don't know." Elise's voice was so quiet that Lewis could barely hear her. "I don't think . . ."

"Are you in heaven?" Lewis asked, suddenly desperate for an answer. He glanced around them, trying to appear casual, and was relieved to see that the crowd was so focused on the Vistani and their wares that they did not notice him. Given what he had seen in Mithras Court, he wondered just what might qualify as strange to these folk.

"I am here."

"Were you in heaven, then?" Professor Drake said.

"No."

"What do you mean? You cannot have been to hell!" Panic seized Lewis, weight pressing down on his chest. "You lived a virtuous and good life!" He staggered and nearly crashed into a young couple. He steadied himself hurriedly.

The couple took no notice.

"No, Lewis, I have not been to heaven or hell." She was barely audible. "I am just . . . here."

"Purgatory, then," Professor Drake said, steadying Lewis and returning the cane to him. "My condolences, madam."

"I have never left . . ." Her voice faded completely, and the heat of her ring faded with it.

"You, there!" The woman's voice was powerful, with an unusual accent.

Lewis looked up to see a tall Vistana woman standing before him, her hands on her hips. She wore a blouse that revealed the well-muscled arms of an athlete, while her black pants suggested the legs of a dancer.

"Can I help you, madam?" Lewis slipped his hand instinctively into his pocket and closed it around the Webley. He had no idea who to trust. Something about her was sinister.

"*We* can help *you.*" She glanced at the pocket where he gripped his revolver and smiled. He wasn't sure why, unless she could see through clothing. "Madame Catalena would speak with you." She gestured at a wagon across the ring. It was a deep purple, with many symbols and designs painted on it. A small group of citizens stood nearby.

"The astrological symbols of a seer or fortune teller," Professor Drake said confidently. "I've seen them in Eastern Europe a number of times, among the Romani."

The woman nodded. "A seer, yes. Please follow me." She turned as if their agreement was certain.

Lewis glanced at the professor. The old man was stroking his beard and staring at the distant wagon with one eyebrow raised. Upon seeing Lewis's questioning stare, the professor nodded.

"I believe we should follow her."

"I don't believe we have a choice," Lewis said, surprising himself as he started to follow. He could not help but speculate that she was at least as strong as he, perhaps stronger. Although most of the

Vistani were not particularly large or forbidding, they all looked as if they could defend themselves. If they could be mobilized into a fighting force, he had no doubt they would prove a fierce ally—or adversary.

The crowd gave way, parting as the woman led them around the edge of the circle. Other Vistani offered bows of obvious respect and moved swiftly aside. Their escort stopped in front of the wagon. Now that they were closer to this particular vehicle, Lewis saw that rough wooden stairs led to an opening in the rear of the wagon. More symbols marked each side of the opening, perhaps wards against evil spirits. Unlike the other wagons, a man stood at either side of the stairs with the same dark-eyed wariness as their guide. They nodded to the woman.

"He is here," she said.

"He may enter." The man on the left spoke with a thick accent as he motioned to the steps. Elise's comment about these gypsies had been cryptic, but it demanded consideration. She had not warned him to distrust them, but whatever purpose these Vistani served, it might differ from his own goals. And that might make gaining their assistance difficult. Still, he had to make the attempt.

"Madame Catalena will see you." The woman waved a hand at the stairs.

Lewis took a deep breath and climbed the steps. They creaked ominously, but held his weight. Professor Drake took a step to follow him.

"Not you."

Lewis turned to see their guide pressing her palm against Professor Drake's chest.

"But Captain Wentworth is my companion. May we not speak to Madame Catalena together?" The professor was not foolish enough to try to push past her or the men.

"This is for his ears only," the woman said. "Stand back."

"It's all right, Professor. Mind this for me, will you?" Lewis handed his cane to the scholar.

"If you are certain, then. Take care." The professor looked as if he wished to say more, but thought better of it.

Lewis nodded and turned to the doorway. Steeling himself against whatever might lie within, he climbed inside.

The inside of the wagon appeared larger than Lewis had thought possible. Several brass lanterns hung from hooks in the wooden roof and provided comfortable light. A bookcase filled with leather-bound books stood against the far wall. Symbols he did not recognize covered much of the interior. A small yellow bird cocked its head at him from within a metal cage to his left, and a table rested in the center of the wagon, bearing candles burning in silver candlesticks. A woman sat in a gnarled wooden chair behind the table. Black hair fell past her shoulders in waves, blanketing her white blouse. As she watched him, she shuffled a deck of worn-looking cards that didn't look like any he had ever seen.

Elise would have enjoyed the market, but she would have *loved* this, Lewis thought. The occult had intrigued her and she had loved to have her fortune told. Lewis had indulged that interest by taking her on occasional visits to palm readers and astrologers. He had never considered the belief in such things more than wishful thinking at best, delusion at worst: something for women with Elise's interests to enjoy, but not to take seriously. No doubt she would have chided him for being serious this time.

"Welcome, Lewis Wentworth." She smiled as she motioned for him to approach. Her gaze was not reassuring. "Please, kneel before the table."

"Who are you? How do you know my name?" Lewis did not understand why he was asked to kneel, but did as he was told. He dropped down on the thick rug before her. It was the pelt of a gray-furred animal, although he could not tell what kind. Splayed out as it was, only three appendages were visible; it looked to have had only that many limbs even in life, which made no sense. The rug had no abrupt edge, as he would have expected if a limb had been cut away.

"I am Madame Catalena." Her rhythmic voice took his thoughts away from the mysterious animal hide. She stopped shuffling the cards and put the deck down on the table. Motioning to it with a tilt of her chin, she said, "The cards have told me many things about you and your beloved Elise, but there is more to learn. Please, cut the deck."

"How do you know about Elise?" Lewis snapped to attention, his eyes on her, wondering if this Vistana might truly have information. Perhaps she could explain how Elise could reveal herself to them as a ghost, how she had made contact.

"I told you, I am Madame Catalena," she said. Apparently, this was the only explanation needed. "The tarokka cards told me."

"Are you the leader of the Vistani?" Lewis reached forward, despite his skepticism. If he could get her to talk, to see his point of view about escaping from Mithras Court, he could perhaps get her to help him escape.

"Wait." Catalena reached out to stop him. "Your left hand. It is easier for your spirit to control."

"You did not answer my question." Lewis fought against the soft haze that settled into his mind at her words, but to no avail; he felt himself relax. A small voice in his head wondered what difference his left or right hand could possibly make, but he ignored it.

"I am the head of our clan. And for this moment, I am your conduit to whatever answers the universe and your soul choose to reveal to you."

"I don't understand." Lewis had not come to play cards with a gypsy. He needed answers to specific questions, not vague promises of revelations from his soul. But, he reminded himself, if these Vistani were not the agents of Lord Knight, and if they could move at will through the Mists, then he had to find a way to gain their aid. If that meant playing cards, then he would play cards.

As he met Catalena's gaze, something was so compelling that Lewis could not ask the questions that plagued him. His instincts told him to follow her lead, that she would be more open to him and his cause if he showed respect for her customs.

"Of course you do not. It is my job to teach you, to show you. Perhaps this will aid you in the coming days, perhaps not. Nonetheless, I will try." She nodded toward the cards, holding his blue eyes with her dark ones. "Feel the energy. Let your deep mind choose where to break the deck."

"My deep mind?" When Lewis was twelve, his father had taken him to London to see the circus. That in itself was odd, given his father's distaste for the city, but it was not that which truly drew the memory to the forefront. He and his father had been separated and he had stumbled into the tent of a hunched old woman performing a tarot reading for a local merchant. Quiet as Lewis had been, they had failed to notice him and he had listened in, and had heard the fortune teller speak of her client's *deep mind*. He had never understood what that meant. Had he asked his father, he would have been whipped for listening to such trash.

"Your soul—the voice that speaks to you in your mind, warning you of danger or urging you to action." She arched one delicate eyebrow. "That is your deep mind."

"I call that instinct." Lewis bristled at the condescension her expression implied. "We are born with some—we learn more through hardship."

"Call it what you will." She shrugged, but her eyes locked onto him with great intensity as if she were trying to see inside him. "Use it to choose a card now."

"Very well." Lewis longed to dismiss this woman and her claims as mere superstitious drivel—yet she knew things about him and Elise. He had witnessed too many incredible events over the past days to dismiss anything as fanciful. He reached out and touched the deck with his left hand, leaving it there for several seconds. Then he slid the deck apart, laying the top half next to the bottom. He watched the gypsy for any reaction.

Madame Catalena glanced at the deck and arched one eyebrow. She tapped her right forefinger on the tabletop and nodded.

"Have I chosen well?" He wondered how she could know without looking at the cards. Flimflam artists in London had a number of tricks, lines they could say, to appear all-knowing, but this was Mithras Court. Anything was possible here, and he doubted that she had to rely on the lies of London fortunetellers for her earnings.

"We shall see." She stacked the deck together into its new order and drew the first four cards. She placed them facedown in front of herself in a long line and turned over the first card. "This is your past." She tilted her head as she examined it.

The picture depicted a poorly dressed young woman whose face was emotionless and whose pockets hung empty. A shadow loomed next to her and she seemed ignorant of the danger. At the bottom of the card were the words THE BROKEN ONE. Lewis had never seen the card on his many outings with Elise. It gave him a chill.

"Is this supposed to be me?" He gripped the table tightly, holding back his impatience before it could turn to anger. "Is this some kind of joke?" She clearly mocked him.

"This is how your inner soul views your past. It reveals one choice that changed the course of your life and caused you great pain." She reached out to touch his hand gently. Her eyes revealed sudden sympathy. "You blame yourself for her death, but it was not your fault."

"How could you know these things?" Lewis gritted his teeth. Elise's death *was* his fault. Had he been with her that night, she would be alive.

"Because *you* know them." She removed her hand and reached for the next card. "Shall I continue?"

"Yes, by all means." Her knowledge of him, whether from the cards or from another source, had been accurate, and his doubts were fading. He watched eagerly, a desperate hope blooming that he might learn more.

"This represents the recent past." She turned over the next card. It showed a swordsman reaching out to choose from a trio of blades—one white, one black, and one gray. At the bottom of the card were the words THE SOLDIER. Lewis gasped. He had never seen this card, yet the meaning was evident. It was an obvious choice for Madame Catalena to select if she could manipulate the cards to show him what she wished.

Yet it was also who he had truly once been.

"I see great inner strength and determination in the person you have become, perhaps because of this tragedy." Her face showed a stoic curiosity as she observed him.

"I have a purpose, one inspired by Elise's death, if that's what you mean." Richard Bailey would die slowly, begging for mercy that would never come. Lewis clenched his fists.

"I speak of something deeper than a simple plan," Madame Catalena said sternly. "You have great resolve in all that you do—rallying the troops in the India campaign, or countermanding Lord Rothschild's order to charge during the occupation of Egypt."

Lewis felt the blood drain from his face, bewildered that she could know such things. Her statement that he had always been driven was an easy guess, but there was no way she could know such specific details about his military service. His opinion of her shifted in a heartbeat to one of respect and admiration. He leaned forward with rapt attention.

Catalena studied him, her expression one of satisfaction. She knew she had impressed him and gained his respect. In Lewis's mind, that made her more useful, but also more dangerous. He had not decided that the Vistani were his enemies, but should they prove to be, knowledge of him could weaken his position. She raised her eyebrows in question.

"Please, continue." Lewis nodded eagerly, intent on learning more.

"This card represents the present." She turned the third card, revealing the image of a wizard in a hooded robe, mystical energy swirling about him. The words read THE WIZARD. Lewis could not guess what it meant.

"Very interesting." Catalena watched him intently. "You are on a quest for knowledge, for enlightenment."

"After the last card, I would hardly call that prophetic." Lewis frowned, wondering again if she was playing games with him. To mention such specifics and revert to generalities made little sense.

"Some of my words have many interpretations. It is for you to determine what they truly mean." Catalena's mouth tightened at the corners as if he had irritated her.

"You're being evasive." Lewis crossed his arms, though the posture hardly seemed impressive while he was on his knees.

"Perhaps you would care to leave?" she asked, a challenge in her eyes.

Lewis thought about it, but realized that he had to stay, had to know what other secrets she held. He shook his head solemnly, signaling his defeat.

"Good." She tapped the deck. "Now for the future, something of concern to you, no?"

Lewis eyed the fourth and final card warily, wondering if her next comments would be vague gibberish or useful revelation.

Catalena turned the last card, pulling him away from his musings. The picture showed a woman on a horse with fog swirling wildly around her. The lettering at the bottom read THE MISTS.

"That's not a tarot card!" Lewis exclaimed. The other cards had seemed odd, but this . . . "What kind of deck is this?"

Madame Catalena's eyes blazed, then cooled to embers. "Not tarot cards. *Tarokka* deck. The tarokka is attuned to the Vistani. Much more power than the playthings of your world." She sighed.

"As I thought," she continued, tapping the card. "You are in great danger." She watched him, expressionless, waiting for his reaction. Lewis suddenly felt as if he were being tested, but did not know why—or what his reaction should be. He opted for honesty.

"Of course, I'm in danger. All of Mithras Court is in danger!" Lewis slapped the table. "You're toying with me, madam! Either you know something or you do not. My military service is a matter of public record. It could have become known to you, and as that is the only relevant information you seem to possess . . ." He felt foolish for believing in her, even for a moment. He stood up, determined to leave—clearly, there was no reasoning with a charlatan, and he questioned whether her people could truly pass through the Mists. If they could convince people that they were great seers, what else could they convince them of?

"Very good, Lewis Wentworth. I indeed know many things. My reading has revealed a great deal to me." Catalena's eyes narrowed and anger showed there. "I will tell you this—not all citizens of this place are threatened by Lucius Knight, and not all newcomers are destined to die."

"Go on." Lewis frowned but remained still. If he had successfully run through some kind of fortune teller's gauntlet, then perhaps she would reveal more.

"Your enemy, the Snake . . ." Catalena leaned forward, her eyes intense. "He, too, is a newcomer. Unlike you, he aligns himself with evil, with the lord of this place."

"Lucius Knight."

"Yes."

"But Frederick knew of Bailey—how could the Snake be a new-comer? Surely he left Mithras Court to murder Elise and returned later with myself and my companions. It is the only explanation that makes sense." Lewis watched her for any hint of deception, but saw none.

"The Vistani move through the Mists. We know who enters Mithras Court, and we know that no one has left in all the years this place has existed." Madame Catalena paused, her fingers drumming on the table as if it aided her in thought.

"You control passage through the Mist . . ." Lewis narrowed his eyes. He had believed Frederick when he said he knew of the Snake. He further believed that Knight and his minions did not have the means to leave Mithras Court, for surely they would have escaped long ago. That left only one conclusion. "If, as I believe, Bailey came from here to London to murder Elise, and if you are the only ones who can grant escape from Mithras Court . . . " He slipped his hand into his pocket, his fingers closing over the Webley. "You allowed Bailey to come to London, and as a result, he killed Elise!"

A strong hand gripped Lewis's wrist from behind, its crushing force making him release the pistol. A knife appeared at his throat, its sharp blade pressing against his flesh with just enough force to frighten him.

"Do not move." Lewis recognized the other woman's voice. He had not heard a hint of movement behind him, nor of anyone on the stairs to the rickety wagon. He had no intention of moving, lest he decapitate himself on her weapon.

"It is all right, Zuza." Madame Catalena waved her off. "Captain Wentworth's concerns are justified. He is new to this place and has not yet learned the truth." She fixed Lewis with a stern gaze. "The

Vistani have an understanding with Lucius Knight. He leaves us alone, lest we cut the flow of food and supplies to his citizens. And we will never, under any circumstances, help any of his subjects to escape through the Mists."

The knife slipped away and the hand released his arm. Lewis turned to see Zuza glowering at him. He swallowed and returned his attention to the seer, considering his next words carefully.

"Do you expect me to believe that?" Lewis rubbed his wrist. He could believe the part about Lucius Knight leaving them alone. They controlled the flow of goods to Mithras Court, but for them to promise not to aid his trapped subjects in their escape seemed cruel. Why make such an agreement with an evil force like Knight?

"Yes. It is the truth."

"If you can pass through the barrier, then why . . . do you come here?" Surely there were better places than Mithras Court. Why should they bother to come at all? The fact that they did could indicate that they did care about what happened to Knight's subjects, he supposed, but then why would they refuse to assist the citizens? Lewis sighed. These Vistani did not make any sense.

"As I said." She tapped her fingers on the table. "We bring goods to the people of Mithras Court. In turn, we are compensated very well."

"Are you jailers, then?"

Madame Catalena laughed at that, her mirth flowing forth almost like sunshine. It burned through Lewis's pain, and for an instant he felt whole and happy. It quickly faded, however, as she sobered.

"We are moving away from the truths you seek. We will not help you or your companions to leave. You know this. I see it in your eyes. Therefore, your questions do not revolve around my people or even the Mists any longer. In your heart, I see only your wish to know more about your nemesis—the man with the snake tattoo—and his lord and master, and how you can take your vengeance upon them."

"Yes." Lewis wanted to deny it, but she had seen through to his core. The Vistani would not help him escape. And as much as he wished to learn more about these strange gypsies and their relationship to the barrier around Mithras Court—his desire for information about his true enemies overshadowed that. "If Lucius Knight does not control the Mists, then how did he achieve mastery over Richard Bailey? How did he bring him—and us—here? Surely he had a hand in that?"

"I cannot answer that." Catalena leaned back in her chair. "Perhaps he found a way to influence you and your fellow passengers—to bring you to that train station at that moment. Perhaps it was merely fate."

"I do not believe in fate," Lewis said angrily. As for influencing them, Professor Drake had admitted that he had dreamed of their enemy just as Lewis had dreamed of him the previous night. He wondered if the others experienced the same thing.

"Then you are a fool." Catalena shrugged. "Fate controls much that happens to us all."

"And if it was not fate, if Lucius Knight influenced us to board that train?" Lewis asked. "How would he know that we would arrive here? How could he predict the Mists?"

"The Mists brought you and your nemesis to Mithras Court. As to the reason—I cannot make a guess. Ours is not to question the will of the Mists." She pulled a shawl about her shoulders.

"You speak as if the Mists are alive." Lewis suddenly remembered his terrifying encounter in that soupy wall of fog.

Madame Catalena did not answer, but stared more intently at him.

Lewis's brain swam with confusion as the memories of his encounter in the Mists swirled through his mind. He felt suddenly dizzy and a spike of pain shot through his thigh. The room shifted, spinning slowly as if he had absorbed all he could of the place and the insanity that accompanied it. "How can any of this . . . how can I . . . he . . ."

"Focus on me, Lewis Wentworth." Madame Catalena leaned forward and her dark eyes bored into him. "Channel your inner strength." Her voice was soothing, hypnotic, as it had been at the beginning of their conversation.

Her eyes pulled him back from the edge of his confused state. The spinning ceased and the fog in his mind cleared.

"You have another question—one you fear to ask." She motioned for him to come closer.

Lewis obeyed, kneeling before her. He leaned in close to her and she reached out and took both of his hands in hers, resting them on the table. Warm energy surged from her, flowing up his left arm, through his torso and down his right arm, as if a circle had formed between them. Lewis's body tingled and the hair on his arms rose. He did not ask his question of his own will.

"Why is Elise here? And why can I see and hear her?" A weight lifted from his chest. Those questions required answers more than any others.

"She has always been with you, Lewis, bound to your pain as it revolves around the circle of your love. In this place, many things are possible, even speaking to the dead. Cherish your moments with her, for you are both in grave danger. Anything could happen." She released his hands and leaned back.

"What danger? Why are we here? Why does Lord Knight wish us harm? Why—"

Catalena waved him away, looking tired. "We are finished."

Lewis stood up.

"Can't you help my companions and I escape from this place?" he pleaded. "After I've completed this purpose of which you spoke?"

"No." She looked past his shoulder and strong hands grabbed him from behind, practically lifting him from the floor.

Zuza half-dragged, half-carried him to the door and tossed him out. Lewis tumbled down the stairs, rolling as he hit the ground. He winced as jabbing pain lanced through his thigh and his shoulder. He landed in front of a concerned Professor Drake.

"Well, that did not appear to go well," Drake said, holding out a hand to help him up.

CHAPTER SEVENTEEN

"Very interesting," Professor Drake said as they pushed through the crowd. He watched Lewis for a few moments, then held out the cane. "Captain—you look as if you need this." Lewis took it gratefully. His leg throbbed from kneeling in the Vistana's wagon.

Lewis had related the tale of his tarokka reading and what he had learned from Madame Catalena as they strode through the busy street, moving steadily away from the wagons and toward the Mists. He saw no change in Drake's expression when he suggested that some of the Vistani might be inadvertently, or purposefully, aiding their enemy.

"Clearly, we can expect no further help from them." The gypsies' unwillingness to help weighed heavily upon Lewis.

"At least we can be assured that they will not aid Lucius Knight in his plans for us." The professor frowned, despite his optimistic statement. "Not more than their agreement requires, at any rate. But I fail to understand—if they can pass through the Mists, why will they not aid us in our escape? It seems an unfair agreement, to let people die in exchange for the right to trade here."

"Perhaps they will offer assistance when I fulfill whatever purpose they believe I have here. Beyond that, I do not think they will be forthcoming with any additional information." Lewis moved to avoid a youth in dirt-smeared trousers who stood near several boxes, his shoe shine cloth held at the ready.

"Do you have any inkling of what this purpose might be?" The professor did not look at him, and Lewis wondered if the evasion was intentional.

"No," Lewis said, deciding to trust Drake for the friend he was. "As far as I am concerned, my *raison d'être* is to kill the Snake, set Elise free, and escape from this place, but that hardly seems like the

178

purpose Madame Catalena hinted at." Lewis was still frustrated by the fortune teller's ambiguous talk. "I do not know, but I fear I shall learn the truth of it soon. Perhaps before it is too late."

"That does seem likely." The professor paused and glanced around before he finally settled his attention back on Lewis. "There is something I find difficult to believe in all of this."

"Just *one* thing?" The sarcasm was unmistakable.

"Indeed. I find this notion that Lucius Knight could have influenced this Bailey fellow, and perhaps the rest of us, to board our fateful train, quite impossible to believe." The professor's speech was labored as they maneuvered through the crowd. "If he does not control the Mists, how could he have known our journey would end in Mithras Court?" He frowned. "Yet the idea that it could be fate is even more ludicrous."

"I agree. Neither theory seems believable." Then again, nothing about Mithras Court made sense. They walked through a nightmare, but they could not deny that they were there. It was not some sort of shared hallucination—it had to be real, yet it could not be. Elise, he added to himself, was another facet of this mystery. Her ghostly apparition was incredible, but Lewis could not question that she had reached him from the beyond.

"Do you believe these Vistani when they swear that neither they nor Lucius Knight control the Mists?"

"I do not believe that Madame Catalena lied to me about anything. Something in her eyes said she told the truth." Lewis thought that sounded foolish, but it rang true for him. He could not express it well, and he knew that the gypsies might bend the truth, or omit some of it, but he did not think they had lied to him.

"What do you make of what she told you about your wife?" Drake's tone became curious rather than thoughtful.

"What do you mean?" Lewis stopped to stare at the older man. It seemed that Drake suspected something that Lewis had not.

"I'm sorry, Captain." Drake stopped. "I simply meant that when Madame Catalena told you Elise had always been here, that sounded surprisingly similar to what Elise told you."

"Yes. Perhaps . . ." Guilt swirled through Lewis's anger. His voice became regretful. "Perhaps I have held her back." His stomach churned at the thought that his unwillingness to let go of her death could have trapped her spirit.

But he loved her still, he always had, and he could not, *would* not accept that a love such as his could be responsible for her miraculous appearance in Mithras Court.

A tiny part of him could not stop thinking that he had been responsible, and that part called him coward for refusing to acknowledge his guilt.

"Rest easy, Lewis." Drake put a hand on his shoulder. "The pain of your loss is natural. If it is true that she has become ensnared by it, then all who have suffered a loss could say the same about their departed loved ones. You merely have the benefit—or curse—of becoming trapped in this place where it is possible to speak to the dead. Once we leave, as your soul heals, you will overcome it and set her free. You cannot blame yourself for loving Elise so deeply."

The friendly use of his first name surprised Lewis. It embarrassed him as well, however. Only a short time ago, he had considered the man might be, if not an enemy, then at least not an ally, let alone a friend. Yet Drake was treating him as a great friend. Lewis thought about what the professor had said, and it made sense. Everyone missed their loved ones—everyone wished their loved ones were still with them.

"You're right. Thank you, professor." He clenched his fists in frustration. "I have read stories of the disturbed spirits of murdered men and women. They roam the land or their places of execution, trapped between worlds until their deaths can be avenged."

"I have heard such tales as well," Professor Drake said evenly. "If there is truth to the tales of the dead rising from the grave, as we have seen here in Mithras Court, then perhaps there could be truth in those old yarns as well."

"It's possible Elise has remained trapped between this life and the next because the man who murdered her runs free." Lewis felt his doubt and confusion diminish. "Bailey must die. It is not vengeance that matters. It is the only way she can be set free."

"You could be correct." Drake thought for a moment. "I must

point out that other stories say that distraught spirits merely require the truth of their deaths to become known. In this case, that has happened."

"I am not certain what 'become known' means, but I am certain that I am correct. There is no doubt in my mind." But there *was* doubt in his soul—he could sense it there, whispering to him, trying to be heard. He was as angry as ever, and he had no intention of letting Bailey escape.

He changed the subject. "We should continue to the barrier." At the far end of the street, he could see that the crowds thinned and the daylight dimmed.

"What about finding Frederick?" Drake looked back the way they had come, but the big man was not visible in the crowd that still thronged the street.

"He will have to wait." Lewis strode onward with new determination.

As the crowd melted away and the din subsided, the buildings they passed became shabbier. A junction appeared at the edge of the fog, difficult to see in the dim light. Several slovenly men and ladies skulked about the streetlamp nearest to the intersection.

A young girl sat on the cracked steps leading to one of the dilapidated terrace houses. She tossed some jacks down before her, but did not appear to have a ball to go with them. She looked at them forlornly, picked them up, and ran into the building.

"I don't like the looks of this street." Professor Drake turned in a circle, taking in the full scene.

"Nor I." Lewis handed his cane to the scholar, then reached into his pocket, his hand caressing the barrel of the Webley. He reminded himself that the revolver's six remaining bullets would not last long. He needed ammunition, but had seen none for sale in their travels. He wondered if Lord Knight prevented the sale of weapons or firearms.

On the other hand, Lewis realized, people got their ever-present firearms and ammunition from somewhere. But even if he could not locate an outfitter, he would not deal with the Vistani for bullets.

As they neared the intersection, a street sign emerged from behind a veil of grit, its worn lettering marking the crossroads of Bacchus Way and Knight Street. Lewis paused in the center of the road as an odd smell—damp earth mixed with rotting vegetables—assaulted his nose. He put his hand to his mouth and took in their surroundings, trying to identify where such a stench could come from.

Ahead, he could see that the next block had been nearly abandoned. Chunks of brick and mortar, broken glass, and other trash and debris littered the street. Only two dented lamps, one with a large crack in its globe, illuminated the way. To the right, the street ended barely a dozen feet away in the Mists. The buildings in that section were gutted, scorched, and in ruin as if anything near the Mists suffered from decay. But clearly, something terrible had happened there far beyond what he had seen in Mithras Court. Lewis was reminded of artillery damage, yet he had seen no evidence of that type of weaponry. It looked like the relic of an ancient war.

"Bloody hell." Lewis shivered. "Well, we can't leave that way."

The professor held a handkerchief to his mouth as defense against the stench. He lowered it to speak. "And ahead?" The old man peered beneath his bushy white eyebrows down Bacchus Way.

Lewis followed his gaze and squinted into the murk. "I see only fog, but I'd wager more of the same."

"We should investigate." The professor motioned forward with the cane. "We must eliminate all doubt." Lewis thought the certainty in his voice—that the man had not admitted that they were trapped here—was odd, but it was a reasonable tactic. If nothing else, they knew that this place could change in surprising ways.

"Sound thinking." Lewis stepped in front of the man. Duty did not change in the face of illogical thinking, and his duty to protect Drake was clear. He could feel the threatening, ominous weight of the Mists up ahead. He realized suddenly that he did not want to investigate further. Everyone they had encountered said that the Mists were impassable, and he was not inclined right now to doubt their word. The hair on his arms rose, and he felt as if something within watched and waited, hoping they would dare to enter. He drew the revolver. "Stay close."

He walked slowly forward, conscious of shadowy figures slipping about at the edges of the fog. They were not the undead, for it was still daylight. They were likely thieves and cutthroats, with little choice but to prey on the weak to survive. Lewis made certain they could see his weapon; the strangers kept their distance.

"There, I see it." The professor halted after a few dozen feet and pointed.

"Damn." Lewis came to a stop. The filthy fog gave way to the unyielding solid gray of the Mists. He had expected it, but still found it surprising—and disappointing. He raised his pistol reflexively. After a moment, as the two stood looking at it, he said, "There is something menacing about even the mere sight of that barrier."

The professor shivered. "I think we've done all we can here. Let us return to the inn."

Lewis nodded and they backed away. He turned after a few paces and hurried to the intersection, all the while feeling Mists behind him like a weight between his shoulders. He paused in the middle of the street. The sounds of the market had died down as if the intervening fog had thickened, and indeed, as he looked back the way they had come, he could barely make out the people milling about the lamppost. In the fog, the odd stutters of their movement made them look like the walking dead.

"Come . . ." The whisper of a dark voice sent chills down his spine and he spun, falling to one side to dodge the attacker.

There was no one there..

"Hello?" Lewis swallowed, turning toward the unexplored side of Knight Street. He tightened his grip on the gun, but the street was empty. He peered into the fog and still saw nothing—but now he felt a presence like a burden on his back. Whatever his eyes said, someone was there. Something watched them.

Drake had not heard the voice. Lewis stared into the gloom, hoping it had been one of their companions, but he knew it was not. None of them would have used that tone, or failed to identify themselves. The voice had been far too close to be someone shouting from a distance.

On each side of the road one street lamp, taller than the ones they saw in other parts of the Court, rose up on a wrought-iron stalk, shaped like a bending tulip. Unlike the elegant terraced homes of many of the other streets of Mithras Court, these were low, squat stone structures. Lewis had the distinct feeling that people were hiding behind those stout doors, watching them through narrow windows, but he could not see movement within. Yet the feeling of eyes on him persisted.

"Is anyone there?" Lewis stepped forward, gun ready—he did not wish to be defenseless, but shooting an innocent would be equally bad.

"Where are you going?" The professor followed him by a pace.

"Something is strange about this place. It's different from the rest of Mithras Court." Lewis moved forward, eyeing the fog ahead of them. Although it was still daylight, the fog seemed thicker, swirling despite the lack of breeze. The air hung heavy and stale, as if the street were somehow untouched by the motion of the wind, undisturbed by the passage of footsteps. Lewis's limbs felt heavier, as if he walked through water.

"It is odd." Drake's speech sounded slower than it should have. Lewis thought he was enunciating to combat the strangeness of the place. "I find these Roman structures interesting, given the name of this district." Lewis wondered if Drake had noticed his slurring words.

"My district . . ." the voice whispered, far away yet right behind them. Goosebumps raised on Lewis's skin as the voice crawled over his nerves.

"Lucius Knight," he said quietly. Hearing the voice again, feeling it again, Lewis remembered it from his nightmare. Though it had been hot then and was cold now, he remembered the way it had felt in his dream, and dread filled his stomach. If this were as bad as his dream had been, he would go mad. He would not be able to stop it, would not be able to face what Knight could do to him.

"Yes." The echoes in Knight's tone promised slow death.

Lewis stood his ground, though it was difficult. He had a growing desire to run as fast as he could, anywhere, so long as it was away from this place.

"What do you want of us?" Professor Drake's voice quavered, but he did not turn to flee. Lewis took strength from having such a man at his side as they faced their enemy squarely.

"Your obedience, your pain, your lives . . . and more." Knight spoke in a low voice, but his cackling laugh was unmistakable. "I will see you soon."

"You *will*, you son of a whore!" Lewis ran forward despite his limp. This man, this creature, whatever he turned out to be, had ordered Bailey to kill Elise. He would pay for the crime he had commanded. Lewis would crush the life from both of them!

Knight's laughter drifted on the fog, matching volume with the ebb and flow of the air, and he sounded no longer like he was whispering in their ears, but was everywhere in the Court at once.

"Captain Wentworth!" Drake called, trying not to become lost in the fog. "Wait!"

Lewis ignored Drake, pressing on. The swirling vapor scraped his skin, scratching at him as if whatever lay ahead corrupted the air even more than simple coal soot ever could. Occasional lights shone from the stone buildings, but not a single person was visible. Oddly-shaped street lamps, each of them resembling a different flower, stood at regular intervals, lighting enough of the lane to see the path ahead. Lewis slowed, not wishing to stumble upon the Mists again.

The street ended at a broad, grassy park. The road forked to the right and left, likely forming a square around the area. Lewis swiftly crossed to the park, pausing as he reached the edge.

A gust of driving wind cut through him, making his coat flap behind him and sweeping the fog away to reveal a small forest of tall oak trees ahead. A dirt road cut through the wood. Two tall Romanesque obelisks rose up at least ten feet, one on each side of the road. A metal sign hung from the one on the right; the name *Knight* was etched into its surface. It swung back and forth, banging against the stone as the wind pushed it.

"An odd place to find a park of this size." Drake caught up and leaned on the cane, trying to catch his breath.

"Even though we don't know its true depth, I agree. The fog

surrounding it might make it appear larger than it truly is." Lewis looked at his boots. It was odd to feel grass beneath his feet again. He had no idea how long it had been since he had walked in Hyde Park. But surely that had been before Elise had died. The park always reminded her of the estate, and she had insisted on going there often, even in the rain. She would remove her shoes and run across the lawn as if it were her own backyard. Twirling, she would laugh and reach out to him, beckoning him to follow.

He sighed at the memory. If only she would reappear, he might share such an experience with her one last time. But though he hoped for it, her ring remained cold against him.

"The trees are strange." The professor's voice interrupted his reverie as he pointed to the nearest—a huge, gnarled oak.

Lewis pushed his desires away and focused on the forest. *Ancient* described the massive trees, he thought, guessing that a dozen men would need to clasp hands to encircle their trunks. As they drew closer, he saw that their bark was blackened, charred as if a fire had burned through the underbrush. And yet the area around them was choked with plant life. The branches started just above his head, and large, reddish-brown leaves sprouted from them, brushing against each other and forming a canopy overhead that gradually meshed with the fog.

It had been December in London when he boarded the train, and the city had seen a light snow. The trees near Lewis's modest home in Coniston Court had been bare for over a month. Here, the landscape matched the middle of autumn. Lewis had barely noticed before, having spent so much time running from the walking dead and whatever skulked in the shadows. It was more proof that they were not in London. He sighed and looked up.

"And old," Lewis said. "There is something familiar about the way they cluster along this field." The scene nagged him as he tried to remember what the trees reminded him of, and he merely looked at them for several minutes. He'd almost dismissed the question from his mind when it came to him. "The tapestry."

"Of course!" Drake stepped closer, keeping an eye on the wood before them.

"This forest matches the scene in the tapestry at the Laughing Gargoyle. The only thing missing is the hovel." But a closer look revealed a faint indentation in the ground where the hovel would stand.

"I see the resemblance, but it *could* be a coincidence. The trees have grown older and larger since that tapestry was woven." Drake frowned. "If you're correct, then perhaps the wolves in the tapestry are here as well. We should be cautious."

"I've been cautious since the moment we arrived in Mithras Court." Something was unnerving about the forest—something he couldn't identify. He could feel the burning-eyed gaze of Knight on him. He glanced into the trees, but saw nothing. "Knight is in there. I can feel it." Still, he did not bring his revolver to bear. There was no target and *somewhere in there* could encompass quite a bit of land.

"Yes . . ." Knight whispered, clearly taunting. "I am waiting for you."

Lewis took an angry step toward the dirt trail—he would teach the lord of Mithras Court a valuable lesson when he killed him and the Snake. His fear fell away as revenge clouded his mind. Safety and patience be damned—he would set Elise free.

"Do not listen, my love!" Elise cried. "His words are poison!" Her ring burned against his chest.

"What do you mean?" Lewis jerked to a halt. Turning in a circle, he searched for her, but saw only the trees and the fog. "Why can I not see you?"

"Do not enter that wood." She did not answer his questions.

"Why does Knight wish us harm?" Drake looked around, trying to locate her.

"Elise!" Lewis turned more slowly, hoping to see her, but the wedding ring had gone cold as the soft echo of her voice faded.

"I say, Captain!" Lord Crandall's voice echoed across the clearing.

"Steady now!" Lewis turned toward the new voice, sighting a pair of individuals emerging from the thick fog to the left. As the figures coalesced, Lewis recognized Lord Crandall and Gregory. He relaxed, albeit slightly, when he saw them. These arrivals were friendly, but Lord Knight was still out there.

The men hurried across the grass, their coats fluttering behind them in the breeze. Gregory held a worn musket across his arm. Two bags, one presumably for powder and the other for musket balls, hung at his side. Lord Crandall gripped an ornate flintlock pistol in his hand.

"Ease yourself, Captain Wentworth, we are all friends here," Lord Crandall said as they neared. He studied Lewis's face. "You appear rested."

"As well as anyone can rest in this place." Lewis lowered the Webley. "How did you fare?"

"From the looks of the circles beneath Drake's eyes, about as well as you." The gentleman smirked grimly at the professor, but returned his attention to Lewis. "We found no break in the Mists. I'm beginning to believe that the entire perimeter of Mithras Court is wreathed in the stuff. I'll reserve my final judgment until we hear from the others."

Lewis had expected that answer, though he had hoped it was wrong. Had it been as simple as finding a hole in the Mist, the citizens of the Court would have done so long ago. His own explorations had found nothing to make him think that other searchers would find something else. "You've acquired some weapons." He inclined his head toward Crandall's pistol. "If somewhat antiquated." Any weapon was better than nothing, and they would certainly need them.

"Yes. One shot is better than none, I thought." Crandall held the pistol, running a hand along its surface. "It is a very nice piece. It will make a fine addition to my collection."

If we can ever leave this place, Lewis thought. He had committed himself to aiding them in finding an escape from the place, but he had to consider the possibility that there was no way out. He shook his head. Every jail had a door, and every door had a key. They simply had to figure out that key and how to use it.

"It's a shame we couldn't find anything more modern." Lord Crandall let the flintlock drop to his side. "We asked the shopkeeper who sold these museum pieces to us if he had any bullets for your Webley, but all he had were musket balls and powder. He suggested we talk to the Vistani."

"The Vistani were not forthcoming with an offer of assistance," Lewis said. "We had an encounter with them, and they do not provide anything other than conversation." He still did not understand how they could be so cold, so cunning as to profit from the people of Mithras Court and remain unfeeling to their plight.

"Indeed?" Crandall raised his eyebrows in surprise. "Were you able to glean some useful information?"

"I learned that they are not aligned with Lucius Knight, and that neither they nor he controls the Mists." He explained his dream about Knight and finished with Drake's admission of having dreamed about the man and the train station in the days leading up to their fateful train ride.

"That said," he continued, "it appears that Knight has the ability to influence our world and its occupants, through dreams. He may have drawn us all to the train station two nights ago with the intention that we would arrive here."

"So, this Lucius Knight contacted you!" Lord Crandall glared at Professor Drake.

"A dream does not constitute contact. And Captain Wentworth has dreamed of the lord of this place as well," Professor Drake said. "If you must question me, then you should question him as well. For all we know, each and every one of us has had a similar experience."

"Gentlemen, this is fruitless. I suggest we cease this bickering and regroup." Lewis said, fixing both men with a stern glare. If they wished to be treated like first year cadets, then he could oblige. He had hoped for better from Professor Drake, though could understand how Crandall's incessant verbal attacks could wear on him.

But before he could suggest a direction more fruitful than pointless arguing, his thoughts were interrupted by the sight of a dark shadow flitting between the nearest trees, just at the edge of the grim forest. A reflex brought his weapon up, though there was nothing to aim at.

"Is something there?" Gregory aimed his musket toward the wood. He squinted into the forest, but the shadow had gone.

"I am not certain. Mithras Court has me on edge, I think." Lewis relaxed only slightly when nothing else appeared.

"Is there truly no way to negotiate with these Vistani?" Lord Crandall eyed the forest with the wariness of a man facing a vicious animal.

"The answer to that is a resounding no!" The familiar voice echoed off the buildings around them. Whoever he was, he sounded far away. But he'd clearly heard their discussions, and had to be much closer.

Lewis turned, the gun coming around, but he saw only Edgar slogging across the field. The Bainbridges followed a few paces behind, looking bedraggled; they were clearly exhausted. Unlike Lord Crandall, they did not carry guns, though Thomas carried a mop handle in one hand. Relief at their survival overrode his surprise at the sight of them.

"Explain yourself." Lord Crandall's voice carried across the field. Crandall glanced at Edgar, his lip curled in derision.

"We saw some of those dirty vermin emerge from the Mists," Edgar said as they neared. "I tried to negotiate safe passage out of here, since obviously they can pass through unharmed." He wiped the sweat from his brow with his meaty hand.

"What you mean to say is that you attempted to bribe them," Lewis translated for his companions, though he doubted that they needed his help to understand the implications of Edgar's statement.

"Call it what you will, but the fools weren't buying." Edgar's jowls shook and he waved his arms in irritation. "I just don't understand the people in this place. They don't care about money at all."

"And why should they?" Bainbridge asked as they reached the group. "In this self-contained place, how much value can money truly have?"

"They use some form of currency." Lewis said. He had seen the hectic marketplace, but had not thought to pay attention the kind of money they had been using, so focused had he been on locating Frederick and the Vistani. "I don't know what it is, but the market was very busy, and people were paying in coin, not barter."

"An astute observation," Professor Drake said. "I tend to agree. I would expect such a place to rely more on barter than a single monetary system."

"I don't mean to interrupt." Lord Crandall's contempt called all attention to him as surely as if he had stepped into the group's center. He flashed an annoyed glare at the professor and Edgar and raised his pistol—for a heartbeat, Lewis was certain he intended to shoot someone. "But what are we all doing here in this field at the same moment? Did none of you go to your assigned areas?" His sneer clearly labeled them all cowards.

"You did not arrange to meet here?" Lewis's blood turned to ice. He had thought it mere coincidence that he and the professor had happened upon the others. That led him to another conclusion— this was a trap.

He looked to the forest involuntarily, expecting to see horror befall them from out of those grim trees. In his estimation, there was little true coincidence in life, and Mithras Court seemed to hold none. They had been led to this place.

"No. We saw the road that led here and came into the park after surveying the boundary." Lord Crandall's eyes flicked to the forest. "There was something strange about it and we deemed it worthy of investigation."

"A street back, we heard you speaking to a woman and followed your voice." Gregory held his musket in a ready grip as he, too, warily surveyed the forest.

"I'd guess that you were conversing with Elise?" Lord Crandall asked.

"Yes. She warned us to leave this place," Lewis said quietly. In hindsight, her advice had been sounder than he'd realized. He wished he could summon her rather than waiting for her to contact him.

"We heard the lot of you babbling as well." Edgar waved at them, managing to convey both distaste at their discussion and annoyance. "Judging by how close you sounded, I'd have thought we would find you much sooner."

"The water vapor that forms fog does allow noises to carry far- ther," Anne said, in a tone that suggested she was speaking to her students. She pulled Thomas's coat about her tightly and glanced at the woods.

"If all of us ended up here, then it follows that Reggie and his wife should have found their way as well." Professor Drake rubbed his beard thoughtfully. "They could be in trouble."

"Or perhaps they are in league with our enemies," Edgar said.

"Never." Professor Drake shook his head. "They have proven themselves stalwart allies."

"Did you hear any other voices besides ours?" Dark foreboding bloomed in Lewis's mind. If Reggie and Mary were not here, they might already be dead, but there was little to do besides wait. For the moment, he was more concerned about the trap they had all walked into.

"Other than a few locals, no." Thomas said.

"We must leave immediately." He spoke quietly so as not to panic them—or to arouse the attention of whatever had set the trap. Lewis motioned them back in the direction he had come. He knew the road on the other side, and this was no time to explore. "Quickly." Every second counted.

"But what about Reggie and Mary?" Anne had clearly not recognized what they'd wandered into. The only expression on her face was concern, and Lewis hoped they could escape before it became fear.

"We can't help them right now." Lewis took a few steps ahead, studying whether their path was still safe. "We must leave at once." His eyes went back to the woods. He was stunned that they hadn't been attacked yet. "Move!"

"I believe the road we came down to reach this park is the shortest route back to the inn." Thomas spoke in a low voice as understanding of their situation dawned upon him. He gripped his mop handle more firmly, and took Anne's hand.

"Very well. Form up behind Mr. Bainbridge." Lewis planted his feet and pulled back the Webley's hammer as he focused on the woods. "I'll cover our escape."

"Ah, but the trap is sprung!" Richard Bailey stepped out of the forest, drawing a thick black cloud with him like a cape. He stopped in the center of the dirt road, between the two obelisks, and straightened his modest gray coat as he smiled at them menacingly. "It's time for some—"

Lewis raised his Webley. He could not miss—Bailey could not escape justice. He fired. "For my wife, you murdering bastard!"

Time slowed to a crawl as a gout of flame marked the bullet's exit. The slug hit Bailey in the chest and blood sprayed as it tore through him. A crimson stain spread across his white shirt, over his heart. He staggered a pace but did not fall. Lewis watched him double over, coughing. He held his finger on the trigger, ready to shoot again. Bailey straightened up, a grin creasing his features. He shook his head the way a father might scold a child.

"That's twice you've tried to kill me." Bailey put his finger into the hole in his chest and laughed. "I think I'll take a turn now." He raised his arms and the dark cloud swirled thicker about him, rolling over his shoulders, around his torso, up his legs. The snake tattoo on his forearm writhed like a live thing. The hissing that Lewis had heard the prior evening filled the park, and the wound in the man's chest healed as Lewis watched, transfixed. Bailey took a step toward them.

"Shoot!" Lord Crandall didn't wait, but fired at point-blank range with a flash of gunpowder. A second, louder shot echoed through the park as Gregory, down on one knee, fired his musket.

Lord Crandall's pistol ball hit Bailey in the shoulder. Gregory's shot caught him in the abdomen. The impacts knocked him flat, the dark cloud obscuring him. Lewis had no doubt the Snake would laugh these shots off as well. Bailey's gurgle of pain mingled with the hiss of the myriad snakes hidden in the murk.

"He's dead. He has to be dead!" Edgar's voice shook and he sounded like he was trying to convince himself. "No one could survive that!"

"What does it matter?" Thomas had frozen, dropping Anne's hand to grip the mop handle more tightly. "The snakes are coming, even if their master is not!"

"Edgar's right. Not even the dead monsters get up after such a barrage," Drake said. He sounded warily confident, and Lewis glanced at him.

But they all froze at the voice. "Nobody except me gets up from that." Bailey was a mere silhouette in the cloud, but Lewis could see enough to watch him sit up and slowly climb to his feet. The others saw it as well.

"Run!" Lewis held his ground and fired again. "Now!"

"Follow me!" Thomas grabbed Anne's hand, pulling her with him as he ran toward the road. "Come on!"

"The guns are useless!" Lord Crandall caught Lewis by his coat and waved his flintlock toward the road. "It's time we leave, Captain."

"Hurry!" Edgar called from up ahead.

Lewis backed away as swiftly as he could, never taking his eyes from his nemesis. For an instant, Bailey seemed content, even amused, to merely watch from his black shroud. His lip curled in a nasty grin as the cloud flowed over him. The hissing of the snakes grew to deafening proportions, but he made no other move.

Somewhere ahead, Anne screamed and others joined in. Lewis kept his attention on the man who had slain his wife. He stopped suddenly, and took aim at the man's head. If such an injury could destroy the walking dead, then perhaps . . . he fired once more.

"For vengeance!"

Bailey jerked back but did not fall. After a moment, his grin grew wider and he waggled one finger at Lewis. "That feels lovely!" He stepped forward as a dark cloud shadowed his features.

"My God!" Lewis stared numbly as the hole in the man's head closed up. New skin formed over the wound until barely a blemish remained. The shot had not even slowed the Snake.

A cold dread rooted Lewis in place, and his hands shook as the truth crashed over him. The man who had killed his wife, the man whose death Lewis had planned and attempted—this man could not be killed. His quest could not succeed. Elise would remain trapped forever.

Frustration clawed its way up his throat, pulling a ragged scream from him.

"Not God. Lucius Knight." Bailey drew closer, his feet gliding across the ground without steps. The dark cloud swallowed him from behind as it rolled toward Lewis. Lewis did not move, did not run. He merely stood there, his hand limp at his side with the realization it could do no good.

"Captain, snap out of it, man!" Lord Crandall's voice boomed across the park; it wasn't possible to tell where he was, even if Lewis had been able to take his eyes off Bailey.

"Listen to your friend!" Elise's ring warmed him, jolting him out of Bailey's reach.

"Elise!" Lewis stepped back another pace.

"Run, my foolish love! Your life depends on it!"

Her insistence doused his sudden apathy. Turning his back on the man he had sworn to kill, he ran, doing his best to ignore the pain shooting through his sore shoulder. He spotted Lord Crandall at the edges of visibility.

"Keep moving!" Lewis waved him away, surprised that the man had stopped. He waited still, until he could fall into step next to Lewis.

Ahead, he could see Professor Drake and Gregory where the fog thinned. He saw no sign of the Bainbridges or Edgar, and he thought about the screams he'd heard. Lewis pounded after them, his booted feet thudding in the damp earth of the field, panic driving him in spite of his limp. But as fast as he ran, the snakes still neared, their hisses echoing around them in a cacophony of doom.

"The cloud is getting closer!" Lord Crandall said.

"As are the snakes!" Lewis glanced over his shoulder and gasped as he realized that dark vipers were mere yards away, closer than they should have been. Shadowy things moved along the ground, like whitecaps on an approaching wave, but this tide, he was well aware, was made of death. Somewhere in the center, Bailey walked among it, commanding the serpents—and Lewis could not stop him. His hands balled into fists as he tried to figure out a way to stop the Snake, but he could only run.

"We shot that fiend!" As Crandall matched Lewis's pace, lines of worry creased his features, and even his walrus moustache drooped as if the situation had dented his once impervious bravado. "He should be dead—dying, at least."

"Perhaps he's already dead." Professor Drake jogged at the edge of the lane that ringed the park, near one of the side streets, clutching at his side as if he had a stitch from the run.

Lewis hoped the old man had stopped only to allow them to catch up, for if this sprint had winded him, the scholar would not last long. He wondered if any of them would survive in the face of an enemy they could not kill, could not keep down. At least the dead things stayed down when they were shot in the head. At that thought, his fear burst, surging through him, filling him with panic and the desire to get away, to save himself, abandon Elise, the others, and escape what he could not fight.

His boots met the paving stones of the street, their soles adding to the cacophony of sounds reverberating against the buildings on either side of the road ahead. Whirling, only a stride out of the park, he caught a glimpse of a shadowy figure in the cloud and could not stop himself from firing again, despite the uselessness of the attempt. He had no other way to attack the man, but he could not accept his fate passively.

"You are an excellent shot, Captain Wentworth!" Bailey's voice echoed around them, distant and close at the same time. Lewis had the sinking feeling that it did not come from the figure in the cloud. "You've hit the bull's eye with every round!"

"Who are you, Bailey? What manner of creature is impervious to bullets?" Lord Crandall demanded. Were they not running for their lives, Lewis would have laughed at the affronted tone in his voice.

Disembodied laughter answered him.

"We aren't going to make it." Drake glanced past Lewis at the growing storm on their heels. "We must take shelter." He gestured toward the buildings with the sword.

"These street lights do not appear to offer any protection from this creature." Lord Crandall turned toward the nearest door. Pounding on it, he shouted, "I say, open up! We require immediate aid!"

No answer came. Lewis did not find that surprising.

"Keep moving," Lewis said. "They can't help us!"

"What about your wife?" Professor Drake's practical question belied his fear. "Can she not intervene as she did before?"

"She told me to run!" Lewis felt the air around him go warm as the oncoming cloud pushed over him.

"For God's sake, we have a woman out here!" Edgar was banging his meaty fists against a door to their right. Had the vapor overtaken them, surely Lewis would not have seen the man. He could barely make out his rotund frame. Thomas and Anne stood with him, slamming the planks of the door madly. They seemed most interested in breaking the door down; whatever had frightened them so badly was not forgotten. A light could be seen through the narrow windows on either side of the doorway.

Lewis realized with a chill that no other house had a light on. If these residents would not help them, he was not confident that anyone else was near enough to help them.

"Leave us alone," a woman cried from within. "There's no help for you here, or anywhere else in Mithras Court!"

"Keep moving!" Lewis's heart slammed against the inside of his chest as the hissing redoubled with the woman's words. The fog hesitated at the edge of the park. The scene was reminiscent of his dream, he thought, but while the light had saved him in those nightmares, here it did not frighten the serpents, and it would not help against a creature like Bailey. His mind groped madly for an answer. Perhaps a blast from a cannon could obliterate the man. If only his lancers were there!

Edgar looked past Lewis and his eyes bulged; he turned and ran. Thomas and Anne caught sight of the cloud and followed him, their screams mingling with the thunder of the oncoming storm. As Lewis watched them run, frozen in place, the cold crashed over him, engulfing him in its damp darkness. The force squeezed his chest like a vise, knocking the wind from his lungs and sending him sprawling into the professor. They fell hard against the pavement, and agonizing spikes of pain shot through Lewis's shoulder and leg. But the worst was yet to come—his gun slipped from his fingers, skittering out of reach.

He opened his mouth to scream, but managed only a low croak between gasps. The stinging fog pushed gaseous tentacles into his mouth, his nostrils, even his eyes. Cool, scaly forms slipped over him as snakes slithered across him. They squeezed against him, moving easily. Panic tore into him, ripping through his soul as his life, his quest for vengeance, flashed before him. The serpents grew heavier as hundreds of the creatures crawled over him, the first ones never leaving, joined by more and more. His panic dropped away as he realized that he was going to die. Joy touched him as he thought of joining Elise and he closed his eyes, seeing her twirling in her white dress on the grassy fields of Hyde Park, waiting easily now for the end.

CHAPTER *EIGHTEEN*

A woman's blood-curdling scream ripped through the fog. A man's throaty cry joined it, echoing against the buildings lost in the murk. As they faded, Lewis became aware that the snakes no longer moved over his body, and he blinked at the startling revelation that he was alive. He stared up into a light haze, lighter than the ever-present fog of the place. A glowing lamp resembling an iron flower hung over his head, its light pushing back the fine mist.

The screams, he realized, had been the sounds of people dying.

"Dear God, what happened?" Professor Drake sat up slowly on Lewis's right. His expression was a mix of wide-eyed bewilderment and barely-controlled fear.

Lewis gingerly rolled onto his side and pulled himself to his feet, turning to view the aftermath. Drake appeared rumpled, his coat smeared with dirt and grime; his hair was awry and his beard was studded with blades of grass, but he seemed none the worse for wear. He stood up slowly on wobbly legs, brushing off his coat and leaning on the cane. A half-dozen feet away, Lord Crandall lay curled on the ground, his back against the blocks of the nearest building, his pistol clutched in one hand. His eyes were closed tightly and he shook—whether from chills or fear was impossible to judge. The structure against which he lay drew Lewis's attention.

It sported half of a stone turret, rising above the square that formed the main building. Had they gained entry, it might have made an excellent defense; Lewis doubted if even Bailey could get through those walls. Turning his attention, he saw Gregory sprawled face down in the gutter a few feet away, one hand still gripping his musket. He twitched; Lewis could not decide whether he was alive or dead.

If the thick fog was any sign, Bailey had swept away from them, moving along the street in the direction of the pub. In its wake, Thomas lay on the thoroughfare as if tossed like a leaf in the wind. He flailed at the air around him, still trying to stop the snakes. Panic-stricken, his hair sticking out in every direction and his clothing disheveled, but he did not appear to be injured.

Lewis found no sign of Anne or Edgar, and he suspected he knew who had shrieked—and why.

Fear wrapped its icy hands around his chest, and he dared to wonder at the fate of their lost companions. Too many people had already died in this place, and he saw their faces in his mind, staring at him accusingly as if he could have saved them, but he could not think about that now. . It was vital that the survivors regroup immediately, lest they leave themselves open for another attack.

"Lord Crandall," Lewis kept his voice steady and firm. "Lord Crandall, the storm has passed."

Crandall's eyes opened. He blinked and reached up to brush the sweat from his face.

"I'm alive?" Focus came back to his incredulous gaze as he took in his surroundings.

"Indeed you are." Professor Drake said.

"But the snakes . . ." Lord Crandall stood up slowly, but swayed and dropped his flintlock. He managed to steady himself without falling. "They were all over me."

"As they were all of us." Lewis shivered at the memory. He would not soon forget the terrible events of the past moments.

"Did your wife save us, then?"

"It wasn't her." As much as he wished it had been, her ring had remained cold. "They passed us over. We must leave this place, lest they return to correct that."

"Of course." Lord Crandall's voice was no longer commanding, but he managed to sound in control of himself. "Thank you." He bent down to retrieve his pistol; as he stood, his gaze fixed on the area behind Lewis.

Lewis turned and spied his revolver where it had landed against the opposite building, a two-story brick structure with a stout double door. Eyeing both directions of the street warily, he hurried to the weapon and retrieved it. Revolver in hand, he backed away and cracked open the gun to count his remaining bullets. His heart chilled as he realized he had only two rounds left.

"Bloody hell." Gregory had recovered while Lewis armed himself. "What in the name of all that is holy was that?"

"There is nothing holy in this place." Lord Crandall approached him and handed over his pistol. "You'd best reload us."

"Whatever it was, bullets appear to be of little use," Professor Drake said.

"Bailey could have killed any of us, perhaps all of us, but he did not." Lewis added. "Apparently, he was not here for us." Lewis pointed down the street.

"Where is Anne?" Thomas asked, but he did not wait for an answer before shouting her name. He staggered to his feet and peered into the fog, at the buildings to each side, and settled his gaze on Lewis and the others. "Help me find her!"

Lewis scanned the fog as he reached Thomas, searching for any sign of their friends—or their enemies. He found no hint of either. The street remained clear, the homes on either side closed. The residents remained safely behind closed doors.

"We must find them!" Thomas took a step forward.

"We will." Lewis caught him by the arm and pulled him up short. Given the lack of bodies, it was possible, he thought, that the others might still live, though their screams had sounded final. But that proved nothing. "You must tell us what happened." Information was vital to any military action. Surely, since Thomas had been closer to them, he would know something, have seen something.

"Can your wife find them?" Thomas asked. "She must know where they've been taken."

If they're alive, Lewis thought. "If she knew, she would tell me." Lewis said. "Tell us what happened."

"They're gone," Thomas said, breaking the silence and the tension. "The snakes took them."

"What did you see?" Lord Crandall shifted to face the man.

"It was colder than any fog I've ever felt, even at sea." Thomas shivered. "The snakes rolled toward us like the water in the wake of a ship. Edgar and Anne were right here with me, our backs against the wall—we'd tried to gain entry into a house. We tried to run, but we were too late. The fog broke over me, knocking me to the ground. They both screamed, and . . ." He stopped, staring at memories. Lewis knew they would haunt him for the rest of his life. Thomas looked at them again, his eyes bright with tears.

"What?" Professor Drake put a comforting hand on the man's shoulder. "It's all right. Tell us."

"I saw something . . ." Thomas's eyes were haunted. "A snake, as thick as a fist, came out of the cloud and wrapped itself around Anne's ankle. Another grabbed Edgar, and they . . . they dragged my wife away. It happened so fast . . ." Thomas wiped the tears from his face and straightened. "Tell me what to do! How do we get them back? Surely there is a way." But he did not sound certain—he asked for a miracle and he knew it.

"They might still be alive," Professor Drake commented. Lewis wondered if he realized how slim the possibility might truly be.

"Yes, yes." Thomas's composure slipped again as hope came to his eyes. "We should arm ourselves and mount an attack on those responsible!"

"Arming ourselves is an excellent idea," Lewis said. "However, launching an attack against an unbeatable foe is suicide. We must first find them and learn more before taking any action." The memory of hundreds of dead Zulus, with their hide shields and spears strewn about the blood-spattered plains, came unbidden into his mind, and he pushed away the thought. In Mithras Court, he and his companions were the Zulus against an overwhelming and superior force. He did not wish to die the way the Zulus had.

"The Captain is correct." Lord Crandall crossed his arms over his broad chest. "Sound military strategy relies on knowledge of one's enemy. We are sadly lacking in that area. We must learn more."

Lewis looked at the gentleman in surprise. Not only had he

disagreed with nearly everything Lewis had said, but the man had gone out of his way to usurp his authority at every chance. Perhaps he had been so horrified by the Snake's assault that he was ready to acquiesce to Lewis's experience. He recovered a stoic expression and nodded at the man.

"We must return to the Laughing Gargoyle," Lewis said. Given their immediate need for information, the time had come to find Frederick and learn everything from him.

"What about Reggie and his wife?" Professor Drake asked. "Should we not search for them?" In the heat of the moment, Lewis had forgotten about the laborer and his wife. Their absence from the park did not bode well.

"Where would you have us look?" Lord Crandall fixed him with a challenging stare. "Mithras Court is not so small that we could easily find them."

"I assume that they were supposed to return to the Inn after investigating their section of the Mists?" Lewis glanced around the empty street, wondering if their enemy still watched.

"Yes." Lord Crandall inclined his head.

"Then we can look for them upon our return."

"And what then, Captain?" Thomas said. "How will going to the inn help us in any way?"

"Frederick is there." Lewis answered both questions by tapping his revolver. "This might not have any effect on Richard Bailey, but it will prove quite influential against our reluctant innkeeper."

"I see." Professor Drake frowned at the weapon; clearly, resorting to threats of violence against an ordinary citizen of Mithras Court was distasteful.

"An excellent idea." Lord Crandall nodded grimly. "He *will* tell us what we need to know."

"And then?" Thomas breathed out slowly.

"If we learn what we need, we can formulate a plan. Come on, everyone. Let's keep our pace brisk." Lewis accepted his cane from Drake and moved into the fog, never turning back to see if they were following; the sounds of their shoes on the stones was enough. Not even Lord Crandall argued.

=====MC=====

"What was that thing?" Gregory kept pace next to Lewis in the center of the old road. "That Bailey fellow—surely he's not a man. Is he a demon, a devil—or something else entirely?"

Lewis had seen dozens of men fall in battle and he knew that no human could survive the wounds Bailey had sustained. Given what he had seen of Mithras Court, it was not a stretch to imagine that the Snake was not human.

"He could be either of those—or neither," Professor Drake said before Lewis could answer. The old man rubbed his beard as he glanced around the street. "Mythology is full of stories of creatures that are more than men."

"Well, that is unenlightening, though certainly mysterious." Lord Crandall smirked at the professor. Lewis was not about to let their argument flare.

"That's enough." Lewis focused a baleful gaze on the gentleman. "And speak softly." He had not seen a single living soul since their attack, but that did not mean that there weren't spies about. "Professor, can history tell us anything about these creatures? You called them the minions of Mithras before." His tone was barely above a whisper as he glanced at the buildings to either side.

Drake frowned. "I'm afraid not. In the mythology, there is no mention of any preternatural abilities of these creatures, nor is there any mention of men controlling or transforming into them."

"What the devil are you talking about?" Lord Crandall sounded distracted as he peered into the gloom ahead, his flintlock ready. Thomas carried his mop handle, but kept silent.

"These minions of Lord Knight, and the fact that this place is called Mithras Court cannot be a coincidence." Drake shifted nervously.

"And what of these walking dead?" Lord Crandall inquired. "Are they mentioned in this mythos as well?"

"Not that I am aware of." The professor grew quiet.

"I take it there is no mention of ghosts in these Mithraic stories?"

Surely the professor would have volunteered such information had he known the answer to that question. Still, Lewis had to be certain. If the man knew anything that might help free Elise, he had to know. One thing held true in every war. No one could predict what information would be crucial and what useless.

"I'm sorry, my friend." The professor shook his head. "There is nothing in the mythology to explain how your wife can be here with us now. But many things are at work. This is not the pure myth. If it were, I fear Lord Knight would be Mithras himself."

Lewis waited for the professor to say more, but he offered nothing.

"Perhaps there is more at work here than this Mithras." Thomas said.

Lewis considered their encounters with the walking dead, the raven, and the snakes. It appeared that these creatures all worked in concert with one another, doing the bidding of Lucius Knight, but that explained little. How could any man control such creatures? It spoke of dark magic that he would have never considered prior to his entry into Mithras Court. Now, he could think of few other explanations for the things he had seen.

He kept silent as they traveled toward the next crossroads, pondering Mithras Court and gleaning no answers that seemed satisfactory. A few people appeared, moving about their business and doing their best to ignore Lewis and his companions. The locals seemed to move away as if they knew what had befallen them, or what would soon befall them.

Lewis paid them little heed as he searched the buildings, hoping to find an outfitter where they might purchase bullets and firearms. Guns would not help against Bailey, and most likely not against the other minions, but they had proven effective against the walking dead. One good shot to the head and those foul things went down.

"This is the street we took to arrive in the park. I can lead, sir." A somber Thomas Bainbridge gestured to the left as they approached an intersection. The older buildings gave way to the newer terraces they had become accustomed to in the Court. The street sign attached to the last flower-shaped lamp post indicated that the cross street was Minerva Lane. Thomas paused and looked at Lewis.

"Very well, Mr. Bainbridge." Lewis clapped a hand on his shoulder. "If there is any way we can save your wife, we will do it. I swear to you. You know that I understand your pain." The odds of finding them alive and saving them were not in their favor, but he could not bring himself to tell the man that. If Thomas did not know that, then hope would help. And if he did, it would be taken as a courtesy.

"Thank you, Captain Wentworth." Desperate hope brightened Thomas's face, as Lewis had hoped it would. "And allow me to express my condolences on the loss of your wife as well."

"Thank you." Lewis nodded. Although the odds might be against saving their two missing companions, he would give it his all. If they could be saved, then he would find a way to do so. "Lead on."

"Of course." Bainbridge took the lead. Lewis followed a pace behind.

Dozens of citizens soon came into view. They strolled the streets, peering into shops, walking pets, carrying bundles. An occasional cab rolled past, adding hooves to the auditory symphony. Minerva Lane appeared moderately prosperous, with an array of shops mixed among terrace houses and a few cafes and pubs. Normally, Lewis would have felt strength in being among the citizens. Here, their motives were suspect and his anxiety increased. Any one of them, perhaps all of them, could be working for the enemy. He did not wish to speculate on what people had to do to stay alive in such a place.

"What does one need to do to find an outfitter in this place?" Lord Crandall waved at a blacksmith's shop in annoyance. "Surely *someone* in Mithras Court must have weaponry and equipment."

"If the burned-out buildings the professor and I discovered are any indication of modern warfare, then I agree." Lewis adjusted his grip on his gun. "Frederick will tell us where to find them."

As the fog thinned near the end of the street, the train station appeared. Lewis slipped his revolver into his pocket, but kept a firm grip on it as he tried to prepare himself for what was to come. He was a soldier, he had been trained in the art of war, but to assault a citizen seemed contrary to all he had learned about a soldier's duty to protect civilians. He wondered what Elise would say, and hoped for a moment that she would appear and tell him herself. Her ring remained cold. Lewis would welcome her appearance for any reason, even to chastise him, just to look into her eyes once more.

Thinking of her, wishing for her to appear, sparked a memory from his meeting with Madame Catalena.

She has always been with you, bound to the circle of your love, the gypsy had told him, and again he wondered if his grief and pain might have caused Elise to become trapped between worlds. What if it had nothing to do with Bailey? He narrowed his eyes, turning away from his doubts. Regardless of the reason she had appeared to him, it had been wonderful to see her again. And should it prove to be he who was to blame, that elation would override his guilt as would the fact that her appearance had saved him and his companions more than once since their arrival in Mithras Court. Surely, that could not be a bad thing.

"Captain?"

At the sound of Lord Crandall's voice, Lewis realized he stood at the bottom of the inn's steps. He glanced up at the four-story structure and looked at the gentleman. Concern furrowed the man's brow and he appeared red-faced with embarrassment, a surprising expression on the man who, up to this point at least, had shown himself to be a posturing, self centered fool.

"What is it?" Lewis readied himself for a barrage of criticism.

"We are about to break the law and threaten a citizen," Lord Crandall said, quietly enough that their companions could not hear. "This is not something a gentleman does. There is no honor in it."

"Neither is it something a good soldier should ever do," Lewis said. "This situation is unique, and given the nature of this place, I believe we should treat all citizens as enemies. Their unwillingness to help us has aided the enemy, and it seems likely that at least some of them are actively working at counter purposes to us. They must be treated as enemy soldiers unless proven otherwise. Our goal is too important."

"They might simply be afraid for their lives." Professor Drake stepped silently up to them. He had overheard—or guessed—what they spoke of.

Fear was no excuse, Lewis thought. Fear kept men in chains and he would not accept that.

"Captain Wentworth's right," Lord Crandall said, his voice an angry hiss. "By accepting this way of life, by allowing some of us to be captured or killed and doing nothing to help us or even warn us, these people have proven that they truly are our enemies." He raised his pistol and waved it toward the inn door with a grim nod. "Frederick most of all."

"Thank you, Lord Crandall." Lewis hid his shock at the gentleman's support. Having the man in agreement felt almost as odd as just being in Mithras Court, as if yet another law of the universe had been turned upside down. "We will take this slowly, Professor. We are not criminals, but mark me . . . when the time comes, I will do what I must." Lewis put his Webley into his pocket. "I suggest, though, that we put our weapons away. We don't want Frederick to suspect anything before we are through the door." He glanced up at the daylight filtering through the thick fog.

"There are most likely some patrons inside." Lewis frowned. "Lord Crandall, if you and Gregory could keep them at bay before they can draw weapons, I'll handle Frederick myself." He took a breath and climbed the stairs.

The door was unlocked. Lewis opened it and led his companions inside without incident. The common room stood empty. The chairs rested upside down on the tabletops, and the stools were on the bar. The hearth was cold and dark, and only two dim lamps provided light. After a moment, Lewis strode across the room, looking for any hint of their host, but saw none.

As he neared the tapestry in the back, he slowed, then paused. Josephine and Ben had vanished from the tapestry, and four flesh-colored blots had appeared before the hut. They were blurred and indistinct, clearly still forming, but Lewis knew with cold certainty what it meant. Despair crossed his heart—the four forms could only be Edgar, Anne, Reggie, and Mary.

Chloe appeared as if from nowhere, standing behind the bar and watching them with a thoughtful expression on her face.

"Have you seen Frederick?" Lewis asked, wondering how she had reached the bar without them seeing her enter.

She pointed at the worn wooden stairway to the right of the tapestry. "He went upstairs about half an hour ago."

Lewis looked up. The narrow stairs ascended into shadow; a closed door was visible at the top. He glanced sideways at Lord Crandall, who had crossed the room silently. The gentleman nodded grimly, drawing his flintlock in emphasis. Lewis turned to Professor Drake, standing on his opposite side. The old man looked at him, a curious expression on his face, and after a moment he shrugged.

"Very well." Lewis turned to his companions. "Gentlemen, I suggest Lord Crandall, Professor Drake, and I handle this," Lewis said crisply. "Thomas, remain here with Gregory—keep a sharp eye out for any trouble."

"I understand, Captain." Gregory raised his musket. "I'll keep things honest. I'd give anything for a modern weapon, though."

"Agreed, but we must make do with what we have available." Lewis had already wished he had a Gatling gun, or some sticks of dynamite. But that was not possible in Mithras Court. He refocused his attention and slowly climbed the stairs, taking care to be as quiet as possible.

The wood creaked beneath him as he tried to move quietly. He went slower, breathing calmly, as if even the air movement might give them away. He reached the top, confident that although the wood had groaned, it had not given them away.

"He's here," Lewis said, his voice barely a whisper. "He has to be."

"Then we will interrogate him." Lord Crandall narrowed his eyes in deadly earnestness. "The time for evasion has passed."

Lewis reached out and the worn doorknob would not turn. "It's locked."

"Then a quiet approach is impossible," Lord Crandall said, a grim expression on his face.

"Can we break it down?" Professor Drake said from behind.

"Perhaps," Lewis said, but he could hear the doubt in his own voice. He launched himself at the door, throwing his shoulder into it, knocking it open to reveal a long, dimly-lit hallway beyond. A half dozen doors on either side stood closed. A candle burning in a small sconce on the right side provided a dim glow, while at the far end, a slash of brighter light spilled forth from a partly open door. As Lewis's eyes adjusted, a large form took shape at the back of the hallway as Frederick stepped out to face them.

"That's far enough!" Frederick said, and Lewis saw that the inn-keeper's pistol was aimed at them.

Lewis aimed his Webley at the innkeeper's chest and advanced several paces. He could feel the determination on his face; he had no intention of obeying Frederick.

"There are three of us to your one." Professor Drake stepped forward, sword at guard. "Do not force a confrontation you cannot win."

"There is no reason for bloodshed," Lewis said calmly. They needed to take the man alive to get answers to their questions. "But we insist that you tell us everything you know about Lord Knight, his minions, and Mithras Court."

"And why should I do such a thing?" Frederick made no move to lower his weapon. "Do you really think, after all you've seen here, that you could possibly frighten me as much as the Raven? Or Lord Knight himself?"

"More of our friends have been lost, taken by that Bailey fellow and someone we don't know," Professor Drake said. He sounded the voice of reason, and Lewis hoped the innkeeper would listen. "We do not ask you to fear us. We ask you to help us in our time of great need. Before it is too late."

"It was too late the moment you arrived in Mithras Court." Frederick met Drake's gaze levelly. "For all of you."

The man's statement angered Lewis. In war, the battle was not over until all possibilities had been exhausted and he had not remotely reached that point. He would not, *could* not give up. Nor would he ever accept defeat the way these people had. But before he could say anything, Crandall spoke.

"You let us be the judges of that." The floor creaked as Lord Crandall shifted his weight.

"You don't understand. I've done all I can to help you." Remorse tinted the innkeeper's tone, but Lewis heard no hint that he intended to comply with their request.

"I'm afraid we must insist." Lewis stepped forward slowly, prepared to bring the gun up, trying to make the man understand. He did not wish to kill him, not even after Frederick's failure to warn them had caused the deaths of so many of the survivors of the train ride. "You have answers we need." He paused beneath the candle and locked eyes with the man.

"That's far enough." The innkeeper held his pistol steady, and Lewis realized they did not have much leverage over Frederick, given the horrors of Mithras Court that the man lived with daily. Still, he might be persuaded.

"We don't have time for games. Tell us how to fight these minions of Lord Knight and where they've taken our friends." Lewis cocked the Webley. "Or this conversation will turn foul."

"If I knew how to fight them, don't you think I would?" Frederick's gun dipped. "I can't tell you anything more than I have . . . *he'll* know, and he'll punish me and my family."

"Who will know?" Professor Drake said. "Lucius Knight?"

"Eventually, yes." The man licked his lips nervously. "The Raven first, of course."

"Another of Lord Knight's minions, no doubt," Lord Crandall said matter-of-factly.

"Aye. And if I tell you any more, he'll know it. He is ever watching this inn, and ever listening to me." Frederick's voice dropped to a loud whisper. "As surely as he did last night, he already knows what is happening here. I can't tell you anything else. I have daughters to think about." He sighted down his pistol. "I will not let them be hurt. Or worse."

"We can fight this enemy together." Lewis said. "But we need your knowledge and assistance to find better weapons and plan an effective strategy."

"You don't understand what you're asking of me." Frederick's eyes narrowed and he took a step toward them. "I can't . . . I *won't* tell you anything else!"

"We do not wish this to become violent." Lewis fixed his attention on the man's eyes. "Please, lower your weapon and talk to us." He stepped forward slowly.

"Stay back!" Frederick's eyes widened and his voice shook. "I don't want to kill any of you but I'll defend myself. I swear it!"

"Put that pistol down and tell us what you know." Lord Crandall drew closer. "We can protect you against them."

"You couldn't even save your friends. How can you protect us? And what makes you think we need your help? Just leave us be!"

Lewis blinked at the man's statement. He had not considered that they might not wish to be helped. Even if they had adjusted to life in the Court and had come to accept it, they surely could not pass up a chance to fight back and escape.

"We're offering you the best chance you're likely to receive." Lewis drew himself up to his full height. "I am a trained soldier and a military strategist. With the right tools, we can defeat this enemy. No one is truly invincible."

"Long ago, some cowboys thought that as well, and they didn't last two days! Don't you see—Knight and his servants are unbeatable! No amount of knowledge of planning can change that! We're all cursed!" Spittle flew from his mouth.

"Who?" Lewis arched an eyebrow, but stopped moving lest he provoke Frederick into shooting at them.

"Two murderous American gunslingers." Frederick's shoulders relaxed slightly, but the gun remained steady. "They came here a dozen years ago and thought they could rule the place. The minions made short work of them and they were far more cutthroat than you ever could be!"

Lewis wondered how many people had been trapped there over the years, and it sent a shiver down his spine. Despite the fear, he had to believe it was possible to take their fight to the enemy. Everyone had a weakness. This man had to know something useful.

"You sound like a frightened woman!" Lord Crandall closed the distance by another pace, stepping ahead of Lewis. Lewis groaned at the man's foolish attempt at shaming the innkeeper, but before he could speak or try to stop him, Crandall finished. "Snap out of it, you pathetic coward! Drop that pistol, now!"

"No!" Lewis could see trouble coming, but it was too late, and he watched helplessly as Frederick squeezed the trigger.

A flash lit the hallway, burning into Lewis's eyes. The report of the gun was ear-splitting in the closed space. The candle went out and a gasp echoed through the hall. Worst was the sound of a body dropping in darkness.

Lewis's eyes fought to adjust to the dim hall. Slowly, he refocused in the light of the far doorway. Lord Crandall lay on his side, clutching his right leg as blood slowly pooled around him; Frederick stood just beyond, his gun hand at his side, eyes wide in shock as if he were surprised at what he had done. Without waiting for him to recover, Lewis leaped forward, hitting him across the head with the Webley. The big man's eyes rolled up into their sockets and he dropped to the ground next to Lord Crandall.

"Are you all right?" Professor Drake went to the gentleman's side.

"Concern for my well-being? From the man who nearly ruined me?" Lord Crandall muttered through clenched teeth. "Surely you jest."

"I don't know what you're talking about. I am merely concerned that one of our number has been injured." The professor bent down to look at the man's leg. "A flesh wound. The bullet passed through."

"Disappointed you'll not be rid of me yet?" Lord Crandall snapped angrily.

"This is no time for arguments." Lewis wondered how the professor could have brought ruin to Lord Crandall, but pushed his questions aside. "Professor, please go fetch the other men." He reached down to tear off a strip of Frederick's shirt and set about the task of dressing Lord Crandall's wound.

CHAPTER NINETEEN

"You are making a terrible mistake." Frederick's voice was calm and measured now. "If anyone sees us out here, the Raven will know, and he'll come for you. He might already be on his way."

The big man was tied securely with ropes, his hands behind his back. A red lump had formed on the side of his head where Lewis had hit him with his pistol. His clothing was disheveled and his shoulders slumped in defeat.

The group stood at the head of the stairs to the train station. Lewis faced the innkeeper and the others encircled them. In the fog, Lewis could barely discern the shapes of the buildings around the square. It would be virtually impossible for anyone to see them. Even if they did, he had Frederick's pistol loaded and in hand. Gregory had proven to be swift on the reload, not only working easily with his own gun, but with Lord Crandall's and Frederick's. Despite its age, the gun was in good working order. Using it would help Lewis conserve the remaining Webley bullets.

"I think not," Lord Crandall said. He leaned against Gregory. His leg wound had been superficial and the bleeding had stopped, but standing was painful. Lewis had wanted him to stay behind, but decided Crandall was entitled to be a part of this.

"Tell us about Lord Knight, his minions, and where they have taken our friends." Lewis repeated his earlier question. "Do this, and upon my word as a soldier, we shall release you."

"I've watched you." Frederick spat at Lewis's feet. "You're desperate, and you're doing something none of you is cut out for. You aren't villains, and even if you could convince yourselves to kill me, you would never harm my daughters. That's all I care about."

214

"You don't know us at all." Gregory moved into view, his weapon in plain sight.

"I'll do whatever I must to save Anne." Thomas pushed past Lewis and glared at the man. "By God, I'll push you down these stairs myself if it would save her!"

"I don't believe these men would let you do that." Frederick glanced at Lewis. "Would you, Captain? You are a Captain, right? Sworn to protect the innocent?"

Lewis frowned. No one in Mithras Court, other than the children, was innocent. They had given up and given in to the enemy, and that made them collaborators in Lewis's eyes. "We are not criminals—we are men of honor. What you fail to realize is that this is war, or as close as one might come. In war, men of good conscience are sometimes forced to do the unconscionable." He did not like it, but there it was: the inescapable truth glaring at them.

"You won't harm my daughters, and we both know it. I can see it in your eyes." Frederick raised his chin defiantly.

"We won't have to." Lewis stared at the man and glanced down the stairs.

"You wouldn't." The innkeeper's eyebrows rose.

"Gentlemen—if you would, please." Lewis motioned to Gregory and Thomas, who flanked the innkeeper. They both looked as though they would rather be somewhere else, but under the distaste he saw only resolve.

The men stepped forward, taking Frederick's arms and moving him a pace closer to the tunnel stairway. The gas lamps on the landings below were extinguished, but it was impossible to know whether by accident or design. Lewis wondered if it had been part of Knight's scheme to make it difficult for the survivors to return to the station.

They had anticipated that problem.

Lewis motioned to Professor Drake. The old man nodded and produced one of the lanterns from the Laughing Gargoyle.

"What in the name of hell are you doing?" Frederick struggled against his bonds, but Lewis and Gregory had tied him up securely. The muscles that hoisted kegs and crates could not loosen the sturdy knots.

The lantern threw a bright glow on their group as Professor Drake adjusted the light to direct its beam. He entered the tunnel, that terrible place where their nightmare had started a mere two days ago, and shined the light into the depths. Lewis heard hissing as the monsters within undoubtedly backed away from the light, retreating into the shadows. He took several steps toward the tunnel, never taking his eyes from Frederick's. Lewis turned, drawing his gaze away from the terrified innkeeper, and looked down the stairs. He took a deep breath and steadied himself with his cane.

Perhaps a dozen feet down the stairs, Lewis could see the walking dead. They stood at the edge of the light on the first landing, clawing at the glow of the light before them and hissing. Their rotting faces turned upward toward Lewis, sensing the presence of the living. He shivered, wondering what such a hideous state might feel like. Could those poor souls remember being alive?

"You won't do this. I took you in, fed you, gave you shelter from the elements and the undead!" Frederick interrupted Lewis's thoughts, his face red with near hysteria. "Have you no decency?"

"You also kept us from the truth of this place, an action which has cost several lives." Lord Crandall leaned toward him. "You'll hardly get sympathy from us."

"Bring him closer," Lewis said, looking at Thomas and Gregory. They moved him a pace closer to the stairway.

"I had no choice!" Frederick's veins popped as he struggled against his bonds. "The Raven . . . he would have slain my family had I warned you. You can't free yourselves, let alone all the Court—why would I be so foolish as to take your side?"

"Tell us what we wish to know." Lewis kept his voice low, calm, and serious as he stepped in front of the man, momentarily blocking the creatures from the innkeeper's view. "I promise you—we will protect your family to the best of our abilities."

"Don't you understand? There is no protection!" Frederick looked from one to the other frantically, hoping that one of the others might help him. Seeing no solace, he glared at Lewis. "Only the Vistani know the weaknesses of Lord Knight's minions, and they'll never tell you! I should know! They would not help us when we tried to fight back! Even Dragos, who offered us supplies, would not tell us!"

"Even if that is true, you know more than you are telling us." Lewis frowned. "Do you know where the Snake has taken our friends?"

Frederick shook his head but said nothing. Fear tugged at his features, his cheek twitching. Soon, Lewis thought, he would crack.

"To the first landing, gentlemen." Lewis motioned toward the depths below.

"Right, Captain," Gregory said. They pushed Frederick toward the first step, waiting for Lewis and Professor Drake to advance ahead of them. Frederick had an unobstructed view of the staircase and of the corpses gathered there, hissing.

Lewis swallowed slowly, pushing his fears away. With Drake and the lantern at his side, he descended into the depths. The rank stench of decaying flesh assaulted his nose immediately and he nearly gagged. But he pressed on. If they were to save their friends, they had to endure the horror below long enough to force Frederick to speak.

"Dear Lord!" The professor slowed for an instant before hurrying to catch up.

"You can't do this!" Frederick said. "Somebody help me!"

"You warned us—no one in Mithras Court will lift a finger to help us, and you know they won't help you." Lewis paused just above the first landing. "And yet, you did. Curious, that."

"Indeed," Professor Drake said, sounding thoughtful. "Why *did* you help us?"

"I can't tell you!" Frederick struggled, his face so red it looked as if he might explode. "Please—he'll kill my daughters!"

"Why would the Raven kill your daughters for answering a simple question?" Lewis asked, genuinely curious.

"Please, I must not answer!"

"Leave him on the landing, then." Lewis nodded to Gregory and Thomas.

"No!" Tears streamed down Frederick's face.

"Then tell us how we can save our friends. Or we will leave you to these monsters! Your daughters will have no father, and you will have taken the coward's way out, leaving them to suffer in this place while you are comfortably dead! Is that what you want for them?"

"You don't understand!" Frederick sobbed.

"Then make us understand!" Lewis leaned forward, his face within inches of the other man. "Why does this Raven watch you? Why did you aid us when we arrived?" He paused, but no response came. "How can we help our friends?"

Frederick closed his eyes, squeezing them tightly as if he could wish away the terror surrounding him.

"Gentlemen, please back away." Lewis motioned to the others.

"Captain, are you certain?" Thomas looked at the walking dead, crouched at the light's edge mere feet away from Lewis and the professor. They watched and hissed, pushing against each other.

"Go up the stairs, Thomas." Lewis straightened. "Trust me."

Thomas and Gregory retreated slowly, pausing midway between the landing and the top. They waited, watching, Gregory clasping his hands before him nervously. Thomas opened and closed his fists repeatedly and looked as if he were trying to hold himself together.

"You're bluffing." Frederick steadied his voice. "You won't do this to me. You won't."

"Professor, if you would climb until the edge of your light is there." Lewis motioned to a point at the edge of the landing, mere feet from where he stood with the innkeeper.

"As you wish." Drake backed slowly upward. As he climbed the worn stairs, the light receded with each step he took.

The monsters hissed as they inched forward within the shadows, their forms becoming clearer with every step. Six of them had gathered. Flesh hung loosely against bone on several, giving them an aged appearance. One looked more like a skeleton in tattered clothing than a person. A man and a woman in the fore had wounds visible on their skin. Their upper class clothing, torn in places, was somehow familiar. Lewis realized with horror that he gazed upon some of his less fortunate fellow passengers. They looked at him with empty eyes, opening their mouths and snarling. Could they hate him for surviving? Their burning anger was palpable.

"Captain Wentworth, you must release me!" Frederick's broad chest stretched against the bonds as if he thought his girth might burst the ropes. "Please! You don't know what you are doing!" The dead reached for him, their clawing fingers barely a foot from his legs. Their dead expressions were terrifying—there was no humanity there, only animal hunger.

"Help us, and I'll do as you ask." Lewis kept his tone calm and emotionless, though the walking dead chilled his insides as if he had swallowed ice. These sad remnants of humanity reminded him of the fate they would suffer if they did not fight back or escape. He pointed the pistol at them, knowing that if the lantern were extinguished, he would need to move swiftly to save himself.

"I . . . can't!"

"Retreat another pace, Professor." Lewis stepped behind Frederick.

"Of course."

The darkness closed in on the innkeeper as if it hungered for his flesh. The dead came closer until their claws nearly reached him. The fetid odor of decay and death floated upward, intensifying the putrid smell of the air. Lewis put his handkerchief up to his face and leaned forward to speak to Frederick.

"One more step and they'll have you," he said. This would be the moment Frederick would surrender . . . if indeed he would surrender. Possibly, Lewis had misjudged the man's resolve, and he might truly be willing to die to save his family.

The dead hissed and the burning hunger in their empty eye sockets scorched the atmosphere. Lewis's face flushed as if the air had grown warmer around them. A salty trickle of sweat dripped down his face. This was an incredible gamble; should it backfire, they would all perish. Before he could berate himself for risking innocents, Elise's ring grew warm against him.

"Do not harm this man." Elise's voice jarred Lewis. "You will need him." He blinked and looked around, but did not see her. Judging by the lack of a response from the others, only he had heard her this time.

"You have five seconds before I let them have you," Lewis said, ignoring her warning. When he reached three in his mind, the inn-keeper spoke.

"All right!" Frederick took a tiny hop backward. "I'll help you. Just get me out of here!"

"Swear on the lives of your daughters." Lewis held his ground. If they were to believe him, then his promise needed collateral. He did not think Frederick would break such a vow.

"I swear!"

Lewis straightened and motioned for Drake, relieved that he could end this madness. The old man joined him, the light from his lantern pushing back the darkness and the dead, who shrank away with angry rasps. Lewis let out a slow breath, thankful that he had not needed to do more, and glad that nothing had gone awry.

"We're listening." Lewis made no move to untie Frederick. He would let the man prove he would keep his word.

"I offered you my help when you arrived," he gasped as if out of breath, "as a result of my role in the rebellion so long ago. I am Lord Knight's greeter to all newcomers into Mithras Court. It is my job to provide a safe haven for a limited time."

"I sense you are not happy with that arrangement." Lewis saw anger in the man's eyes behind the fear. "You are as a slave, yes?"

"Yes." Frederick eyed the monsters nervously. "We've been here for thirty-five years. At first, we resisted Lord Knight, but in the end we were powerless to stop him and his servants. They slaughtered many of us, and they forced oaths of allegiance from the survivors."

He paused and looked ashamed, even through the fear—Frederick kept glancing at the dead that clustered near the edge of the light, near the warmth of the living. "My duties," he said, "also include reporting on the comings and goings of newcomers. Each night I must meet with the Raven and tell him what I know. I have done so faithfully, unable and unwilling to aid any of the poor souls whom the Mists see fit to bring here, and yet the Raven still does not trust me. Still he watches me."

"So it is the Mists that bring people here, not Lord Knight?" Lewis said. He had believed Madame Catalena when she had told him this, but Frederick's confirmation quashed any remaining doubt he had, however small.

"Aye. Lord Knight is as trapped here as the rest of us." He struggled against the ropes again. "If the Raven finds out I've told you this, he'll do more than kill me. He'll see to it that my daughters become the walking dead, and then he'll feed me to them!"

"No one else is going to die!" Lewis glared at Frederick. "No one else."

Frederick sobered, looking at Lewis with the faintest touch of hope in his eyes. He glanced at Gregory. "Maybe I am a coward, but I have my daughters to think of. I'm not willing to risk their lives . . . not after what Lord Knight did to their mother." He shivered and tears brimmed in his eyes.

What have we done? Guilt numbed Lewis's chest, but he forced it back. He had done what he had to do.

"What does this have to do with finding the others?" Thomas's voice was nervous as he came down the stairs. He moved toward Frederick and started untying the ropes.

Lewis wanted to tell Thomas not to allow his hopes to grow, for having heard their screams and seen them in the tapestry, he doubted that they were alive. Still, he had to be sure, had to see them with his own eyes, for what if the tapestry showed unconscious or sleeping forms? What if, in its mockery, it could trick them with such a ruse?

"I can't tell you any more . . . they will hear . . ." He looked at the dead. "The dead are the eyes and ears of Lucius Knight . . . he does not focus his attentions on more than a few of them at a time, but the more we talk of these things, the greater the chance of him knowing. He looks for his servants, you see."

"Then we'll return to the inn," Lewis said. "The dead can't hear us inside, can they?"

"No, but the Raven and his birds watch the inn day and night." Frederick slumped against the wall, overcome with exhaustion. "If you can tell us nothing else, how will you fulfill your promise to help us save our friends?" Professor Drake rubbed his beard thoughtfully, his eyes watching both the innkeeper and the dead.

"I must show you." Frederick turned his head and locked eyes with Lewis. "I will take you to a place where you can help your friends tonight, just before first night."

"Why should we believe you?" Gregory crossed his arms.

"He speaks the truth." Elise's voice was a whisper in Lewis's ear. "He is trying to help you, but someone compels him to silence. He must *show* you."

"I see no deception in him." Lewis tilted his head in acknowledgement and glanced around. "We should leave this place quickly."

Thomas nodded, hard at work on the bonds. As his hands became free, Frederick helped pull the ropes off and took several steps to stretch his legs. He looked at Lewis.

"What next? What is our destination?" Lewis felt the weight of the dark hunger lurking behind them. He began moving up the steps.

"We should return to the inn, gather lanterns and oil, and wait until just before first night." Frederick glanced at the dead. "We must hurry."

"Very well. We will do as you say." Lewis mounted the stairs, glad to leave the gaping tunnel and the ravenous dead behind them. If and when he escaped this place, the images of the dead would haunt his dreams until the end of his days.

CHAPTER TWENTY

"How do we know we can trust Frederick?" Safely back in the parlor of the Laughing Gargoyle, Lord Crandall leaned back on the sofa, his leg resting on the cushions. Blood had seeped through his bandages, but the wound seemed to have closed. The immediate danger was past.

Lewis stood at the door to the common room. The serving girls moved about, tending to the four patrons who had recently arrived. Frederick was nowhere to be seen, but Lewis believed the man would appear in time to help them. The vow the innkeeper had taken on the lives of his daughters, combined with Elise's support for the man, carried great weight with him.

If only he could really talk with her—if only she would return for more than a moment. *Talk to me, Elise. Please.* He had missed her so much for so long, and although he could miraculously speak to her, he could barely discuss anything, could not truly enjoy her company, her conversation, her buoyant spirit. She did not answer his thoughts and he gave up, turning to the others.

"The man gave us his word." Professor Drake worked to adjust one of three lanterns on the floor. Lewis was glad for the man's attentiveness to the task; they would need all the lamps in working order if they were to remain unmolested by the denizens of Mithras Court after dark.

"You would talk to me about a man's word? Incredible." Lord Crandall glared at the professor. Lewis tensed. This was not the time or place for an argument, but curiosity over the men's feud got the better of him.

"Do you mean to impugn my honor, sir?" Professor Drake paused in his task. Perhaps the professor had finally been pushed too far.

"Not yet."

"You've antagonized me since our introduction." Drake spoke with the frustration of a parent whose child was banging a toy incessantly. "Why do you bear me ill will, Lord Crandall? Do not think to evade this question. I *will* have an answer, if you please."

"January, 1857." Lord Crandall's eyes flashed with anger.

"What the devil are you talking about, man?" Drake set down the lantern and looked at him in confusion.

Lewis remained silent now. So far the men had avoided examining the topic, but if this conversation would resolve it, he would not stop them again.

"You really don't know, do you?" Lord Crandall slowly stood, taking care not to put pressure on his wounded leg. He stepped forward and glared down at the professor. "Let me provide you with another clue. Missing artifacts from an archaeology dig in Rome, 1857."

"The temple of Minerva?" The professor blinked in surprise.

"Very good, professor." Lord Crandall looked around the room at the faces of their companions. "In 1857, my family's fortunes had fallen into, shall we say, a less than favorable condition. In an attempt to remedy that situation, I spent what remaining monies I had on an archaeological expedition to a small temple being excavated outside of Rome. I'd arranged for the British Museum to purchase whatever artifacts were discovered, at a handsome profit for myself." He paced a bit.

The professor's eyes widened as Crandall spoke.

"Yes, I see you remember." Lord Crandall scowled at the man. "*You* made arrangements with a local magistrate to intercept that crate. You absconded with the most valuable artifacts."

"Is this true, Professor?" Lewis was surprised that the man could have been involved in something illegal. To learn that he could have perpetrated such an act threatened his trust.

The professor's face turned crimson, though Lewis could not be sure if it was embarrassment or anger. He bowed his head in defeat.

"I did not realize it was you from whom I liberated those items.

Nor did I know it would cause you financial woes." Drake's voice was quiet and remorseful.

"Financial woes!" Crandall loomed over the man. "You sullied my good name as my various promises fell apart and friends and colleagues called in their debts. You nearly ruined me! I was forced to sell my family's estate and move to a home in the city. I had to let go of my staff, save for Gregory, and was forced to liquidate most of my assets!"

Lewis watched and waited, wanting to learn more.

"If you knew of this from the moment we met, why did you not say something?" Professor Drake asked.

"In the heat of battle, a soldier does not attack his fellows lest he place his entire battalion in jeopardy!" Lord Crandall said, his anger boiling over.

"And yet you have argued many points with Captain Wentworth, at least until the Snake attacked us," Thomas said from the other side of the room.

"Lord Crandall was merely doing his duty as a member of the gentry to assume the mantle of command," Gregory said.

"Please, gentlemen. There is no point to this!" Lewis said. "If we are to survive, then we must put all differences aside, at least until we have escaped from this place. Nothing good can come of this dissension and I will have *no* more of it!"

"Lord Crandall." Professor Drake slowly stood and looked into the man's angry eyes. "I ask you to please accept my apologies. Perhaps there is no excuse for my behavior, but I will tell you that I did what was necessary to honor the memory of my brother, God rest his soul."

"Why should I believe you?" Lord Crandall glared at the man.

"Because I have proven myself a stalwart ally to our group since our arrival here." Professor Drake looked at the man calmly. "It was no secret that you did not like or trust me. Were I truly your enemy, I could have killed you on several occasions and no one would have been the wiser."

Lord Crandall stared at the man for nearly a minute, as if trying to decide what action to take. Sweat beaded on his forehead and his moustache drooped. Finally, Crandall's shoulders relaxed.

"I'll accept that. For the moment." The harshness in his eyes spoke volumes. Had this taken place a century earlier, Lewis thought, a challenge to a duel would have followed. He was glad that neither man had seen fit to escalate to such a foolish situation.

"Very good, gentlemen. Let us not speak of this again. We have more important matters to attend to," Lewis said.

Professor Drake nodded.

"Agreed." Lord Crandall said.

"Since we are in agreement that we can trust Frederick, at least for the moment, does that also mean we can trust his daughters?" Gregory asked.

"I believe we can." Lewis glanced out the door and saw Chloe and Jenna still moving about the common room.

Upon returning to the pub, the innkeeper had explained the situation to his daughters. Although Chloe and Jenna were frightened by the knowledge that their father would lend aid and thus endanger them all, he had convinced them that they would not be harmed. They had scowled at Lewis and gone about their work.

"If any of them are lying to us, I'll shoot them." Thomas gripped the arms of his chair so tightly that his knuckles turned white. Lewis could understand his anger. Everything hinged on Frederick and his family honoring their promises. If they had lied, or Frederick intended to betray them, then all hope of saving Anne and Edgar would be gone.

The man's anger resonated with Lewis's thirst for vengeance, which in turn made him think of Elise. He desperately wished he could hold her hand once more, but he would settle for being able to have a conversation with her. That was denied to him, for she did not reappear, and she had not answered his whispered questions.

"If they were to lead us into a trap, then I hardly think it will matter," Gregory said. He held the musket in one hand, ready to use it in an instant.

"I seriously doubt that he's willing to betray us. If any of us survived such an event, he knows it would mean his death. Considering what is at stake, I do not think he would risk betraying us." Professor Drake was readying the final lantern.

"He will not betray us." Lewis felt as confident as he sounded. Frederick meant to keep his promise. He was sure of it. "Now, I suggest we prepare our weapons and ready ourselves. Lord Crandall, are you well enough to travel?"

"It is only a flesh wound. I shall be fine. Even if I was not, you need me. I have experience with firearms and I'm an excellent shot." Lord Crandall displayed his flintlock. "I will participate fully."

Lewis could not argue with that; he needed all the men he could muster. He glanced at Lord Crandall's flintlock and touched the pistol in his own belt. He had not allowed Frederick to take the weapon back. Thomas had asked about acquiring additional pistols, but given the ineffectiveness of firearms against Lord Knight's minions, Lewis doubted it would matter. They would find other methods in the final confrontation.

A knock drew his attention and he turned to the door as Frederick pushed it open slowly. He entered with a nervous glance at them. The innkeeper wore a dark green tunic and a black cloak, unlike the leather vest he normally wore over a white shirt. Lewis concluded it was for camouflage. A lantern dangled from his right hand, and he held a cutlass in his left.

"Night is approaching," he said somberly, pointing to the windows, although the drapes were drawn and they could not see outside. "Are you ready?"

"Indeed we are." Lord Crandall said.

"If you mean to go through with this, then I must ask something of each of you." Frederick stepped toward them.

"We're listening." Professor Drake said.

"*We* are listening." Lord Crandall said.

Frederick ignored them. "You must promise to remain absolutely silent and do exactly as I say or you'll place us in danger. If they hear us, this will all be for nothing." He frowned. "This is very dangerous, even with our preparations."

"We are aware of the danger," Professor Drake said. "Even so, we must help our friends."

"I will take you to them and show you how to set them free, but if you don't listen to me when the time comes, you risk death from our enemies." Frederick glanced at Professor Drake, Lord Crandall, Gregory, and Lewis. "Can you agree to this?"

"We will do as you say." Lewis understood that in the field it was important to heed the men who knew the terrain or had intelligence of their mission. He frowned, for he also knew that no plan survived the field of battle. Some of them would likely die. "We are ready, then," he added, retrieving a lantern and looking expectantly at the innkeeper.

"Do not light them until I tell you." Frederick started for the door. "Follow me."

"Where are we going exactly?" Professor Drake held a lantern in one hand.

"Back to the wooded park where the Snake attacked you." Frederick did not wait for a response as he stepped through the door into the common room.

Lewis dropped a hand to his pocket, feeling the comforting weight of his Webley. He had only two shots remaining, short of a reload for the pistol. He exchanged a nervous look with Lord Crandall and Professor Drake, but followed the innkeeper, conscious of his companions hurrying after him.

He wondered what had become of Elise. She did not appear to answer his query.

=====MC=====

"I cannot believe we are here again, given what happened earlier today," Professor Drake said to Lewis as they strode down the ancient street where they had been attacked by Bailey. The old man's face seemed paler than normal. "It seems the height of foolishness to return where we know they watch."

"Then again, this could be the last place they would look for us." A shiver slid down Lewis's spine as he glanced at the squat stone buildings to either side, where the two people they sought to rescue had been taken—or killed. He hoped his guess was correct, that no one would think to look for them in the place that had caused them pain and taken such a toll on their group.

Although the fog prevented him from seeing far, he knew the end of the street had to be near. The open field and the forest beyond would be only a short distance away.

"When first night falls, all talk must stop." Frederick glanced up at the fog-enshrouded sky.

Lewis followed his gaze and noted that already the sun's light had dimmed, and the shadows drew closer as the fog thickened. He drew the musket pistol, catching sight of the street's end as he looked to the path ahead. The crossroad that divided Mithras Court and the park was free of traffic, even pedestrians, though the distant sound of hooves and the occasional shout reminded him that they were not truly alone. A chill wind whipped up as they reached the street, swirling the fog away suddenly, and the grassy field and the massive oak trees of the forest beyond materialized as if they had not existed a moment ago.

"It's time." Frederick paused at the edge of the park and turned to face them. "Hood your lanterns and keep your mouths closed. If we are spotted, it will mean the death of all of us."

"We understand." Lewis passed his cane to Professor Drake and shielded his lantern. Its beam vanished, leaving only a dull glow around the base. Next to him, Drake followed suit, plunging them into near-total darkness.

"Let's go." Frederick stepped onto the empty field, crossing it swiftly. He turned away from the dirt road at the last minute, moving along the forest's edge, where a barely-visible path cut into the trees.

Lewis peered into the wood, surprised to see that the area between the trees was choked with dark vegetation. Surely the massive tree trunks would have prevented underbrush from growing there. The faint odor of decaying leaves reached his nostrils and he had the strange sensation that the plants themselves watched him. He shook himself and focused on Frederick.

The innkeeper paused a few dozen feet from the dirt road. He glanced back. A small trail led into the forest, a dark and ominous hole in the thick underbrush. He motioned to it.

"This is where we go," he said. "Do not fear. The dead will not walk this path, whether it is light or dark."

"Why is that?" Thomas said from the rear of the group.

"I'm not sure. Some say this is an ancient path worn by the druids themselves and that nothing can grow on it because of primeval magic." Frederick shrugged. "I only know that the dead avoid it and nothing will grow across it."

"We'll accept your word," Lewis whispered, quietly enough not to alert the dead.

"Lead on," Lord Crandall whispered.

Frederick entered the wood. Professor Drake followed a few steps behind. Lewis hurried after them. The rich smell of mold and rotting wood intensified and the air grew damp and colder. It was a forbidding place, and Lewis did not envy Frederick his position in the lead. The trail appeared well-maintained—the cut underbrush left Lewis to wonder if there were people living in the woods, perhaps using the trail as refuge at night. He saw no one else, however, and the remaining daylight vanished within two steps, plunging them into near darkness. Lewis could barely see the dim shapes of the two men in front of him, let alone anyone hiding in the forest. Panic clawed at him, but he forced himself to stay focused and alert, and swiftly realized the forest was calm and silent on either side. Frederick was correct; none of the walking dead moved about.

Behind him, the occasional crunch of leaves or crack of twigs reminded him that the rest of his companions followed closely. He hoped that they could remain true to their words and do as Frederick said, for he believed the man's warning of the dire consequences of disobeying him. Although he could not see or hear the dead, that did not rule out the possibility that they were there, or that there were other things to fear.

Several minutes of travel brought them to the edge of a large clearing. The rough outline of a house-sized foundation marked the end of the path. Beyond it, dried and dead soil, completely devoid of any plant life, covered the area. Two dark mounds of freshly-turned earth rose up in the clearing's center, looking like giant ant hills. The forest beyond appeared as ancient and darkly foreboding as the one through which they had come. Discovering ancient ruins in the woods might once have intrigued and excited Lewis when

Elise had been at his side, but nothing was so enticing about the scene before him now.

Frederick put his finger to his lips. He stepped inside the boundary of the ruined structure, halting in the middle of the rough stone foundation and motioning for them to join him inside. He watched them enter the border one by one, his shoulders relaxing a little more as each person joined him. He breathed a sigh as soon as they had all entered.

"It's safe to talk now. This foundation is hallowed ground, the only place that remains free of the dead in Mithras Court," he said. "Not even Lord Knight and his minions can see us, as long as we remain inside this building."

"This was a church?" Professor Drake asked.

"Churches were destroyed by Lord Knight and his minions years ago." Frederick chuckled humorlessly, looking at the foundation around them. "This is something much older. No one's sure who built it."

"Perhaps the druids," Professor Drake said.

"Maybe." Frederick shrugged. "All I know is that it works."

"This is very interesting." Lord Crandall waved his flintlock in a loose grip. "But what the devil are we doing here?"

"You asked me to help you save your friends, did you not?" Frederick stared at him. "This is where they will be."

"In the middle of these woods?" Thomas swept a hand over the clearing.

"Aye." Frederick looked up. "It's dark now. They'll be here soon."

"Why would they come here?" Lewis did not doubt him, but an explanation could help them. "Especially given that this clearing is adjacent to the church that not even Lord Knight can touch?"

"I don't know why they do it here."

"Why they do what?" Thomas snapped his head around in shock as he focused on the innkeeper's statement. Lewis thought the phrasing odd, and tensed for action.

"Tell us what they do here, exactly," Lewis said, gripping his weapon tightly.

"It is better that you see for yourselves. Do not leave this place until I say so."

"Right." Lewis studied Frederick. He appeared nervous, but not so scared as he would be if he were about to betray them. The thought that these invisible walls might shield them from view was ludicrous—as ludicrous as the walking dead or the bulletproof Snake. For the moment, Lewis believed the man. His thoughts were interrupted as he heard movement on the far side of the clearing. "Quiet, everyone. Someone's coming!"

"They can't hear us. But why take any chances? Now watch, all of you." Frederick stepped closer to the edge of the foundation and peered ahead. "You must see this."

Four torches appeared abruptly, bobbing through the woods, and with the light they provided Lewis could see a small gap in the underbrush. As the procession drew closer, Lewis recognized the blue coats and helmets of the Metropolitan Police. They stepped into the clearing, forming up in front of the mounds. He was shocked to see the gray-haired Inspector Newton. Lewis did not recognize the other three officers.

Newton eyed the clearing and the foundation, his gray eyes narrowing as he scrutinized the spot where Lewis and the others stood. But as Frederick had predicted, he did not notice them. Lewis breathed a sigh of relief at their security.

"Inspector Newton," Lewis said quietly. It made sense that the man who had once sworn to protect the citizens of his district would ally himself with Lord Knight. Perhaps he thought that doing so kept them safer, but it did nothing to aid newcomers, and in fact, endangered them.

"Everyone in Mithras Court serves Lord Knight one way or another." Sorrow tinged Frederick's voice. He looked at the ground as if he could not bear to meet Lewis's eyes. "It is inevitable."

"What are they doing?" Thomas stepped closer. "Where is Anne?"

"Watch."

The last of the light faded from the sky and would have plunged them into complete darkness were it not for the torches carried by the officers. As if it were a signal, the distant moaning of the undead echoed through the trees, closer than Lewis would have liked. The earthen mounds shifted and soil slid to either side.

"What in the name of God!" Professor Drake took a step back.

"What's happening?" Thomas's voice shook.

Lewis's chest tightened. As he watched, a familiar gloved hand shot up from the nearest mound even as feet pushed up from the second pile. A sickening feeling crawled across Lewis's stomach as he watched creatures slowly unearth themselves from their graves while the officers stood silently watching.

"Oh dear Lord . . ." Gregory said.

"No, it cannot be!" Thomas said. "Anne!"

As the pair rose from their graves, Lewis's heart shrank into a ball of dread. True to his word, Frederick had delivered them to their lost comrades. Each bore the injuries of their death. Dozens of red welts marked snake bites on Edgar and Anne, and suddenly it all became clear to Lewis. The dead in Mithras Court all rose to wander the darkness and the shadows. This was why he recognized the undead creatures on the train station's stairs and this was how these walking dead always seemed to be around. Not even death could set one free of this place. The truth froze Lewis in place and for an instant, even had he wished to shoot at them, he could simply not move.

"What's happened to them?" Lord Crandall whirled toward Frederick, accusation in his voice as if the innkeeper had caused their deaths and resurrections.

"They're dead!" Frederick said, glaring at them all. "And they belong to *him* now."

"What do you mean?" Lewis watched as the pair staggered on unsteady limbs toward the officers.

"Look!" Frederick pointed behind the corpses.

"Welcome, my friends. Do not be afraid." A tall man in a black coat and hat stepped forward, his aquiline features giving him a bird-like quality. One finger bore a diamond ring of obvious worth, and the fine cut of his clothing would have marked him as a noble-man in London. A large black raven perched on each shoulder. He seemed to pull a thick dark fog with him like a cape.

The dead hissed, shying away from the torches held by Newton and his officers, and moved toward the Raven. They bowed their heads to him in acquiescence, demonstrating rudimentary intel-ligence, as Lewis had suspected.

"You will follow these officers. They will take you to Lord Knight, your new lord and master."

"Do you understand now?" Frederick scowled. "Everyone who lives in this place serves Lord Knight, in life and in death. There is no way to resist a man who can enslave your corpse."

"You told us you would help us save them!" Thomas grabbed Frederick by the lapels. "You bastard!"

"This isn't helping!" Lewis grabbed Thomas and pulled him off the man. "It's not his fault!"

"But Anne!" Thomas cried. "Look at her!"

"It's Knight's fault! He is the true villain!" Lewis released him and met his distraught stare with a steady gaze. "Save your anger for him!"

Thomas glared at him for a moment, then his shoulders slumped in defeat. "You're right. I know you're right." To Frederick, he said, "I'm sorry."

Frederick shrugged.

Lewis turned back to watch the officers, the dead, and the man in the top hat. As Frederick had predicted, none of them, dead or living, noticed their group, not even with Thomas's shouting. He desperately wished for Elise to appear. He needed her guidance more than ever. She might be able to explain what they were seeing. At the very least, she would offer him comfort in the face of the horrifying realization of the dead.

"You *can* save them," the innkeeper said. "If you have the stomach."

"How?" Thomas shook. "How can we save them from this?" His anger slipped to tear-streaked sorrow, but he did not waver.

"One bullet to the head and they will not rise again." Sympathy shone in Frederick's eyes. "If you truly love them, if you truly want to save them, then you must kill them."

"No . . ." Bainbridge blinked back his tears and stared into the clearing at his dead wife. Lewis shuddered at the pain of having a loved one torn away; he could not imagine to the horror of seeing a loved one rise from the dead, a mindless walking corpse. Pity surged through him. He wished he could do something to spare the man from it.

A chill swept through him at the realization that Frederick had kept his word. He had provided them with a terrible opportunity to save their friends. He stared at their broken comrades and worked up the courage to raise his pistol.

CHAPTER *TWENTY-ONE*

"Do you see what you're up against? The Mists around Mithras Court are endless and deadly. No one here will offer you the slightest aid, and even the Vistani will ignore your cries. Help isn't coming, and not even death offers you a way out. Fighting is pointless. You must surrender to his will. It's the only way to save yourselves." Frederick motioned toward the clearing.

"There will be no surrender." Lewis turned to the innkeeper, bringing his pistol up and aiming at him. "Is that clear?"

"Idiots! I'm trying to help you." Frederick glanced at the pistol, his eyes darting between the weapon and the scene unfolding in the clearing. "I could have let you die, but you convinced me to help you. That's what I'm doing by showing you the pointlessness of fighting. You have to give in to join Lord Knight—it's the only way. He might go easy on you if you go to him now!"

"I swear to you on my wife's grave that you will die if you attempt to undermine our position." Lewis pulled the hammer back.

"I have done what I promised. I have shown you how to help your friends." Frederick clenched his teeth. "If you want to save them, you have to kill them."

"Kill Anne? This is madness!" Thomas looked frantically at Lewis, tears streaking his face. "Can't your wife help them, Captain?"

"I don't think so. I'm sorry." Lewis shivered uncontrollably as his face flushed with fear and rage. The rushing sound that rang through his ears in battle echoed once again, grounding him, even in this sea of insanity and horror.

"Anne . . ." Thomas said, so softly that Lewis barely heard him.

"We must destroy these foul creatures and their master." Lord

Crandall brandished his pistol. "Can we not shoot them from the safety of this area?"

"Bullets won't cross the foundation," Frederick said. "I've tried. Even if they did, they would do nothing against the Raven. He's invincible."

"No one is invincible." Gregory glowered at Frederick as if he were to be his target rather than the Raven, Newton, or their dead friends. Lewis did not protest. Frederick had done as he had promised, yet he had been deceptive with them.

Lewis thought that Gregory might be wrong.

"No . . ." Bainbridge said, staring at Anne from the boundary's edge.

"Go now, children of death." The Raven's voice was thick with joy. "Your master awaits!"

The dead moaned in response, turning slowly toward the policemen.

"This way, men." Inspector Newton motioned toward the trail down which they had come. Although the burly man's voice was confident, his face was pale and his expression was haunted as he turned away from the scene. The dead shambled after the officers slowly, staying at the edge of their torchlight.

"Can we truly destroy them?" Professor Drake said, his voice steady. "How do we know that they do not return later, even after being shot in the head?" He had drawn the sword form the cane and held it ready.

Lewis nodded. For all they knew, Knight could resurrect the dead over and over again. He shivered at the hideous thought.

"When you burn them, or put a round through their heads, they don't come back," Frederick said. "But if you're asking me whether their souls are set free when they're destroyed . . . I don't know. Anything is better than this . . . anything."

"I must help Anne!" Thomas wrenched the flintlock from Lewis's grasp and darted forward.

"Stop him!" Frederick lunged for the man. "He'll get us all killed!"

"Wait!" Lewis dived after him, catching Thomas's jacket, and they hit the ground hard. But as the others ran to help, Thomas leaped up, free of his coat, and crossed the foundation. A shimmering green curtain of light appeared, forming a wall above the foundation for an instant. It vanished with a faint pop that echoed around them. It hadn't stopped Thomas and he entered the clearing, running for his wife.

"What's this?" The Raven turned, his black eyes focusing on Thomas.

"You there, halt!" Newton spun, drawing a flintlock in one fluid motion. His men were slower as they drew their own weapons, but if Thomas were to survive, it would take a miracle, for he ran straight for the dead.

The dead stopped, sniffing the air and craning their necks toward him. Edgar clawed at Thomas as he passed, gnashing his teeth like a carnivorous animal. As he got close to her, Anne raised her arms in a parody of an embrace, but her dead, fogged eyes stared vacantly, and that stopped him. Thomas raised the pistol. Newton saw his hesitation and aimed his own gun, finger tightening on the trigger. Lewis could do nothing, shocked into stillness for that crucial moment.

"Wait, Inspector!" The Raven focused his dark eyes on the officer and his men. "Let this be their first blood!" He grinned.

The inspector and his men stopped as if they were marionettes whose cords had been cut. They lowered their guns almost as one, and they watched the drama without expression.

"We must aid Thomas." Lewis gritted his teeth, reached into his pocket, and drew the Webley.

"Captain, don't be a fool," Frederick hissed. "He's lost!"

"We cannot allow him to become one of these abominations!" Lord Crandall said. "We must put an end to their suffering, and keep Thomas from joining them."

Anne reached for Thomas, but the teacher did not fire, even though she was nearly upon him. Lewis had to act lest the poor American die at his dead wife's hands. The thought of Thomas having to slay his own wife wrenched his heart. He met Frederick's fearful eyes with defiance and vowed silently that he would permit no more death as he aimed his Webley.

"Good-bye!" He ran forward. The barrier glowed green as he

crossed it, sending a tingling sensation through his entire body. Lewis was through it, ignoring the Raven and running directly between the nearest officer and Anne. He raised his revolver and fired. The bullet pierced the side of her face as her arms closed around Thomas. She dropped, dragging him down with her.

"Stop!" The Raven's voice was angry, even frantic.

Out of the corner of Lewis's eye, he saw the tall man gathering the dark gloom about him the way Richard Bailey had, but he did not wait for the Raven to attack. Instead, he fired his last round at the nearest officer. The bullet hit the policeman in the abdomen, and his coat immediately showed his life's blood pouring out. The man screamed as he fell backward and landed on the ground with a dull thump. His pistol dropped nearby.

Lewis allowed his momentum to carry him forward and dropped the useless Webley into his pocket. He hit the damp earth a few feet from the officer. He grabbed the man's gun, more ancient than any he had seen, and brought it around, aiming at the next officer.

"You will all die for this transgression!" The Raven seethed. "Kill them!"

Lewis felt the heavy darkness moving toward them, heralded by dozens of flapping wings and the cawing of myriad ravens. Their time was nearly out. The second officer turned as Lewis launched himself off the ground, catching the man's firing arm and spinning him to face Inspector Newton, who was frozen with surprise at the turn of events. Lewis gripped the man's hand over the flintlock and squeezed as hard as he could. The officer fired at Newton.

Newton gasped and dropped; the shot had hit him in the leg. He wasn't dead, but he could not pursue.

"Help me!" Bainbridge shouted, somewhere behind Lewis.

Thomas wrestled with Edgar's corpse. The dead banker had wrapped his unyielding arms around the other man and was trying to rip his throat out.

Another shot rang out and Lord Crandall burst from conceal-ment, his pistol raised. "I am setting you free!" The corpse fell sideways, taking Bainbridge with it, but he seemed uninjured. Lewis marveled at his luck.

"You will all die!" The Raven screeched like a dozen birds squawking together. The sound sent shivers rolling up and down Lewis's spine.

Lewis struggled against the officer, a burly man with black hair and a crooked nose. He had overcome his surprise and was fighting back. Lewis flipped his pistol around and hit the man in the side of the head. The officer dropped to one knee. and Lewis saw a second flintlock sticking out of the man's belt. He dropped his empty weapon and grabbed the loaded one.

"Your friends have been set free!" Elise said, her voice blaring across the clearing even as her ring burned against his chest again. "Leave these foul men and run for your life, my love!"

"No!" Lewis said, anger burning through him. Such evil as these men performed could not be justified under any circumstances, in war or in any other situation. He turned and planted his left fist in the officer's cheek, knocking him flat even as he grabbed the man's pistol. "These men deserve death for allowing this horror to continue!"

"For the love of God, Captain Wentworth!" Professor Drake shouted from within the ruins. "Retreat!"

Lewis was surprised he could hear Drake through the barrier. He whirled around just in time to see the Raven becoming barely more than a shadow as he stepped backward into his cloak of darkness. Hundreds of birds broke free as if they had been part of him, and in a few seconds, the clearing was completely enveloped by wings and swirling gloom as the menacing flock rolled forward. Lewis realized that Bainbridge still struggled to extricate himself from Edgar's grip, mere feet from the Raven's fluttering cloud. Lord Crandall stood between the teacher and the church's foundation. Gregory ran forward to help Bainbridge. They would make it before the storm overtook them—but not if they hesitated.

"Run!" Thomas said. "Forget about me! Anne is dead already. It doesn't matter!"

"We're not leaving you!" Gregory hoisted him away from Edgar. Lewis approved; he would lose no more to this place if he could help it.

Lewis aimed the ancient police pistol into the center of the dark cloud and ran forward, moving toward the safety of the shrine. He fired into the murk, knowing it would not kill the flock, but hoping the shot might slow it down. The pistol exploded in a burning flash, flying apart, the concussion knocking Lewis to the ground. His hand stung and was blackened by powder, but he was not badly burned. The birds shrieked louder, overshadowed only by the Raven's cackling laugh. Dirt whirled as if a dervish had taken hold of it, blowing it into a frenzy. Soil and grass pelted Lewis as the Raven closed on his companions.

Bainbridge was free, his hesitation gone. He pushed Gregory toward the foundation and ran with him. Lord Crandall had already stepped inside by the time Gregory crossed the boundary with Thomas.

The Raven stopped, drawing himself up until the cloud of wings and shadow towered over the clearing. The shriek of the birds and the flapping of wings rose to the fury of a cyclone.

Lewis hauled himself to his feet and galloped through the underbrush, but even at full speed, he knew he would never reach the sanctuary before the Raven was upon him. The cloud surged forward, between him and his goal. It halted, blocking him from safety, and the cackling grew louder.

"Stay right there, you filthy whoreson!" Inspector Newton shouted. Lewis felt certain that the man had trained his weapon upon him.

"Do not fire, Inspector!" The Raven's voice echoed from all over the clearing. "He would be the greatest prize of all for our master!"

The cloud rolled toward Lewis, its incessant crowing penetrating his ears and driving fear into him. Shadowy wings and snapping beaks danced in the murk, but Lewis saw no sign of the man. Even if he had carried his loaded weapons, they would do nothing against this nightmare that bore down on him. He closed his eyes and braced himself for the inevitable, his heart sinking. If he died, he would become one of the walking dead and forever be separated from Elise.

"Leave him alone!" As if his thought had summoned her, Elise's sudden shout resonated as loudly as the Raven's voice.

Lewis blinked and saw her shimmering form standing between him and certain doom. Her blue nimbus glowed so brightly that Lewis had to raise an arm to shield his eyes; she radiated a star's light. She raised her hands, pushed her palms toward the Raven, and the electric crackle of preternatural power joined the din of the storm. Green lightning ripped a hole through the maelstrom, drawing a ragged scream from the Raven and his birds. Lewis could again see the shrine—and that Elise was drawing her power from its sanctified ground. Lewis's companions stood within the ruin, watching in amazement.

"By all that's holy!" Newton gasped.

Elise spread her arms wide and the lightning danced from one hand to the other. She worked it as a potter would mold clay, until she held a glowing green sphere. She hurled it into the cloud, where it exploded in a blinding emerald light.

The Raven's scream pierced Lewis's ears. He felt a heavy thud and the clearing went quiet. Only the distant murmur of the walking dead broke the silence.

The dark cloud had vanished and the Raven lay sprawled next to the unmoving corpses of Anne and Edgar. His breathing was ragged and his chest rose and fell, but scorch marks and rips marred his once-fine clothing. In some places, the fabric had burned away completely, revealing pale flesh and the tattoo of a raven on his left forearm.

Elise, still shimmering, though not quite as brightly, stood over the Raven, her ghostly arms at her sides as she stared down at Lord Knight's minion.

"Dear Lord!" Professor Drake staggered from the protection of the shrine, coming to stand near Lewis.

"Steady now, Inspector." Lord Crandall, his flintlock in hand, limped into the clearing, aiming his weapon at the injured police officer. Gregory followed a step behind, his musket at the ready.

"Who are you people, really?" Inspector Newton said. "You—whose ghostly servant commands such power?"

"We are not a group to be trifled with, you cowardly dog!" Lord Crandall pulled the flintlock's hammer back, but paused when Newton spoke.

"Did the Mists send you?" Newton's eyes brightened.

"We were abducted by your Mists, if that's what you mean, and we're none too happy about it!' Lord Crandall said. "If I were you, I would not question further. Rest assured, we are in charge."

If Elise could command such powers, then the gentleman's assertion was correct—however, Lewis knew the fortunes of war could change swiftly and unexpectedly. He came to his senses and roused himself from staring slack-jawed at her.

"Elise!" He hurried over to her, pausing to look at the injured Raven for an instant. The man still breathed, but appeared unconscious. Lewis shuddered to think that such an onslaught had not killed him. Truly these minions were powerful, and their small group should not tarry long there. He glanced at Elise and gasped at the intensely bright love pouring forth from her as she watched him. The look brought tears to his eyes as he realized that she had pushed through the veil of death to save his life. He wished he could save her from her incorporeal existence, but he had not the slightest idea how to do so.

"Lewis." She smiled triumphantly, her delicate features as beautiful as ever. She reached toward him, but paused and frowned, suddenly remembering that they could not touch.

The Raven stirred and birds squawked from the trees.

"He is not dead," Elise stated. "You and your friends must leave this place at once."

"Surely, he will be dead soon," Lord Crandall said.

"There's no time for discussion!" Elise focused on Lewis. "We must run!"

"We?" Lewis blinked, surprised that she would include herself.

"I've absorbed energy from the shrine." She smiled wanly. "It allowed me to aid you, and it has given me the strength to remain with you for a time, but I shan't be able to help you like this again. You must hurry." Elise's eyes grew larger as she stared into Lewis's in the way only she could, in the way that she always had. "The Raven stirs, and your time is running out!"

Love shone in her eyes, and Lewis wanted nothing more than to close his eyes and bask in her love's warmth, to imagine that he stood with her at the altar on their wedding day, safe and sound. But doing so would damn them both. He cast another look at the Raven and saw the minion's flesh mending. Elise was right. They did not have much time. They never did, not in life, and not in this place.

Lewis took a deep breath, steeling himself against the future. Despite their victory, the reality of the walking dead and the power of the Raven lent credibility to Frederick's assertion that their enemy was too powerful for them to defeat. He would not give up, but he had to consider the possibility of defeat. He waved to Lord Crandall and motioned to the two surviving officers. It was time to choose a new course.

"Lord Crandall—Gregory—please reload your weapons." He turned to Drake. "Professor, if you will retrieve the lanterns. Thomas—the pistol?" He paused. "Where has our innkeeper gone?"

Frederick had slipped away, and they saw no sign of him in the fog. They set to their tasks swiftly, and in a matter of minutes had gathered within the sanctuary. Lewis checked the condition of his Webley and redeposited it into the pocket of his coat. Thomas returned Lewis's flintlock, which had not been fired. Newton and the two officers tended to their wounds within the safety of the ruins. They had no quarrel with Lewis and his companions, and likewise he felt no threat from them.

Lewis felt certain that Lord Knight would know what they had done. Another battle was likely. He took in the oddly hopeful glint in the policemen's eyes every time they looked at Elise. They wanted to believe that fighting back and winning might be possible.

Lewis risked a last glance at their dead friends. They lay where they had fallen, battered and twisted caricatures of the people they had been. He bowed his head and offered silent thanks to the builders of the shrine, wondering if he could have done more to safeguard his companion's lives had he known about this place sooner.

"You did everything you could, love. You almost spent your own life," Elise said. He was not surprised that she had read his thoughts.

Lewis met her gaze again. "There's so much I wish to ask you."

"And there is no time. There is never enough time." Elise offered him a gentle smile, but her brow furrowed. "We must leave now."

"Very well." There would soon be time to talk to her, Lewis decided. He summoned the others. "Stay together and follow me." He turned and stepped out of the shrine, onto the trail.

"Where do you propose that we go?" Lord Crandall pushed ahead to walk by his side. "We have very little in the way of allies in Mithras Court." Lewis thought it surprising that the gentlemen thought they might have any allies at all.

"For the moment, we're going to get away from here." Lewis held up one of the lanterns, allowing its light to penetrate the vegetation as he moved forward. The truth was, he had no idea what to do. His quest for vengeance stalled with the realization that he could not harm the Snake—or any of Lord Knight's minions. As far as he knew, his quest could not succeed and if that proved to be true, then he would have to reevaluate his very existence. If he could not kill Bailey and his master, what then *could* he do? He pushed the thought away. There had to be a way, and he had to find it. Bailey had to die!

The distant baying of dogs broke the silence and jarred Lewis from his grim thoughts.

"Another of Knight's minions comes!" Professor Drake said. "We must move faster!"

"He's right, Lewis." Elise motioned to the path. "Hurry!"

"This way to the inn!" Lewis pointed with his flintlock and hurried down the trail, uncertain that his destination was wise, but knowing they had no options. He debated going to the castle-like home where they had been attacked by the Snake earlier that day, but dismissed that. They could not hope to break down that door, and those inside would never allow them entry. Elise floated over the ground beside him, her insubstantial form passing through the underbrush and tree trunks. If she thought his idea was a bad one, she did not say.

"I can't see taking shelter at the Laughing Gargoyle. Perhaps the Vistani will aid us?" Gregory said. "Surely under these circumstances . . ."

"They won't," Elise said, and all heard her. "The Vistani cannot."

"Why is that?" Lewis watched her. "Why, Elise?"

"I do not know for certain. They have rules they must follow in order to pass through the Mists. Perhaps this is one of them." She bowed her head. "I'm sorry, love, that is only a guess."

"We must find a way out of Mithras Court, not merely hide like craven dogs," Lord Crandall said.

But my quest! Lewis thought. Yet he knew Crandall was right. Escape was more important—if they could find it. Still, to turn his back on revenge was difficult.

"Yes—if only we knew the way out!" Professor Drake's speech was less refined, more disjointed, than normal. The man clearly had seen too much. Lewis frowned at the thought. The old man had truly become the closest thing he had to a friend in years.

"Your wife is correct, Captain," Lord Crandall said. "Your quest for vengeance can only result in the death of the rest of us, and that I will not abide."

"How can I leave Bailey alive?" Lewis clenched his teeth.

"Lewis, swear to me that you will forget about retribution and find a way to escape from this place!" Elise's eyes held him with her rapt gaze. "It is a pointless venture, and I cannot bear the thought of you remaining trapped here!"

Agony struck Lewis like a slap across the face. For two years, his sights had been set on one goal—a goal that he had thought would set Elise at peace. His world turned upside down.

"What you ask is difficult," he almost yelled. "How dare you ask this of me. This quest is my life!"

She gazed at him gently, as if she understood and he didn't.

Her tenderness gave his defensive anger pause, and he realized what he had said. His revenge was all he had left to his life. He had told the truth—he did not, he realized, live. Not the way he had with her, not at all. He was simply a body seeking vengeance, and that was no honour to her at all.

He was unprepared for the panic that flooded him. So long he had searched for the Snake. How could he simply walk away? What would he replace the vengeance with? How would he live without her? His goal and his bitterness had consumed his world, burning away all joy and opportunity until there was nothing left. He *had* nothing else. There was only the rage and the vengeance.

"Promise me this as you once promised to love and hold me forever." She locked eyes with him, her voice quiet but no less urgent.

His chest ached, as if someone stood on him, but he suddenly felt completely empty. He had nothing. "I . . ." Lewis's resolve buckled. "I promise."

He looked up and her bright blue eyes met his. He saw happiness and peace that surprised him as he felt warmth flow back into him, and his ache lessened. The weight upon his soul lifted. He felt himself let vengeance go, and he realized that she had just saved him again.

Lord Crandall cleared his throat. "Well, Captain, that has been settled. What do you recommend we do?"

"If the Vistani will not aid us," Gregory said, "and the Mists surround the entire perimeter of Mithras Court, then we're trapped." He paused to catch his breath. "We need to think differently about the problem—we cannot use the streets."

"The entire perimeter . . ." Lewis glanced over at Elise, barely ducking a low branch. "That's it!" The surface was encircled, but there was more to Mithras Court than these few city blocks!

"Yes, Lewis!" Hope shone in her eyes.

"We have not considered something since our arrival." Lewis stopped, drawing the little group together and raising his lantern so they could see each other. "Perhaps we can leave the same way we arrived."

Drake gasped as he realized what Lewis intended.

"The electric train." Lewis turned and hurried through the underbrush with a renewed sense of purpose. Perhaps thwarting Lord Knight's plans to kill them was vengeance enough. Surely that would enrage their enemy and he would suffer a defeat, however small.

Chapter TWENTY-TWO

"Are you daft, man?" Lord Crandall caught up to Lewis.

Lewis ignored Crandall's question. The drone of the walking dead and the baying of the dogs grew louder with each step. He watched the trail warily, the bright light of his brass lantern pushing back the darkness.

"No, the captain has something there," Professor Drake interjected. "Given the horrors we witnessed in the train station, I seriously doubt Lord Knight will expect us to return there. He thinks he has total control because of the dead."

"An excellent point." Lewis had not considered that aspect. "More importantly, it is the way in which we arrived."

"But who will pilot the train?" Lord Crandall inquired.

"Once on board, we can improvise."

"I believe I can figure out how to operate the engine," Thomas said. "But how do we know it will run at all?"

"Because there was power flowing to the tracks after we arrived in Mithras Court," Lewis answered.

"By God, there was, sir!" Thomas's eyes widened. "Meaning that the electricity is still flowing from London! There must be a connection that can take us home!" His eyes grew sad, and Lewis knew he must be thinking of life in London without his wife.

"And potentially, a way out," Lewis said, not wishing to engage in a conversation of loss. Still, he could at least see his friends safely out of Mithras Court as he had promised. A sliver of hope flared within him that he might succeed. He refused to allow his hope to grow. It was a plan of desperation. Lord Knight might not look for them in the station immediately, but if they could not use the train to leave, they could not hide there forever.

"I hardly think that whoever built this place or trapped us here would have ignored the tunnel," Lord Crandall said. "It is surely a dead end."

"Have you a better idea?" Professor Drake said.

"Not at present," Crandall admitted grudgingly.

"I suggest we get there as swiftly as possible, instead of bickering about it." Lewis pushed ahead on the trail, but slowed as the edge of the park came into view.

Dozens of dead men and women lurked at the entrance to the trail, watching and waiting. As the lamplight met their broken and battered bodies, they recoiled, shrinking back into their fellows. They hissed through decaying jaws and stretched their clawed hands toward the group. Lewis halted, his pulse pounding through him as he looked into their dead faces. Not recognizing any of the corpses brought him scant relief, for whether he knew them or not, they were equally deadly. Doing his best to defy the fear he felt, he stepped forward slowly. Remaining here meant certain death, as the other minions would be upon them swiftly, but that did not mean that leaving through the mass of dead appealed either. He gritted his teeth, gripped his flintlock pistol tightly, and pressed onward, trusting to the lamp's light.

"My God!" Thomas said. "How many of the damned things are there?"

"Too many." Lewis's light pushed back the dead the way a ship cuts through the sea. Elise floated beside him, and he saw that the shambling corpses shied away from her even more than the lamplight. Lewis's breath caught in his throat as he realized that at least a hundred undead occupied the field. A profound anger and hatred burned from their sightless eyes. Lewis had felt the anger before, but something was different about it. It was as if Lucius Knight himself directed his ire through them.

"How can there be so many of them?" Professor Drake stayed close to Lewis.

"If there are apparently thirty-five years worth of the dead, how can there be so few?" Lord Crandall spoke quickly, sounding annoyed.

"The poor souls." Elise's eyes brimmed with tears. "I can see them, tiny flickering lights in the centers of their bodies, trapped forever. Oh, Lewis, it's so distressing!"

"There is nothing we can do for them." Fear gnawed at Lewis's insides. He glanced at her and saw tears streaming down her glowing cheeks. "I'm sorry, love, I didn't mean—"

"I should be sorry," she said softly, so that only he could hear. "I'm sorry I boarded the train that night, sorry I went to visit my friends when you wished to remain at home. I'm sorry I died. These two long years have taken away the warmth I once saw in your eyes."

Lewis stumbled on a root in the path as her words gripped his heart. The lamplight bobbed as the lantern swung like a pendulum in his grip. How could she feel such guilt? She had done nothing wrong. He opened his mouth to answer, but could not. Her love had saved him after the horrors of war, had brought him back from the brink of the cold dark place into which his soul had sunk. Their marriage had been warm and filled with joy, and when that had been taken from him, his spirit had returned to its prison as vengeance had taken hold of his every waking thought. In the end, his quest had chipped away at him until only anger and hatred remained. He realized she still watched him, her mouth moving in silence as if she searched for the right words.

Lord Crandall shattered the moment. "Does no one in Mithras Court lie at peace in death?"

"I . . . don't know," Elise answered. Conflict etched her once serene features. Lewis knew instantly that she knew more than she was admitting.

"You have seen something," Thomas said, sounding hopeful. "Please, tell me Anne has been set free."

"I saw . . ." Elise's eyes held a plea for help as she stared at Lewis. Lewis knew that her evasion was meant to cushion the blow for Thomas.

"Stay together, everyone," Lewis said, interrupting their discussion. He motioned at the dead around them with his flintlock as he carefully stalked across the grassy field. "I suggest we move in pairs so our lanterns offer better coverage."

"It is all right, Lewis." She smiled wanly at him and turned to face Thomas. "I saw the tiny flickering lights of their trapped souls . . ." She brushed away the ghostly tears from her face. "They vanished when they died their true deaths."

"What does that mean?" Thomas's voice shook.

"I am not certain, but I hope that they have moved on." Elise bowed her head sadly. "I hope."

"I can see the street!" Professor Drake said, interrupting them, much to Lewis's relief. He sensed that Elise had held something back, something bad. Perhaps there was no escape for the souls of the dead . . . and if so, the last thing they needed was for Thomas to learn that fact until they had time to escape. Once they were safely out of Mithras Court, there would be time for such talk.

"There." The professor pointed toward the road where they had been attacked by the Snake.

As if in response, the baying of the dogs echoed off the buildings.

"I suggest we focus on reaching the station before Lord Knight's other minions overtake us!" Lord Crandall said.

"Agreed. Stay close!" Lewis felt a twinge of relief as they moved out of the park and onto the moderately lit streets of Mithras Court, as if it were a small victory. The dead made no effort to follow them.

He tried to focus on their destination, but his eyes kept wandering to Elise. The distraction made him more vulnerable, but he did not care. Seeing her after so much time apart was like food to a starving man. He could not deny himself that one small joy while trapped in this hellish nightmare.

They left most of the dead behind as they hurried down the cobblestone road of Venus Lane. They saw no other citizens, nor did they see any of Knight's minions. Only the hissing dead lurking in the shadows at the edge of the light and their own hurried footsteps broke the silence. The dead watched with a burning hunger that made Lewis's skin tingle. He tried not to think about them, instead focusing on the buildings they passed. The stone structures remained dark and most likely bolted against the evils of the night. Light spilled from an occasional window, brightening the fog-enshrouded street only slightly.

Moments later, they entered the more modern section of Mithras Court. After a few minutes, they arrived at the edge of the square in front of the Laughing Gargoyle. It surprised Lewis that the dogs had not yet overtaken them, and that no other minions appeared. They clearly deliberately paced the survivors. Such a thought did not bode well. Perhaps, he thought, they had managed to surprise them by heading to the inn.

"I do not detect anything unusual," Gregory said, his voice barely a whisper.

"If our enemies are anticipating our movements, they will be expecting us to return to the inn. I suggest we make for the train station at once." Lord Crandall pointed toward the opening at the center of the square next to the tall statue of the unnamed soldier.

"Elise?" Lewis glanced at her. "What do you think?"

"You must choose, love." She offered him a supportive smile. "You have always known what to do. Do not falter now."

"We go forward," he said, bolstered by her words. "We must remain silent. And for the love of God, everyone remain together!" He nodded to Elise, offering her a brief smile, and then strode into the square.

=====MC=====

"Where the devil have they gone?" Lord Crandall paused next to Lewis on the second landing of the descending tunnel.

"I don't know." Lewis raised his lantern and peered into the gloom. No fog clouded the tunnel, and the walking dead were absent. The foul stench of decay and death remained. The atmosphere felt stale, the way the air in a sealed mausoleum would feel. Next to him, Elise's brilliant glow brought him slight comfort against the dread that was growing in his mind. He forced himself not to focus on her and kept his eyes fixed on the path ahead.

"It is like walking inside an ancient tomb," Professor Drake murmured. He pulled his pocket watch from his vest and turned it over in his hand as if it gave him comfort.

Lewis glanced at his fellows. Lord Crandall scowled while Gregory stood alert, musket ready. Thomas held his lantern high and positioned himself so he could watch their rear.

"All of you, remain alert." Lewis stepped onto the platform, continuing toward the train.

"Was that meant to offer encouragement?" Elise frowned. "I doubt you spoke with such a lack of enthusiasm to your men in Africa."

"This isn't the Zulu war, and these aren't soldiers," he whispered so only she could hear. "It was meant to keep them focused on our objective."

"They are scared, Lewis, just as you were when you were a young soldier," Elise said, her voice chastising.

"This is a war, and we must win it," Lewis spoke loudly enough for all to hear, "by escaping."

"Whatever the outcome of this attempt." Lord Crandall's voice echoed down the tunnel. "Spoken like a true soldier, Captain."

Elise narrowed her eyes in clear disagreement, and for an instant he imagined that they were back in their London home, embroiled in an argument over something trivial. That was merely another facet of their bond, and it reminded him profoundly of what he had lost. He turned away, sorrow in his eyes, and walked on in silence.

No undead waited to assault them, but the stench and bloodstains on the brick walls remained as proof that they had been there. Were it not for the dim light, Lewis might have thought it just an ordinary train tunnel.

A bright light appeared at the end of the stairwell. The gas lamps of the platform burned brightly, pushing away the shadows. That perhaps explained the absence of the dead—there was nowhere for them to hide.

They found the train's engine and passenger car on the tracks, and to Lewis's relief, they appeared undamaged. The doors stood wide open as if to welcome the passengers back. The electric lights in the cars glowed as brightly as the gas lamps of the station.

Lewis paused as he reached the station. He tightened his grip on his pistol and wished again for more bullets for his Webley.

"We have power!" Thomas moved to hurry forward.

"Wait." Lewis reached his arm out to block the man, stopping him fast. "This is unsettling," he said. Nothing was normal in Mithras Court, and yet something felt wrong.

"What do you mean?" Thomas said "We're free!"

"It smacks of an ambush," Lord Crandall said.

"I see nothing, man or beast." Gregory trained his musket on the ticket booth where the first of them had been slain two nights ago. "Even the corpse inside the ticket booth is absent."

"Indeed." Lewis could not shake the memory of how the vast grasslands of Ulundi had seemed safe until the Zulus rose up from the tall stalks and attacked. He shivered, then shook his head at the absurdity of comparing their situation with the plains of Africa. He caught Elise's attention.

"I don't see anyone." She closed her eyes for a moment and then opened them. "I don't feel the angry, unquenchable hunger of the dead, nor do I sense any of Lucius Knight's minions."

"Can we assume that you have sensed these things in the past?" Lord Crandall asked.

"That seems obvious." Professor Drake crossed his arms.

"I am not taking anything for granted." Lord Crandall turned an angry glare on him.

"The answer is yes." Elise inclined her head.

"Then it's time to leave." Lewis lowered his gun. "Thomas, get to the engine, inspect it for damage, and see if you can figure out how to work it. The rest of you—to the passenger car."

"Move!" At Lewis' shout, they sprang into action, hurrying across the platform. Lewis hung back, watching every corner of the station, looking at each shadow cast by every pillar, corner, and structure in the place for the slightest hint of danger. Lord Crandall and Gregory moved with the fluidity of soldiers, sweeping their weapons back and forth methodically. All of their efforts were unnecessary—they remained alone in the station.

Thomas darted to the engine and examined the gauges. He whistled. "Everything looks in order, and if I read these gauges correctly, we have power coming straight from good old London!"

Lord Crandall and Gregory hurried into the passenger car. They did not sit, but gripped the hand railings tightly. Drake stepped up with the sword drawn. Lewis paused several feet from the door.

"Captain?" Professor Drake halted at the car's entrance and turned to face him.

"I need a moment, if you please." Lewis waved him on.

"Of course." Professor Drake looked at Elise. "I understand." The scholar disappeared into the train.

"Lewis?" Elise hovered next to him. "What is the matter?"

"How can I let you go?" He had lost her once and was not prepared to do so again. She had helped him release his need for vengeance, but she could never cure him of his love for her and his desire to remain with her.

"Lewis, this has been borrowed time. You must leave—there is no other way!"

"But—"

"You must leave!" She frowned. "If you remained here and were to die . . . I've seen the flickering souls of those walking dead. I do not think we would ever be reunited, and I cannot bear that!"

"Lewis." Professor Drake stepped out of the car. "Forgive my eavesdropping, but Elise is correct. You must let her go . . ."

"But I've been so alone for so long. Days have seemed like years, and years have been decades. How can I face the remainder of my life alone?"

"I'll be with you forever, my love . . . and when you die, an old man in your bed . . .we shall cross over together to whatever lies beyond." She reached out and brushed her hand against his cheek, his face tingling with the warmth and love of her gesture.

"How . . . how can I let you go for a second time?" Lewis's eyes stung with bitter tears. "I've been so alone for so long and now that I've found you, I can't just walk away."

"You know I am right, Lewis. Now, do as I say. You can still talk to me . . . wherever I am, I'll listen." She blinked away her sorrow and smiled at him. "Now go!"

"How many men have the opportunity to say good-bye to their loved ones?" Professor Drake said kindly, returning to the train car.

He turned back. "You have been given a true gift."

"You're right." Swirling pain wrapped around Lewis's heart and squeezed. They were right. *She* was right. Love pierced his agony with new warmth. It was time to say good-bye. He slipped his pistol into his belt and reached out to Elise. Their fingertips touched, and although hers slipped through his, the contact warmed him.

"I'll be with you," Elise said. "Everywhere."

"I know." Lewis wondered if that could be enough. He straightened. It would have to be. He turned toward the engine. "Thomas, show us just how good you are—get this train moving!"

"Understood, sir!"

Lewis climbed aboard. Elise remained at his side as he slid the metal door shut. It latched into place with a loud click and he set down the glowing lantern, grabbed the overhead brass bar, and peered through the window. The light from the back of the train flowed into the tunnel. It was difficult to see where they were bound from his angle, but Lewis was able to clearly see the platform. A low hum emanated from the engine, growing louder. Slowly, the train moved backward and the station slid past them, replaced by the brick walls of the tunnel.

"The way looks clear." Thomas's voice echoed from a brass tube at the front of the car.

"Very good." A lump formed in Lewis's throat as he looked at Elise. If they succeeded, this might be the last time he saw her for a very long time, perhaps ever. Mithras Court had shaken the foundations of his beliefs, and although he was not ready to believe in God, he surely believed in something. If spirits could exist, then he had seen evidence of some form of afterlife. He could only hope that he would find her again . . . someday.

"You don't need to say anything." Elise answered his unspoken words with a gentle smile.

"I might not see you again for . . . well, forever," Lewis said. The car rocked gently on its tracks, moving ever faster. "How can I not say anything?"

"But you *will*, Lewis. This experience has proven that." She glanced at the others. Lewis realized that they had been staring at them for several moments, their eyes questioning. "All of you, listen to me. You will see your loved ones again. There is something more beyond the veil of life. I am proof of it." She smiled at them.

The car rocked to the side, jolting them out of their discussion. Lewis tore his eyes away and glanced through the window. The wall curved and he realized that they were nearing their point of entry.

"We're nearly there!" Lord Crandall said, looking in the same direction.

"Agreed. Any moment now—if it is going to happen," Lewis said. "We're rounding a bend in the tunnel." He resisted the urge to close his eyes so he would not have to watch Elise vanish. Instead, he stared at her beautiful face, taking it in and etching it into memory.

"Good-bye, Lewis. I love you." Tears flowed down her glowing cheeks. "I'll be waiting."

"Captain Wentworth!" Thomas's voice was panicked as it suddenly came over the speaking tube, interrupting them.

"What is it?" Lewis moved to the speaking tube.

"The Mists! They're in the tunnel and we're heading straight for them! We can't stop in time!"

"Then the Mists really are everywhere." Lord Crandall turned toward Lewis. "Above and below. We must stop at once."

"No." Lewis leaned into the tube. "We keep going, Thomas." If electricity could continue to flow from London, then there had to be a way through. Perhaps all they needed was the protection of the passenger car that had brought them.

"Are you daft, man?" Lord Crandall crossed the car swiftly, glaring at him. "You remember what happened when we went into the Mists before. We're lucky to be alive!"

"We have no other choice! The electricity flowing through these tracks has to be coming from London. That means there's a way back!" Lewis narrowed his eyes. "We go on!"

No one argued the point.

"Ten seconds!" Thomas yelled. It was hard to hear him over the din of their passage through the tunnel. The walls flashed past as the car increased speed.

"Good-bye." Elise mouthed the words.

"I shall see you again." Lewis smiled at her wistfully, wondering how long it would be before they next spoke, and wishing that he truly believed they would.

An odd popping sound filled the train, far louder than the hum of the electric engine and the creak of the wooden car. The Mists poured through every opening, every seam in the wood, filling it far more rapidly than when they had come to Mithras Court two nights prior. It scratched at Lewis's flesh, scraping against him with the coarseness of sand. Elise flickered and then faded from view.

"Elise!" Lewis called to her, but knew it was too late. His time with her, his second chance, was over. He was alone again. He bowed his head and felt himself moving with odd slowness, as if wading through syrup. An unnatural, mind-piercing screech reverberated through the car. Something thumped against them from the outside; to Lewis, it sounded as though undead pounded against the walls, the door, the ceiling, to gain entry. The train car vanished abruptly and Lewis found himself floating, alone in the Mist with no discernable up or down. He became disoriented as the world slowly spun, and the screeching was suddenly unbearable.

He heard his friends screaming.

Pain seared his shoulder injury and spread through his entire body as if an electrical storm raged and the lightning struck inside him.

Then the Mists vanished as swiftly as they had come, and Lewis found himself face-down on the floor of the car. It bounced and shook as it careened at dangerous speed, and Lewis realized that they had not escaped.

Chapter TWENTY-THREE

The car lurched and came to an abrupt stop with the shriek of metal on metal. Somewhere, something wooden shattered. Lewis was thrown forward and pain lanced through him when his shoulder slammed into the front wall of the car. He dropped to the floor, stunned for a moment. A cry pierced the air around him, calling him to his senses.

"Fire!" Gregory bellowed. "Lord Crandall, wake up!"

Lewis blinked and forced himself to a sitting position. The car was a twisted wreck. It leaned at an angle against the wall so the passenger door was above them. The lights were flickering and flames engulfed the wooden bench. Judging from the broken glass, one of their lanterns had shattered.

He hauled himself up and spied Professor Drake lying on his back, clearly stunned.

"Come on, Professor!" Lewis grabbed the man's arm and pulled him up. "We must get out!"

Drake shook his head and looked stupefied for a moment, but then gathered his wits. He stood on shaky legs, bracing himself against the wall of the car.

"The door is jammed!" Gregory pushed against it. He threw his shoulder into the door. "Help me!"

Lord Crandall hurried over to him and they hurled themselves at the door. The metal groaned, but the door did not give way.

"Captain, if you please." The men heaved against the door again, not waiting for Lewis's reply.

Lewis crossed the slanted floor, navigating the incline and the debris carefully to reach them. He wedged himself between them and all three pressed with their combined might. The door opened with a final crunch of metal, swinging outward just as the heat from the flames reached them.

"Everyone out!" Lewis said. "Gregory, keep that lantern going! Move! And take care around the electrified tracks!"

Lord Crandall climbed out. Gregory handed him the lantern and scrambled through the opening. Professor Drake followed, still slightly dazed. Lewis pulled himself out, away from the flames that were burning ever closer. He hit the ground on his feet, leaving him free to survey the damage.

The passenger car was bent and burning, but it was in better condition than the twisted wreck of the engine. It must have slammed into a wall at incredible speed.

Lewis ran over to it, his stomach twisting as he realized Thomas was not on the platform.

"Thomas!" He climbed up the side of the wreckage and peered into the engineer's compartment. He nearly retched at the sight of Thomas's broken body. The man had been crushed to death as the back of the engine had crumpled against him, mashing him into the front of the car. His destroyed form slumped over the gauges, his sightless eyes staring to the side in their last fearful look.

"Do you need help, Captain?" Professor Drake inquired. "Is Thomas—"

"He is dead," Lewis said, his tone defeated. They had no time to mourn, for they were now exposed in a dark tunnel with only one good lantern to keep the dead at bay.

"Lewis?" Elise said.

Lewis was not surprised to hear her voice, but it buoyed his spirits in the face of yet another tragedy. He saw her hovering behind him, concern on her face.

"He's dead." Lewis tried to hide the elation he felt at seeing Elise again. He did not wish to dishonor Thomas's memory.

"What the devil happened?" Lord Crandall brushed his coat, dust and soot falling away. "Surely this train cannot achieve such speed."

"The Mists brought us back." Lewis glanced down the tunnel where the flickering lights and the dancing flames cast dim light back the way they had come. The Mists blocked the exit, looking like a menacing cloud rather than harmless vapor.

"We have gone from one option to none." Lord Crandall turned to Lewis. "All right, Captain. What now?"

"We go back." Lewis glanced down the broad tunnel toward the station. He saw the glow of the gas lamps on the platform a good half mile distant, barely visible. "We stay in the light and return to the inn." There was a slim chance they might be able to rally the other patrons to aid them in their defense against Lord Knight, but at the very least, the stout door would repel all but the most determined attackers.

"And what if Frederick denies us entry?" Gregory said.

"We have exhausted our options. The inn is the only thing left."

Lord Crandall stroked his moustache, gripping his pistol tightly. After a moment, he nodded his acquiescence. Gregory fell in behind Crandall and held the lantern out to the professor. "You'll be needing this."

"Thank you." Professor Drake took the lantern and turned expectantly to Lewis.

"Then we are agreed. Stay close to the lantern." Lewis stepped over the nearest track and negotiated several pieces of twisted wreckage. He strode along the dirt floor toward the distant glow of the platform. Elise glided beside him, filling him with a comfort he knew he should not feel.

Yet he could not deny his feelings. He had resigned himself to leave her behind once again. Now that she was back, how could he not feel some joy?

CHAPTER TWENTY-FOUR

The walls of the tunnel lacked the soot and scoring that was caused by the older steam power locomotives. Given that the City and South London Railway was barely two years old, and that electric engines did not belch black smoke, all was as it should be. It meant, Lewis thought, that this section of tunnel had truly once belonged to London, though he could no longer convince himself that it still did. Lewis felt that home had never been so far away.

"I'm glad you are still with me." Guilt flashed across Elise's face in the downturn of her lips. Not quite a pout, Lewis had always thought it endearing. "I know you're in danger and I want only for your safety. But I have dreamed of being able to talk to you."

"I am glad of it. If I am truly damned, at least I have had these past days with you." Lewis smiled at her. "No matter what happens, seeing you again has been a gift."

"Oh, dear Lord!" Professor Drake drew the group up short and stared at the tunnel wall to their left. He leaned forward on the cane and examined it, mouth agape.

"Professor?" Lewis turned toward him, his weapon ready.

The scholar had stopped near a darkened indentation in the wall. He leaned forward to examine a small alcove just large enough for a man. Nothing was interesting about it that Lewis could see, and any delay concerned him.

"What are you on about now?" Lord Crandall halted several feet away. "We do not have time for idle curiosity."

"We're here. We're really here." Drake's voice was quiet—too quiet to be intended for the other men. He leaned closer and lifted the lantern. "Knight is not his name."

Lewis saw a narrow opening in the bricks at the back of the alcove.

Older granite stones, perfectly fitted, formed a narrow passage that was shrouded in darkness.

"Professor?" Lewis peered into the dark opening.

"This is my fault. It's entirely my fault." His words were quiet, disbelieving. He straightened, turning to face the others, his voice growing louder, steadier. "This is the tunnel. This is the Roman ruin."

"I think you'd better explain yourself." There was a dangerous tone to Lord Crandall's voice as he interrupted.

"I created Mithras Court." Professor Drake looked at the alcove and its mysterious passage. "I was uncertain before, but there is no doubt now. This place was created by me."

"What are you saying?" Lewis asked, wanting not to believe. He had come to admire the man, to consider him a friend, and not merely for their shared sense of loss. To hear him take responsibility for the place sent a chill through Lewis; equally as frightening was Lord Crandall's glare. Lewis stepped between the men.

Drake looked as though he were about to speak, but no sound came out.

"Professor, you must tell them." Elise hovered nearby. "There is power in truth."

Lewis remained silent, though he wished Drake would take Elise's advice. The tension in their small group could be quietly defused, or it could explode and plunge them into chaos. He had seen such things in war; fear and confusion could rip like a panicked beast through the tightest of units. He had heard stories of regiments fighting each other as tempers flared and he was very aware that the four of them on the platform were not as close as a unit in war was.

"As I've told Captain Wentworth, I once had a brother named Thomas. He was a member of the 13th Light Dragoons." The professor looked at Lewis as he paused.

"What has this got to do with us and Mithras Court?" Gregory asked. He did not sound particularly curious.

"My brother was slain in the disastrous Charge of the Light Brigade during the Crimean war. I was devastated, and my life became aimless as I focused only on my grief. When I met some of his surviving friends months later, I was informed that my brother's death had been no accident." Another pause, and Drake looked at Elise. "They claimed that a Colonel Merriwether had deliberately sabotaged the engagement and was responsible for Thomas's death. And the deaths of eighty-seven others."

"Who?" Gregory asked.

"Colonel Lucius Merriwether!" Drake glared at him.

"I take it the first name is no coincidence?" Lewis asked, understanding dawning on him.

"No. Clearly. Merriwether changed his name." Drake bowed his head.

"That makes sense, I suppose," Gregory said. "Merriwether is hardly a name that commands the ominous respect Lord Knight enjoys."

"Then you know Lord Knight, knew him," Lord Crandall's tone was dangerous.

"Yes." Drake's tone of defeat did not cool Lewis's rising anger.

"You knew of Lord Knight prior to our arrival?" Lewis could not keep himself from glaring at the man. "And you did not tell us?"

"I did not know until now."

"Explain yourself, Professor, and be quick about it." Lewis shifted so he could see both Drake and Crandall, hoping he would not need to intervene between them. "We have a limited supply of lamp oil and time." Lewis hoped that something in the tale would redeem the man, but feared it would not. He tightened his grip on his pistol.

"I did not wish to believe Thomas's friends. But my curiosity won out, and I delved deeper into the mystery. What I learned shocked me to the core of my being. Merriwether had come from a family of farmers and had risen as high as possible for such a man. Angry at his superiors for their haughty treatment of him, frustrated by the fact that those gentlemen and lords would always outrank him regardless of their abilities, he began to scheme for a way to destroy them. He made a dark pact with a great evil—"

"What do you mean, evil?" Gregory spat his question.

"I do not know—perhaps the devil himself." Drake frowned. "That is not important. The result of this black bargain is what matters. Merriwether promised to deliver one thousand souls to this evil in return for lordship over a land. By the time I learned of it, he had nearly done so."

"Are you daft, man?" Lord Crandall's lip curled into a sneer. "How could he kill one thousand men?"

"By countermanding orders, redirecting needed supplies, and creating confusion within the ranks. When I had gathered the proof of this, I took it to my brother's friends and we debated over what to do with the knowledge. We concluded that no one would believe our story, for our evidence was purely hearsay. The story of a pact with dark powers would be too incredible for the common man to believe.

"We decided something else, too—that prison or even death would not be enough of a punishment for this criminal. On that day, we chose to curse the man's soul for all eternity, for if the dark powers were real, we reasoned, so might be the power of a curse. I studied ancient rituals and rites and happened upon a Roman curse of the God Mithras. It required several items, including an original copper curse tablet—"

"A curse tablet such as the one you stole from my shipment of antiquities," Lord Crandall interrupted.

"Yes. That was the reason that I needed your Roman artifacts. I donated most of them to the British Museum, but kept the copper tablet. I altered the text of the curse engraved on it, added to it, and then located a Mithraeum, an underground shrine to Mithras, left over from the days of Roman Britain. With these tasks completed, Thomas's friends and I performed the ritual. Nothing appeared to happen during our incantations, but when we completed the curse, there was a flash of blinding red light. When it faded, we found ourselves in an alley in Whitechapel, and we could not locate the Mithraeum again. The passage that led to it had vanished from the sewers through which we had entered. I never heard further word of Colonel Merriwether, and assumed that our curse must have trapped him—or at least, if it had failed in that purpose, it had killed him."

"And you believe this is that passage?" Lewis motioned to the alcove, wondering how Drake's story could benefit them. If he was the one who had cursed Lucius Knight, he must have some notion of how to fight the man. It gave him renewed hope in their continued survival.

"I am certain of it. Look." He pointed to the wall where Latin writing had been carved. "I carved those letters to mark the passage as part of the curse. This is the place. This rail line, however it came to be, has bisected the old Roman tunnel.

"So you see, my friends, this entire affair is my fault. My curse somehow created this place—not just imprisoning Merriwether, but the citizens of several neighborhoods as well. I have caused countless deaths and endless suffering that surely rivals Merriwether's crimes." He watched the others with stoic reserve as if waiting for their reaction, as if he had admitted his guilt and would accept whatever came next.

"You realize, of course, that you must die." Lord Crandall said it so matter-of-factly that Lewis blinked. It sounded as if the anger the man had directed at the scholar fell away, and a sense of right and wrong had dictated an action regardless of how anyone felt about it. Lewis heard a loud click as Crandall cocked his pistol. He raised it and pointed over Lewis's right shoulder, giving him a clean shot at the scholar's head.

"Wait—don't!" Elise said.

Lewis gasped as he realized the man's intent. As the gentleman pulled the trigger, Lewis brought his arm up to deflect the flintlock, unsure whether he would be fast enough.

A bright flash and a loud crack assaulted the four men. The musket ball missed Professor Drake's head by inches, striking the wall with an ear-shattering sound, ricocheting to strike stone again and embedding itself in the opposite tunnel wall. The echo reverberated down the tunnel into the distance. Lewis brought his pistol up, conscious of Elise's frustrated expression off to his right. "What the devil are you doing, man?" Lord Crandall dropped the discharged flintlock and clamped his hands over Lewis's weapon, forcing it down and away. He shouted, "Gregory, shoot!"

"Stop!" Lewis struggled against the man's strong grasp. "We need him alive!"

"He must account for his crimes!" Gregory raised his musket. Elise glided between them, knowing that a bullet would pass through her, but perhaps hoping that the servant would not shoot a woman, ghostly or otherwise.

"You must not do this!" Elise said. "Professor Drake must live!" The light danced as the lantern swayed in the professor's nervous hands, stretching the shadows against the walls.

"Gentlemen! I order you to stop," Lewis said, his voice level. The tone of command was unmistakable.

"I can bring this terrible affair to an end!" Drake's free hand rose in a supplicating gesture, and he stared at Gregory's rifle with hope and horror on his face. "I know that now!"

Still locked in a struggle for his flintlock, Lewis struck Lord Crandall in the face. Dazed, the gentleman released his grip on the pistol. Taking advantage of the moment, Lewis whirled around to aim his weapon at Gregory's face.

"I *will* shoot!" Lewis pulled the hammer back. "Enough!"

"All of you, *stop!*" Blinding blue light pushed back the darkness as Elise's nimbus flared.

Lewis lowered his pistol and brought a hand up to shield his eyes from her burning anger, thankful that she had saved them again. Lord Crandall and Gregory ceased their posturing to shield their eyes as the light drained the fight out of them. When all weapons were down, Lewis allowed himself to breathe again.

"Tell them, Professor." Elise's luminescence faded to a soft glow.

"If we can locate that copper tablet, I can reverse the curse and end all of this." Professor Drake moved slowly out from behind Lewis to face the others. "I can destroy Mithras Court and return these poor souls back to where they belong. I can end this!"

"Why should we trust you?" Lord Crandall's knuckles turned white as his fists clenched.

"I have no reason to lie, especially now. I am in as much danger as the rest of you, perhaps more if Lucius Merri—er, Knight figures out who I am." The professor's shoulders slumped as he turned away.

"What do you mean—more danger than us?" Gregory's eyes

narrowed as if he were trying to ferret out deception in what Drake had said.

"I dreamed of the train that brought us here many times over the past few weeks. I must believe that Knight was luring me here to take his revenge."

"Perhaps we should allow him to take you," Lord Crandall said, arching an eyebrow. His expression was deadly serious.

"Enough discussion." Despite all that had happened, Lewis did not believe Lord Crandall was serious. Nonetheless, he had to control the situation. "This is the best option we have. We must help the Professor reach the tablet and reverse the curse. With luck, that will set us free."

"Do you believe you are capable of doing this?" Lord Crandall looked pointedly at the professor.

"I do not know for certain," Professor Drake said, after a moment's thought. "But there is every chance I can. And," he added, "what else is there?"

"Very well. I shall assist you as I can, for the moment." Lord Crandall glanced at Gregory. "And so shall you, Gregory."

"Very good, sir." Gregory nodded.

"Lead on, Professor." Lewis motioned toward the side passage. "Lord Crandall, if you and Gregory could bring up the rear."

"Wait." The gentleman picked up his empty flintlock. "Let me reload first."

"Of course." Lewis glanced at Elise and breathed a thank you, for she had certainly saved them from killing one another.

With all weapons loaded and ready, the professor led them into the passageway. Lewis had grown accustomed to the lack of fog in the tunnel, but the air felt different between the Roman walls—somehow cooler, and even cleaner. It was fresh, but he could not help but wonder if it was older as well. His feet were loud on the ancient Roman paving stones, despite his best efforts to move in silence. The professor negotiated the tunnel with the clear expertise of one who had been there before.

"Why did you wait so long to tell us, Professor?" Lewis peered into the darkness ahead where the lantern's glow did not reach. He wondered if more of the dead awaited them, or if Mithras Court had other horrors to unleash; it seemed unlikely they would make the journey unmolested. Tightening his grip on the pistol, he pushed the thoughts away. They had no choice but to carry on; regardless of the consequences, this was their only hope of escape.

"I was not certain if this place could truly have been created by my curse, until I saw this passage."

"But surely you must have suspected," Lewis pressed.

"Yes." The professor glanced over his shoulder for an instant. "I am sorry, Captain. I have been a coward."

"The important thing is that you can try to correct this now." Lewis could understand the guilt the scholar must feel, for the professor was not the only man with blood on his hands. So many Zulus . . . dead in the attack in which Lewis had been a participant and a near casualty. Was he any better than the Professor? Had he redeemed himself over the years? He had lost himself in Elise's love after the war and in his quest for vengeance after her death.

"But so many have suffered, so many have died . . ." Drake brought Lewis back from the past.

"And you will pay your penance by reversing this curse and saving them." Elise's form brushed against the wall. Part of her vanished inside it, a reminder that she was still a ghost, that soon Lewis would no longer be able to speak to her if their plan succeeded. He lifted a hand toward her, wishing he could touch her for just a moment. It was almost torture to have her so close and not be able to feel her against him, to kiss her, to hold her hand. If only their plan could bring her back from the dead, erase her murder from history. But it could not. All it could do was set Lewis and his companions, and hopefully Elise's spirit, free.

"I agree with that, madam. He *will* pay," Lord Crandall said. The tone of menace was still there, and still unmistakable.

"Quiet. Someone is up ahead." The professor spoke in an urgent whisper as he stopped short, pointing to another light spilling around a sharp bend in the corridor.

"How?" Lewis raised his pistol, every muscle in his body tensing for battle. Mithras Court did have more to throw at them.

"Can Merriwether, or Knight, or whatever you wish to call him, have beaten us here?" Gregory asked quietly.

"I . . ." Elise closed her eyes for a moment. "I do not sense the presence of his minions or any of the walking dead."

"A pity you could not have employed such an ability earlier," Lord Crandall frowned at her.

"I did try." Elise flashed angry eyes at the gentleman. "I was not strong enough, did not know what I could do in this place. As I have learned, I have aided you when my abilities could help."

"Forgive me. The tension of the situation has affected my sensibilities." He bowed stiffly.

"Hood the light," Lewis hissed, pointing to the lantern.

The Professor did as he was bid.

"Now we go forward and see who waits for us." Lewis aimed the gun ahead of him. "I'll take the lead." He stepped forward slowly, careful to keep his footfalls silent. Whoever was up there had to know they were in the tunnel, but they did not need to know exactly where Lewis and his companions were.

Despite the difficulties in moving silently along the paving stones, Lewis did the best he could. As they drew closer, he could hear whispering, and a moment later, a rough stone arch to their left marked a new passage. Lewis flattened against the wall and motioned for the others to do the same. Slowly, he edged along the ancient surface until he neared the opening and could peer inside.

Chapter TWENTY-FIVE

A long, low chamber stretched as far as Lewis could see. The far end disappeared in darkness. Marble reliefs depicting Romans adorned the walls, along with ancient Latin symbols. A stone altar occupied the center of the room. An oil lantern rested there, and Lewis's eyes widened as he saw Frederick, in his dark cloak, and the Vistana, Dragos, standing on either side of it. Lewis stepped boldly into the chamber, his weapon aimed directly at Frederick's heart.

"Gentlemen, remain perfectly still, please," he said.

Frederick swallowed and froze, but Dragos looked unfazed. He merely watched them with an unconcerned grin on his face. The black-haired man still wore his gold-buttoned coat and dark trousers, and Lewis could see the missing pinky finger on his right hand.

"What the devil are you two doing here?" Lord Crandall stepped up next to Lewis, his weapon aimed at the innkeeper.

"Waiting for you." Frederick stood straight. "Dragos knew you would come."

"I think you'd better explain yourself." Lewis kept his weapon trained on him.

"It's true." Dragos's eyes widened as he spied Elise emerging from around the corner.

"I thought you couldn't speak," Gregory said. He had drawn up next to Lewis, his musket leveled, just in time to hear Dragos.

"That's what we all thought." Frederick motioned to the gypsy. "We believed he'd lost his mind when he was banished by the other Vistani and couldn't talk—at least, nothing that made sense. Apparently, we were wrong."

"I saw all of you in the tapestry. The professor, the captain, his ghostly wife. The time had come," Dragos said abruptly. "I have waited for the scene to change—to reveal to me what I must do to redeem myself."

"Just what in God's name are you talking about?" Lord Crandall said. "How could you possibly be waiting for us here? And how could you know about us?"

"Frederick told you of our revolt long ago, and how I helped the citizens of Mithras Court in their struggle against Lord Knight." Dragos leaned on the altar. "And how I was banished from my people."

"He has told us that much," Lewis said. "What has that to do with us or Elise?"

"I have been away from my people for a very long time. Even so, I know that the curse of Mithras Court is endangered by your presence. This is the curse that you, Professor, set upon Lucius Merriwether, who calls himself Knight, and upon all who live here." The Vistana looked at the Professor with knowing eyes. "Your curse killed him and banished him to this place, and he seeks his revenge against you. It is no coincidence that you are here." He turned and looked at Lewis, and let his eyes settle upon Elise.

"What are you saying?" Professor Drake stepped closer to the Vistana. "That Lucius Knight has brought us here? Your people said it was the Mists."

"The beast who is Lucius Knight seeks to escape from Mithras Court. Even now he rages against his bonds," Dragos said. "I believe he has brought you here to aid him in that goal."

"I can believe that Lord Knight manipulated the Professor through his dreams." Lewis glanced at Professor Drake. "But what about myself and the others?"

"He influenced others, who in turn took actions that ensured you would be on the train." Dragos glanced nervously at Elise. "Your wife's death was no random killing. Lord Knight sent the Snake to her for this purpose. For this purpose alone."

"How did your wife's death bring you to the train?" Lord Crandall turned to Lewis.

"I have ridden the rail line every night since she died," Lewis said. "Two years have come and gone. I had hoped to find her killer there, with a great deal of luck. If what Dragos says is true, it was only a matter of time before I would find myself in the company of the Snake."

"Yes." Dragos nodded approvingly. "You do not need to end the curse to be free. It is possible to alter it . . . to shrink it. It will reshape around Lord Knight alone, and release all those souls who have been trapped here for so long. He need not go free." Dragos stepped toward Lord Crandall. "I speak the truth."

"You have not explained how you knew we would be here," Elise glided into the room, her radiance brightening Lewis's heart as well as the Mithraeum.

"The tapestry that showed the field before Lord Knight's dark wood . . . it changed when you encountered the Raven," Dragos said. "It revealed the Professor standing within the ancient shrine, and Lewis there before the gathering storm, bravely facing the most powerful of Lord Knight's minions. Then it showed you, brave ghost, wounding the Raven, and the tapestry changed, showing all of you standing inside the Mithraeum."

"Then you knew of this place?" Professor Drake sounded startled.

"The Vistani know."

"The Professor's curse created Mithras Court, but what do I have to do with this?" Lewis demanded, anger rising within him. He was infuriated at the implication that he, Elise, and the others had a part to play in the events that were unfolding. "And what does my wife have to do with it?" He did not like being manipulated any more than he liked surrendering his free will.

"Elise was the first soul to come to this place since it was created." Dragos stepped closer and studied Elise hungrily, as if he was a man desperate to claim her. Lewis drew himself up and stepped between them.

"Easy, gypsy." Lewis lowered his pistol, but his tone was stern. "Elise is not some prize to be won or lost."

"Forgive me. I never thought to see a pure soul again." Dragos bowed deeply.

From the first time he had seen her, Lewis had been instantly attracted to Elise's spirit.

He had heard it in her voice as he lay in the hospital, barely conscious. It had brightened his days for years afterward. And he found that especially in his darkest hour, it offered a respite of light. The gypsy had seen what they all saw.

Lewis kept his weapon on the man. To take anything in Mithras Court for granted was to invite death.

"What's different about her? Hundreds of the walking dead roam this place. Surely they have souls." Gregory lowered his musket, the tension in him easing.

"She is . . . untainted." Dragos looked down for an instant.

"What are you saying?" Lord Crandall drew closer.

"The souls trapped within the dead here can be set free," Dragos said. "But even in death, they are cursed."

"So many lives destroyed because of you." Lord Crandall stared at the professor, his look filled with more pity than anger. Lewis wondered at that. Had Lord Crandall finally witnessed the same tired remorse in Drake's eyes that Lewis had seen? Drake's desire to make amends was genuine; Lewis was sure of it.

And just as Lewis sought redemption for the mistakes of his past, he felt it vital to give Drake that same chance.

"I'm sorry. I am so sorry." The professor looked at Lord Crandall. "I swear I will set things right."

"Yes. You will, and I will see to it." It was a cold threat. Lord Crandall turned away from the Professor, clearly disgusted.

"Why would Knight need a pure soul?" Icy fear ran through Lewis at the realization that whatever Knight wanted from Elise could not possibly be good. "And what does he need of me?"

"Knight's motives are beyond me." Dragos shifted uncomfortably in place. He raised his chin defiantly. "You have no time to understand, only time to act. We must move quickly if we are to stop him. If morning comes before we are in place, we cannot succeed."

"This doesn't make any sense," Professor Drake said. "Even if Knight can reverse the curse, he will still be dead. Nothing can change that."

"You can be certain that whatever he has planned, it is not good for any of us," Frederick said. "I think we must do as Dragos says and stop him."

"I am forced to agree." Lord Crandall nodded, though he didn't look pleased. "If there truly is a way to keep the evil lord trapped, setting us and the other people of Mithras Court free, then we must try. Give us this copper tablet and let us be done with it."

"You're too late," Frederick answered, pointing to the empty altar. "Knight's minions took the tablet long ago."

"Then how—" Lord Crandall stared at the empty table. "How are we to defeat him?"

"We must retrieve it from the belly of the beast." A smile spread across Dragos's face, revealing his perfect teeth and his lack of sanity. "We must enter Lord Knight's manor house and steal it."

"How in the name of heaven and hell can we do that?" Lord Crandall paced between Lewis and Dragos. "Even if we could get past his minions and the walking dead, we would not know where to look for it."

"The tapestry will show us the way. Watch." Dragos retrieved a large pack from behind the altar. He loosened the drawstrings and pulled out a large bundle of rolled cloth. He opened it on the stone altar, revealing a black woven fabric with gold fringe along the edges.

"Like that hideous tapestry at the inn?" Gregory's face twisted in revulsion. "But it has no picture."

Dragos glanced down. "This will show us what we want to see. The tapestry hanging in the Laughing Gargoyle shows us what Mithras Court wishes us to see."

"How does it work? Where did you get it?" Lewis stared at the cloth. He had never before believed in such things, but having seen the tapestry at the inn, he did not doubt the man.

"The Vistani have many mystical ways." Dragos stood looking over the fabric.

Lewis and the others leaned over the cloth. Unlike the scene of the hovel and the woods on the larger tapestry, this was completely black. Colors slowly emerged in the cloth, as if someone were stitching new patterns as they watched. Slowly, a map outlined in white revealed the floorplan of a large house. Above it, more squares formed another floor of the home, and next to that, a third level. A cellar appeared beneath the first floor.

A red thread snaked through the cloth, forming a line leading from the second floor all the way to the cellar and then out through some kind of hidden tunnel. Walls formed around the red line, flanking it as it moved to the edge of the tapestry. Prior to reaching the edge, several more squares appeared. These, Lewis thought, probably represented terrace homes in the neighborhood, or possibly outbuildings.

"There is a secret passage?" Lewis frowned at the map. They could not possibly be that lucky. Nobody and nothing had been kind to them in Mithras Court—certainly not Lady Luck. Something so convenient had to be a trap. Lewis wondered why Dragos would lead them into a trap. He surely could not be aligned with Knight.

"The Vistani hold many secrets," Dragos said. "We have the means, if you have the will."

"Is there no other way?" Lewis looked at Elise, searching for her thoughts. "If Lucius Knight has brought us here for a reason, should we really deliver ourselves to him?"

"There is no other choice," Dragos said. "If we do not obtain the copper tablet and alter the curse, Lord Knight will hunt us down until we are all dead."

"I thought he could not attack the Vistani," Lord Crandall said. Lewis watched the gypsy intently as he answered.

"Normally, that is true. I, however, have been banished. Now that I have shown myself to be more than a mindless fool sitting in the Laughing Gargoyle, he will look for me as well." Dragos frowned. "At least when he realizes that Frederick and I have decided to help you."

"I see." Lord Crandall tweaked his moustache. "Why must we use this tunnel to obtain the tablet?"

"You've seen Lord Knight's minions and the walking dead," Frederick said. "We couldn't get near his manor above ground. There is no other way."

"Won't he expect us to use the tunnel?" Lord Crandall asked.

"I do not believe he will. The Vistani can help, by making it appear as if you plan a full assault," Dragos said. "And Lord Knight does not know we have learned of this passage."

"Elise?" Lewis asked, turning to her. He sought her insight, or some indication as to whether Dragos told the truth.

"I cannot say if what Dragos has said is true or false, love."

"Can't, or won't?" Gregory turned, curious. "I mean no disrespect, madam, but we should know if you are withholding information. In the past, you have told us you could not answer our questions, yet later we learned that you indeed knew more than you let on."

Lewis resisted the urge to leap to her defense. Whether he liked it or not, Gregory's question was valid. Elise had been able to tell them much, and her refusal seemed strange.

"I . . ." The corners of her mouth tightened, as if she were fighting against something. "I can't answer that."

"Elise, what is it?" Lewis stepped toward her, fear gripping his chest in a vise at the thought that she might have withheld information or lied to them. If either were the case, he knew she had to have a good reason. Anything else would be impossible for her.

"Lewis, there are things I am not permitted to say, at least not now." She bowed her head in defeat. "It is not from a lack of wanting. I simply cannot speak about certain subjects. I do not know why."

"Permitted by whom?" Lewis reached out to touch her, but lowered his hand. He gritted his teeth in frustration. "Does Lord Knight or the Vistani have some kind of hold upon you? Are either of them preventing you from speaking?"

Elise looked at him but did not respond. That was telling enough.

"There are rules in Mithras Court—even for ghosts," Dragos said with a wise nod. He pointed to the tapestry. "We must not lose sight of our goal. This is the only way."

"If Dragos says it's the only way, it's the only way," Frederick said, nodding grimly. "He proved himself tenfold by disobeying the other Vistani and helping us rebel against Lord Knight." Lewis saw that Frederick did indeed trust the Vistani. Whether that meant

Lewis could trust them, he did not know. "If Dragos says that Lord Knight will not expect us to go through the tunnel, then he believes it to be true."

"Belief in something does not make it correct," Lewis said, though he understood Frederick.

"I agree. As far as I'm concerned, you are both suspect." Lord Crandall narrowed his eyes. "Yet if the alternative is to await death, I suggest we make the attempt."

"We will be watching you both." Lewis offered Elise a smile meant to convey his support. It felt false, though, with his distrust roused, and it felt more unpleasant than he could really say that he did not quite trust her. He couldn't fix it, he thought, as he turned back to the others. "That said, I believe we must make this attempt, and we must trust you."

Lord Crandall turned to practicalities. "Captain Wentworth's Webley is out of ammunition, and all we have are a musket and two antiquated flintlocks. How do we fight such a superior force?"

"Madame Catalena waits for us." Dragos folded the tapestry and tucked it into the bag. "She will help."

"I thought the Vistani had to remain neutral because of your arrangement with Lord Knight, or these Mists," Lewis said. "Madame Catalena refused to offer any aid before."

"Things are different now." Dragos looked levelly at Lewis, and he could plainly see the pain etched in the Vistana's worn features. "She cannot ignore your pleas any longer—not in the face of prophecy. She will provide you with more information and help."

"What prophecy?" Lewis asked, wary of such things despite her soothsaying.

"An old prophecy goes back decades here. When the tapestry shows this Mithraeum, the curse will be in jeopardy. A second prophecy tells about a man with two souls. There is more that I do not understand, but I know this: you, Lewis, and your ghostly wife are important somehow. Madame Catalena must lend you aid even if the Vistani cannot get involved."

Lord Crandall asked, "What help can she possibly offer?"

"Perhaps she will provide weapons. I do not know for certain," Dragos said.

"What good are weapons against Lord Knight's minions?" Gregory asked. "So far, Mrs. Wentworth is the only one who has been able to slow them down. Guns will work against the walking dead, but not against the minions."

"Madame Catalena knows their weaknesses." Dragos slipped the bag over his shoulder, dismissing their concerns as unimportant. "She will tell you what she knows. I will see to it that she obeys her own law." He frowned, a look that Lewis took to mean that he was not fond of the Vistana clan leader.

"You don't like her, I take it," Professor Drake said.

"She is my wife," Dragos said levelly. "And the one who banished me."

"Isn't love wonderful?" Frederick said dryly.

"Indeed?" Lord Crandall glanced at Lewis and flashed him a concerned look.

"Your own wife banished you for aiding Frederick in his rebellion?" Lewis swiveled to face the Vistana.

"Aye." Dragos sighed. "The Vistani are forbidden from interfering with Lord Knight's laws. I violated that covenant, failed at the attempt to free myself, and was punished accordingly."

Lewis saw truth in the gypsy's gaze. He nodded grimly. If the Vistani would truly aid them, and if the curse tablet was necessary to escape from Mithras Court, they had little choice but to follow the Vistana's plan. Yet Lewis did not like it. It seemed too convenient, too simple—something that should have been tried in the last thirty-five years. If they had means into Lord Knight's home, surely they did not need the curse tablet to attack him. But perhaps they required it to truly defeat him, and for that, they would need Drake at least. Lewis knew they had no other options.

Still, thinking about it, Lewis considered that he did not trust the Vistani any more than he trusted Frederick. The things that people had to be willing to do to survive in a place as harsh as this did not suggest that they were entirely trustworthy. If only there was another choice . . . He sighed at the thought. There wasn't. Even if he could accept that Dragos and Frederick were willing to help the survivors, he was not certain he could trust Madame Catalena and the rest of the Vistani. Regardless, he could see no other option than to try their plan, and to do it with their eyes open and their wits about them.

"Lead on, Dragos." Lewis motioned toward the exit to the ancient temple.

Chapter TWENTY-SIX

With two lanterns now, there was less danger of being left in the dark even though there were more of them. They exited into the larger train tunnel. It was still free of the dead. Lewis glanced behind the group and caught sight of flames; the train wreckage was still burning. He bowed his head, remembering Thomas, and followed Dragos toward the station.

A slight smirk played at the corner of the gypsy's lips. If he had truly been banished and speechless for over thirty years, the possibility of reprisal would certainly be cause for a grin. Or possibly, the survivors had stepped into Dragos's trap. In sharp contrast to Dragos, Frederick's face was slick with sweat, and Lewis did not think it was from exertion. His eyes flicked left and right as if expecting an attack at any moment.

They reached the platform without incident and found the gas lamps fully lit and the station empty. Without the train at rest on its tracks, the chamber felt like an enormous empty tomb. At that thought, Lewis wondered if Thomas would rise again as one of the walking dead. He thought about asking the Vistana, but opted to hold his tongue. It did not matter how people became the walking dead—it only mattered that they did, and that Lewis and his companions would free the trapped souls if it was possible to do so.

"This way—please, hurry." Dragos waved them toward the edge of the platform. He led the way to the stairs that would take them to the surface of Mithras Court.

Lewis put a careful hand on Dragos, stopping him near the foot of the stairs. "That's odd," he said, gesturing. The gas lamps in that passage glowed brightly. "This passage was dark when we descended."

"Indeed." Lord Crandall tweaked his moustache and drew up next to Lewis. "Someone clearly knows we are coming."

"Who controls these lamps?" Lewis scrutinized Dragos, searching for any signs of deception.

"Lord Knight," the gypsy said, his expression stoic. Lewis noted with some annoyance that his face was hard to read. But for all that, he thought the Vistana was telling the truth.

"Then he is aware of our presence?" Professor Drake rubbed his beard nervously.

"He certainly is now." Dragos frowned at the glowing lights. "It does not matter. The Vistani can confound Lord Knight's scrying abilities. It is part of our deal; we bring in the supplies, and he does not watch us." Dragos looked at Elise. "When your wife revealed herself to the Raven, Knight's attentions became fixed on you. A soul of such purity stands out like a beacon."

"Are you saying Elise is the reason his minions continue to find us?" Reflex made him fear for Elise's safety—yet what could harm a ghost?—but without question, his foolishness had forced her to take action against the Raven.

"No," said Dragos. "I think he did not know she had come until his Raven saw her, though I think he wanted her for his own reasons. But she is not the only reason they are able to find you."

"Everyone in the Court acts as the eyes and ears of Lord Knight," Frederick said. "He'd have known where you were anyway."

"This is true." Dragos agreed with a nod.

"You knew?" Lewis turned to Elise. He felt like a fool for not having realized the degree of scrutiny they were under. He should have known; sound tactics required information about the enemy. "That if you showed yourself to Knight's minions this would happen? That I was putting you in danger asking for your help every time they attacked us?"

"I did not know it. I knew it was a risk to let them see me, though." She paused to study him. "I see your guilt, Lewis. Do not blame yourself."

"I am a fool." He had acted one, he knew, no matter how much she excused him.

"No, Lewis. You tried to help your friends." She beamed at him, pride in her bright eyes. "There is no shame in an honorable act, and I would expect no less of you."

"I suppose that is true. But I wish I had not revealed your presence." He smiled, a little wanly, and wished he could touch her, though whether to reassure her or himself, he was not certain. He had never thought that simply holding her hand could equal the intimacy they had once shared. But now, looking at her, he would have given anything just to hold her hand.

When he looked away, Dragos stared impatiently at him. "Enough talk. We must go now." Without waiting for the others, he started up the stairs, quickly disappearing from sight.

Lewis glanced at Lord Crandall, but the gentleman merely shrugged.

"We apparently have no choice. Stay together and remain silent." Lewis nodded to the others and climbed after the Vistana.

The stairs were still devoid of the living and the dead. At the top, they found the square completely empty. The dim shadows that normally marked the edges of the light had vanished, leaving only quiet vapor behind. Lewis turned in a complete circle outside the tunnel entrance and frowned. He could not pretend that the absence of the dead was at all reassuring.

"I don't understand." Professor Drake stopped to catch his breath near the entrance. "Where have the dead gone?"

"Lord Knight has called them," Dragos said, matter-of-factly. He stood a few feet away, watching the small group come out of the tunnel.

"Called them where?" Gregory held his musket at the ready as he looked around the square, but true to Dragos's statement, nothing hostile could be seen. No dead, no minions, and no civilians.

"I am not privy to Lord Knight's wishes." Dragos squinted into the fog ahead of them. "I only know, for I have seen it before, that he has called his dead to him."

"Then perhaps he does not know where we are, after all," Lord Crandall said. Lewis thought it had the tone of a man trying to convince himself. "Would he not have his dead here to meet us, if he knew where we are?"

"Then why would he have turned the stairway lights on?" Lewis wished he had a box of bullets for the Webley. A Gatling gun would be nice, too, while he was wishing. He smiled at the thought, but the truth of the situation crushed his humor. "No, our enemy moves against us even now. I am sure of it. Wherever these poor corpses have gone, it is to our detriment."

Dragos nodded. "I agree with you—wherever the dead are, they have been called by Lord Knight, and he will use them against us. We must not dally here. Madame Catalena awaits us at the market." He moved across the smooth stones of the square, heading for Bacchus Way, not waiting to see if they followed.

"I'll meet you there shortly," Frederick said. "There's something I need." He looked toward the Laughing Gargoyle.

"Where are you going?" Lewis looked at him. He was gratified when Frederick's eyes widened with no small amount of fear. The man should fear him.

"I have additional weapons for us. I've been saving them, in case I'd have a reason to use them, and now I believe I do." Frederick halted and watched, waiting for approval.

"Very well. Go." Lewis waved him off, but wondered if they would see Frederick again.

Frederick nodded and hurried toward the inn.

Lewis followed Dragos and the others.

"Do you truly trust him or this Vistana?" Lord Crandall spoke softly as Lewis caught up to him.

"I'm not certain who to trust. For the moment, their interests and ours seem to coincide." Lewis glanced at Elise.

She watched him, a curious expression on her face, but did not offer an opinion. Lewis wondered if it was her choice to remain silent or if she was compelled to not speak. He wondered what she knew and how it might affect them, but there was no way for him to find out.

"Let us take care, then. It seems to be all we can do." A short, humorless laugh, and Lord Crandall turned, following the gypsy.

"And to think, I had planned to relax," Professor Drake flashed Lewis a conspiratorial smile.

"After the past days, I will never take anything for granted again. I think I will see danger at every turn." Lewis glanced at the others. "If we do find our way home. I do not think I will forget our time here."

"When you have returned to London, that will change." Elise hovered at his side as he crossed the square. "You will learn to trust again, learn to live again. You will learn to love. You must, my dear, for you are not living now."

"Is that prophecy, or just your hope?" Lewis's tone was harsher than he had intended, but the thought of loving again was preposterous. Only one woman could ever capture his heart, and as he looked at her ghost, he knew no other woman ever could. He had been a wounded soldier who had found his perfect bride and she had healed his pain and given him a new life. Given the pain he had suffered since her death, he did not see how any woman could possibly fill the gaping hole in his heart.

Elise frowned at him but did not answer.

Lewis hurried onward, dismissing the conversation. He knew he was trying to protect himself from what she asked him to face, but he could not countenance the thought of loving another.

Bacchus Way stood deserted. The tents and booths of the market were gone, the flags and pennants had been furled, and the shop doors were closed. Lewis suspected that those doors were barred. Crumpled papers blew across the street. Bits of food and other debris littered the street here and there. The fog ebbed and flowed with the wind, undulating at the edge of the soft lamp light.

Dragos did not hesitate. He strode down the center of the street, fearless of discovery. Lewis watched the Vistana with respect and concern, thinking that his boldness was not entirely from the fact that they had likely already been discovered. Regardless of his bold attitude, Lewis watched every shadow, every movement at the corner of his vision, as he walked down the street, some distance behind Dragos.

"I do not like this," Gregory said, behind Lewis. "Still not a soul, living or dead. Such silence has me on edge, waiting for the trick to end."

Ahead, the fog parted to reveal the wagons exactly where they had been that morning. Zuza and four other Vistani stood waiting. When she saw them, Zuza waved. Behind her and her men, in the square formed by the wagons, Lewis noted twenty or so of the dark-skinned men and women, standing around a fire.

"Welcome, Dragos." Zuza said when they neared. Her voice was low. "You are expected."

"I am honored." Dragos bowed deeply and hurried forward to meet her. Lewis was surprised when Dragos stopped a few feet back; he had not seemed reluctant to see Zuza until he stood still.

"I did not believe Madame Catalena when she told us to expect you." Zuza looked at him with something akin to contempt. "Many of us were too young to remember, but all have heard the story of your fall from grace."

The older man to Zuza's right glared at Dragos and spat on the ground, as did one of the others. A third man offered the Vistana a tight smile and a nod.

"So it would seem." Dragos straightened, an arrogant grace Lewis had not seen in him before, as he met Zuza's gaze squarely. "We must see Madame Catalena at once."

Zuza nodded but did not move aside. Instead, she glanced at Lewis. Then she caught sight of Elise. Her eyes widened, and Lewis thought she might drop to one knee in reverence. It lent credence to Dragos's assertion that Elise fulfilled some Vistani prophecy.

"So, it is true," Zuza said, her voice even quieter. "Lewis Wentworth has two souls."

"What are you saying?" Lewis stepped in front of Elise, prepared to defend her. Dragos had said something of the sort, but Lewis hadn't taken it seriously.

"You heard me, no?" Zuza frowned at him.

"What do you mean, 'two souls'?" Lewis crossed his arms. He didn't want to look weak in front of her, but she gave the impression that she thought him nothing, or slightly less.

"Madame Catalena is waiting for you, Lewis Wentworth . . . and your ghost." Zuza moved aside and motioned them forward with a wave. "She will explain. This time, she says, you will listen, because now you believe that she can see."

"I would speak to this gypsy woman as well," Lord Crandall pushed past Professor Drake to stand next to Lewis.

"Yes?" Zuza looked him up and down, a look that sized him up like livestock and found him wanting. She shook her head. "But you are not important. Captain Wentworth and Professor Drake will come with me. The rest of you," she looked at Gregory and Frederick, "will go with my men. They will give you better weapons." Without allowing Lord Crandall to respond, she spun on one booted heel and moved into the circle of wagons.

Lewis hurried after her as she walked into the inner circle toward Madame Catalena's wagon. The other Vistani watched with curious expressions that ranged from awe as they saw Elise to clear disdain at the sight of Dragos. Some of them muttered amongst themselves and Lewis heard the words "traitor" and "spirit," among others, some in a language he did not understand. He glanced sidelong at Elise, who glided smoothly with him, her face a mask of concentration as she set her sights on Madame Catalena's wagon. Dragos met the angry and occasionally relieved stares of his fellow Vistani with dignity, looking at each of them until the other turned away first.

As they neared the wagon, the door opened and the older woman stepped out. She glanced at the Professor and frowned, then looked at Elise. She stepped down from the wagon and stood before them with her hands on her hips. Her dark eyes focused on Dragos for a moment and her mouth tightened. Lewis could not decide if she looked at him with disgust or anger.

"My wife, I have returned." Joy and fear flashed across the gypsy's features, but he was quickly inscrutable again as he looked at her.

"So it would seem." Madame Catalena nodded in satisfaction. "It is good to see you. And you." Madame Catalena turned on Lewis, her dark gaze like a knife. "You return—older, wiser, and with the truth standing beside you." She inclined her head to Elise.

"I understand the Professor's part in the creation of this place, but I do not know why the rest of us, my wife's spirit included, have been brought here," Lewis said levelly. "I would agree with you, but I do not know all I need to."

"And you, Dragos, are you ignorant as well?" She did not look at him, but instead glanced across the square.

"I know what must be done," he said. To Lewis, the comment seemed cryptic, but she accepted it at face value.

"Very good." She focused on Elise. "And you, ghost . . . do *you* understand?"

"Her name is Elise." Lewis's face flushed with anger at her rude behavior. Elise deserved greater courtesy.

"Her name *was* Elise," Madame Catalena said sternly. "Now, she is more than that. And less."

"You speak in riddles, exactly as you did before." Lewis frowned, wishing that for once, she would say what she meant. He was a military man and accustomed to dealing directly. Her subterfuge frustrated him.

"I know only what I have learned from following Lewis around Mithras Court," Elise said, when Madame Catalena made no reply to Lewis.

"And yet, you sense that there is more, no? You see what Lewis sees, but you see more as you experience this place." Catalena arched an eyebrow. "I sense that you tell them what you can, but there are things you cannot say, words that will not form on your lips." Lewis thought the Vistana's expression seemed neither upset nor happy—simply curious.

"I . . ." Elise glanced at him, looking for help. "I have told Lewis and his friends that there are things . . . things I cannot say."

"I do not accuse you of it. I simply state it as truth." Catalena watched her for a few seconds and nodded as if satisfied. "Tell me, what is the first thing you remember after the Snake murdered you?"

"Endless darkness." Elise frowned. "And then . . . I was with Lewis, in his study in our home. I tried to talk to him, to make him hear me, but he could not."

"I'm sorry." Lewis turned to her. "I wish I could have offered you comfort." He could not know which moment she spoke of; many times, he had sat in his study, staring at his bookshelves numbly, wishing for her to walk through the door, nearly convincing himself that she would.

"It was you who needed my comfort," Elise said. "I watched you playing with my ring and then finally slipping it onto the chain around your neck. It nearly broke my heart."

"I wanted something of you close to me." Lewis bowed his head, but even as sorrow threatened to overwhelm him, anger and rage pushed it aside. The mention of her ring conjured the moment she had described in his mind. It had been only days after her death, mere weeks before he took on his quest to find her killer. "The Snake and his master must pay for their crimes," he said, his voice nearly a whisper. "You have told me not to seek vengeance, but I cannot abandon it, love. I cannot leave them unpunished."

"And they shall be punished, if you can alter the curse." Catalena fixed him with a knowing gaze. "It is up to you and your companions. We cannot force you, though we will provide you with information and other help."

"I thought you said you could not interfere—that there was a balance that you needed to respect?" Lewis asked.

"Lucius Knight is changing the balance. His actions grant us additional freedom which we can use to help you now." Madame Catalena frowned.

"Then perhaps you could enlighten us as to what Lucius Knight plans to do?" Professor Drake said. "You seem to know exactly what is going on."

"Enlightenment comes in small doses," Madame Catalena said with a smile. "I know that Lord Knight brought you three here for a reason. I can guess that it is his desire to be free of his prison and that he hopes to use you toward that end." She blinked at Drake.

"Do you mean me, or all of us?" the Professor asked, turning away under her gaze.

She flashed a grim smile at him. "Lord Knight knows you are here, Professor Drake. He will be looking for you as much as the Captain and his ghostly wife."

Drake swallowed and Lewis saw sweat beading on his forehead. Lewis turned away, refocusing on the Vistana.

"If Lord Knight needs all three of us, then why would we wish to deliver ourselves to him?" Lewis needed something more concrete if he was going to risk their lives on this dangerous plan. Their idea of infiltrating Lucius Knight's home was flawed at best. Surely the tunnel was well known, surely Knight would expect them to go there. And if that were true, then surely Madame Catalena was deliberately sending them to their deaths . . . but why?

"You are concerned that Lucius Knight can find you through your wife's spirit, yes?" She glared at Dragos for an instant. Her husband crossed his arms and raised his chin defiantly, but said nothing.

"Among other things," Lewis said. That one concern hardly captured all of his fears, though it was the one that demanded attention. "The undead have vanished, and it seems likely they have been ordered to capture us or prevent us from doing what we are attempting. Why should we walk right into their arms?"

"Because I will give you this." She reached into a deep purple pouch tied to a bright red sash around her waist and retrieved the grayish-white feather of a large bird. She handed it to him. "This token will make it impossible for Lord Knight to find you thought Elise."

"If I were him, I would protect the secret entrance revealed to us by Dragos's tapestry." Lewis accepted the feather, tucking it into his coat's inside pocket, though he could not help but wonder why Madame Catalena had not given him the token earlier. Surely she must have known that Elise was with him and that Knight could track them. The only explanation was that she wanted things that way, for purposes only she knew.

She glanced up at the dark fog overhead. "First night will end early. When dawn arrives, you must be ready to take action. Knight and his forces are weaker during the day. You have seen this."

"Will that make a difference, should we confront one of his minions?"

"Not unless your ghost can conjure the lightning again. Killing them should not be your goal. You need only slow them down long enough to retrieve the tablet." Madame Catalena frowned as if speaking to a petulant child. "To kill them, you would need silver."

"Then let us find some," Lewis said. "Surely there must be—"

"There is no silver in Mithras Court. Lord Knight forbids it, and his minions watch for it. Spies who report it are well rewarded." She shook her head. "I am sorry. We are surrounded by traitors."

"Will this help?" Professor Drake held his silver pocket watch out in front of them. It glinted in the lamplight.

Catalena's eyes widened in clear astonishment, but she said nothing, taking it from him and feeling the weight in her hands.

"Can your people turn that into musket balls?" At the sight of the watch, hope infused Lewis, sparking new life into his thirst for vengeance as the prospect of killing Richard Bailey became possible. He had given up that quest, turned away from it as Elise has requested, but the minions had been invincible and impossible to defeat. The playing field had just been leveled. For him to ignore his new chance at vengeance would be cowardly and dishonorable.

"Yes. This can make one, perhaps two silver bullets." She handed it to Zuza. "Take this to Garen at once."

"Yes, Madame Catalena." Zuza hurried across the circle, toward the Vistani around the fire.

"Rest now, my friends." Catalena motioned to Dragos. "At first light, Dragos will lead you to the entrance. Once there, you must continue without any of my people."

"Dragos won't be joining us?" Lewis frowned. "But he has the map." Betrayal came to Lewis's mind at the realization. If Dragos went with them, it would be the best proof the Vistani could offer that they were serious about this assault. He wondered at the terms of the Vistani's agreement with Lord Knight, but resolved not to trust Dragos or the other Vistani. Not until they proved themselves worth trusting.

"He will draw it for you on parchment." Catalena glanced at Dragos. "You will not need him once you reach the entrance. His absence would arouse suspicion."

"I will draw it now." Dragos bowed and departed in the direction of a dark green wagon.

"Go now. Join your friends." Catalena pointed to the far side of the fire where Lord Crandall and the others could be seen inspecting firearms. "Zuza's man, Radu, will have additional provisions and weapons you may desire." She turned to leave.

"Wait." Lewis reached for her but before his hand could touch her blouse, she slapped it away and took a step back.

"We are done here." Catalena narrowed her eyes. "I do not think we shall meet again, Lewis Wentworth." She disappeared into her wagon, drawing the flap shut behind her.

"That woman is infuriating," Elise muttered, then added, so quietly that only Lewis and Drake could hear, "These Vistani serve their own purposes. Be wary of them."

"We will." Lewis reached out to her, let his hand pass through her, and then turned. "Let's rejoin our friends and prepare ourselves."

"Oh, dear," Professor Drake said quietly, sounding worried. When Lewis looked at him, Drake was looking across the circle.

"You!" Lord Crandall's shout came as a surprise. He strode toward them angrily, past the crowd of Vistani around the fire, and Lewis felt the Professor stiffen beside him. There had been no provocation for the attack, he thought wildly—the men had put their feud aside. Lewis had no time to ponder it. Crandall descended upon them like a mad wolf.

"Trust me," he hissed quietly. But his face contorted so swiftly that Lewis thought he'd imagined it. Crandall was in full bait, his face red, as he said "You are a thief, Drake!"

"Excuse me?" Lewis blinked in confusion at the man's sudden rage.

The gentleman pointed at Professor Drake and shouted, "Son of a whore!"

"What have I done now?" Professor Drake raised his chin in defiance and stepped into Lord Crandall's path. "I have no other secrets for you to have discovered!"

Lord Crandall closed to within inches of the professor, leaned in, and glared at the man. His hand slipped to the pistol in his belt and he exhaled slowly, as if struggling to keep his temper under control. Lewis moved to place a restraining hand on the gentleman's shoulder, but Crandall shrugged it off.

"It is your fault we are here! Your fault that so many have suffered and died!"

"I have told you that I am sorry, that I truly feel the pain of it all. What more do you wish of me?" He looked upset, guilty, but Lewis noted he was beginning to get angry, pushing back against Crandall's attack.

Lewis felt the heat of curious stares as the Vistani turned their attention to the fight. Those closest stepped toward them, forming a loose circle as they gathered around. They whispered among themselves, and although Lewis caught only pieces of their conversations, he realized suddenly that they were placing bets.

"Lord Crandall, I hardly think this is the time—"

"It is always the time, Captain!" The gentleman whirled on Lewis, eyes blazing. "And *you* can certainly not claim any high ground in this argument, sir! It is your ghostly *whore* who has brought this upon us!"

A crimson veil dropped over Lewis's eyes as he struck Lord Crandall with the full force of his anger behind his fist. Pain shot up his arm as he impacted with the man's cheek bone. Crandall stumbled and fell as Lewis shook out his hand. He had hurt the impertinent bastard; no one called Elise that . . . *no one.*

"Enough!" a harsh female voice yelled from behind them.

"Lewis, stop! It's all right!" Elise added.

"No one says such things about you!" Lewis shook off Professor Drake, who had grabbed his arm in the chaos.

"I said *enough!*" the woman's voice roared. Strong hands closed like a vise around each of Lewis's arms as someone lifted him off Lord Crandall. Zuza's eyes were dark storm clouds, her face a scene of fury. Lewis's own rage faded to disgrace at his loss of control; provoked or not, it was inexcusable to meet Crandall's words with fists. Not wishing to further embarrass himself, he stilled, watching Zuza carefully, trying to make it his own choice to end the fight.

"Zuza!" Dragos's voice cut through the moment. Lewis glanced over his shoulder and saw the man standing next to them. "Release him." Dragos looked up at the woman.

"As you wish." Zuza breathed out slowly as she lowered Lewis to the ground. She turned and extended a hand to Lord Crandall, still on his back from Lewis's blow.

"Leave me be!" The gentleman batted her wrist aside and stood on his own. A red welt had formed on the man's cheek, but he did not seem angry. Rather, he was red-faced with shame. "Professor Drake, please forgive me. I do not know why I did that. I think this place is rather more disturbing than I had thought." He bowed stiffly. "Captain—likewise, my apologies to you and your wife."

"Accepted," Elise said, hovering closer. "Perhaps Knight is to blame?"

"Or perhaps Mithras Court has taken its toll on us all." Lewis's anger subsided at the truth of their situation. "This is not the time for bickering. We must act as one if we are to survive."

"Agreed." Lord Crandall dusted off his clothes. Straightening, he gestured at Gregory and Frederick, where they stood near the supply wagon. "Let us get you better weapons and plan our strategy." He fixed Lewis with an odd look, winked, and stalked away.

Lewis watched him go before he glanced sidelong at Elise and Professor Drake. Elise said nothing; the professor merely shrugged. Taking that as acceptance of Crandall's apology, Lewis hurried after the gentleman. Neither Dragos nor Zuza followed.

CHAPTER TWENTY-SEVEN

"Silver?" Lord Crandall lowered the Winchester he had been inspecting. "If only I'd brought some with me, but I spent my last bit of silver coin buying my train ticket."

Lewis had joined him across the compound at one of the wagons. Several crates and sacks lay about, holding dried food, clothing, oil for the lamps, and a number of weapons provided by Frederick, who had rejoined them moments earlier. The innkeeper stood to the side, a proud look on his face as if he had done them a great service. Lord Crandall gripped his rifle tightly, studying it intently.

"As did I," Gregory said.

"Perhaps we were manipulated into spending our last silver," Lewis said. He was certain he had possessed silver coins as he had boarded the train. When he had arrived in Mithras Court, he had not bothered to check. He'd looked just then, and those coins had vanished. He eyed the weapons, noting with relief that they were not simple muskets.

"Fine weapons," Lord Crandall said. He shook himself suddenly. "I nearly forgot—Frederick brought this as well." He thrust a wooden box toward Lewis.

Lewis recognized the box of Webley bullets right away. He took it greedily, opened it, and counted the shells. The box was full, and he counted twenty-five rounds. He withdrew his revolver from his coat, dropped open the cylinder, and reloaded it. He slammed it home and spun the cylinder. Satisfied, he slipped the weapon and remaining bullets into his pocket, and turned to Frederick.

"Where did you get these rifles and the Webley cartridges?" The answer did not matter, but curiosity got the better of Lewis.

"When newcomers arrive, I am the first person they meet. As such, I can take stock of what they have . . . and I sometimes am left with their items." He bowed his head for a moment as if guilty, but lifted it to look at Lewis. "The Winchesters came from the American cowboys I mentioned. They thought to seize power in Mithras Court . . . they lasted a day. I was fortunate to be nearby when they died. As to the Webley cartridges, an old police constable came through several years after the cowboys. The Mists had taken an interest in him—he got drunk and admitted he had murdered his partner to cover up his morphine addiction. I could not save his pistol, but I salvaged his ammunition."

"Unfortunate for them. But a boon to us." Lewis clapped the man on the arm. "Well done."

"What do we do now?" Professor Drake asked. "Do we follow the Vistana into that tunnel? Does that seem prudent?"

"There is much to this plan that does not sit well with me," Lewis said. "As Lord Crandall mentioned, this could be an elaborate trap. At the very least, our goals and those of the Vistani might not align as well as they would like us to believe. For the moment, we have little choice but to follow along. They are correct in their assumption that an assault to the manor would be suicide. I do believe them when they say that obtaining the tablet is the only way to defeat Lord Knight." Lewis looked from Professor Drake to Lord Crandall.

"But knowing that this could be a trap makes us ready for one," Gregory pulled back the lever of his Winchester, sliding a bullet into place in the chamber.

Lewis turned to look at him, and noticed a crate hidden beneath a tarp under the wagon. The cloth had pulled back slightly, and he read the word Dynamite. "What the devil?" He straightened, catching sight of Lord Crandall and looking at him meaningfully.

"They've forbidden us from taking any of that," the gentleman said.

"Yes," Zuza said, "that is not for you." She had split off from the crowd and joined them without Lewis even noticing. He wondered if she had overheard his suspicions over her people's motivations. He decided it would not matter.

"Do you wish to aid us or not?" Lewis motioned to the crate. "Explosives could be of immense help to our cause." Out of the corner of his eye, he saw Elise watching in silence, wearing a frown.

"It is forbidden." Zuza watched him, her eyes admitting no chance to bargain or even to question.

"Then I question your motives, Zuza." He spoke despite the risk of provoking her.

"Our aid must even the balance that Lord Knight has disrupted. Were we to give it to you, it could tip that delicate equilibrium in his favor." She crossed her arms in emphasis, her expression stern.

"We're talking about ending the curse upon which this place is founded," Professor Drake commented. "And you're worried about a balance?"

"This is one of the rules we must follow. We *will* not break it. Nor will you question it." She swiveled to look at the scholar, her gaze putting a pointed emphasis on her words.

Professor Drake nodded slowly. Lewis saw little point in challenging the Vistani in their own encampment. His arms had gone rigid and the grip on his pistol was tight with tension and frustration. He loosened his hand and rolled his shoulders casually.

"We seem to be your pawns," Lord Crandall remarked, looking thoughtful, and as though he didn't like the conclusion he was reaching.

"We are all pawns." Zuza moved away, leaving the gentleman sputtering indignantly.

They all watched her as she left. Several men joined her in conversation halfway between the fire and Lewis's group. Lewis strained to hear what they were saying but could catch nothing of their discussion. He thought it had to do with the mission they were about to embark upon, but could not be certain.

He looked up at the fog above and thought it appeared brighter.

"We have perhaps an hour to prepare," he said. "Rest if you can. We must all be at our best when the sun rises." He looked at Elise and wondered how many more times he would lay eyes on her. If they were successful, she would likely depart as she crossed over or went wherever spirits went. If he died, he would become a mindless corpse staggering around Mithras Court, perhaps forever. Would she stay with him if that happened, and would he retain enough of himself to remember her? He doubted that, from the walking dead he had seen. None had shown a spark of anything other than burning anger.

The frown she had been wearing for several hours deepened. She looked at him, saying nothing, but with a glance at the others, she said, "I will be with you, Lewis. I will help as much as I am able. But this time, I will also try to keep you safe." She smiled as she looked at him, both love and tenderness in her eyes.

Lewis mouthed "thank you" to her, and rechecked his Webley. He had said his good-byes to her, but after tearing himself away from her in the tunnel hours earlier, he did not think he could bring himself to go through that parting again. He would not say good-bye again, regardless of what happened.

=====MC=====

"Is there nothing more you can do for us?" Lewis asked. He and his companions gathered inside the compound of wagons just after dawn. Frederick, a flintlock in his hands, and Dragos, with no weapon, had led a small entourage of Vistani out to meet them. Madame Catalena, Zuza, and two other guards joined them.

"We have done all we can. To do anything more would risk destroying us all." Madame Catalena turned to Elise. "Ghost, I sense your fears. You need not worry about bringing Lord Knight's minions down upon your group. The feather will protect you from being noticed until any of his true minions lay eyes upon you. Should that occur, the spell will be broken. But by then, I think," and she smiled kindly, "they will know where you all are."

"I shall remain invisible." She flashed Lewis a smile and vanished before his eyes, but her voice touched him gently. "Do not fear, my husband. I am still with you."

"I know, love." Lewis understood her decision, though he still did not trust the Vistani. He did not think they necessarily had his best interests at heart, and thought of the old adage: "the enemy of my enemy is my friend." Surely his group and the Vistani had the same goal, to defeat Lord Knight. Setting themselves free in the process was a great reward—and that was what he questioned. Would they allow them to leave? Would their departure even be possible—or would their altering of the tablet simply tighten the bonds on Knight without releasing them or the other trapped residents of the Court? He tightened his grip on his Webley and turned his attention to the clan leader. If and when their treachery occurred, they would be prepared for it.

"Madame Catalena, how am I supposed to alter the curse tablet if we retrieve it? I have a few notions of how it might be done, but I have no idea if they will work," Professor Drake said.

The Vistana woman gazed at him a long time. "The curse can be changed, if you use this." She reached into her pouch and withdrew a small scroll of yellowed parchment. She handed it to the professor. "When you have the curse tablet in hand, read from this paper. You will shrink the curse to the confines of Lord Knight's home. You will set yourselves, and the citizens of Mithras Court, free."

If you're telling us the whole truth, Lewis thought. He refrained from voicing that thought, content for the moment to see how the game played out.

The Professor opened the paper and read it silently. His eyes widened as understanding dawned on him, and he nodded as he rolled the paper and tucked it away.

"I believe this will work." He beamed and stood straighter than he had since escaping from the train station. His conscience was relieved at finding a solution. "Yes, this will do the job . . . at least, I think it will."

"You're not certain?" Lord Crandall said with a frown.

"I am not an expert in the results of curses. Until this one worked, I did not even think they were real. It appears to do what they promise. That is the best I can tell you," Drake said.

"That's good enough, Professor," Lewis said. The scholar surely would have recognized a ruse.

"What if we should encounter the Snake, or Lord Knight's other minions?" Gregory inquired, hefting his rifle. "These will not be of much use."

"Then you will use these." Catalena held out her hand, and Zuza passed her two silver musket balls. "These are all that could be fashioned from the Professor's watch, but it might be enough."

"But there are four minions," Professor Drake said.

"Nothing else can be done." Catalena looked at him levelly and folded her hands.

"Very well, then." Lord Crandall took the silver balls and handed them to Gregory. He pulled his antiquated pistol from his belt. "Gregory, please load the silver into my flintlock, as well as the Captain's."

Lewis handed his pistol to the man. As the servant loaded the weapons, Lewis looked at the Vistana before him. He studied her pale features, searching for any signs of deception, but saw only grim determination and conviction.

He didn't trust her expression. He still had the sense that something was wrong—the mission had come together far too easily.

"Can this really be done?" he asked, curious to know how she would answer.

"Yes." She smiled. "Dragos will guide you to the secret tunnel entrance. Should you survive and succeed, you will return to London—we will not meet again."

"And if we do not survive?" Lewis gazed at her. That had always been the other option, but she had never before suggested the possibility. He wasn't sure whether he preferred the certainty the Vistana had previously displayed, or if he preferred this realism about their fate. Even if the Vistana did not influence that fate.

"Then you will be dead. Or worse."

"Well, then. Thank you for what aid you have rendered." Lewis turned away from her, not wishing to reveal his distrust. If she already knew, he could do nothing, but if she did not, he could, perhaps, convince her that he suspected nothing. He glanced at his companions and said solemnly, "No matter what we might encounter, do not panic. If anyone attempts to flee without my direct order, I shall shoot you myself. We *must* remain a cohesive unit if we are to have any chance of success." He had given that exact speech to his men the night before the Zulu spear had hit him. To their credit, none of his men had broken ranks during the battle, and one of them had pulled Lewis onto his horse, risking his own life to save his commander. Lewis hoped his raw group would live up to that success.

"Follow me." Dragos nodded farewell to Madame Catalena, then glanced at Lewis and stepped into the fog.

Wishing that Elise were visible at his side, Lewis followed the gypsy.

Chapter TWENTY-EIGHT

"That is the way." Dragos pointed to the yawning stairway below them.

Lewis risked a glance around the dark alley into which the gypsy had led them. Nestled between two brick homes, the long, narrow lane led from Knight Street back into the gloom. They neither saw nor heard a single man, woman, or monster, as on the rest of their swift journey through Mithras Court.

Lewis could not shake the increasing sense that every being within the Mists knew what was about to happen. The thought was chilling; it could reveal foreknowledge of their plans, not just on Knight's part but on the part of all the citizens of the place. He looked into Dragos's dark eyes, but saw only stillness there.

That did little to ease his fears. As he had already perceived, much more was at work than either Madame Catalena or Dragos had told them. For the moment, though, he felt they were safe enough. Surely a betrayal would come only when they had achieved the objective of reaching the tablet.

"How will we find our way once we descend into this tunnel?" Lewis looked for a change in the man's expression but saw none. Dragos's eyes were still emotionless, his thoughts hidden.

The Vistana withdrew a folded paper from a pouch at his side. "As Madame Catalena promised, here is the map provided by my tapestry. It will guide you true."

"Excellent." Lewis took the paper, unfolded it, and examined it. Satisfied that it resembled the tapestry he had shown them earlier, he handed it to Professor Drake. "If you would navigate, Professor."

"Of course." He took it carefully, saying, "I shan't let you down."

"Then let's go." Frederick eyed the hole. Lewis thought he looked nervous, but he was not surprised. They were finally making the move to attack Lord Knight directly. Though the prospect filled Lewis with a savage eagerness, the innkeeper likely had different feelings about it.

"You seem nervous, innkeeper." Lord Crandall, with his Winchester across his arm, stepped closer to the man. "Do you know something we are unaware of?"

"Isn't what we already know enough?" Frederick drew himself up, pistol in hand. "What we are about to do is foolhardy. Unlike you, I have proven my commitment to the Court's freedom by trying to end Lord Knight's rule before. I remember the cost of failure. I would just as soon get it over with."

"Of course." Lord Crandall nodded, but his expression did not match his kindly tone. Looking at Lewis, he said, "Captain, we shall follow your lead."

Lewis paused for a moment in the hope that Elise might whisper to him, but she remained silent, as he knew she should. The hair on his arm rose suddenly, as if her ghostly hand had brushed it, and perhaps it had, he thought with a smile. He steeled himself and glanced at his companions, then settled his gaze on Frederick.

"We will do our best to keep you safe." He turned to Dragos. "Thank you for your help." The sooner they were rid of him, the better. They needed to speak freely, without the Vistana overhearing.

"Of course." Dragos bowed deeply. "I shall return to Catalena's side." Without waiting for another word, the gypsy turned and disappeared into the fog at the edge of the alley.

"Professor?" Lewis motioned to the scholar's lantern. As the only man without a rifle, he would carry their source of light.

"Very well." The old man opened the lantern, lit it with a match, and then closed it again. He held it high and nodded. Once again, he carried Lewis's cane.

"I don't like this one whit." Lord Crandall spoke quietly, sweeping his weapon around them. "This tunnel is not as deserted as we were led to believe. I had expected it to be more remote—entirely forgotten. This looks as if it has been used in the past weeks."

"A moment." Lewis peered into the fog where Dragos had vanished. When he was satisfied that the man had truly gone and he could speak without fear of discovery, he turned on Frederick.

"Now we can speak plainly, yes?" He looked directly at the innkeeper.

"What do you mean?" Frederick's expression was nervous.

"Do I really need to ask the question?" Lewis arched one eyebrow. He had little patience for subterfuge, especially now that the Vistana had left.

"I don't know what—"

"No more lies, no more evasions." Gregory swung his rifle around, aiming it at the big man; he looked serious. "What are the Vistani up to?"

"I don't know what you're talking about." Frederick did not even attempt to raise his weapon. "I know only what they told you." His voice had a slight tremor in it, and he looked uncomfortable with the questions.

"Of course you don't." Lewis said. "I question their motives and this plan, innkeeper. And I question *you*."

Frederick did not answer.

"You have an air about you that reminds me of a soldier marching toward certain death." Lewis stepped closer to the big man and glared at him. "Am I correct?"

"If you are, then there's nothing you can do to threaten me," Frederick said. "According to you, I am already dead."

Lord Crandall made an inarticulate noise that reminded Lewis of a growl. "Tell us what you know, you impudent wretch, or so help me, I'll splatter your brains against that wall!" He raised his rifle threateningly.

"There is nothing you can do to me," Frederick repeated, defiance in his voice.

"Easy, Lord Crandall." Lewis put his hand on the gentleman's arm, gently pushing the rifle off aim. "Stay sharp."

"But this is clearly a trap!" Gregory said.

"It was a trap before we came here with our reluctant innkeeper," Lewis said. "I do not, however, believe that any harm will come to us until we are in the manor. Further, since the Vistani clearly need us to retrieve the tablet, I do not believe that any betrayal will occur until we have taken possession of it." He paused to look at Frederick. "Knowing that, we can spring their trap on our own terms once we have the tablet. The question is, Frederick, how far will you go to preserve the Vistani's secret?" Lewis narrowed his eyes at the innkeeper.

"Try me." Frederick's voice shook ever so slightly.

"We shall." He turned his attention back to the group. "We have no choice but to continue on until we learn the truth. We need that tablet, and I do not believe we have any other options. Since we know that a trap will be sprung, we will undoubtedly be more careful than the Vistani and this wretch expected,"—he looked dismissively at Frederick—"and I believe we can succeed as long as we look sharp. Once we have the tablet in hand, we will have leverage against both Knight and the Vistani. We must continue forward. Are we in agreement?"

"I concur." Lord Crandall hefted his rifle. "All we can do is make the best of this, with caution."

"I am with you," Professor Drake said as he looked at Lewis.

"Very good, sir," Gregory said. "I'll keep Frederick in my sights."

"You realize I can hear you." Frederick stepped into line behind Lewis.

"Yes." Lewis strode forward. "You realize that your opinion does not matter to me."

The innkeeper frowned, but said nothing.

"Then let us proceed." Lewis, with Professor Drake at his side and his revolver held ready, slowly descended into the dank depths. Lord Crandall and Gregory followed behind Frederick.

Cobwebs brushed against Lewis's head and he heard small creatures skittering on tiny feet away from the light—and the sound of something larger moving through muck. The light revealed a low ceiling held up by ancient beams. Webs hung in every corner like silk stalactites, while dust motes hovered in the air, looking suspended in time. Thick, damp mud covered the ground, making it impossible to determine if there had ever been a stone floor to the place. Smeared footprints covered every inch of it, marking the passage of unknown beasts.

A passage led away into the darkness. As they paused, a loud crash came from behind them. Lewis whirled around and realized that the door above had been shut. They heard the sound of metal sliding against metal as the thick bar slid home, locking them inside.

"We're trapped!" Gregory brought his rifle up, though there was no target, and Lewis was sure that the thick metal bar could not be shot off with a gun.

"This was to be expected," Lewis said coolly. He had not thought that the Vistani would trap them down there, but that made a certain amount of sense. "They do not wish for us to have second thoughts." He glanced at Frederick but saw the same concern as before. If he knew this was going to happen, he did not give any indication of it.

"What do we do?" Drake asked.

Lewis turned toward the tunnel. "We go on. Our goals have not changed, though we must proceed with the utmost caution."

"And what if this is the trap, the betrayal?" Lord Crandall asked.

"The Vistani need us to reach the tablet alive," Lewis said, sure of himself. "It is the only logical solution to our problem. We must be safe, for the moment." He motioned toward the tunnel. "Let us continue."

Drake fell into step beside him and they moved forward.

The light pressed back the darkness, revealing more of the narrow passageway that had clearly been built by ancient Roman, it might or might not have had something to do with the cult of Mithras. Remnants of that once-great empire lay hidden all over England. Lewis focused his attention on the path ahead. As they moved, he became aware of the stench of rot and decay, not just of wood and earth, but of flesh and blood. It teased at first, merely the faintest aroma, but quickly grew more prominent.

"My God, what is that smell?" Professor Drake held the lantern before him like a talisman warding off evil.

"I believe we all *know* what that is," Lord Crandall said grimly. "The walking dead are here—or have been. Very recently."

A sudden fierce wind whipped past them, blowing their coats behind them. Before Lewis could say anything, he heard the low moan of the dead accompanying the wind, far closer than he would have liked. He stopped, bringing the others up short with a raised hand and peering into the gloom at the light's edge. Shadowy pockets of deep darkness shifted ever so slightly, making him uncertain what might be there. He breathed Elise's name in silent prayer; she would be very welcome at his side. She did not appear, but even with the risks of her appearance, it was disappointing.

"Do you see something?" Lord Crandall raised his Winchester.

"I'm not certain." Lewis squinted at the darkness and took two steps forward. As the Professor followed and the light moved, so too moved the shadows. The shift was accompanied by the soft sound of feet dragging in the mud.

"We are not alone." His voice was calm, but he could not ignore the terrible dread that pressed upon him—all those undead, all waiting, more silent than he had ever heard them. He wondered if the Vistani had known this would occur or if Knight had somehow learned of their plans. If the numbers of the dead were few, then this might be merely an obstacle—and was not totally unexpected. His feet felt weighed down by cement blocks, and he hoped he would not need to move swiftly. "There."

"The walking dead?" Gregory kept his voice low, but it resounded nonetheless through the hallway, and Lewis heard the dull echo in the distance.

"It seems likely," Professor Drake raised the lantern higher, but it did little to help. A sudden wind caused the flame within the glass to flicker and dim.

Fear churned in Lewis's stomach, and all he could do was raise his pistol, aiming at the shadows; the wind gusted stronger and the lamp's light danced mockingly on the walls. The gun was no defense against the wind, nor against so many undead. He cursed himself for believing that the tunnel would be empty. He was still convinced that the Vistani needed his group to succeed. Such an immediate and obvious betrayal made no sense . . . unless Knight had outmaneuvered them all.

"They knew we were coming." Lewis turned to Frederick. "Why would the Vistani do this to us? It doesn't make sense! I expected the trap to come later."

"I don't know." The innkeeper shrank back from him. "Maybe Lord Knight discovered our plans?"

"And how would he do that?" Lord Crandall said, his voice dangerous.

"I don't know," Frederick repeated. "But if you thought this was a trap, then why come?" he asked.

"Sometimes," Lewis said, with a serious look in his eyes, "people who lie to you tell you the truth by omission. I do believe that the curse can be altered as Professor Drake thinks it can. As long as we were prepared for the trap, we could not be surprised by it. Until this point, we have been pawns in the Vistani's plans. That ended when we decided to go on, even knowing we were walking into a trap."

The dead moaned and hissed, drawing his attention.

"I did not think they would spring anything upon us until we had the tablet," Lewis said, fear gripping him.

"None of this makes sense." Lord Crandall glanced sidelong at Lewis. "Why would the Vistani allow Frederick to give us these weapons if they meant for us to be captured?"

"We cannot know what their true goals are." Professor Drake had to shout to be heard over the rising wind.

Lewis looked at Frederick, and the big man was far more nervous. Whatever the Vistani's true plans were, he had to know more. He frowned and pointed his gun at the innkeeper. "Believe me when I tell you this—I will feed you to the dead if you do not immediately tell us all you know." The wind whipped up again, tousling Lewis's hair and snatching his voice away, but from the look on Frederick's face, he heard the command.

Frederick looked at him for a moment; something in Lewis's face convinced him that his threat was serious. "They promised to transport my daughters to another domain, one called Borca, if I came here with you. It's safe there."

"That was easy," Lord Crandall said. "I thought you would be evasive again." Lewis nodded his agreement and stared at the innkeeper.

"Was it?" Frederick turned toward him, anger burning in his eyes. "We've been manipulated and used by Lord Knight and the Vistani for thirty-five years, and I'm tired of it. They agreed to free my daughters, a promise I am convinced they will not break. When they give you their word, they always keep it."

"They've clearly lied to us!" Lewis protested.

"But they gave you no word to break," Frederick countered. "And now that I've led you here, I am free of my obligation to them and to Lord Knight. For the first time in thirty-five years, I can make my own decisions without fear of repercussions to my family. I am tired of Mithras Court, tired of Knight, and tired of the Vistani. Most of all, I am tired of living in constant fear. To answer your question—yes, this is a trap, and yes, I will help you!" He paused to catch his breath. "The Vistani need you to get the tablet. But they believe the only way to get you through Lord Knight's defenses is to allow you to be captured."

"So these dead will not kill us?" Lord Crandall sounded incredulous.

"All I know for certain is that Lord Knight needs Captain Wentworth and Professor Drake alive. I do not know about the rest of you." Frederick frowned. "I would guess that you do not matter."

"When we get to the tablet, what then?" Lewis asked.

"You would do as they asked, and change the curse as the Vistani wish," Frederick said.

"Will that set us free as they have said?" Lewis asked, doubt clouding his mind.

"I don't know." Frederick meant it—Lewis was certain. "What do you intend to do now?" He watched, his eyes wide, but filled with a desperate hope that Lewis might save him.

"We shan't allow you or anyone else to be taken or killed." Lewis swiveled forward. The other men followed suit, bringing their guns up. Before they could shoot, Lewis ordered, "Hold your fire. We are in a bad tactical situation. The minions cannot be far behind these dead."

"What shall we do to escape?" Gregory looked to Lewis the way a soldier looked at his commander. He glanced at Frederick and handed him the musket he carried, keeping the Winchester for himself.

The dead made no move to advance into the circle of light. Lewis watched them for several seconds, then snatched the feather Madame Catalena had given him from his pocket and thrust it at Frederick. "Does this really work? Does it shield Elise from Lord Knight's vision?"

"I would guess that it is just a feather." Frederick bowed his head. "No doubt the Vistani thought it would get you to accept their trap more easily. Or perhaps they thought it a joke to appease you."

"Then I add my light to yours!" Elise appeared abruptly, though her glow was dimmer than before. "Now, my love. You must go back the way you came—the dead are only before you. Now, run!"

Elise's radiance pushed back the darkness and the dead recoiled. But the wind howled louder and faster, blowing dirt and debris into Lewis's face, making him squint. The lantern dimmed and Elise's nimbus faded, as if the wind was more than just air—as if it fed on light. The sound of skittering feet suddenly rose, joining the howl.

"What the devil is that?" Lord Crandall asked, his tone no longer one of demand but of fear.

"It's the Scorpion." Frederick's voice was truly panicked.

"We run, but carefully. Professor, stay in the center. Gregory, take the point. Lord Crandall and I will cover the rear."

"There's nowhere to run!" Frederick said. "Dragos locked and barred the entrance. Ten of us couldn't open it!"

Lewis had expected treachery, but he'd thought that dropping them into the trap would be sufficient. Locking the door had seemed pointless, since they had no other options but to try the tunnel. Now, however, he knew the truth, that the Vistani did indeed wish them to alter the curse, but that they believed that the only way to get them to it was by allowing them to be captured. Damn them for their ability to see a bigger picture.

"If the door is locked, then we are truly trapped," Drake said grimly.

Lewis faced the gathering storm and gritted his teeth. "Then we fight." And we die, a small voice added. He glanced at Elise. He saw no sign of the fear she had to be feeling; only love shone in her eyes. If this was to be his end, their end, then he could think of no better way to go than fighting by her side.

"Not yet, Captain. Gregory appropriated several sticks of dynamite from the Vistani." Lord Crandall smiled smugly.

"That's impossible. They'd never part with it!" Frederick said.

"That was the point of my argument!" Lord Crandall turned toward the Professor. "That is why I attacked you, despite our resolution. We needed a diversion."

"One stick should open the door," Gregory murmured thoughtfully. He pulled a red stick of dynamite from his coat and held it up, examining it.

"Now we run!" Lewis pointed down the tunnel as the skittering grew louder. "Move back to the cellar—hurry!" He was still baffled by his misread of the tactical situation, but he had little time to dwell on it. Escape was now their primary concern. Once they left the depths of the tunnel, they could regroup and figure out what options remained open to them, if any.

Frederick, surprise and sudden hope on his face, fled back the way they had come, almost before Lewis finished speaking.

"Slow down!" Lewis called. "The light!"

"You're right." Frederick stopped at the edge of the light, perhaps ten feet away. He exhaled slowly, trying to calm himself, and raised the musket. He nodded as if ready to perform a measured retreat.

The wind increased around them as the lights dimmed and the scorpions closed. They moved as swiftly as they could while staying close together. Lewis's men stuck with him, even Frederick, blazing the trail ahead of them and staying controlled and within the light's circle.

A scream brought them up short. Frederick skidded to a halt in the dirt and brought his musket up as a section of the nearby wall opened inward as if of its own volition. Dozens of dead hands reached out to grab hold of him.

"Frederick!" Lewis aimed the Webley as clawed hands tightened their deadly grip. The innkeeper's musket fired, its ball ricocheting off the wall.

"Professor, bring the light!" Lewis said. He fired the Webley and moved forward. The bullet struck a creature, causing it to release its grip on Frederick, but two more filled the gap, drawing the innkeeper into the shadows of the doorway.

"Captain!" Frederick's shout weakened as clawed hands tore at him and a spray of blood flew.

"I'm here, my friends!" Drake hurried after Lewis. The bright glow from his lantern pushed back the dead, but they did not release their grip on the innkeeper. Instead, they pulled the big man into the gap of the doorway, using him as a shield against the light.

Lewis fired into the mob of corpses as they dragged Frederick inexorably into the side passage. No one was going to die again. He had considered the man a dubious ally until mere moments earlier, but since he had decided that Frederick had truly aligned himself with them, he could not let the man die.

Another of the dead fell away, but another filled the gap.

"Elise! Help us!" Lewis called, wondering where she had gone.

"I am here!" Elise glided next to him, her glow dimming. Even with her added light, the monsters pulled Frederick deeper inside.

The crack of shots echoed through the tunnel as the others fired from behind. Lewis hoped desperately that they would not hit one of their own.

"Captain!" Frederick wailed, his voice a muffled gurgle.

"Oh, Lewis!" Elise said. "Help him!"

"I'm trying!" Lewis fired again and grabbed the front of Frederick's shirt. He pulled hard against the dead, but slowly gave ground as their superior numbers dragged the two of them through the doorway.

The howling wind blew stronger. Their lantern dimmed against it and Elise's glow faded. Lewis knew he was losing the man, and if they did not leave him and run, he would not be the only one to fall. Yet

Lewis could not abandon him. No one else would die—no one!

"There are too many of them!" Lord Crandall yelled. "There is nothing we can do! The Scorpion is nearly on top of us!"

Time slowed to a crawl as Lewis struggled against the tide of corpses. In that moment, he realized he had to let the innkeeper die in order to save them all. He released his grip on the man's shirt. The dead pulled Frederick deeper into the secret passage. And then he was gone.

"Damn you!" Lewis fired until he ran dry, hoping he had struck the innkeeper in the head, hoping that he might at least save the man from rising again. Another life had been lost—another man he had tried to save. Mithras Court mocked him again.

"Keep moving, Captain!" Lord Crandall caught up, slapping him on the arm and jarring him from his misery. "Go!"

The wind was so fierce that the men could not hear one another without shouting. Ominous dread settled over Lewis as the Scorpion pressed down on them, and the atmosphere felt tainted; the minion was affecting his ability to focus. He turned away from the opening in the wall and hurried along with the others, gasping in relief as the cellar came into view ahead of them.

"Form a firing line while Gregory plants the dynamite!" Lewis reloaded swiftly, trying not to fumble the bullets under the onslaught of the dead. "Lord Crandall, prepare to fire your silver shot!"

They did as he instructed, moving with soldierly precision. Gregory passed his Winchester to Drake, who set the lantern on the floor so that he could hold the gun, but his movements were stiff; clearly he was unused to using such a weapon. Gregory ran into the cellar while Lord Crandall turned and took up a position next to the Professor, aiming his weapon at the dead beyond Lewis. He raised his Webley as he turned. Elise hovered at his side, lending her meager light.

"Elise, what is wrong? Your glow has faded even more!" Lewis had not thought Elise could be endangered, but her dimming glow made him wonder if she were under some form of spiritual attack. He feared for her soul.

"I don't know!" Panic crossed her ghostly features and tears brimmed in her eyes. "Something saps my strength!"

"The Scorpion comes!" Professor Drake raised Gregory's Winchester as a cloud of roiling shadow coalesced from the darkness. It mimicked the tumultuous storms of the Snake and the Raven.

Lewis swallowed. They would quickly find out if the Vistani had lied about the efficacy of silver. If it had no effect, then they all would soon be dead. He took a deep breath and watched.

To Lewis's relief, the Scorpion slowed, but he could not tell how the minion had detected the threat of their presence. Then the cloud stopped, shrinking back a little, as if the creature were suddenly afraid, as if it could feel the silver.

"It's set!" Gregory shouted as he ran from the stairway at the exit. A few seconds later, he tapped Lewis and Lord Crandall on the shoulders. "Cover your ears and get up against the walls!"

Lewis did as he was told, clapping his fingers over his ears as he pressed flat against the wall. The others followed suit, all save Lord Crandall, who covered one ear so he might keep his pistol aimed at the Scorpion.

The dynamite exploded with deafening force, sending flame, splinters, and chunks of stone and debris in all directions. Pain lanced sharply through Lewis's right arm as a piece of metal embedded in his bicep. His head smacked against the stone, not hard enough to knock him unconscious, but the room tilted sideways and he hit the ground. Lord Crandall was pushed past him, striking the opposite wall hard, and Professor Drake fell forward, dropping the rifle. Worse, he tripped over the lantern as he fell.

Lewis watched the lantern land on its side and go out.

"Lewis, get up!" Elise said. "Lewis!" Panic filled her voice, and for a moment he could not understand why—until he remembered where he was. If he died at the hands of the undead, he would become a mindless shambling monster.

He fought against his injuries, his swimming head, and the ringing in his ears. The room still spun, but came swiftly under control as he forced the pain away. He rolled, came up into a crouch, and spotted his Webley lying nearby. He grabbed it, raising it into position just as the cloud recovered, growing in size. In the center of the hallway, Lord Crandall tried to stand with the help of Professor Drake. His pistol with the silver ball had landed between them and the Scorpion's storm. Lewis realized that Crandall was all they had for defense at that moment.

"Lewis!" Elise pointed at the furious tempest and moved to float between them. She raised her arm and appeared as if she tried to channel some power, but her glow only brightened slightly. The cloud did not slow.

The dim light from the open exit, combined with Elise's ever-waning glow, was barely enough to keep the dead away, but with a jolt of dread, Lewis realized it would not stop the Scorpion. He reached for his own pistol to fend off the creature, but Gregory had leaped into action. The man dived forward past them, hitting the ground and rolling. He grabbed the lost pistol and brought it around as the roiling cloud loomed over him. Their enemy filled the entire hallway, preventing them from seeing beyond it. The skittering of the scorpions ceased, plunging the room into silence. Before he could fire, a scorpion's tail slammed out of the cloud, piercing Gregory with a grotesque spray of red as it impaled him, the tip protruding from his chest.

Gregory gasped in shock, blood pouring from his sputtering mouth. He looked at Lord Crandall and, oddly, a look of sheer embarrassment passed over his face. With a tiny part of his brain, Lewis noted the oddity, that Gregory knew he'd failed.

His voice rasped, the sounds only half formed, as he said, "I'm sorry, sir." But as the Scorpion jerked him backward into the cloud, he fumbled the gun, bringing it to bear. As he vanished inside the maelstrom, a shot resonated through the tunnel, the sound nearly too loud for the stones to contain.

An inhuman screech tore the air and the cloud recoiled, paused, and retreated in the opposite direction. It left only a trail of black ooze and a broken corpse. For an instant, Lewis thought it was their enemy, that the silver shot had done its work, but it was Gregory, his body lying in a pool of his own blood, his eyes staring sightlessly at the ceiling.

"Gregory!" In a rage, Lord Crandall fired at the retreating cloud but his bullets caused no harm. "Filthy whoreson!" He fired with each step he took, despite the growing crowd of the dead that filled the hall. With dawning horror—would this place never cease to frighten?—Lewis realized that the room was nearly dark. The dead were safe to attack them.

Lewis leaped across the hall and grabbed Lord Crandall by the arm, pulling him backward. "He's gone! Don't let his death be in vain!" With only Elise's feeble glow to hold the dead at bay, they had but seconds to escape. And they had no time to mourn, though Lewis wished to mark the servant's sacrifice—such bravery deserved recognition.

As if his words had galvanized them into action, the dead shambled forward, unsteady at first, but gaining strength and speed as Elise's light dimmed nearly to darkness.

"Bastards!" Grief was etched on Lord Crandall's face. "He was my friend! We must take his body with us!"

"We must *go!*" Lewis fired into the throng of the dead, dropping one. "Snap out of it, man! He would not wish your death added to his!"

"Gregory comes with us." Lord Crandall's voice was firm as he fired again, then his rifle merely clicked as the hammer fell on an empty chamber.

The moan of the dead grew louder as they shuffled forward, closing the gap slowly but inexorably. Every step they took matched a dimming flicker of Elise's light, and the companions teetered on the balance point; if they did not move instantly, they would be dead in moments.

Lewis saw the pain etched in Lord Crandall's face and his own emotions nearly overwhelmed him. So many had died, so many had suffered, and it had to end. His eyes flicked to Gregory's broken body and in that instant, his sympathy overwhelmed him. He slipped his pistol into his pocket and knelt beside Gregory, hoisting him onto his shoulder. He hoped to God that the stalwart servant would not become one of the walking corpses before they could carry him out into the light, but the memory of the church and the ritual they'd seen steadied him as he lifted the body.

"Professor, cover us!" Lewis saw that the old man had retrieved and aimed Gregory's rifle, ignoring the broken lantern at his feet. "Lord Crandall, get your wits about you, man! Reload and *move!*"

"Get behind me, my friends!" Professor Drake fired the weapon; the shot was off target, but the dead fell backward nonetheless as he fired again.

"I'm with you, Captain!" Lord Crandall backed away swiftly, reloading his Winchester as he moved.

"Get back, foul things!" Elise glided past Lewis, again placing herself between him and the advancing dead. Her glow had faded even more and she was little more than a wisp. She roared with exertion as she raised her arms, her nimbus brightening, but only slightly. "Run!"

The dead shambled toward her but moved slowly. Lewis ran into the cellar, negotiating the debris of cracked stones, fallen beams, and splinters of wood and metal, all the while balancing Gregory's body over his shoulders. He nearly fell, but despite the chunk of metal still protruding from his bicep, he reached the stairs. He climbed with strength born of desperation, swiftly reaching the top. The thick metal door that had blocked their way lay to the side of the entrance; the metal bar that Dragos had used to imprison them had blown several feet onto the worn stones of the alley.

The fog at both ends of the lane made it impossible to see what might lie beyond, but for the moment, the diffuse daylight offered protection from the dead. Lewis staggered several feet from the doorway and lowered Gregory's body to the ground, seating himself next to the man. He watched as Elise, her form shimmering in and out of sight, floated over to him. The professor and Lord Crandall followed, still firing into the cellar as they backed up the steps. They were covered in dirt and debris, and they bled from minor cuts, but on the whole they appeared unharmed.

"That bastard will pay for this!" Lord Crandall's face was so red he looked as if he might explode. He dropped to his knees beside Gregory, lowered his Winchester, and reached out to close his servant's eyes. "I am sorry, my friend."

"If we can get the tablet, I can fix this!" the Professor said abruptly.

"Are you daft?" Lord Crandall whirled on him, eyes blazing. "You can't bring him back from the dead, can you?"

"Alas, no." Drake bowed his head. "But I can prevent Knight and his minions from killing anyone else. If we can just reach that tablet."

Lewis groaned inwardly. He saw little chance of them reaching the tablet—in fact, he wondered if they might survive another night. Their only hope of escape had dissolved away. He gritted his teeth as frustration at his failures nearly overwhelmed him. He could think of no way to overcome Lord Knight. Then he realized that one option had not been completely exhausted. There were the Vistani.

"Bah, we cannot get anywhere near that tablet! And if we cannot leave this place, then we are truly doomed!" Lord Crandall spat.

"No—I believe we are not." Lewis spoke calmly even as he pulled the metal fragment from his arm. The pain seared his flesh, but he fought against it. He tore a piece of fabric off of his dirt-smeared shirt and dressed the wound. Elise watched him with concern but he ignored her, focusing on the pain. "We can't give up. If the Vistani promised to take Frederick's daughters somewhere safe, they can take us there as well. We'll force them to help us, find our way back to London and return with a battalion of the Queen's soldiers to set Mithras Court to rights!" Professor Drake reached over to tie off his bandage.

"Does it hurt?" Elise asked, gliding over to him, her face a mask of concern as if she desperately wished she could help.

"I'll live." Her concern made him feel better, but he did not wish to feel better. He would need his pain, his anger, if he was to keep himself focused and effective. He turned away from her and looked at his companions.

"What about the two of you?" he gestured at Lord Crandall's scratched and bloodied face, and Professor Drake's blood-smeared scalp. "Do you require attention?"

"I am fine." Lord Crandall's leg wound had started bleeding again, but he gave no indication of concern.

"I'll weather this storm as well," Professor Drake said. It did not sound competitive, something Lewis was both pleased and perplexed by, but if they had truly been able to set aside their differences, he would not complain.

"Then it is time to take this fight to the Vistani." Lewis reloaded his Webley. "They are going to help us, by God." The gypsies had set them up, betrayed them in the hope that they would be captured. Whatever their true reasons, they had caused the deaths of Frederick and Gregory. They would be held to account.

"Yes." Lord Crandall looked up, a sliver of hope in his eyes. "We'll make them pay for this outrage—for their lies and their cowardice. We will have our own back."

"But there are so many of them," Professor Drake said. "How can we hope to convince them of anything?"

"They are powerful, Lewis," Elise said, her worry deepening.

"Men with nothing left to lose can accomplish much," he said grimly. "All we need do is take Madame Catalena hostage and they will do whatever we ask of them." Lewis sighed. Again, this place would force him to act as a bandit. Taking women hostage was hardly honorable, but they had no choice.

"And how will we do that?" Professor Drake asked, stroking his beard thoughtfully.

"We will find a way." Lewis was far past reason. The Vistani were the key to gaining access in and out of Mithras Court, and he would turn that key.

"Yes, Lewis. Find a way!" Elise reached for him, pausing as her hand passed through his shoulder. "Make them heed you!"

Lewis felt a slight tingle as her hand touched him, though he could not be sure it was her. The abrupt tolling of distant bells broke the silence, growing louder with every passing second, and Lewis realized it was a sound he'd heard in this place before—one that did not herald good news.

"Second night is upon us." Lord Crandall's voice was almost reverent as he looked at the fog.

Lewis realized that the diffuse light was indeed faltering. And he realized that they were in a race against time, even more than he'd expected. Soon Lord Knight's minions would be even more powerful, and the Vistani would depart—his trio had to leave with them, if they were to survive. Even with the remaining silver bullet, he did not think they could stand against an attack by the minions.

"We've not a moment to lose," Lewis said sharply. He looked at Gregory's body and said, "Take the dynamite and let us make haste to the gypsy camp!"

Lord Crandall nodded, naked sorrow on his face, and reached into Gregory's torn coat, retrieving two dynamite sticks. He stood and took aim with his rifle at Gregory's head, but tears streaked down his face.

"What are you doing?" Professor Drake's eyes widened and he recoiled a little.

"I cannot allow him to become one of those mindless things." The gentleman chambered a cartridge, but hesitated.

The bells grew louder, the sky darker, and Lewis knew they could not wait any longer.

"Leave him or shoot him, but decide," he ordered, wanting to give the man an excuse not to shoot his dead friend. He could only imagine the horror of having to shoot someone he cared for to prevent them from rising again in such a terrible place. "We must go now. The Vistani will be leaving. It might already be too late." He hurried to the end of the alley and saw that Knight Street was completely empty, an eerie silence over the area as the bells fell silent. In the distance, he could hear horses' hooves striking the cobblestones.

"Are the wagons departing?" Professor Drake asked.

"I think so." Lewis peered into the street, panic rising within him. The Vistani were their only chance of survival. They had no option but to fight their way free, just the three of them.

A single shot rang out in the alley behind them and Lewis knew the deed was done. It was a sad affair, but it bolstered his respect for Lord Crandall. Lewis turned and saw the gentleman lower his rifle. Gregory lay in a pool of blood that had not been there a moment earlier. Lewis did not look for long, not wishing to see the man's shattered remains.

Lord Crandall bent to retrieve Gregory's ammunition, then hurried to join the others at the end of the street. The distant baying of dogs sounded, a new terror to be faced.

"The Dog," Professor Drake said. His voice was nearly a whisper.

"You must run!" Elise said suddenly, her voice sharp. "Run for the Vistani, Lewis!"

Her voice urged him on, launched him forward. His arm throbbed, but pain no longer concerned him. If they could not reach the Vistani in time, nothing would matter. Darting along the empty street, he raced against the waning light and the approaching dogs. He veered onto Bacchus Way, and in moments, he neared the area where the Vistani had made their camp.

As he had feared, but had hoped not to see, their wagons were gone.

Lewis peered into the fog-enshrouded gloom ahead of them, then closed his eyes and listened. The creak of wagons and the sound of hooves echoed in the distance. It was difficult to discern which of the streets the Vistani were taking. But slowly, his senses found his prey. He pointed past the junction of Knight Street, to where Bacchus Way vanished between the rundown buildings.

Without pausing for the others, without even caring if they understood, he started running as fast as his limp would allow. If he could catch up to them, he could force them to take his friends with them—if he could not catch them, they would not live through the night.

He tore through the intersection, dashing through the trash-strewn neighborhood. He barely noticed the damaged buildings on either side. No little girl was playing, no thieves skulked in the shadows—he found no sign of anyone at all. As the light faded to night and the gas lamps slowly brightened, he did not even see the dead.

As he left the glowing lamps behind, he saw the front of the last wagon move into the Mists, slowly disappearing. It was only coincidence, he told himself, that it was the same section of the Mists into which he himself had stepped the previous night. The memory sent a shiver down his spine. He ignored it—there was no time for anything else. Half of the wagon had vanished, and only four Vistani guards followed. He recognized them.

"Zuza!" Lewis yelled, pointing his Webley at her. His voice reverberated between the buildings. "Stop—or I swear to you on my wife's grave, I will shoot you!"

Still a few dozen feet ahead of him, the Vistani paused as their last cart disappeared in the murk. They turned slowly, and Zuza looked at him expectantly.

"Take us to London!" Lord Crandall raced up beside Lewis, his Winchester aimed.

Professor Drake sighted awkwardly down Gregory's rifle as he took up a position opposite Lord Crandall. Lewis doubted if the man could hit even the wagon, let alone the Vistani, but Zuza could not possibly know that.

"You must help these men!" Elise insisted, gliding forward, stopping short of Zuza.

"You do not understand." Zuza sounded as though she expected no less of them. "We have done all that we intend to do. Your destinies lie along a different path."

"If by not understanding, you mean we do not comprehend your betrayal, then you are correct." Lewis squeezed his finger ever so slightly, feeling the tension of the trigger. "Take us with you, or help us. Those are your only options, short of death."

"Indeed?" Zuza simply smiled as she stepped backward into the Mists; she vanished instantly, and her men were scarcely slower. Lewis held his fire, certain of the futility of shooting into the Mists. Such an act would only waste their valuable ammunition.

"Damn you!" Lord Crandall shouted, though he put up his rifle without shooting.

"You have no honor!"

"But we do," Zuza said. She stepped from the Mists leading three horses. A small lantern hung from the saddle of each, casting welcome light. She paused in front of them.

After a moment, she looked directly at Lewis. "We have done all that we are able to." She handed the reins to Lewis.

"Why have you feigned assistance, only to send us to our deaths, and now offer additional help, but not the help we've asked for?" Lord Crandall kept his rifle trained on her, but Lewis thought the weapon was less worrisome to Zuza than the man meant it to be. "What are you after?"

"We serve." She bowed and walked back toward the Mists.

"Stop!" Lord Crandall fired a shot, clearly meant to miss her. It ricocheted off the paving stones, but Zuza did not flinch, let alone stop.

"Hold your fire!" Lewis reached out and put a restraining hand on the gentleman's arm. If the Vistana was willing to help them, he would not see her dead.

"If I were you," Zuza turned toward them and craned her neck, listening, "I would hurry." And Lewis realized that the baying dogs were suddenly much louder; ice water filled his veins as he realized that the minion closed on them.

Again, the gypsy stepped into the Mists and vanished.

"I don't understand." Professor Drake glanced in the direction of the dogs' barking. He shifted nervously. "What do we do now?"

"I don't care what their goals are. They could save us . . . and they could have saved Gregory." Lord Crandall glared at Lewis. "You should have let me shoot her."

"I understand your anger, Lord Crandall, but we have clearly received all the aid these Vistani will offer. We cannot bring back the dead, and more than likely, we cannot even save ourselves. There are two options left to us. We can hide and wait for the minions or the dead to take us one by one, or we can do something that Lord Knight will never expect." Lewis divided the reins, handing one set to Professor Drake and the other to Lord Crandall. "We can attempt a frontal assault. Perhaps with the horses . . . we will be able to breach their defenses. Perhaps."

"That is suicide." Lord Crandall's face went white as he considered the idea.

"Perhaps. But a soldier such as yourself should agree—dying in battle would be better than running away."

"Soldier? What gave you the idea that I was a soldier?" Lord Crandall was bewildered.

Lewis was struck speechless for a moment. "You were in the Transvaal War—you mentioned spending time in the Transvaal. Is that not true?"

Lord Crandall put a hand to his forehead. "The Transvaal. Yes. No. I mean, yes, I have spent time there. But we undertook an expedition to hunt rhinoceros and warthog. I have never been part of her Majesty's armed forces. I suppose big-game hunting has given me some skill with firearms."

Lewis stared at him, dumbstruck. His entire mental picture of Lord Crandall took on a new shape. "Yes. Well." Lewis swallowed. "In that case, I hope we can be of a similar mind. If we are to die, then I would prefer to do it on my terms."

"I'm not so certain that we must die. If Knight brought us here for a reason, then he might need us alive," Professor Drake said. He sounded thoughtful, and Lewis realized he might be right; he hadn't considered that they'd been told that Knight had brought them here for a reason. He'd had no intention of doing anything the heinous lord of this place wished, and when they'd had the secret route, it had seemed they wouldn't need to. But now—perhaps they could use that information to their advantage.

"So far, we know only that he brought you and Captain Wentworth here for his nefarious purposes. So you see, Professor, even if that is true, and he might wish to take you both alive, I am expendable." The gentleman glanced back the way they had come. "To hell with it. To hell with the Vistani, to hell with Lucius Knight. And to hell with you, Professor Drake. Gregory's life will be avenged." He took the reins and swung up onto the horse easily.

The baying of the dogs grew louder. Lewis knew their time and options had run out. Elise hovered several feet away, frantic concern on her ghostly features. She frowned.

"Lewis, don't do this."

"I want only one thing." He turned away from her and patted the pistol in his belt. "If Lord Knight truly is a ghost, then I cannot harm him. Richard Bailey, on the other hand, might be a powerful minion, but this silver bullet . . . he will die this night." He climbed up into the saddle of his horse, feeling the familiar comfort of such an animal.

"Lewis, nothing good can come of this." Elise glowed brighter as she glided closer. "This will only speed up your death. Perhaps if you hide long enough, you can find another way out of Mithras Court?"

"There is no way out of Mithras Court, Elise." Lewis looked at her, his expression stoic. "If we can succeed, then perhaps I can set you free by killing the man who murdered you." Surely that much would be possible. If he killed Bailey and she was not freed, it would mean he was the reason she remained trapped between worlds. His death would surely solve that problem, even if he remained trapped in Mithras Court as a walking monster. Either way, she would be free.

"You don't know that his death will help me," she said quietly. "And I don't want you to die trying to find out."

"It will help me." Lewis had trailed Bailey for two years. His desire for revenge had taken many turns since arriving in Mithras Court, but it was all he had left.

Elise looked stricken, but underneath, she looked proud—she looked loving. With a gentle smile, she vanished, but her ring did not cool; it remained warm against his skin.

The Dog was close now, but did not seem to be getting any closer. Lewis wondered if the silver shot in his flintlock had caused the minion to slow its advance.

"It's been a long time since I've ridden," Professor Drake said, interrupting Lewis from his thoughts. He climbed into the saddle without aid, though he looked slightly awkward as he moved. He held the rifle aloft and glanced at each of them. "Once more unto the breach, dear friends."

"Once more," Lewis echoed, conscious of their impending doom, but certain that his silver shot would keep the minion at bay whether he fired or not.

"Once more." Lord Crandall raised his chin in defiance of Mithras Court. "Once more."

Lewis turned the horse and spurred it to a gallop. Lord Crandall and Professor Drake formed up on his flanks. Elise glided along behind them, floating over the ground with ease. Lewis pushed her from his mind as the anticipation of battle sent shivers through his body. He smiled with the joy of true purpose: the destruction of Lord Knight and his minions.

For the first time since the Zulu War, he felt ready for what lay ahead.

CHAPTER TWENTY-NINE

Hot air shot out of his horse's nostrils as Lewis guided the beast down the empty street. He felt the rhythm and power of the horse as it maintained a steady gallop. He held the reins with one hand, his pistol with the other. With his two companions formed up on either side of him, he suddenly felt as if they might actually succeed. Very few enemies could withstand an organized cavalry charge, even one as small as this. They would crash through the dead, who lacked any ability to stand against determination and light, and Lord Knight's minions alike, killing any who got in their path.

The howl of the wind and the sound of the dogs increased as they thundered along Knight Street. Judging by the volume, the creatures had nearly matched their pace and were closing in. But as long as they kept to the horses, Lewis did not believe the minion would be able to overtake them.

"There's something up ahead!" Lord Crandall said, alarm in his voice.

Lewis focused forward and saw human shapes in the park just past the flower lamp post. His eyes widened as he realized that they were the dead—hundreds of them stood waiting all across the field, as they had earlier that night, though more had gathered since then. Lewis and his companions realized where the walking corpses that had been absent throughout the rest of Mithras Court had gone. They had been in this park, waiting.

The understanding that Knight planned the park to be his killing ground, or a point of capture, made Lewis nervous, but he could do nothing about it. They could only delay the inevitable. There was only one way to reach Lord Knight's Manor, and it was the road that ran along this dead-infested field.

"What do we do?" Professor Drake shouted.

"We stay together and keep going!" Lewis knew full well that shambling creatures would be hard-pressed to move out of the way of galloping horses. They had strength in the dark, but they had no ability to stand against something as powerful as a horse.

"I can help!" Elise spoke in a soft tone, but Lewis knew that all of them heard. Her glow flared brightly as she appeared in front of them, and her tactic was surprisingly effective. The dead parted before them, scrambling to get out of her way. To Lewis, it felt almost too simple, as if they were part of a prearranged choreography, as if Knight had anticipated their assault. He gritted his teeth. It did not matter—they were committed to this course of action, and there was nothing left for them to do.

"Hold your fire unless they get in front of us!" Lewis said, hoping that awareness of the trap would allow them to overcome it. "We do not want to obstruct our own path!" The other two showed no sign of preparing to shoot the dead.

Their horses pounded onto the hard-packed dirt and grass of the field before the looming forest. They headed directly for the gap between the two stone markers that identified the road to Lucius Knight's estate. Despite the clear path before them, their horses slowed, refusing the road. It was not the dead, Lewis thought—the dead had fallen well back with the passing of the light, and none of them appeared on the dirt road that entered the forest.

The hounds grew louder as the horses slowed down, but Lewis and his companions entered the forest safely before they were caught, the horses moving at a slow gallop.

But safety was not to be had. The instant they passed the obelisks, the lanterns went out, as if a giant hand had reached out and extinguished them, leaving only Elise to light their way. Not even afterimages marked the lamps' absence.

"Lewis, I'm fading! I can't hold on to—" Before she could finish the sentence, Elise winked out altogether for a moment, reappearing at barely half her strength. Lewis watched her, his heart thumping against his chest as panic sought to overtake him. He had not thought a ghost could be injured, but the exertion evident on her face, the pain there, made him think otherwise. Had he endangered her by this brash plan? It was too late to turn back, for the dead closed ranks behind them, perhaps as Knight had intended. They had to continue.

The darkness swallowed them as they rode beneath the archway formed by the intertwining branches and thick dark leaves of the trees overhead. The road remained free of the dead by virtue of the magical properties the forest possessed, as it had earlier on their way to the druidic ruins.

Lewis's horse reared—perhaps against the darkness, perhaps against something unseen. It slowed their progress, but he urged the mount forward, if not as quickly as he wished. He kicked the horse, spurring it on, but it fought him. He saw that the other horses balked, and the inexperienced Professor Drake looked to be in serious trouble.

"Damn it, beast, move!" Lord Crandall dug his heels into the stallion's sides, to no effect.

"There's something wrong with . . ." Professor Drake paused in mid sentence. "They're in the trees!"

Lewis looked up and saw human shapes clinging to the branches, dozens of them. Even in Elise's feeble glow, he could tell they were the dead. With the light as dim as it was, they no longer feared to attack.

As if they recognized that they had been spotted, they dropped upon the group like giant spiders.

A flash and boom signaled that Drake had fired just as one of the dead jumped at Lewis. He swiveled in his saddle and fired, hitting the creature in the head as it landed. Lewis fell backward, almost dropping his revolver. His training and experience in the saddle allowed him to remain on the horse.

"There are too many of them!" Lord Crandall fired, swiftly and with precision despite his near panic.

Two more of the monsters dropped upon Lewis. One landed behind him, raking the back of his neck with skeletal claws, but it did not get a firm seat and fell off the horse. Lewis was not so fortunate twice. The other landed squarely on his back and wrapped its gangly arms around him. The woman, her face half missing, gnashed her teeth and pulled, trying to unseat him. He slammed her in the jaw with his Webley. She released him, falling away.

"Captain!" Professor Drake called, his voice panicked and muffled.

Lewis turned to see the Professor dragged from his saddle as two of the things landed on him from above. He fell backward, hitting the ground hard and dropping his rifle. Lewis drew rein and his horse wheeled to a stop; several monsters plummeted to the ground in front of him, missing their aim at him. He spared a quick thought at his good fortune, then spun around in time to see Lord Crandall thunder past, two of the creatures hanging off him.

"Die!" Lord Crandall shouted, bringing his gun up as they disappeared into the fog.

"Professor! Grab my hand!" Lewis shot one of the creatures as it tried to drag the struggling man into the dark forest. It dropped to the ground in a twitching heap, giving Lewis the narrowest margin to save the old man. He fired again, and again, taking more of the things down. As more dropped from the trees, he knew his time was running out.

The old man looked up as the monsters pulled at him. Gashes in his face bled freely, but he fought to stay alive, or at least to remain free. Three more undead shambled toward him, but Lewis plowed through them, the stallion's massive frame knocking them aside with ease. He reached down, locking arms with the professor, and used his momentum to pull the man up into the saddle behind him, kicking at one of the dead that wandered too close. He drew reins again, turning the horse around.

"Hold on!" As soon as Lewis felt the professor's arms around his waist, he spurred the beast. The horse reared, kicked two more of the dead away with a sickening crunch, and leaped forward.

"It is too late!" Professor Drake yelled. "The dogs are upon us!"

The wind howled and the dogs became deafening, mere yards behind them. In the commotion, Lewis had not realized how close they had come. He could feel the dark storm cloud that the minion generated, rasping against his skin as it neared. Elise was so faint that Lewis could barely see her, but they could do nothing for her. He regretted bringing her into this, but he'd had no other choice, and no time to tell her to save herself.

Rifle shots echoed through the wood ahead of them, and were shortly followed by an explosion. Lord Crandall's horse burst forth from the fog in front of them at a frantic gallop, and Lewis's pounding heart faltered as he saw that the gentleman was not on the beast. Seeing his empty horse was like watching one of his soldiers die at Ulundi.

"Lewis, he needs your help!" Elise appeared from behind Lord Crandall's fleeing steed.

The dogs bayed again from behind, no more than a few dozen feet away. Lewis could not risk a look back. He gripped the reins and kicked his horse's sides, urging it to greater speed.

"We're doing all we can!" he yelled as his horse plowed forward.

The fog swirled around them, thicker than before, but suddenly they burst through it as if stepping out a door. They entered a small open field before a massive stone manor house, visible under the light of thousands of twinkling stars. It was the first time they had seen the sky since their arrival, and Lewis felt relief—the world did exist, they were not lost to the fog forever. Somehow, the fog did not touch this place, and the sheer wonder of that was breathtaking. Lewis glanced around the field, a smile of joy on his face even after all he had suffered in Mithras Court. His eyes lit on heavy double doors that stood open, revealing a candlelit hallway inside.

Dozens of the walking dead stood in the field. Lord Crandall, bloodied and battered, stood halfway between the forest and the manor house, in the center of a wide circle of scorched earth and shattered bodies; his dynamite had saved his life. A trail of twitching corpses led from the woods to the blackened clearing as clearly Lord Crandall had hurled a stick of dynamite, blasting the clearing in which he had now taken a brief moment of solace. Unfortunately for him, the dead were pressing close to the edge of his circle. As they moved, they left clear a path for Lewis and he grinned tightly—they could reach the sanctuary of the light thanks to the actions of Lord Crandall.

"I can do nothing to help! I've got nothing left!" Elise cried.

Lewis spied her floating between them and the door to the manor house. She flickered in and out, her glow a feeble shadow of its former glory. He turned back toward their trapped companion and drew in his horse's reins. If Lord Crandall was to be saved, it was up to him. "Elise! Save yourself!" he called. "I'll take Crandall!"

The gentleman stooped, dropping his rifle and pulling out the last stick of dynamite. Lewis watched in horror, unable to stop him—they could make it, they were safe!—as Crandall lit the fuse. He planted it in the ground in front of him. He retrieved his rifle and fired into the oncoming throng of the dead, backing slowly away from the explosive, but not quickly enough.

"Lord Crandall!" Lewis turned his horse toward the man; it slowed to a trot as it spied the dead, fighting his commands, and he cursed. The horse had ridden over the dead so easily—he'd not realized that a mass of the creatures would cause it to balk.

"Forget me, you fools! The way is open! Get inside!" Lord Crandall squeezed the trigger, knocking back one of the dead, but another took its place, and many more approached beyond that one, trying to reach him. The rifle had to be nearly empty.

The fuse burned down, leaving them with mere seconds.

Lewis knew the gentleman was correct, but he refused to accept that. To lose another so close to safety—that, he could not countenance. He spurred his horse forward, even as the dead turned to face them. The howling minion emerged from the forest behind them, a massive storm rolling forward. Dozens of barking hounds hidden in that storm added to the cacophony. Lewis's horse skidded to a halt, nearly throwing them from the saddle. The dead did not appear to notice as they continued toward Lord Crandall, ignoring Lewis and Drake.

"Lewis, hurry!" Elise yelled, floating toward the doorway.

"Go, now! The dog is here!" Lord Crandall pulled the trigger again, but the rifle had run dry. The big man dug a hand into his coat pocket, fumbling for cartridges as the dead lurched forward.

As he watched in horror, Lewis realized he recognized two of the dead. Cold dread swallowed him as he beheld the broken and twisted forms of their missing friends closing in on Lord Crandall.

"Reggie," he gasped.

"And Mary . . ." Drake's voice trailed off as he too realized that truly, no one could escape Mithras Court.

"Oh, dear friends." Crandall finally recognized them also. "I will set you free."

The fuse was almost gone. Lewis turned his horse. He had to retreat—there was nothing he could do to save the man, or Reggie and Mary. Nothing would be served by allowing himself to die. Further, he would not allow Crandall or the others to die in vain.

"Go!" The gentleman offered a crisp salute.

Lewis's breath caught in his throat at the man's gesture. He had seen many men fall in battle, but had never witnessed such unexpected brazen courage. This honorable gentleman's sacrifice would not be for nothing. He turned the horse toward the manor house and kicked hard. It lurched forward, practically leaping into the air as it galloped toward the open doorway to the house.

The explosion nearly knocked them both from the saddle, showering them with bits of dirt and bone, but Lewis barely noticed as necessity drove him forward. He regained control of the horse and guided it toward the house, his resolve only growing.

"Should we really go through an open door?" Professor Drake sounded doubtful. "It seems a bit obvious."

"It doesn't matter now. We need the light!" With another sharp kick, Lewis guided the horse at a run, leaving the chaos behind. The horse slowed again, as if the manor house frightened the creature, but another jab in the ribs from Lewis kept it moving and they quickly cleared the entryway.

They passed into a corridor perhaps twenty feet high, its upper reaches lost in shadow. Closed doors lined the paneled walls, and suits of armor and paintings of ancient warriors in battle decorated the hallway. No people were present, dead or living, though loud chanting echoed around them, emanating from the open door they had come through. A boom sounded—Lewis remembered the clang of being shut into the tunnel—as the door slammed shut and barred their escape, silencing the noises of the park. He did not care about escape—they would only face the horrors of the Court, and they would eventually lose.

He saw what lay ahead and gasped. Through an open door was a great hall—and within the hall stood Richard Bailey and the Raven. A third, heavy-set man stood near, his arm hanging uselessly in a sling. Behind him was a man wearing a colonel's uniform who would have been called average were it not for his faint reddish glow. He looked up as they neared the door and smiled. It was no thing of joy, nor of kindness, and Lewis felt his skin crawl at the sight of that smile, that evil face.

"Welcome, gentlemen!"

The horse stopped hard, throwing Lewis and the Professor from the saddle. They hit the floor in a heap at the edge of the doorway. Lewis's Webley skittered across the floor and out of sight. The horse turned back into the hallway and Lewis fought to stand. His eyes lit on a dark-skinned man, perhaps of Indian descent, waiting in the hall. A fierce dog was tattooed on his arm. He reached up, grabbed the bridle as the horse tried to run past, and twisted—the crack as the beast's neck snapped would last in Lewis' memory to his dying day. The stallion shuddered and dropped like a stone, and the floor shook when it impacted.

"Farewell." The Dog smiled coldly, and his insanity flashed in his eyes for a moment.

Lewis looked for Elise, hoping she might defend them against the minions, but she had vanished. He drew his pistol and waved it at the man. Next to him, Drake could only watch, weaponless. When the Dog saw Lewis's pistol he paused, eyeing it warily. Lewis sneered at him, glad to have wiped the smug smile from the minion's face.

"That's right. I have silver." With nowhere to run, Lewis grabbed the professor's arm and pulled him through the open doorway and into the massive room beyond. He turned sideways so he could watch both the Dog behind them and the others inside.

The audience hall appeared fit for kings, with suits of armor standing near massive marble pillars that held up a huge vaulted ceiling. Swords and great poleaxes hung on the walls. Worn blue and green pennants hung from the distant rafters. A throne sat on a raised dais at the far end of the room, but Lord Knight and his minions stood much closer. The ghastly lord was in the center of a large chalk circle, arcane symbols covering nearly every inch of the floor. At his feet lay the copper tablet, partially embedded in the marble flooring. He laughed as they entered.

"You have one shot that can hurt my minions, Captain. I admire your courage, but surely you realize that you cannot kill all of them. Let alone me."

"What do you want of us? Why have you brought us here, Merriwether?" Professor Drake turned his back to Lewis so he could watch Knight, the creatures in front of them, and the Dog behind them. Lewis held his pistol in front of him like a talisman to ward off evil.

"You of *all* people should know the answer to that, Professor," Knight said. "I need your blood to reverse the spell that enslaves me." He laughed at Drake's startled expression. "Oh, do not fear. I require only a small amount. You should live through the ordeal."

"And what of me?" Lewis gripped his pistol tightly. "Why do you need me?"

"You have the best role of all." He laughed again, the sound grating on Lewis's raw nerves. "I need you for your wife." He paused and his tone was different, wheedling. "Yes, my dear. I know you are here."

In the chaos, Lewis had not realized that his ring had gone cold, but it warmed again as she winked into existence next to Lewis.

"I understand now." She glared at the man, hate in her eyes. "I am not certain how or why, but as I faded out of existence moments ago, I floated in a mist-filled abyss, perhaps within the barrier Mists themselves, neither here nor anywhere else. Knowledge flooded my mind as if someone had granted me understanding." She glanced at Lewis and her hate became fear, etched on her features. "He seeks to switch places with me, trapping the two of us here and allowing himself to escape."

"You are mistaken," Lord Knight said, sounding contemptuous.

"I do not wish to leave this place, for I am but a ghost. I do, however, require both of you. If you agree to my terms, I'm prepared to guarantee all your safety. All you need do is surrender to my will."

"He's lying," Professor Drake whispered. "I know the curse, and I do not believe it can use a soul as pure as Elise's for any purpose."

Lewis's anger simmered. This man had ordered Bailey to kill Elise, and had likely brought them all to Mithras Court. If Drake's story were true, then Knight was responsible for the deaths of hundreds of the Queen's soldiers as well. He would make no agreements with this fiend. Whatever his plans, Lewis would thwart them. Even if he could not kill their ghostly enemy, he could certainly kill his instrument . . . the Snake.

"I do not care what this cursed bastard says," Lewis hissed. "He will not use us, nor will I allow him to use Elise." He would be damned if he allowed any harm to come to Elise.

"By all means, discuss my offer amongst yourselves," Knight said, his red eyes blazing with amusement. His voice turned hard as he added, "I give you thirty seconds."

"Professor, were you truly unaware that a place such as Mithras Court would be created when you cursed this man?" Lewis pressed his back against the scholar's, his hands steady, his flintlock pointed toward Bailey.

The scholar paused. His voice had the ring of truth to it. "Had I known, I never would have done this thing."

"Then I am honored to die with you." Lewis glanced at Elise, attempting to share in a single look a lifetime of love that he—they—had missed with her death. He would not be cheated of an afterlife with her as well. He was going to die, they were going to die, and would be trapped in the Court forever as the living dead, he hoped, however that even that terrible outcome would set her free somehow, for not only would he kill Bailey, but he himself would die. Whichever of those outcomes set her free was irrelevant, for she would be free in either case.

"Good-bye, my love," Elise said, realizing that he intended to sacrifice himself.

Lewis smiled wanly at her.

"You have made a decision?" Lord Knight said.

"Indeed." Lewis paused, looking away from Knight, trying to allay his suspicion, but when he spoke, it was not to surrender. "Now, Professor!" Lewis ran forward. Drake moved with him, though he had no gun of his own. Lewis noted with grim pleasure that the minions retreated to the edge of the circle. They feared his silver, perhaps, but they feared him for certain.

"Take them!" Lord Knight's angry roar filled the room, but no one moved.

"Take this!" Lewis spun away from Lord Knight, certain that they could not harm the man, but just as sure that Bailey would die. He brought his pistol up. Perhaps in the confusion, Drake would reach the tablet.

"No!" Bailey gasped as he realized Lewis's intention, but it was too late for the minion to defend himself.

Lewis fired the flintlock. The round struck Bailey in the head, the silver carving easily through his skull. An expression of horror froze on the Snake's face. He stood for a moment, seemingly unharmed, then collapsed in on himself, not so much falling as slumping to the ground.

He did not move.

Richard Bailey, the man who had murdered all that Lewis cared about, was dead, and Lewis's expression turned exultant. Whatever happened next did not matter—vengeance had been served. But he was not done. He pushed Drake ahead of him.

"Professor, the tablet!" If either of them could reach it, they could end this. He looked directly at Lord Knight and smiled.

"You filthy whoreson! How dare you strike down one of my generals!" Lord Knight shook his fists. "You shall suffer a thousand tortures for this indignity!"

Lewis ignored him, his eyes fixed on the copper tablet at Knight's feet. He leaped for it.

"Lewis!" Drake said, but Lewis could not look.

The Scorpion leaped forward, catching him just shy of the chalk circle. He batted Lewis's empty pistol aside and reached for his throat. Lewis twisted, but the man clamped strong hands around his neck.

The Scorpion yanked hard, the chain slipping out from beneath Lewis's shirt. The chain snapped with a small musical sound. Elise's ring sailed across the room toward the door, and hit the floor with a gentle chime. Lewis tried to spin toward it and catch it, but could not raise his arms as the minion held him pinned. He could only watch as his connection to Elise skittered away.

The Scorpion punched him in the face. Pain ricocheted through his skull and his vision went black. The world spun sideways and he hit the stone floor hard, expelling the breath from his body. The Scorpion reached down, grabbing him by the coat and lifting him easily off the floor.

"Release me!" Lewis kicked the man, punched at his arms, but he might as well have been hitting an oak. The Dog held the professor in a similar fashion; the old man's scalp bled and a bruise formed on his cheek. Elise glowed feebly on the other side of the scholar, watching them with tears brimming. As Lewis caught her eye, she smiled sadly, but said nothing. He did not understand her sudden silence.

"Bring them into the circle!" Lucius Knight commanded. "Time grows short! The Mists are coming!"

The door burst open and a fierce wind blew through the room. The Mists poured into the chamber the way they had filled the train car, and Lewis's spirits rose for a moment—perhaps the Mists had chosen to aid them. He wondered if that explained Elise's expression. If the Mist did somehow speak to her, or influence her.

Despite Knight's fear and concern, Lewis doubted that the Mists had come to their aid. They merely swirled about them as the Dog dragged Drake into the circle and the Scorpion hauled Lewis inside, despite their struggles. Lewis looked longingly at the flintlock, mere feet away, but even if he had been able to reach it, it was empty.

Knight chanted in Latin, words Lewis didn't know, though he could guess their meaning. The Mists curled forward and the minions' faces turned from fear to eager anticipation. Lewis did not understand anything that was happening. He steeled himself for his fate, whatever it might be.

Drake surprised him, gasping, "What?" Lewis tried to glance at the other man to find out what had startled him, but he did not have to wait. "Lewis, he's not trying to escape!"

A backhand from the Dog silenced the Professor, and his head lolled to the side as he lost consciousness. Seizing the chance, the minion drew a curved blade, grabbed Drake's forearm, and sliced a long gash that bled instantly. The pain brought Drake around, his eyes fluttering open as he screamed, but it stopped nothing. Lewis could only watch in helpless horror as the first drop of Drake's blood struck the floor and a wall of shimmering red energy lit the border of the circle. It vanished instantly. Lewis could not even guess at its significance, but the minions seemed to know.

"The vessel!" Knight pointed impatiently at Lewis. "Hurry!"

"Aye." The Scorpion stepped forward, dragging Lewis with him.

"Damn you!" Lewis beat the man's arm, scratched at his flesh and bit his hand, but the minion ignored the attacks. Lewis took another tack. "Elise, help us!" He glanced at her imploringly, but the Mists had nearly reached her. She stood watching, waiting. Lewis did not understand and had no time to try.

"Now!" Knight ordered.

The Scorpion drew a dagger and grinned demonically. The minion plunged it into Lewis's chest. Intense pain exploded through him and a red haze dropped over his vision. Every breath sent a jolt of pain through his body. His fingers and toes tingled, and his strength vanished.

The Scorpion dropped him. As Lewis hit the floor, he saw the Mists envelope Elise, a tiny tendril reaching for her ring where it lay near her feet. The red walls of the circle flared to life again as bolts of crimson lightning shot out in every direction, blinding him for a moment. When his vision cleared, the Mists had vanished—as had Elise and her ring.

"It is done!" Lord Knight bellowed, and the triumph in his voice rang off the walls. He laughed madly, looking down at Lewis. "So, you think you will die and become one of my mindless undead servants? That would be too kind a fate for you. Far too kind." His grin was pure evil.

"Bastard," Lewis gurgled, blood oozing from his mouth. The pain faded as his body grew numb, and terrible cold settled over him.

"No easy death for you, Captain Wentworth. You shall serve me." Knight's ghostly form knelt beside him, the man eyeing him with clear amusement. A red flame shot from the lord's hand, striking Lewis in the forearm. He hissed but felt no pain. A tattoo of a snake formed on his arm, growing rapidly. As it did, Lewis felt his strength returning, his wounds healing, a newfound power coursing through his veins. He did not understand why Knight would heal him. Reveling in his newfound power, he realized something, something unwelcome. Although he retained some semblance of free will, he knew he would obey Lord Knight's commands, whether mental or verbal, without question, for the rest of his life. He had been enslaved by the lord.

Like Bailey before him, he had become the Snake.

He wanted to scream, tried to struggle, but could not find the will to do either. His body was not his own as he slowly stood, bowing his head. After a moment, he could talk and move again.

"Why?" he asked quietly.

Nearby, the Scorpion made no move to stop him.

"You, like the Vistani, thought I sought to escape from this place, but why would I wish to do such a thing? I am dead, and nothing can change that." Knight smiled.

"What, then?" Professor Drake sat on the floor, cradling his bleeding arm. Lewis startled at his voice. He had not realized his friend still lived. It gladdened him, though given their fates, he was not certain he should be happy either of them had survived.

"Good Professor, I should thank you for providing me with a kingdom, and subjects to rule." Knight frowned. "You made one mistake. You did not make my domain large enough for my liking. In fact, the small size of Mithras Court has mocked me every day for the past thirty-five years. With the help of Elise's beautiful soul, however, that has been remedied."

"You used her soul as fuel for your spell?" Drake gasped. "You truly are a fiend."

"Mmm . . . yes."

Anger raged within Lewis, demanding that he kill the man, do whatever was necessary to banish him to hell, but as he turned to Knight, he was incapable of doing anything to harm the ghost. Tears streaked down his face as he realized he had not only failed Elise in life, but in death as well. He had no reason to doubt the lord's statement that Elise was gone—he could not see her, and he missed the comfort of her ring. Surely her soul had been destroyed forever. He bit his lip, drawing blood.

"Now, let us go forth and see our new domain. Dog, bring the Professor. I would not want him to miss this. He'll be our guest for the rest of his life, and we will never know when we might need his services again." Knight glided out of the circle, his eyes alight with an evil gleam. "You, too, Snake . . . attend."

Lewis stepped forward, his mind frantic to free himself from Knight and to attack him with his newfound strength. But with each command from his new master, all he could do was obey. He struggled to stop himself with every ounce of strength he had, but his soul was as locked as his will. As they left the room, he spied the Webley, lying in the hallway. He scooped it up, as Knight clearly allowed him, but all he could do was slip it into his now-tattered coat.

CHAPTER **THIRTY**

Night still gripped Mithras Court in its dark embrace. In the diffuse glow of the street lamps, Lewis saw that Bacchus Way was empty. He caught sight of the citizens watching from their windows, fear written on their tired faces.

As they neared the intersection at Knight Street that would take them to the Mists, Lewis braced himself for what he would see there, knowing he would learn for certain that Elise's soul had been destroyed. He knew that Knight's spell might have failed, but he knew better. He had seen the energies burst forth. He had felt Elise's absence. He knew what had happened.

"Elise, I am so sorry," he whispered.

"She would be happy to know that you still live," Knight said, laughing.

"You killed her . . . twice, now." Lewis glared at the man with all the hatred he could muster, but he had to settle for angry looks, not the revenge he'd dreamed of. It was the only hostility he was allowed.

"Yes. And your hate is refreshing, Captain. I shall have to put that to good use." He smiled, motioning to the cross street up ahead. "And now, we shall see my new domain!"

But when they rounded the bend, Lewis heard Knight gasp.

Lewis stopped short, his eyes widening in shock. The fog had parted, and the wall of the Mists that he had seen just a day ago had retreated, but it had not vanished.

Instead, it had moved back perhaps a hundred yards. Revealed was not the stone road that Lewis's expedition into the Mists would have suggested. They saw no sign of the creatures that had infested the Mists, and Lewis wondered briefly whether they had moved back with the Mists or if they had been hallucinations. What was revealed was clearly not the land that the lord had envisioned, and Lewis smiled, even as he looked upon the dreariest swampland he had ever seen. A dirt road ran from the cobbled street into the Mists winding between two mosquito-infested ponds. Lewis smiled wider. Anything that thwarted the dark lord was acceptable to him.

"No!" Knight hurried forward, stopping just inside the Mists, disbelief on his face. "This is not possible!"

"On the contrary. This is very possible." Madame Catalena emerged from the Mists, Zuza at her side. Lewis's heart skipped a beat when Elise appeared with them, glowing as brightly as ever. "Did you really think we did not know what you planned?"

"Curse you, dirty gypsies!" Knight glared accusingly. "How?"

"You made one fatal error in your scheme." Catalena held out her palm, and a small circle of gold was revealed—Elise's wedding ring. "It was not Lewis's *body* to which Elise was bound."

"The ring." Lewis gasped with the realization. "That is why it warmed when she was near!"

"Yes." Catalena looked at him with sympathy. "You have done us a service, Captain Wentworth. I am sorry for the outcome, but fear not—this was not in vain." She closed her palm around the ring, then opened it again. Her palm was empty. "Elise is free. If you know nothing else from your time here, know that."

"I love you, Lewis. I will watch you from afar and hope for your redemption." Elise smiled sadly. "Good-bye." She faded from sight.

Joy blossomed in Lewis's heart as he realized that his sacrifice had not been for nothing. She, whom he had loved these many years, loved in life, loved beyond death, fought for—she was free. His voice was quiet as he whispered, "Go, love . . . and remember."

"No!" Knight dropped to his knees, throwing his hands skyward. But Madame Catalena wasn't done.

"We shall honor our pledge to take Frederick's daughters to safety. And I think we shall meet again, Lewis Wentworth." Catalena turned to Knight and her voice was notably harsher. "Enjoy your new kingdom, Lord of Mithras Court!" Without waiting for a response, she and Zuza stepped into the Mists and vanished.

And Lord Knight screamed as Lewis threw his head back and laughed with joy.

In the shadow of the Last War, the heroes aren't all shining knights.

PARKER DeWOLF

The Lanternlight Files

Ulther Whitsun is a fixer. When you've got a problem, if you can't find someone to take care of it, he's your man—as long as you can pay the price. If you can't, or you won't . . . gods have mercy on your soul.

Book 1
The Left Hand of Death

Ulther finds himself in possession of a strange relic. His enemies want it, he wants its owner, and the City Watch wants him locked away for good. When a job turns this dangerous, winning or losing are no longer an option. It may be all one man can do just to stay alive.

Book 2
When Night Falls

Ulther teams up with a young and ambitious chronicler to stop a revolution. But treachery may kill him, and salvation comes from unexpected places.

July 2008

Book 3
Death Comes Easy

Gangs in lower Sharn are at each other's throats. And they don't care who gets killed in the battle. But now Ulther had been hired to put an end to the violence. And he doesn't care who he steps on to do his job.

December 2008

TRACY HICKMAN
PRESENTS
THE ANVIL OF TIME

With the power of the Anvil of Time, the Journeyman can travel
the river of time as simply as walking upstream, visiting the
ancient past of Krynn with ease.

VOLUME ONE
THE SELLSWORD
Cam Banks

Vanderjack, a mercenary with a price on his head, agrees out of
desperation to retrieve a priceless treasure for a displaced noble. The
treasure is deep within enemy territory, and he must survive an army of
old foes, a chorus of unhappy ghosts, and the questionable assistance of
a mad gnome to find it.

VOLUME TWO
THE SURVIVORS
Dan Willis

A goodhearted dwarf is warned of an apocalyptic flood by the god
Reorx, and he and his motley followers must decide whether the
warning is real—and then survive the disaster that sweeps
through their part of Krynn.

November 2008